SCAVENGE THE STARS

TARA SIM

HYPERION

Los Angeles   New York

First Edition, January 2020
10 9 8 7 6 5 4 3 2 1
FAC-029191-19326
Printed in the United States of America

This book is set in Bembo/Monotype
Designed by Torborg Davern

Library of Congress Cataloging-in-Publication Data
Names: Sim, Tara, author.
Title: Scavenge the stars / Tara Sim.
Description: First hardcover edition. • Los Angeles ; New York : Hyperion, 2020. • Summary: After Amaya rescues a mysterious stranger from drowning, she reinvents herself to seek revenge against the man who ruined her family and stole the life she once had.
Identifiers: LCCN 2019011660 • ISBN 9781368051415 (hardcover)
Subjects: • CYAC: Revenge—Fiction. • Justice—Fiction. • Identity—Fiction. • Fantasy.
Classification: LCC PZ7.1.S547 Sc 2020 • DDC [Fic]—dc23
LC record available at https://lccn.loc.gov/2019011660

Reinforced binding

Visit www.hyperionteens.com

AS ALWAYS: FOR YOU, FATHER

TO INHERIT THE SKY,
YOU MUST SCAVENGE THE STARS.

—REHANESE PROVERB

1

The most basic rule of water: Better to be above than below.

—*THE VIEW FROM SOUTHERLY: A MARITIME HISTORY*

The first thing Silverfish had learned on board the *Brackish* was how to hold a knife.

Not the useful kind that could gut a man, but something smaller, duller, and better suited for a child's grip.

The second thing Silverfish had learned was just how much a fish's innards could stink. How the odor clung to her hands for days after she'd worked the gutting deck, where offal and grime stubbornly adhered to the ship's lacquered wood.

She had been forced to get used to these lessons over the last seven years, embittering and eroding her like salt on stone. Now as Silverfish worked, the wailing of seagulls above her as familiar as a lullaby, she ignored how the slime of a sturgeon stung her withered hands. Although she had once again been assigned to the foulest corner of the ship, she couldn't help but smile.

In a few days' time, she would never have to scrape fish guts again.

The *Brackish* creaked around her, as if in resentment. Out of habit, she scanned the deck for Roach. The Water Bugs—the other children—scurried about on the lower deck or climbed into the netting to fix loose ropes and retie knots. The younger Bugs were good for climbing and getting into small spaces, while the older ones like her were used for manual labor: stitching up sails, scrubbing the hull, hauling cannon fodder on the gun deck.

She finally spotted Roach up in the mainmast, his long, lanky body perched precariously above the riggings. He had gone up there plenty of times, but Silverfish still felt a swoop in her belly and the instinct to pray to her father's gods. A dark stain lingered at the foot of the mizzenmast where Mantis had fallen only a few months before. Mantis had been the nimblest of them all, but when he'd lost his footing and tumbled down, there'd been nothing graceful about it. His bones had made a resounding *crack*, a sound that had followed Silverfish into dark and suffocating dreams for weeks afterward.

There hadn't even been time for final rites. The Bugs had merely hauled his shattered body overboard, hardly daring to pause their work lest the captain decide to add the time they wasted to their debts.

Roach noticed her and gave a two-finger salute, a familiar gesture that meant *I'm all right.* It was their routine, a sort of call-and-response. Forcing down her worry, Silverfish saluted back before shooing away a seagull that descended low enough to see if it could steal a snack. It settled again on the railing at the end of the gutting line where Beetle worked.

Beetle was the smallest and youngest among them, barely eight years old. The girl didn't even know how to swim yet. The hilt of her knife fit awkwardly in her tiny hand, her fingers constantly readjusting themselves as she struggled to open up a fangfish. Her wispy brown hair stuck to the sweat on her face, and blood splattered her thin forearms. The girl snuffled, trying not to cry.

Silverfish hesitated, debating whether to move toward her. As soon as she took a step, a roar came from the lower deck.

"Silverfish!"

Captain Zharo stood at the bottom of the stairs. She forced herself to meet his piercing gaze. She hated having to look at his face, red and blistered from the sun and half-concealed by a gnarled black beard. The rest of his hair was a tangled knot that Silverfish was certain he never washed.

"You take care of that sturgeon, or I'll use you to remind the others how to slice open a belly," he growled.

"Yes, Captain." She bent her head and continued working, but her shoulders didn't lose their tension, even when he stalked away. She watched him from under her lashes as he stomped past the wooden blackboard nailed under the foresail. On it were the names of every Water Bug on board—several crossed out, including Mantis's—followed by a series of numbers. It was how the captain kept track of their debts, calculating how much time they all owed on his vessel.

Out of habit, Silverfish's eyes went straight to her name and the small sum beside it. The price of only a few precious days.

As Zharo passed the board, a twelve-year-old Bug named Weevil waited for him to get out of earshot before fishing something from his pocket: a piece of hardtack.

Silverfish's heart sank.

The hardtack was already halfway to Weevil's mouth when the captain turned and spotted him. He was across the deck in a few strides. The boy dropped the hardtack and tried to back away, but the captain already had him by the collar. Some of the Bugs gasped as the captain pushed Weevil against the railing, half his body leaning precariously above the water.

"You do it again, you're for the sharks," Zharo growled. "I'd kill you now if it didn't mean losing a pair of hands."

Weevil was all too quick to nod his understanding, moaning in fear as he tried not to tumble overboard. With his shirt ridden up in the captain's grip, Silverfish could plainly see the stark, hungry press of his ribs against his skin. Silverfish knew that hunger well, that clawing desperation that lurked between survival and suicide.

Silverfish shouldn't have cared. Weevil knew better than to steal. They were all starving, after all.

Amaya would have cared.

But Silverfish hadn't been Amaya in years. She had left Amaya behind, hundreds of miles away, buried at sea.

It was the first cruelty Captain Zharo had shown her. When she had set foot on the *Brackish*'s deck seven years ago, the man had looked her over, unimpressed, and said, "Who you are and where you came from don't matter. Your name's Silverfish now, and you'll be thankful for it."

She had once thought that beatings were the worst punishment the captain could dole out, but now she better understood what had happened that day, the same thing that happened whenever a new child was brought on board. The captain stripped them all of their names, their lives, everything that made them people.

Because to him, they weren't people. They were bugs, easily squashed under his heel.

Captain Zharo let Weevil go at last, forcing the boy to scramble for a hold on the railing. As Weevil slumped with relief onto the deck, Zharo went back to the debt board. With a single motion, he erased Weevil's sum with an aggressive swipe of his sleeve, the chalk screeching as he increased the amount by two weeks. Then he picked up the abandoned hardtack and shoved it in his own mouth, crumbs spilling onto his beard as he grinned at Weevil and continued on his patrol.

Silverfish lowered her head, puncturing the soft underbelly of the sturgeon she held. She scraped out the red globules of its insides and flung them into the metal pail before her, some of the warm ichor seeping into the open sores on her hands. In the water, the fish's blood turned purple.

The Water Bugs were no better than the contents of that bucket: useless, repellent, easily dumped. She glanced at the end of the line at Beetle, who was still trying not to cry.

Silverfish knew better than to get involved. After a few more days of this, she would leave this festering ship for good.

Beetle whimpered loudly now. She hadn't hardened yet, but she would. She would have to.

What'll the captain do if he comes to shut her up?

Cursing again, Silverfish threw the sturgeon's carcass into the bucket with the rest she'd gutted and moved down the line. Without a word, she crouched beside the girl and grabbed the next fangfish out of her still-full pail, swiping the knife up along its belly. Beetle's whimpers died down to harsh little gasps as she caught her breath. They worked in silence for a while, and Silverfish was content to keep it that way.

Then came a voice, small and broken, from beneath all that wet hair and snot.

"Will you tell me about Moray? You used to live there, didn't you?"

Silverfish nearly dropped her blade. It had been a long time since she'd heard the name of her city spoken out loud. She tried hard not to even *think* it. Memories had a way of creeping up on you if you let your guard down, of taking you by the throat and refusing to let go.

Beetle was waiting for her to go on, her eyes wide and frightened and eager for escape. She was tempted to tell the girl that it was better to simply forget the past and everything you were before.

Silverfish took a deep breath.

"I remember walking by golden, columned buildings. Those might have been the banks in the Business Sector, or maybe the Widow Vaults." She found that once she started talking, the memories, hazy as they were, became insistent. "There were gardens, too, filled with ferns and palms and trees that dropped fruit when they were ripe and heavy. My mother and I would take the bananas, mangoes, and papayas from them for our breakfast. And the water of the bay is beautiful. It's blue and clear, and you can see the coral and fish beneath."

Beetle's eyes were faraway, her lips parted. "Da used to tell me he'd take me there one day," she whispered. "Soon as he got the money to."

Silverfish instantly regretted saying anything. Beetle had only just begun her seven years, and Silverfish was already filling her head with images of a life beyond this ship. Part of her wanted to keep the hope alive in this girl, this tiny flicker of the future. Another part wanted to douse it with seawater, to make her realize that this was now her only reality: blood, guts, and fear.

Debt ruled on both land and sea. Silverfish knew they could never likely escape it.

Beetle's face was red, but her eyes were shining. "You're going home soon, aren't you?"

Home. Back to Moray, to her mother, to everything she had forgotten while trapped on this gray expanse of a prison. Would her mother even recognize her? It had been so long since she was truly Amaya. Would her mother see the girl who used to sing to her rag dolls, who used to leave an offering of milk and herbs for the gods, who used to curl up to sleep beside her? Or would she only see Silverfish, a stranger with deadened eyes and blood crusted under her fingernails? She supposed she would find out in a few days' time.

"Yes," she said, blinking. "I'll go back."

The small, quivering smile Beetle gave Silverfish lasted only a second, but it was enough. She had done the right thing. She had done the Amaya thing.

Then a shout pierced through the air:

"Man in the water!"

Silverfish joined the Bugs who scurried to the railing, many of them still holding their knives. She saw him within a moment: a dark shape bobbing as he tried to stay above the surface of the frothing water. She ran down to the middeck, where the rest of the Bugs were crowding the starboard railing, and squeezed in next to Roach.

Captain Zharo was already yelling at them to get back to work, his hand straying toward his pistol as if itching for an excuse to put a few holes in them.

"There's a person in the water!" one of the Bugs cried.

"Does it look like I give two shits? Let 'em drown and be done with it."

Silverfish gritted her teeth. The man was barely staying afloat, inhaling water every time he tried to open his mouth to call for help.

7

He'd likely been fighting against the waves for a while now and was rapidly losing energy. A goner.

Then something else caught her eye: a flash of gold on his chest. His coat, heavy and black with water, was lined with golden buttons.

A wealthy man. Maybe even a merchant from Moray.

Silverfish inhaled sharply. "Get one of the nets ready," she snapped at the Water Bugs. When they only gaped at her, she swore and grabbed one herself.

Concern creased Roach's face. "Sil," he warned as she threw down the fishnet.

Captain Zharo bellowed behind them, but Silverfish ignored him and leaned over the railing.

"The net!" she screamed down to the man. At first she couldn't tell if he'd heard her over the rushing of the waves, but she released a quick sigh of relief when she saw him weakly cling to the netting. She tried to haul the man up, the muscles in her arms and neck straining. Some of the Bugs, seeing her struggle, hurried forward to help. Silverfish winced as she heard—and felt—the netting tear, but by some miracle it didn't give way.

The man fell over the side of the railing onto the deck. The children scrambled away as he spat up water, coughing and shuddering, before flopping onto his back and lying still.

"Have you completely lost your mind?" Roach hissed as Silverfish knelt at the man's side. He was tall and burly, his skin brown, his jaw lined with scruff. Likely from Khari, her father's country. Bright spots of color studded his shirt like bullet wounds—the ruffled orange petals of marigolds. "You should've let him drown."

"He . . ." Silverfish faltered, wondering what *Amaya* would say. "It wouldn't be right to let him drown."

Roach gave her an incredulous look, his wiry brows furrowed.

A pair of boots appeared before her. Silverfish followed them up to the captain's scowling face, his bared teeth—or what was left of them—stained with tobacco. His hand clenched and unclenched beside his pistol.

Silverfish gave a small nod to Roach, who carefully moved away from her. She began to shiver.

"Have you gone deaf, Silverfish?" the captain growled. When she didn't answer, he smacked her so hard she fell to the deck. One of his rings caught her lower lip. *"Well?"*

The pain was a bright starburst across her vision, and she fought for breath. She licked her lower lip and tasted copper. "N-no, Captain."

"I said to leave 'im be." He cast a disdainful glance at the man's unconscious body. "And now you've gone and torn a net. Repairs cost money, you know."

Silverfish froze. *No, no. Please no.*

Zharo crossed to the debt board as the Bugs scattered to get out of his way. His sleeve was already coated with chalk dust from erasing Weevil's sum, and it left a streak across the board where he struck out her remaining balance. Picking up the chalk, he made it scream against the board, quadrupling her debt.

Zharo's beard split as he grinned at her with those yellowed, decaying teeth. "Looks like you'll be around four more weeks, Silverfish."

She fought back tears. The ever-present pain and exhaustion, the sores on her palms, the stink of rotting fish—it had all been bearable only because of the thought of reuniting with her mother. The only thing getting her through these last few days had been the relief of finally returning home, a dream as sweet and hazy as incense.

Now it would be a month.

The captain nudged the unconscious man with his boot. "Seeing as you thought to pull this trash from the water, he's *your* responsibility now." He tilted his head, then snapped his fingers at a boy, who flinched. "Tear off these buttons and bring them to my cabin. For every one you steal, I'll cut off a finger. Everyone else, back to work!" The Bugs scuttled away except for the boy, who pulled off the man's golden buttons with shaking hands.

Silverfish crouched there, her cheek ablaze with pain, as she stared at the man she had rescued. Blood dripped from her split lip and into the puddle of water around the man's body, each drop unfurling like small purple flowers. Blue sea, red blood.

She wouldn't know who he was—or what he was—until he woke, but when he did, she hoped she'd been right about him.

Surely saving a man's life is worth a few more weeks, thought Amaya.

He better be rich, thought Silverfish.

2

When you're on a losing streak, it's better to call it quits.
You never know when ill luck will follow you
from the tables and through your doorway.
—THE DEVIOUS ART OF DICE AND DEALING

The smell of rotting squid was not helping Cayo's headache.

But, much as he longed to remove himself from the bulbous carcass stuck to the edge of the dock, he forced himself to stay put. The entire port reeked of marine life left to bloat in the sun, but this end of the docks was the worst of it, usually reserved for lesser vessels and unexpected visitors to Moray. Everything the *Miscreant* wasn't.

And yet here they were. Not dock seven, where the *Miscreant* should have already been anchored, but all the way at dock twenty-three. His father's crew was lined up on deck before the gangplank, each of them subjected to the same evaluation by a harried-looking doctor before they were allowed to set foot on the dock. The captain stood in the back with her first mate, the latter rolling a gold sena coin between his tattooed fingers, antsy to disembark. But everyone had to be checked for ash fever before they were allowed into port—no exceptions.

The early signs were dangerously subtle, a fatigue that eventually came with all the chills and aches of a normal fever before gray spots began to bloom on the afflicted person's skin. The only common factor among the victims was that when the fever finally took hold, it began to congeal the blood in their veins, turning their skin an ashen gray. The sickness had started as a small strain people hardly even noticed, until it proved fatal.

Although a tincture had been made to stave off the worst of the effects—available only to those who could afford it—a cure hadn't yet been found.

Sighing, Cayo checked the time on his fob watch. It was his duty to make a manifest of everything they hauled from the holds of their sleek galliot cargo ship, but with everything running way off schedule and the examinations chipping away precious time, the crew still had yet to unload.

His head throbbed and his pulse picked up as he speculated how his father would react to the dock switch. Kamon Mercado did not take kindly to insults.

Cayo glared at the foreign galleon that had commandeered the *Miscreant*'s spot, at the billowing purple sails that had nearly blocked out the sky as it had approached. It was drawing all manner of attention from dockworkers and sailors bustling under a fierce midafternoon sun.

Although he hated to admit it, the ship was impressive. The sides were painted with swirling Kharian designs, but the flag it flew from its bow was that of Moray, a cutlass and rolled-up scroll on a background of green and blue.

A lone figure stood at the bow, staring out at the city that sat in the curve of the harbor like a smile, its multicolored buildings rising victoriously above the crystalline bay. Strange timing, for a foreigner to visit during an epidemic. Perhaps they didn't understand the meaning of the black flags flying over the harbor.

The dock switch didn't bother Cayo, but he knew his father would be displeased. Kamon Mercado conducted business through commands, not requests, and expected his only son to follow in his footsteps. So Cayo had complained about the last-minute change with the harbormaster, with nothing to show for it other than a worsening pressure in his temples. At this rate, he was going to be late for dinner tonight.

Then again, maybe that wasn't such a bad thing.

He began to inspect the few boxes now sitting beside the *Miscreant*, the dockworkers having pried open their tops: bags of spices, a trove of silver amulets marked with the Kharian gods, multihued jewelry boxes studded with tiny mirrors, medicinal herbs and roots, pearl-handled knives, and even a cache of leather-bound books.

When he was younger, Cayo had dreamed of jumping onto one of his father's ships and sailing around the world. Of collecting treasures from the rain forests of the Rain Empire, the lush valleys and harsh deserts of the Sun Empire, the plentiful farms along the Lede Islands.

But that wasn't the life of a wealthy merchant's son. His life was here, under a sweltering sun, trying not to breathe in the stink of the harbor while the workers around him eyed the golden embroidery on his coat.

"The master not coming down today?" asked one of the dock-workers.

"I'll be handling shipments for the foreseeable future," Cayo said.

The worker raised an eyebrow, looking amused. "That so? Mind you don't dirty those pretty boots, then."

Cayo pressed his lips together, fighting back the urge to say something he would later regret. Cayo doubted the man would recognize fashion even if it whacked him in the face and insulted his mother. He knew full well he didn't have the respect or reputation of Kamon Mercado.

"Do you know who that galleon belongs to?" Cayo asked instead. Might as well start trying to earn their allegiance.

The dockworker shrugged. "All I've heard is rumors. Folks saying it belongs to a Kharian noble, maybe even a royal spare. Me, I say it's a spy from the Rain Empire all fitted up like they're from Khari."

Cayo tried hard not to roll his eyes. Although Khari had helped Moray fend off the colonialist control the Rain Empire had once held over the city, he found it exceedingly difficult to believe that a spy would make such a grand entrance. Since Moray was situated between the Rain and Sun Empires, it had proclaimed neutrality for decades, trying to stay out of the empires' multiple wars over the years. But because they had a hold on the best waterways, Moray was still expected to "play nice."

Cayo checked the doctor's progress, the crew impatiently waiting their turn for inspection, before turning back to the dockworker. "Do you think . . ."

But the words died in his throat when he glanced at the end of the dock. Standing there was a familiar figure—one who brought back the smell of smoke, the taste of gin, and the nausea of regret.

Sébastien.

The sun turned his hair bronze and kissed his light brown skin into a golden shade, but as bright as he was, he still symbolized everything that Cayo had given up to be standing where he was now. Although the two of them had flirted plenty in the dens, often sharing a cigarillo out in the alleys, Sébastien had always been more of an enabler than a lover. He was one of the regulars who would join Cayo in the Vice Sector. And that made him bad news, just like the rest. Just like Romara.

Sébastien gestured frantically at him, and Cayo froze, his fingertips buzzing. When he realized the dockworker was staring at him, he cleared his throat. "I'll be right back."

Clenching his jaw, he walked down the dock to where Sébastien stood. Before he could speak, Cayo snapped, "What are you doing here?"

Sébastien swallowed hard. He was perspiring in the heat, his hair curling over his ears. Cayo was always caught off guard by the intensity of his eyes, round and heavily lashed and the most arresting shade of bluish green. Impossible to read a hand in those eyes—impossible to read anything but a reflection of the sea that Cayo so longed to explore.

Now, however, those eyes were pinched in fear.

"Cayo," Sébastien whispered, "it's the Slum King."

Those last two words made a pit yawn open in Cayo's stomach, devouring him from the inside out.

He grabbed Sébastien by the shirt and pulled him close. "Tell him no," he growled in his face. "I'm done. I've paid my debts."

And he had the empty ledgers to prove it. His shoulders tightened miserably at the thought of his depleted bank account, every drop of his fortune bled into the Slum King's coffers. But at least he was free—he had cut all the strings tying him to that monster.

Sébastien was shaking his head, sweat rolling down his temples. "I'm not here to collect for him, Cayo."

Panic was replaced with dread. Cayo let go of Sébastien's shirt. "What did you do?"

Sébastien licked his dry lips. "I . . . might have pocketed some of my table winnings. A few times."

Cayo sighed and pinched the bridge of his nose. *"Bas."*

"I *know*, I messed up! But my rent was due, and I didn't even have enough to buy food." Tears welled in his beautiful eyes. Cayo did notice that his frame seemed thinner than usual. "He cut back my hours because I wasn't dealing well enough, so what was I supposed to do, huh?"

"I don't know, Bas—maybe not steal from the Slum King?"

"I had no choice!"

Cayo bit back the curse that rose to his lips. Unlike Cayo and the others, Sébastien didn't have the luxury of wealthy parents to bust him out of trouble. He'd been an orphan for years, only making a living in the casinos under the Slum King's employ.

It was the side of Moray that everyone chose to ignore, the grit under the glitter. People came to visit Moray for its grandeur, for its casinos, for the lavish veil it draped over the mundane. They didn't expect that lifting the veil revealed the hard truth: That extravagance existed side by side with destitution. That the casinos they loved to frequent caused people to turn out their pockets and become bankrupt, or worse, end up on the debt collectors' lists. The unlucky ones, if caught, found themselves on debtor ships.

Sébastien scrubbed his hands through his hair. "Cayo, if he

finds out, I'm dead. I'm worse than dead. I already spent the money. It's gone."

"What about Philip?" Sébastien's ex-lover was of the lower gentry, not well known but still affluent enough to help.

"He's already given me too much, and I squandered it. I can't go back to him again." He grabbed Cayo by the shoulders. "Please, I need *something*."

Cayo took a small step back, breaking out of Sébastien's hold. He worried that if he let Sébastien clutch on to him a second longer, Cayo would allow himself to be steered right back to the Vice Sector. "You've come to the wrong person. My accounts . . ." He swallowed. "I have nothing."

"But your father—"

"You really think he's going to let me touch his money? After what I did?" He gestured to the *Miscreant* behind him. "It took ages just to convince him to even let me *work* for him."

Sébastien dropped his gaze. "Can't you do *anything*?"

Cayo closed his eyes, but it only made him more aware of the growing sense of dread that had been building in him ever since Sébastien had uttered the words *Slum King*.

He didn't have time for this. He couldn't associate with Sébastien anymore, not if he hoped to win back his father's trust.

He reached into his pocket for the few silver drinas he had left. They were supposed to last him the entire month, according to his father's budget. He pressed the coins into Sébastien's trembling hands.

Sébastien let out a quiet sob of relief. He tried to kiss Cayo's hands, but Cayo pulled away.

"Don't come to me again," he said.

Sébastien nodded and hurried away, not even looking back.

Before Cayo could contemplate the stupidity of what he'd done, his carriage driver trotted up and touched the front of his tricorn.

"Pardon, sir, but we should be heading back now. The lord'll be expecting you."

Cayo opened his mouth to respond when a shout rose behind him. He turned back to the *Miscreant*, where a couple of dockworkers were forcing a man back onto the ship. The first mate.

"I'm *fine!*" the man shouted, struggling against the dockworkers. The captain of the *Miscreant* kept the rest of her crew from coming to the first mate's aid.

The doctor wiped sweat from his brow. "We can't risk anyone with early stages entering the city proper. Cases have already doubled, and we can't have it spreading further."

Ash fever.

Cayo knew how much his father's men made. He also knew how much the medicine cost.

As the first mate raged and fought, Cayo had to look away. His gaze landed on the decaying squid stuck to the side of the dock, now swarming with seagulls.

As he watched, a seagull plucked out and ate its eyes.

Mercado Manor was like a pearl rising from the bed of an oyster, all white and gold and gleaming. It rested on a gentle hill that overlooked the Merchant Sector, which gradually gave way to the harbor and Crescent Bay, flanked on either side by flora and the tall, spidery forms of palm trees.

By the time Cayo's carriage rattled up to the entrance, the sun was mostly gone and the bay gleamed purplish blue. He stiffly emerged from the carriage, sore and a little sunburned.

The footman came out to greet him. "Good evening, sir. We expected you home much sooner."

"I know, I know." Cayo hurried past, the footman keeping up behind him. "I was held up."

"A change of clothes has been laid out on your bed, and there's a basin ready for you to wash before dinner."

"Bless you."

Cayo took the front entrance stairs two at a time, passing under the jutting balcony supported by fat, curling columns of white marble. The iron chandelier above was already lit warmly for the night.

Bursting into the antechamber, he made to run for the stairs when he caught sight of his father on his way to the dining room. Kamon Mercado raised a hand that forced Cayo to skid to a breathless halt before him.

It was easy to see why the workers were skeptical of Cayo when they compared him to someone like Kamon. Tall, handsome, and stern-faced, he was a man who looked used to command. When he wore his finest blue suit and slicked his hair back, it was impossible to ignore the aura of power around him.

Kamon, his hand still raised as if needing to keep the mayhem of Cayo as far from him as possible, looked his son up and down.

"You reek," his father said. "You were supposed to be home an hour ago."

"I know, I'm sorry. There was a mix-up down at the—"

"Excuses don't matter. Get changed, *quickly*, and come down to meet the Hizons. They'll be here any minute."

Cayo's boots squeaked against the gold-veined marble of the

antechamber as he hurried up the stairs. Soria was already descending, an amused tilt to her mouth after watching the exchange. His sister was lovely in a gown of sea-foam green, the waist swathed in green ribbon and her shoulders covered with a small jacket of cream lace. Her long black hair had been half pulled up, the rest of it cascading down her back in elegant waves. She'd even applied glittering powder above the hoods of her eyes, teardrop-shaped and dark like his own.

"Is that a Vritha design?" he asked. He recognized the seamstress's style in the jacket and the scalloped hem.

"I thought it would be appropriate for tonight," she said, spreading the skirt of the dress as if to curtsy. "Not too much, not too little. Subtle."

"It works. Next to you I feel like a dirty shoe."

"Whose fault is that?" his sister said with a playful wrinkle of her nose. Despite her light tone, Cayo noticed she was pale.

"Are you nervous?"

Soria bit the inside of her cheek. She was only sixteen, but when she did that she seemed much younger.

"A little," she whispered. "I've been faint all day."

"It'll be all right." He took her hand and squeezed. "They'll love you. Impossible not to."

Kamon cleared his throat loudly, and they both started. Soria gave Cayo a small, crooked smile before continuing down the stairs.

He didn't even bother to shut the door to his rooms before stripping and pulling on his good suit. He washed his face and combed his hair, then sprayed a good amount of Ladyswoon over himself, hoping to cover up the smell of sweat and salt.

By the time Cayo returned downstairs, the Hizons had arrived. Kamon and Soria stood at the front to greet them.

"Ah, and here is young Lord Mercado," said Duke Hizon. He was a portly man of Rehanese ancestry, by the look of his light brown skin, curved eyes, and thick black hair. He, like his wife and son, wore his best: a black suit with a purple silk undershirt, complete with a traditional Rehanese wrap over his shoulder. His son, Gen, was dressed similarly, while Duchess Hizon wore a Rehanese-style dress of purple silk with a high collar. "Enjoy making an entrance, do you?"

"On a cloud of cologne," the duchess added sotto voce, delicately waving her hand before her nose.

Cayo forced a breathless laugh. "You caught me, Your Grace." He added a little bow. "I hope it was to your liking."

His father flashed him an annoyed look before showing the Hizons to the dining room. Cayo scowled at their backs; Soria saw and hid a laugh behind her gloved hand.

Cayo took a seat between his father and sister at the long mahogany dining table and immediately guzzled his water, parched from long hours in the sun. He didn't need to turn his head to know that Kamon was glaring at him again. One of the dining staff quickly came forward with a pitcher to refill his glass; he made sure to take more respectable sips this time.

"We almost have the deal cinched," his father had told him last night, after looking through his ledgers. "The Hizons are one of the oldest families of Moray and acquainted with the prince. Once your sister marries the duke's son, she'll have a higher status and access to the Hizon fortune. We only need to secure her dowry and set the date."

He had stared at Cayo then, his face hard and unreadable. It was difficult to find in him the man his mother had once loved, difficult to remember a time his father had actually smiled.

"Do not ruin this for us," Kamon had warned him.

Cayo prepared himself for an uncomfortable dinner. Gen Hizon sat across from Soria, occasionally meeting her gaze before looking away again, shy. He seemed altogether too moody and quiet for someone like Cayo's sister, and Cayo held no real affection for him. But Soria seemed content with the match, and he had even caught her and Gen walking through the garden a couple of weeks ago, his sister holding on to Gen's arm.

Tonight, though, Soria wasn't herself. She was likely nervous now that the duke and duchess were there to evaluate her. Cayo didn't blame her; he could feel their judgmental stares across the table and did his best to hide his face behind one of the flower vases.

Thankfully, his father kept them busy with talk of the current political rumors drifting through Moray. Cayo thought back to the ship with purple sails and wondered how long it would take for the city to find out who owned it. As he made his way through the first course, a light stew of scallops, clams, and fried sage, his mind returned to the events of the day. The first mate. The smell of death. Sébastien.

Had he been too harsh with him? He had been furious at the time, but now . . . Cayo knew what it was like to be in that position. To turn every corner expecting a knife to slide between his ribs.

He heard his name and looked up to find everyone staring at him. Duchess Hizon was studying him over her wineglass, her painted lips puckered. It emphasized the wrinkles around her mouth, two deep trenches on either side of a battleground.

"The duchess was kind enough to inquire about your work at the harbor," Kamon murmured beside him. Only Cayo recognized the warning under his words.

Do not ruin this for us.

Cayo inclined his head to the duchess. "It was quite busy, Your Grace. My father has many ships in his employ, as I'm sure you know. Overseeing them is no small feat."

He risked a glance at his father, who dipped his chin slightly. *Good.*

"And what exactly is it you do to oversee them?" the duchess asked, swirling her wine with a practiced hand.

It was an innocent enough question, but he knew better. This was a test. So Cayo carefully explained the process of unloading and sorting inventory, as well as all the numbers involved in bookkeeping. Soria, who had been in quiet conversation with Gen, fell silent at his side, but she wasn't quite listening to him. She was mostly staring at her plate, their soup exchanged for small game hens cooked with rosemary and honey and topped with a hibiscus sauce.

"Good thing you have a young buck like this to help out at the docks," the duke said with a low laugh. "I imagine it's difficult to spend all day in the sun at your age, Kamon."

"Indeed."

"Better that than wandering the city like a scoundrel," the duchess muttered into her wineglass.

Cayo tensed. He felt his father tense as well. Soria kept her head down, picking at her hen.

The duke laughed that low laugh again. "I believe what my wife is saying is that it's good for young Lord Mercado to be in an honest line of work."

"I quite agree," said Kamon, though his voice was strained.

Cayo tightened his hold on his fork but said nothing. Under the table, Soria found his other hand and squeezed. Her skin was clammy with nerves.

When dessert finally came—coconut and brown-sugar rice cakes with a pineapple coulis—one of the kitchen staff came to ask Kamon to select the after-dinner port. Panic swept over Cayo when his father left. The Hizons were eyeing him like two vultures about to pounce on the same scrap of meat.

"I'll go help him," he blurted, scraping back his chair.

He caught his breath in the hall. His heart had been racing since seeing Sébastien. He still couldn't get his face out of his thoughts, nor the terror in his words.

Bas, you fool.

His father was already making his way back toward the dining room. Seeing Cayo, he frowned.

"You're supposed to be entertaining our guests," he said.

"I needed some air," Cayo said. "Father, I . . . I have something I wanted to ask you."

Kamon crossed his arms, head lowering. It was the stance Cayo had come to call the Negotiator.

"What do you want?"

"I was wondering if I could get a larger stipend per month. It doesn't have to be much, it just— What's so funny?"

Because his father was laughing softly, incredulously, while swinging his head side to side. "That didn't take long, did it?"

"What do you mean?"

Kamon pressed his lips together, white with suppressed fury. "What happened to your month's allowance, Cayo?"

Cayo hesitated. "I gave it to a friend. He—"

"Don't *lie* to me," Kamon snarled. "I should have known that as soon as you had a few drinas in your pocket you'd go back to the tables."

Cayo flushed hot all over, his headache returning with a vengeance. "I haven't gone to any of the gambling halls in months! You can go to the Vice Sector yourself and ask around."

"Even if that's true, how am I supposed to know you won't eventually go back to your old habits?"

"I've been clean for six months," Cayo said through clenched teeth. "When are you going to trust me?"

"Respectability doesn't come quick, Cayo." Kamon straightened his dining jacket. "As you've seen with Duchess Hizon. No, respectability is earned, and you have not yet proven yourself."

Cayo was about to retort when there was a loud *thump* from the dining room followed by a scream. Cayo exchanged a startled look with his father before they ran inside.

"Soria!"

She had collapsed to the floor beside her chair, her hair spread about her like a pool of blood. She must have tried to excuse herself from the table before falling. Cayo dropped to his knees beside her and turned her over. She was unconscious, her eyelids fluttering while she struggled to breathe. Gen had gotten out of his chair to try to help, but he just stood there with his hands extended uselessly. The duke stood as well, pale and wide-eyed, while the duchess covered her mouth in shock.

"Soria," Cayo said, cupping her face with his hand. She was burning up. "Soria!"

Then some of her hair fell away beneath a sweep of his fingers, revealing a spot of gray behind her ear.

Ash fever.

25

3

The sea gives and takes, alternating like the tide.
Be careful lest you take too much. The waves remember what you owe.

—PROVERB FROM THE RAIN EMPIRE

The man, as it turned out, was not rich.

He was delusional.

The next morning, Silverfish brought water and a bit of hardtack down to his holding cell. There were three cells in total on the *Brackish*, all used for isolation and starvation to punish the Water Bugs who got on Captain Zharo's bad side. Silverfish had once been locked up for three days without food or water, nearly dying of dehydration only because the captain had forgotten she was down here.

After long minutes of deep, racking coughs, the man she'd rescued just yesterday looked straight at her. Though his face was weathered by long hours between sun and sea, she guessed he was somewhere in his early midyears—though there was something ageless and off-putting about his eyes. A shiver ran down her spine at the intensity of them, how they mapped out her face, her matted black hair, her ragged clothing stained with fish blood and crusted with salt.

"You saved me, huh?" he said, his voice rough and low.

Silverfish crouched before the bars. His dark eyes followed her down.

"And now you owe me," she said.

Several hours later and standing in the surf of the small island that was one of their usual harvesting spots, Silverfish tried not to grind her teeth. She and Roach were diving for pearls today, their last stop before they reached the waters outside of Moray. They only had about an hour and a half of light left, but still she lingered in the shallows, unable to take a deep enough breath to submerge.

Roach stood beside her, limbering up for the dive. The tattoo of a briar patch on the tawny skin of his chest was visible. One of the older Bugs had given it to him a few years ago before their seven years had ended. The same Bug had inked a tiny knife on the inside of Silverfish's left wrist, a reminder to her that she had to be sharp and ruthless. No matter what, she had to *survive*.

"You look ready to spit rocks," he remarked. "Did your new pet piss on the carpet?"

"He pissed on something, all right," she muttered. "My hopes and dreams." She angrily pulled her shirt off, leaving her in only her underthings and the pouch she wore for collecting oysters. She had long ago forsaken modesty, as had Roach, who had once admitted to her that the sight did nothing for him anyway; physical attraction was about as foreign to him as currency from the Sun Empire.

"Such dramatics!" Roach put a hand against his chest, over his heart.

She threw her clothes down, frustration welling in her. "Don't start."

Roach dropped his hand, sobering. "I'm sorry, Sil. What happened?"

She took a shaking breath, staring out over the waves to where the *Brackish* was anchored. The smaller Bugs were on the shore nearby, others finding tide pools to collect mussels, all supervised by Captain Zharo as he stalked the beach with a hand near the whip he kept coiled at his belt.

"I thought . . ." She shook her head, laughing bitterly at herself. "I thought that if I saved that man, he would repay me. That I could pay off my indenture early and finally go home. He had *gold buttons*."

Roach frowned as he listened, nodding that he had seen them, too. She felt suddenly grateful that he was here with her—the familiar strong line of his jaw and the warmth of his green eyes made her feel significantly less alone. "And let me guess," he said. "Turns out he's just broke?"

"He claims," she said, her voice dripping sarcasm, "to be the wealthiest man in the world."

Roach's thick eyebrows shot up. "Oh," he said lightly. "Well, then."

"He's lying, Roach. Or he's delusional." Silverfish ran her fingers through her long, tangled hair, sighing. "He won't say who he is or where he came from, of course. He carries no money with him. He just wants me to bust him out before the captain decides to kill him."

"I'm sorry, Sil. But you *were* the one who decided to haul him up like a bundle of fangfish."

"If I'd known it would come to this, I would have let him drown." Somewhere inside her, she thought she felt Amaya flinch.

"Is that why you volunteered to dive?"

"I might find enough pearls to pay off those additional weeks. It's the only chance I have at getting home in time."

"In time?"

Silverfish bit her lip. The waves were dark and tipped in gold as the sun sank. They pulled at her legs, urging her forward, pointing her north—to Moray.

"My mother's birthday is at the end of the month," she mumbled. "I wanted to be home for it."

Roach let out a long sigh. He put a callused hand on her shoulder and shook it affectionately. "All right. Let's find you some pearls, then."

Silverfish waded farther out with him. Together they swam under the current, toward the shelf of spiky rocks on the island's northwest shore where the fattest oysters were found. The water was choppy this time of day and desired nothing more than to keep her under. She broke the surface and latched on to the nearest rock shelf to collect her breath. She used to love the water in Moray, swimming through its blue, cradling warmth, but the water here was colder and less forgiving.

"Ready?" Roach said over the lapping of water against rock. Silverfish nodded, and they dived. She followed Roach as he swam determinedly down, down, farther from the light and into the inky blue of deep water. Her ears were already beginning to ache, her chest still sore from decompression after the dives she'd made earlier that week. On those dives, she'd managed to retrieve only a few tiny pearls, half of them misshapen.

Today's dive would be different.

It had to be.

The man she'd rescued—he'd told her his name was Boon— might claim to be wealthy, but all Silverfish cared about was whether he could pay her way off the *Brackish*. He was just as Captain Zharo said: a useless waste of food and water.

"What's your name?" he'd asked this morning after giving his own.

"Silverfish."

The response earned her a slight tic of his mouth, almost a smile. "I meant your real name."

"As if Boon is *your* real name? You call me Silverfish or nothing."

That earned her a sharp bark of laughter as he leaned against the wall of the cell, scratching at the dark beard filling in around his jaw. There was a tremor in his left arm that seemed to come and go at random intervals. "Fair enough. Where you from, then?"

"Moray. You're Kharian, I assume?" His accent hinted at it, though it was watered down, as if he hadn't stepped foot in his home country in years.

"You assume correctly." He'd folded his arms, his crusty, but-tonless coat straining at his elbows. "How'd you end up here, then, Silverfish?"

"How does anyone end up on a debtor's ship?" Instead of answer-ing, he'd just stared at her, his gaze as dark as the pitch they used to waterproof the fish buckets. "What, are you looking for a bedtime story? Fine. The debt collectors came for my family after my father was accused of trafficking illegal goods to the Rain Empire in order to pay off gambling debts. Never mind that he was innocent, or that his lies were about as obvious as a whale in the desert. They hanged him for something he didn't do, and all that debt was slapped onto our shoulders."

She had to pause to take a breath, to fill herself with something other than rage and grief. "My mother couldn't pay, so here I am."

Boon had sat there, quietly listening, fingers laced over his stomach. Every so often he would jerk his head to one side, as if shooing away a fly or trying to get water out of his ear.

"Sounds like a real winner, your dad," he said after a while.

"Don't you dare mock my father," she snapped. "Someone like you has no right to judge the type of man he was. And he was a *good* man—one of the best. Unlike some others I've met."

He ignored the gibe. "So how'd this flawless father of yours come to be wrongly accused?" he asked. "How much shit did he have to step in to get it to stain his breeches?"

"He was a pearl merchant." She could still remember riding on her father's shoulders as he brought her to the docks, as he showed her around his ship and let her hold a few small, perfect pearls. She had called them moons, and he'd told her that was his secret—that the earth had many moons, and he knew where they hid under the waves. "He was loyal to the Port's Authority. But they turned around and claimed he was a smuggler."

Boon made a clucking noise with his tongue and jammed a pinkie finger in his ear, wriggling it around. "Doesn't surprise me. The Port's Authority are fickle bastards."

"You have experience with them, do you?"

He examined his earwax-coated finger, even going so far as to smell it before rubbing it on his shirt. "Unfortunately."

"Are you a merchant?" She had held her breath. It was the question she had wanted to ask since pulling him on board; if he was indeed a merchant from Moray, then he might have enough wealth waiting for him on shore that he could easily spare some for his rescuer.

But he had shaken his head, reading the disappointment on her face. "Not anymore. Not that kind, anyway."

She didn't know what that meant, and at that point was too afraid to ask. "Then why were you at sea? And . . . why were you covered in marigolds?" Marigolds were a symbol of death and remembrance in Khari, mostly used in shrines and for funerals.

"Don't have to tell you my life story, do I?"

She scoffed. *Hypocrite.* "Well, the Port's Authority is the reason I'm here. We never even saw any evidence. They were probably protecting one of their own." She shrugged, although the injustice of it still pained her. "Or maybe it was a competition thing. Maybe Chandra's Pearls was making too much profit and it spooked them."

Boon had stared hard at the opposite wall of his cell. His head twitched a couple of times. Then he jumped to his feet so suddenly that Silverfish took a step back.

"Chandra," he'd muttered. "Chandra, Chandra, Chandra." His voice rose until he was practically shouting it, laughing with disbelief. *"Chandra!"*

He'd given a single loud yell and smacked his palm against the holding cell's wall. Silverfish had flinched back, watching as Boon muttered to himself and leaned against the wall while holding his head, his laughter bleeding into snarls.

Then he had lunged for the bars, grabbing them with thick, scarred hands and pressing his forehead against them, dark eyes unnervingly wide. Silverfish had been frozen by that look.

"I see it now," he whispered. "I see it."

"See what?"

"Your father." He had paused then, his grip slackening. He shook his head as if coming to his senses. "I knew him. Arun Chandra."

Silverfish had closed her eyes for a moment, trying to will away the dizziness that was beginning to make the room spin. Arun Chandra. She hadn't heard her father's full name in years. Like Amaya, it felt like a dead thing suddenly resurrected.

For a moment, just a flash of a second, she'd almost imagined she could hear her father's laugh, low and sonorous in his chest.

"You . . . You couldn't have. He didn't . . ." *Consort with the likes of you*, she wanted to say.

He stepped back and ran his hands through his hair. "Chandra. A pearl merchant in Moray, yeah. I knew him before . . ." Boon had looked at her again, hands still tangled in his hair. "You mentioned a gambling debt. Easy to gamble away a fortune in a place like Moray, no? Mayhap your dear dad wasn't a smuggler, but every man carries his sins a different way."

Sins? The man was a mess and had no idea what he was talking about. Silverfish had taken a few deep breaths, trying to calm herself enough to speak.

Finally, she'd said, "I can't believe you thought that would work."

He'd frowned. "What?"

"You didn't know my father. You never met him—you have no idea what kind of man he was. You're just trying to get me to help you escape."

"Now hold on—"

"It was a nice try, but I don't trust that easily. The only way I'd help you is if you had a fat diamond in your pocket. Even then, I'm not so sure."

She'd thought Boon might get angry, but on the contrary, he just gave that harsh bark of laughter again. "Sounds to me like you don't want to face the truth," he had countered. "That your father maybe wasn't the oh-so-perfect man you recall."

Anger had spiked low in her gut, and Silverfish had grabbed the bars. "I don't care what it sounds like to you, or even if you did know him. You say you're wealthy? I say you're riffraff. One of the Landless, if I had to guess." There was a flash of indignation in his eyes. "I don't expect someone like you to understand what loyalty is."

"And you do?" he'd asked quietly.

She had stormed out after that. But his words continued to trail her in her shadow, written in the crinkles of her palms, murmured under the susurrus of the sea. They followed her down into the depths now, cold and dim and haunting.

"Every man carries his sins a different way."

Roach stopped swimming and pointed to an outcrop of rocky reefs below. It was crusted with coral, spindly stalks of pink and blue like small waterlogged trees. Silverfish swam toward it and eagerly reached for the nearest oyster, but Roach grabbed her wrist. He met her eyes and shook his head, pointing again. She followed his finger and accidentally let a few air bubbles escape.

The reef was crawling with cleverly camouflaged rockfish. One bite from them could send someone into shock. Under the waves, that was a death sentence.

Roach was already hauling her back up. Her lungs were starved, so she reluctantly followed until they broke the surface.

"*Damn* it." Roach slicked back his wet hair, water sliding

down his face. "Those rockfish weren't there last time I dove."

"So we just avoid them," Silverfish said. "We can be careful."

"It's too risky."

Silverfish closed her eyes tight. This was their last diving stop until they reached Moray; she couldn't afford to let the opportunity go.

Protector and Punisher, she thought, beginning the familiar prayer to the Kharian gods her father had called upon his whole life, *Trickster and Temptress, Lord of Earth and Lady of Sky, clear my eyes and clear my mind, for I know not what I do.*

"Sil," Roach warned. "I know that look. That's your I'm-reckoning-with-the-gods look."

She opened her eyes and grinned. "Last one down gets to shuck."

And with that, she took another breath and plunged back into the water.

Kicking her legs hard and fast, she descended to the reef. It was difficult to see them, but the slightest motion gave the rockfish away. They blended so well with the rock that she had to make several second and third guesses as to where the rest of the school was hiding.

Ignoring the strain of her heart, Silverfish reached for a small yet easily accessible oyster. She pried it off the reef and tucked it into the small pouch wrapped low around her hips. A dark shape beside her made her start, but it was only Roach. He shot her a reproachful look before he began to carefully harvest.

The sea was alive around her, full of motion and shadow, from swaying kelp to the flash of small fish darting by. She wasn't fooled; she knew all too well the hidden dangers around her, the potential for death amid all this life. She kept an eye out for brinies, a type of poisonous mollusk, as well as a small breed of jellyfish found in these waters that, with one sting, could paralyze someone for up to five hours. One of the Bugs had drowned that way last year.

As she reached for the meatier-looking oysters, the rock beside them shifted. Not a rock at all—a rock*fish*, motionless among the coral.

Silverfish jerked back, heart pounding. *Damn it.*

But these were the biggest oysters she'd found. She had to take the chance.

With her chest tight and vision beginning to darken, Silverfish's hand hovered over the oysters. The rockfish was still; she couldn't even make out its eyes. Was it better to do it fast or slow? What would provoke it less?

The rockfish shifted again. Fast, then.

She grabbed the oysters and pried them off, one in each hand.

The rockfish struck.

Crying out soundlessly, Silverfish spun away as she clutched the oysters to her chest. Roach was there in an instant to pull her back to the surface.

"Fool!" he panted as soon as they could gulp down air. "Did it bite? Are you hurt?"

Silverfish moved her left hand and hissed. There was a slender red line on the side of her palm that was rapidly swelling. It felt like fire. "It didn't bite, but it grazed me."

"We need to get you back before the effects take hold."

She nodded and clumsily pushed the oysters into her pouch with her right hand, her left already too numb to use. A graze like this wasn't fatal, but the numbness would spread, putting her out of commission for at least a few hours.

Swimming back to shore was difficult. Roach took hold of

her waist as Silverfish paddled with her right arm, and together they were able to crawl onto the beach. She tumbled to the sand, breathing heavily.

"I'll get the other Bugs to help carry you," Roach said. Silverfish used her right hand to grab his wrist before he could stand.

"Wait," she wheezed. "Shuck them. Please. Before the captain sees."

Roach hesitated, but the desperation in her eyes was enough to convince him. He opened her pouch and took out the five oysters she had managed to harvest, going back to his discarded clothes to find a shucker.

"If your lungs seize up, you only have yourself to blame," he grumbled as he sat and began to open each oyster. He showed her their insides as he worked. She grunted in both pain and frustration when she saw only small, standard pearls in two of them, and bared her teeth when the next two had no pearls at all.

Then Roach paused, gazing down at the fifth and largest oyster. He met Silverfish's frantic gaze, a grim smile on his lips.

"Congratulations," he said, raising the oyster for her to see.

And inside: the price of four weeks of debt.

With the help of Roach and some of the other Bugs, Silverfish made it back on board the *Brackish*, ignoring Captain Zharo's taunts the entire time.

"Too eager for those pearls, Silverfish?" he'd rumbled as they rowed back to the ship. "Can't imagine why." He laughed at his own wit, the same grating, coarse laugh that always pulled her shoulders up to her ears. "Don't think this lets you off easy. You best be recovered by your next shift, else I'll add another week or two to the board."

Just wait, you bastard, she'd thought, touching the round, smooth pearl hidden in her pocket.

After a couple of hours in her hammock and partially recovering feeling in her left side, she was able to shuffle into the galley later that night, where Cicada was on duty. He grinned at her from behind the grimy counter, a pot of something boiling behind him on the stove.

"Glad to see you up," Cicada said as he roughly chopped some withered onions. His long black hair was rolled into locs, and tattoos of white dots studded his dark brown face in half-moons under his eyes. "Rumors going about saying you was a goner."

"It's only a scratch," she muttered, showing him her bandaged hand. It was still throbbing, but at least she could move it. "I need to feed my charge."

"Sure thing. But first . . ." He poured her a glass of what looked to be heavily diluted lupseh, a popular type of alcohol found in the Lede Islands. How he'd managed to get it, let alone sneak it on board, she had no idea. He pushed the glass toward her with a wink. "Don't tell Cap."

"Cade, you're beautiful." She downed the drink in three sips, shivering in delight as her head went pleasantly hazy. He also gave her a plate of what he called braised lamb shank with onions, but what she knew was actually rehydrated jerky with the last of the shriveled, rotten batch of onions.

She fixed a plate for Boon and went down to the holding cells, where she found him pacing restlessly. There were no portholes down here, and she had to light a couple of torches. He noticed her bandaged hand as she fumbled with the flint.

"You injured?"

"It's nothing." She shoved the plate through the inch between the bars and the floor. He immediately fell on his ass to start shoveling old, weevil-infested rice pottage in his mouth. Big drops of it fell on his pants and shirt, but he didn't seem to care. "It was worth it."

Still chewing, he looked up with bits of rice stuck around his mouth. "Oh?"

She looked at him closely. There was an expression on his face she couldn't interpret. It made her uncomfortable, and she shifted on her feet. Silverfish reached into her pocket, where the pearl rested. She rolled it between her fingers, its shape like a promise against her skin, before she drew it out for Boon to see.

"Absolutely worth it," she said.

Boon eyed the pearl with a distinctly unimpressed expression. "You kidding? I have ones the size of my balls, and you come here flaunting *that*?"

Flushing, Silverfish stuffed the pearl away. "Right, your so-called wealth."

"What're you calling so-called?" He gave her a small grin, devious and somehow boyish. She thought she spotted a weevil stuck between his teeth. "I could lead you to treasure, girl. More than you could possibly imagine."

"I have no need for imaginary treasure," she told him. "Tomorrow morning, when we dock in Moray, I leave this ship for good."

Saying it out loud was like opening a window that had been boarded shut. The force of her yearning made her shake where she stood. Tomorrow, she would return to Moray. She would finally see her mother.

Tomorrow, she would become Amaya.

Boon's eyes widened. "You . . ." He stood, hands tightly gripping the bars. "Wait. You gotta help me escape first. I can't be seen in Moray."

She narrowed her eyes. "Why?"

"Let's just say that if the captain of this here vessel don't sell me to some other debtor ship first, I'm more likely than not to find a dagger through my heart, you understand?"

Though everything about him screamed *liar*, Silverfish knew the laws about how close a Landless could get to port were strict—and she'd heard stories of what happened when those laws were disobeyed. The Port's Authority didn't hesitate to hang those who thought to try to sneak ashore, dangling their corpses on the seawall by the harbor.

Silverfish hesitated. It was her fault he was on this ship in the first place. Whatever happened to him in Moray would be her fault, too. She couldn't become Amaya with that debt hovering over her.

She was sick of debt, sick of owing more than she was willing to give.

Glancing at the dark stairs, she reached into her pouch and pulled out her shucking knife. It was small yet sharp, and—as she'd learned from experience—perfect for picking locks.

She dropped it to the floor while keeping her eyes averted, then kicked it under the bars.

"I can't help you," she said with a furtive glance, expecting him to understand.

Boon didn't make a move to pick up the shucker, but he smiled.

As she turned toward the stairs, his voice followed her.

"If you change your mind about the treasure," he said to her back, "you only have until tomorrow morning. The tides are in our favor. When the water turns orange, remember to swim down."

She looked over her shoulder. He was sitting in the corner of his cell, keeping his gaze on the ceiling while one foot tapped a nervous rhythm on the warped floor. The shucker was nowhere to be seen.

Captain Zharo's eyes nearly fell out of his head when she placed the pearl on his desk, right in the middle of his ledger.

It was fat and lovely, its gray sheen catching the lantern light. Slowly, he picked it up in his dirt-smudged fingers and turned it this way and that. It was like watching a bear handle a teacup.

"I think this more than pays for the torn net," Silverfish said, trying hard not to grin. "And my remaining debt."

Zharo opened his mouth, closed it, and checked the ledger. He squinted up at her, and the fear she had felt earlier while talking to Boon about her father began to crawl its way back through her. She couldn't explain it other than a vague sense of unease—that she was somehow overlooking something.

"It's enough," the captain grunted.

Silverfish exhaled shakily. Relief, warm and golden, threaded through her veins, holding hands with that ever-present fear.

"I can leave tomorrow?" she breathed.

After a pause, Zharo nodded. Silverfish dismissed herself and walked unsteadily down the corridor, unable to stifle her grin any longer.

Tomorrow, Silverfish would die, and Amaya would go home.

4

Try not to wander into Moray's Vice Sector at night,

unless you desire to leave broke and beaten

and betrayed before daybreak.

—A COMPLETE GUIDE TO MORAY'S SECTORS

The soft chime of champagne glasses sounded almost musical in the din of the festivities. Cayo would have preferred the rattling of dice or the feathery shuffling of cards.

But that was the old Cayo. Here was the new Cayo: Tidy, well-dressed, well-mannered. Stuffed into a suit that was far too hot and had a collar so tight it made him want to cough. A respectable merchant's son, or at least playing the part of one.

Except he wasn't here on respectable business.

Rolling his shoulders back in a vain attempt to ease the soreness out of them, he plucked a flute of champagne off a serving tray and wandered through the partygoers, keeping an eye out for his mark.

He forced himself to put on his best smile, the one that showed off the dimple in his left cheek and made girls and boys stammer and blush. A few acquaintances returned his smile, but he merely lifted his glass in greeting as he retreated farther to the edges of the crowd.

High-society parties were usually arranged well in advance, giving the wealthier citizens of Moray enough time to choose the perfect outfit, hairstyle, and arm companion to show off. Contrary to tradition, news of this gala had blown through the streets only a week ago, making everyone scramble for new jewelry and shoes at a speed Cayo hadn't believed possible of the Moray gentry.

Normally, a faux pas of this magnitude would have been greeted with a great deal of harrumphing if not outright societal exile, but it was excused for one simple reason: The party was hosted by Countess Yamaa.

The countess had swept into Moray on her massive purple sails just a couple of weeks ago—the same day Soria had collapsed—and no one could speak of anything else. No one knew who she was, or where she had come from, or why she was here—the mystery had become its own kind of calling card. The only thing the citizens of Moray knew about her was the only thing that mattered: that she had more wealth than god herself had stars.

Would be nice to have some of that, he thought bitterly as he took in the frivolity around him.

Not to be outdone by the last of Moray's great parties, where Duke Irai had commissioned a yacht solely for the purpose of a water gala, Countess Yamaa had situated them in a massive greenhouse floating on a man-made island off the coast of Moray. The glass panels of the house were welded together using beams of silver-studded iron, and beyond the glow of the lanterns inside, the nighttime sky showered the partygoers with starlight. Massive ferns and flower bushes had been arranged throughout the greenhouse, as well as trees bearing small crystal chandeliers in place of fruit. Parrots and songbirds flitted among the branches, making several ladies duck and cover their heads for fear of droppings.

A year ago, Cayo would have been ready to charm the countess until she fell into his arms, just because he could. Today, Cayo was going to confront her about where she could and couldn't dock her ship. He pressed the cool surface of his glass to his hot forehead. His family couldn't afford any chink in the armor of his father's business. Not when the price of Soria's medicine was so steep.

"Cayo!"

He turned toward the sound of his name. The Akara twins, Chailai and Bero, were sitting at a round table lit by a lantern in the shape of a ship. The table was already strewn with empty glasses and cards.

"We haven't seen you in forever!" Chailai cried. The bird ornament in her hair jangled as she moved.

"We had bets going," said Bero. "On whether you were dead or not."

Cayo gestured at himself. "Still here."

"Then you're likely begging for a Scatterjack rematch," Bero said, grinning tauntingly over his cards. "Come on, I have a good streak going."

It was obviously the beginning of one of their typical nights: enough drink to fell an elephant, followed by visiting the casinos in Moray's Vice Sector. The twins—as well as Sébastien and their friend Tomjen—had done it enough times for it to evolve from *indulgence* to *habit*.

But they hadn't drained their fortunes. The twins and Tomjen were old money; their parents were swimming in wealth and had enough sense to pay off the right people to cover up stories of their children's excesses. The Mercados were only a single generation in— Cayo's father had built their fortune from practically nothing—and had not yet picked up the same tricks.

Cayo hesitated. His fingertips buzzed with the urge to feel those cards in his hands, to down the drink he held and join his friends. To not have a single care in the world, so long as he was feeling good. There were so many things he longed to put out of his mind. His father. Soria. Sébastien.

Where *was* Bas? A tremor of worry ran through Cayo, but he shook it off. Bas had been in trouble at the tables plenty of times before—they all had. He'd see his way out somehow. Cayo had already done what he could.

He gripped the champagne flute almost hard enough to break it. He still remembered nights in the casinos like a fever dream, the heat and thrill of the risk, the hum of alcohol in his bloodstream, the high of reward, the low of losing.

Heart racing, he gave his friends an apologetic smile and shrugged, motioning that someone was seeking his attention. He only just registered their disappointed faces before turning toward the back of the greenhouse. He dumped his champagne into a potted plant along the way. Soria would be proud of him.

But thinking of his sister only brought more guilt, despite the fact that she was the one who had convinced him to come to this party in the first place.

"I'd love to give the countess a piece of my mind," he'd told her earlier that evening when she asked if he would go. "I want to see the look on her face when I ask for a reimbursement for the dock switch."

"I see Father's teaching you well. You should go, then."

He had looked at her sitting against the pillows of her bed, noting the circles under her eyes and the shallow way her chest moved when she breathed. For a moment, she'd reminded him of their mother in her final days: the way her face had grown gaunt and pale, how she could barely keep her eyes open. The memory of climbing onto his mother's bed to lie beside her was as fresh as a new wound, even though it had been years since she'd passed. He could still hear his mother's labored humming as her trembling fingers threaded through his hair, feel how his tears had left a cold, wet patch on her nightgown.

Soria read his worry easily.

"I'll be perfectly fine here," she had said, patting his hand as if he were the sick one. "Father is home tonight, and Miss Lawan will be with me."

"But—"

"You've hardly been outside."

Because ever since they'd discovered she had ash fever, Cayo had been worrying himself to the point of exhaustion. Kamon had had enough sense to buy the Hizons' silence, but Cayo had been consumed with Soria's needs, calling for a doctor and putting down the payment for her medicine as soon as possible. For the first time, he thanked the god and her stars for his father's business.

"I'm livid I have to miss this party," Soria had told him. "And that I'll miss you going off on the countess. You better tell me all about it afterward." Her breathing had been strained, her face slightly gray, but still she had managed to smile. "Just don't fall back into old habits, all right?"

Soria hadn't been the only one to try to convince him.

"It's impossible to tell if the Hizons will keep news of Soria's illness to themselves," Kamon had told him this morning. "Now that they've called off the engagement . . ." His father's jaw had clenched. "Before the rumormongering begins, we can still represent our family at functions such as these. We need to keep up our reputation, now that Soria's candidacy is forfeit."

"Are you sure I'm the best candidate for that?" Cayo had asked with a brazen quirk of his eyebrow.

Kamon's answering look had been dark as a storm cloud. "Better a former rogue than a carrier of the fever."

Cayo didn't care what the gentry thought. After everything his sister had done for him—cleaning him up after wild nights in the Vice Sector, lying for him so that their father didn't know where he was, then eventually convincing Cayo to end his service to the Slum King—the least he could do was take care of her. Now, with her engagement to the Hizon heir severed . . .

Rounding a potted palm, Cayo took a moment to lean against it and catch his breath, tugging at his stiff collar. It was too hot in here. As he scanned the greenhouse for a waiter with a pitcher of water, an arm landed heavily across his shoulders.

"Finally, you emerge from your cave! I haven't seen you at the casinos in months."

Cayo rolled his eyes and shrugged Tomjen's arm away. "You know why."

"Oh, trust me, I know." Tomjen leaned in, tapping the side of his pointed nose. His brown eyes were bright and glassy with what Cayo assumed were his first drinks of the night, his black, slicked-back hair already somewhat in disarray. "You're licking your wounds."

"*What?* No." Still, he was filled with a hot, dreadful shame at the reminder of what he'd lost. But this wasn't about pride, not anymore.

Tomjen slapped his back in what he must have thought was encouragement. "I have every confidence you'll win it all back. Look, your glass is empty. Go get another and we'll find some fun. I spy a lovely group of flowers."

Cayo was confused until he realized Tomjen was steering them toward a small group of women. They were dressed in taffeta and silk, in bright colors and jewel-encrusted fabrics that winked in the light as they moved. They really did look like flowers, or a box of vibrant candies.

"Ladies," Tomjen said, showing off his best bow. The young women tittered, one of them using a silk fan on herself. "How may I best be of entertainment to you this evening?"

"We were just about to play some rounds of Bilge Rat," one of them said. "Would you care to join us?"

Cayo's fingertips buzzed again. Bilge Rat had been one of his favorites, the game fast and intuitive, with a card turnover rate so quick that a game could be over within mere seconds. It was one of the more dangerous ones.

"The pleasure would be mine," Tomjen said with another bow, the very model of a wealthy merchant's son. Cayo, in comparison, felt like a diamond that had reverted back to coal. "Cayo, shall we deal these lovely ladies in?"

Soria's warning enveloped him like a shawl. With an effort, he shook his head, forcing that dimpled smile again. "Not this time, I'm afraid."

Tomjen frowned but let it go, eagerly gathering the girls to him and loudly proclaiming that he had the fastest shuffling speed of anyone here. As they left, Cayo temporarily abandoned his search for the countess and found the nearest door. He needed the open air to clear his head.

Outside, he leaned against the thick glass wall and took in a deep breath, studying the canopy of stars overhead. The night was warm and close, the sea dark and quiet compared to the light and bustle within the greenhouse. The moon shone upon the water's surface like a blanket of pearl.

It took him a moment to realize he wasn't alone. A little farther down the wall stood a young woman in an elaborate gown of silver and gold, the formfitting bodice patterned with tiny diamonds in the shape of waves, the full skirt half-covered in a ruched, gauzy fabric. It was the sort of dress Soria would have drooled over.

Cayo smiled halfheartedly at the young woman, who smiled back. She couldn't have been more than seventeen or eighteen, likely an aristocrat's daughter who had been sent to one of the empires for schooling. Her dark, thick hair was swept up into a simple style with a jade clip to hold it in place. He guessed she was of mixed lineage, her skin somewhat darker than those from Rehan and Moray, her eyes more round than curved. Her shoulders were broad and her arms showed a subtle swell of muscle, and her nose was a bit crooked, as if it had once been broken.

"Not one for gambling, my lord?" she said in a voice like gin, clear and strong.

"I'm afraid not. The cards give me calluses."

She laughed, and his mouth eased into a true smile. It had been a while since he'd made a girl other than Soria laugh.

"I'm not one for gambling either," she said. Her lips were dark with carmine, her eyes dramatically lined with kohl. "I'd rather spend my money on useful things. Like a pocket watch, or a hit man."

He laughed weakly, unable to tell if she was joking, but he couldn't look away from her eyes. They were dark and intense, the way the night feels before a storm breaks. It almost felt as if she could read him, as if she already knew the exact suit he held before he could play it. "How are you enjoying the party so far?"

"It's a bit better now that I have a moment to myself." She reached into a hidden pocket of her gown and drew out what looked to be a canapé of puffed pastry sprinkled with sesame seeds. She popped it in her mouth and shrugged. "It's rather stuffy in there, isn't it?"

Cayo, caught off guard by the appearance of the puffed pastry, took a moment to respond. "I agree. Not to mention gaudy." He gestured at the array of plants and tables inside, the silver tureens of food, the fountain bubbling with champagne behind them. "The trivial things one does with a fortune. No doubt inherited."

"No doubt," the young woman agreed, pulling out another canapé and offering it to him. "Want one? They're good. Filled with red-bean paste."

To his surprise, Cayo grinned. His sister would have screamed in horror if she saw food even come *near* a gown as nice as this one. Normally he would have joined her, but he was too distracted by the sheer confidence that rolled off her, like she knew she could get away with anything.

"I'm all right, but thank you."

She shrugged and consumed it in one bite, not bothering to disguise the sound of pleasure as she ate. She licked stray sesame seeds off her fingers, gazing thoughtfully at the bay. Cayo, enraptured, stared at her instead.

"I suppose that's one benefit of owning fishing boats," the young woman said. "Being able to afford good food."

The fizzing, warm sensation in his chest went flat. *Fishing boats* was what the people of Moray said instead of *debtor ships*. Both were technically correct, but only one was honest.

Cayo had learned through rumors that the countess owned some herself. It wasn't a practice that sat well with him, but the unsettling reality was that it lined the pockets well.

"It's a common factor among the Moray gentry," Cayo replied carefully.

"True enough. Take the Mercado family, for instance. They made their fortune on the backs of indentured children, and the heir is a drunken playboy who squanders it all at the tables."

Cayo's mouth dried. The clothes against his skin seemed to burn. Clearly, she had no clue she was speaking to the drunken playboy himself.

Well, then.

"I happen to know that's not true," he said in what he hoped was a calm, light tone. "I believe one of Kamon Mercado's companies supplies provisions to the debtor ships, but only the ones that employ adults. He would never agree to work with ships that used children."

"Are you sure about that? I hear the countess purchased the *Brackish* from him."

The *Brackish*. He'd never heard of it, nor had his father informed him of a recent sale. It unsettled him to think that his father would conduct business transactions he purposefully kept from Cayo's knowledge.

"At least the Mercados keep the debtors fed and know how to respect the Port's Authority. The entire port was reeling when the countess arrived and had the arrogance to not adhere to its rules."

She stared at him in that dark, intense way of hers, idly touching the row of pearls at her throat. "You seem to know quite a bit about the countess already."

"Only what I've heard since her ship anchored." Remembering his reason for coming to this party in the first place, Cayo scowled. "Have you seen her at all?" he asked, squinting through the glass wall behind them.

She shook her head. "I heard she retired early. She was waiting for someone who never showed."

Cayo scoffed. "Figures. Well, whoever this woman is, she needs to learn her place. She can't just roll up to Moray and upend it like a card table. If she isn't careful, she's going to end up reaping what she sows."

The young woman rolled her pearls between her fingers, her eyebrows raised. God and her stars, he needed to dunk his head in that champagne fountain. Maybe he should have gone with Tomjen and the others.

He suddenly realized he'd had quite enough of this party. And with the countess already gone, what was the point?

"I apologize, my lady." Cayo barely remembered to bow. "I'm rather tired. I should be heading home." He turned and made for the boats that would return him to shore.

He felt the young woman's eyes on his back the entire time.

Cayo was halfway home when he ordered the carriage to stop. Needing to cool off after his strange encounter at the party, he told the driver to wait for him while he took a walk through Moray's dimly lit streets, hands in his pockets and eyes on the ground.

He stopped and craned his head back. A streak of purple cut across the sky like a vein. Sailors knew how to navigate by the stars. Cayo had always wanted to learn, but Kamon had told him that a merchant had no need for that. Their lives were made of numbers and ledgers, not sails and compasses.

"Caaayooo."

He tensed at the voice that sang his name from the darkness. A second later, she emerged from the mouth of the alleyway, one gloved hand on her hip and the other swinging a parasol by its handle.

"Romara." He barely managed to hide the dread in that one word.

She gasped in mock surprise. "You remembered my name! I worried. It's been so long." Romara pretended to pout, puffing out lips that had been painted black for the evening. Other than that, everything about her was red, from the elbow-length gloves to her shoes. Even her battered, moth-eaten parasol was a deep burgundy. She wore her dark hair in a messy bun, kept in place by a glittering hairpin.

"You're a little off course, dear," she went on, pointing behind her with her parasol. "You know where the best spots are."

He hadn't even realized his feet were automatically bringing him to the one place he shouldn't be. Tomjen and the twins had gotten into his head with all their talk of fun. He longed for that familiar cocktail of pleasure and danger sending excitement shivering through him. It would be like easing a sore body into a warm bath— something to take the edge off, to smooth out his nerves, to quiet his anxious mind. He could wager the sapphire hanging from his ear in the hopes of winning more. More money he could spare for Sébastien. More money for Soria's treatment.

Just don't fall back into bad habits, all right? Soria's voice whispered in his ear.

"I'm not going to the Vice Sector," he said. "Not tonight." *Not ever.*

Romara scoffed and stepped closer, and he could see now the smudged kohl winging from the corners of her eyes.

"What's the matter, Cayo?" She cocked her head. "Too good for us now, hmm? Good little merchant boys don't gamble, or some shit like that?"

"Some shit like that," he agreed, steadying her as she swayed. Something inside him swayed, too—a feeling similar to seeing Sébastien on the docks, regret and nostalgia tied up into a complicated knot. "Why don't you go home, Romara?"

She scoffed again, flinging her arms out on either side of her. "I *am* home!" She laughed, a high, shrieking sound that made him cringe.

"I mean to your father's."

Romara dropped her arms, a flash of hurt across her face. "I know what you mean, asshole. Don't tell me what to do."

He raised his hands. "All right." The last thing he wanted to do was get on Romara's bad side. As the daughter of the Slum King, all it took was a lazy point of her gloved finger for her father's men to drag away the poor fools who thought to annoy her. Most were never seen again.

At least he had spent enough time at the casinos for them to understand each other. Romara didn't seem to have her own friends; instead, she was prone to flitting among the groups of regulars who wandered into her father's domain. Cayo had often watched her stalk the casino floors like a wary lioness, surprised that she was so young—only about his age. There had been something vulnerable about her

54

then, a hint of uneasiness under the mask of haughty indifference she was so fond of wearing.

Perhaps that was why he had invited her to some of the games he played with the twins and Tomjen and Bas. At first his friends had been terrified of her, shooting Cayo dirty, accusing looks for even daring to get Romara's attention. But when she had told them the best ways to cheat at which tables and which dealers were more easily distracted than others, she had fit right in.

Ever since then, she sometimes joined them during those restless nights, sharing jaaga leaf to smoke together. They had once lain on their backs on the roof of the tallest casino for hours, high out of their minds and complaining about the city spread out around them.

Romara's complaints were always the same: how her father's grasp on Moray was weakening, and how she would one day push him off his bloody throne to rule this city the way it should be.

"Just one hour," she wheedled now, licking at the corner of her lips. Some of her lipstick had faded there. "The Scatterjack dealer they have at the Grand Mariner tonight is one of your favorites. The one with the curly hair."

Again temptation pulled at him, but weaker than before. After his outburst at Countess Yamaa's party, his mind was cloudy, static.

"Not tonight," he repeated with that dimpled smile. "But soon."

She grabbed his chin in her hand, shaking his head a bit. "It better be soon."

Then she tottered back to the alleyway, blowing a sloppy kiss over her shoulder as her heels clacked into the shadows. He thought he heard her laugh drunkenly to herself.

Cayo exhaled wearily and turned back for the carriage. When he finally arrived at Mercado Manor, he felt as if he'd been beaten with a branch. He thanked the coachman and greeted Narin, who held the door open for him with a short bow. The man's face was creased with concern, as it had been ever since Soria's incident.

Cayo crept up the stairs toward his sister's room, his footsteps muffled by the green runner. He didn't want to bump into his father and be interrogated about how the party went. What would he even say? "Oh yes, it was lovely, especially the part where some lady accused you of employing children."

Easing Soria's door open, he found that the candles were still lit in the sitting room, the door to Miss Lawan's connecting room closed. He walked in and peered into the bedroom. Soria was fast asleep in her spacious bed, blankets piled on top of her to help ease the chills that racked her body.

Cayo made his way to her side, bringing one of the candles from the sitting room. Soria's breathing was strained even in her sleep, her cheeks more hollow than usual, her eyelids sunken and bruised. His sister from two weeks ago wasn't here; in her place was a specter of who she'd been.

Cursing softly, Cayo returned to the sitting room and opened the medicine cabinet.

It was empty.

The bottom of his stomach gave out. He forced himself to close it gently, to sneak back out and shut the door behind him without a sound. Then he turned and strode to his father's office.

He was going to go through the ledgers and find the receipt for Soria's medicine, to make sure they had been given the right amount. But he didn't expect to find his father already sitting behind his desk, idly sipping his morning coffee. Kamon blinked at Cayo when he burst into the room, breathless and bedraggled.

"I take it the party went well," Kamon said, lowering his mug and eyeing Cayo's mussed suit. The window at his back was lit with the pale blue of dawn. He'd been out all night.

Cayo furiously pointed down the hall. "Soria has no medicine left. She needs another dose."

Kamon drew a long, slow breath, then took another sip of coffee. Cayo itched to grab his mug and throw it against the wall.

"I can call for the doctor," Cayo said, his own voice strangling him. "I can—"

"Cayo." Kamon fixed him with a long, hard look. "There will be no doctor. We can't afford the medicine."

The ground felt insubstantial under his feet. Cayo swayed a bit, hands flexing uselessly at his sides. "What?"

"We're broke."

Cayo grabbed the back of the nearest velvet-lined chair before sitting—though it seemed more like falling.

"Between you gambling away all your savings, and bad weather in the south delaying some important deliveries, there's nothing left to spare. Things . . . have been a little tight lately." Kamon looked furious to admit it out loud. "And now that Soria's engagement to Gen Hizon has been called off, we have no access to their fortune."

But he'd seen what his father had been saving for Soria's wedding day, a chest full of golden coin and fine foreign silks. "Soria's dowry—"

"Already spent for her medicine."

Cayo's mind was reeling, but he remembered a fragment of the conversation he'd had with the mysterious girl at last night's party. "You had a sale recently. The *Brackish*?"

Kamon looked surprised, which was a feat in itself. He took

a moment to respond, and Cayo wondered if he was deciding whether to reveal that he hadn't wanted Cayo to know about this particular transaction.

"It went cheaper than it was worth," Kamon said at last. "Honestly, I was looking for an excuse to get rid of the thing."

"Father . . ." Cayo swallowed. "Does it—or did it—use children?"

"I don't see how that's any of your concern." His father took a long sip of coffee as Cayo stared blankly at him. "Whether or not it did, it's not under my name anymore, and good riddance. But that's beside the point. The point, Cayo, is that even with making transactions like this to help pay off *your* debt, there's still barely anything left for Soria's medicine. Do you see where this is going?"

"No, I don't." Cayo's voice crept higher, louder. "What do you mean?"

Kamon sighed and looked up at the ceiling, as if to fortify himself.

"Today I'll be dismissing Miss Lawan and the kitchen staff, as well as the maids," he eventually said. "We can't pay their salaries any longer."

Cayo's chest tightened. He already felt nauseous after being up all night, but now that feeling grew, the revelation dawning on him like the unmistakable glare of the sun at his father's back.

His mother used to sing a song about a farmer whose crops all withered. When he asked her once why she sang it so often, she had shrugged and told him that it was the way of life. Nothing could stay; everything was temporary. You could never trust what you had, only what you were capable of.

They had been rich. He had grown up receiving everything he could possibly want.

And now they had nothing.

"We . . . We have to do *something*," Cayo croaked. "We can sell the manor, or—"

"Cayo." Kamon took another long breath. "The fever has already progressed quite a bit. We didn't catch the early stages in time. Even if we sold everything we own, what good would it do? Buy Soria a few more months? A year, at most? She had her shot with the Hizons, and the sickness took that from her—from us. She is the sea on a windless day, preventing our ship from going forward. Do you understand?"

Cayo sat there with his lips parted. He couldn't believe what he was hearing, thought that maybe he *had* gotten drunk at that party and everything around him was only a blurred distortion of reality.

"What are you saying?" he whispered.

"I'm saying that, though I love Soria dearly"—Kamon paused, his jaw tight and his throat working to swallow—"I have another child to think about, a blood heir who can inherit our family's Vault when I'm gone."

Cayo pushed himself to his feet, knocking back the chair. His father looked up, startled.

"How can you think this way?" Cayo spat. "Are Soria and I nothing but a business venture for you? One of us has been a spare all along?"

"That's not how I meant—"

"If you truly loved your daughter, you'd be fighting tooth and nail for her!"

"You don't think I know how to fight tooth and nail?" His father stood as well, his eyes bright with fury. "I did that in order for you to live the only life you've ever known, one filled with velvet and gold. I did that to buy this manor, to give us status, to bring us up in the world. But you, Cayo—you know nothing of fighting. You simply take and spend. And now here we are."

Cayo stormed out, slamming the door behind him. How dare his father insinuate he was the reason Soria could die? He wouldn't let her. He *refused* to let ash fever take her from him. They had already lost their mother to sickness. Cayo could not survive going through it a second time.

Dizzy, he leaned against the wall and slid to the floor, resting his forehead on his knees.

Just don't fall back into bad habits, all right?

"I'm sorry," he whispered to the hallway. To Soria. Because he knew there was only one way to get the money he needed—only one way to save her life.

He had to once again play for the Slum King.

5

When Neralia fell from the kingdom in the clouds, she held her hands
out to the stars who had forsaken her. Their winking gazes turned away,
and the water rose to claim her, sheltering her from their disdain.

—"NERALIA OF THE CLOUDS," AN ORAL STORY ORIGINATING FROM

THE LEDE ISLANDS

It was strange how seven years could fit inside a pack.

Silverfish looked around her hammock for the fifth time, but everything she owned had been stuffed inside her bag already: a hairbrush, a change of clothes, a rock that was shaped like Moray's Crescent Bay.

Her stomach was a squirming mess, her head buzzing from lack of sleep. She tried to tell herself it was a good thing—her body recognized an opportunity. But it mostly set her teeth on edge, the anticipation tingling down to her fingers.

Today, the *Brackish* was docking in Moray.

Today, she would be free.

Just in time for her mother's birthday.

Silverfish unwound the frayed linen bandage from her swollen hand, revealing the small knife tattoo on her wrist. Flexing her fingers, she checked the cut from the rockfish, red and puffy yet on its way to healing.

Survive.

For seven years, she had survived. She had done anything she could to dance out of death's way in preparation for this moment. And now her reward would be her mother's face when she saw her daughter walk through the door.

Some of the Water Bugs were already awake and watched her in the predawn light. She smiled, but most didn't smile back. Beetle, however, scrambled off her hammock and ran to her. The little girl threw her arms around Silverfish's legs, her thin body shaking as she hid her face against her thigh.

Silverfish's hand hovered above the girl's back. After a moment, she settled it on Beetle's shoulder.

"Don't go," the girl whimpered against her leg. She could feel Beetle's hot breath through the tattered fabric of her trousers.

Silverfish took a deep breath and sank to one knee before the girl.

"One day you'll be able to leave this ship, too. It won't be today, or tomorrow, but that day will come. And you'll walk away with your head held high." Silverfish gently jostled her shoulder. "Remember that, all right?"

Beetle pressed her lips together to prevent them from trembling as she nodded. Silverfish briefly cradled the side of her head, not remembering until after she pulled away that that was something her father used to do.

"Anyway, I'm not gone just yet," she told Beetle as she headed for the door.

She lingered in the companionway, wondering if she should check on Boon. His words still whispered in her mind, following her into nightmares of treasure chests filled with nooses and gambling halls soaked with blood.

Gritting her teeth, she turned away from the stairs leading down to the cells. He wasn't her problem any longer.

Out on the deck, she took a deep breath of clean salt air. The morning waves danced silver; last night's wind had settled into a light breeze. It carried the distinct scent of land, dry and green and oddly foreign. A ship was never quiet, but in the early stages of dawn it was the calmest it would be before the Bugs swarmed the deck and Zharo began to bellow orders.

Roach was already up; she wondered if he'd also had a hard time sleeping. He leaned against the railing, his back to her. She passed under the debt board to reach him and couldn't help but scan it for her name. Her sum had been set to zero—the pearl had been enough. Something large and messy swelled within her at the sight, a relief so strong that it threatened to consume her.

Roach turned when she was close. His expression was complicated. She could tell he didn't want her to go, though he would never admit it out loud. Her only regret escaping the *Brackish* was leaving him behind.

His seven years would be up in six months. He would make it until then.

He had to.

She raised their two-finger salute, which he returned before taking her hand in his. Calluses hardened his palm and fingertips, his knuckles protruding like mountains. She brushed her thumb across their peaks and valleys, and he smiled sadly.

"You'll meet me in Moray?" she asked.

"That's the plan." He enveloped her in a hug, and she allowed herself to be engulfed by it, closing her eyes and holding him tight. He was her best friend on these waters. Her only friend.

"Silverfish!"

They both started and pulled away. Captain Zharo emerged from the cells, screaming her name like he was a demon she had tricked out of consuming her heart. When he stormed up onto the deck, the Bugs tentatively followed, their eyes wide and fearful. When Zharo finally spotted her by the railing, he pointed a stubby, grimy finger at her, a silent summons written across his flushed face and the stiff set of his shoulders.

Roach grabbed for her hand, but she shook her head and he inched away. No doubt the captain wanted to frighten her one last time. She would not give him the satisfaction.

"Today is a big day for you, Silverfish," the captain said, one hand lingering near his hip as he leered at her. They were situated under the gutting deck, the smell of dead fish overpowering. She doubted she would ever get the stink off her. "Or it would have been, had you not double-crossed me."

She tightened a hand around the strap of her pack. "I don't understand."

Zharo bared his decaying teeth. "D'you honestly think I'd let you off this ship? After you done let a *spy* escape?"

Boon. He must have used her shucker to free himself before anyone had woken.

"I don't know what you're talking about," she said, trying to keep her voice from wavering.

"Your little catch," he said. "The spy you plucked out of the waters. He's gone."

"He's not a spy," she said, "he's Landless."

"With those gold buttons? Don't think so. And guess what, Silverfish? Your debt's gone up again." He hungrily licked his bottom lip, his dark eyes as heavy as a touch. "No fat pearl's gonna do it this time. But I'm doin' you a favor, see? You finally get to see your mama."

Zharo took out his pistol and aimed it at her. The Bugs who had crowded against the railing behind him yelped and scampered away. Roach cursed and edged closer to her.

But Silverfish was frozen before the pistol's black, hollow eye, sighting her right where her heart was beating a frantic rhythm in her chest. The iron muzzle glinted gold in the waxing dawn light.

Her breath came faster, rattling in her chest, but she refused to step back. "Wh-what do you mean, get to see my mother?"

He tsked. "Forgot to tell you, didn't I? She breathed her last three years ago. A nice peaceful death, in her sleep. Or so they told me."

A ringing started in her ears. Silverfish numbly looked around, as if seeking someone to confirm if it was really true. The Water Bugs were still cowering, Roach looking on in terror. He met her eyes and shook his head.

Dead.

Her mother was dead.

She couldn't be. Silverfish was going to come home for her birthday. They were going to walk through the gardens of Moray and eat the fruit off the trees. She was going to become Amaya again, a girl curled up in her mother's arms, safe from what the world demanded of her.

But the world was empty and cold, and she was alone.

She finally took a step back. Zharo chuckled and took one forward.

"I would've told you sooner, but you were such a hard worker," Zharo said. The satisfied way he said it, almost like a compliment, was like a hand squeezing the nape of her neck. She shuddered in revulsion. "Was even able to scrape off the top of your earnings for myself. And I would've let you off this ship if you hadn't gone and rescued that bastard. Really, you brought this on yourself."

She had often wondered what she would do if the captain ever attacked her with serious intent, had taken to practicing the motions with Roach or when she was alone: grab his gun, hit his arm where it was weakest, force him to drop his weapon. But she couldn't move, couldn't send a message to the rest of her body to cooperate.

The sun was beginning to rise, deepening the thin dawn light to a fierce, burning orange. The waves caught the light and turned the sea into a roiling fire.

When the water turns orange, remember to swim down.

That was what Boon had said, after all his talk of treasure and finding out the truth about her father. Silverfish took another unsteady step toward the railing until it hit her back, and again Zharo pursued. She could hear the ocean churning below.

"Your seven years are finally up, Silverfish," he said. He cocked the pistol's hammer back. "Be sure to send my regards to your mama."

He pulled the trigger.

The Bugs screamed at the bark of the pistol, but Silverfish had already launched herself over the railing. She fell for what seemed an eternity before she hit the water, knocking the breath out of her.

Remember to swim down.

Silverfish had dived for enough pearls—she knew how to swim down. She kicked her legs furiously behind her, her arms stretching, reaching toward the depths. She left the orange waves behind and swam into the gloom, the water growing dark enough to become another enemy.

Her sense of direction was scrambled; her lungs burned for air. Even as the pressure grew in her ears, even as spots flew across her vision, she kept swimming. Bubbles escaped the corners of her mouth, her chest seizing painfully.

Internally, Silverfish was screaming. She had nothing. No one. And now she was going to die because some Landless nobody didn't know what he was talking about.

No.

She did have one thing left: a new goal.

If she lived, she was going to kill Captain Zharo.

Survive.

Silverfish used her fury and her grief to keep swimming, to slice through the water like a blade. Her limbs were cramping, her vision darkening. Still she swam down, consciousness leaving her bit by bit.

Then she felt it—a tug.

A riptide.

Her father had once told her that you could only see the way forward when all other options have failed you.

Silverfish didn't hesitate. She flung herself into the riptide's path, letting the water whisk her out of the dark and into the unknown.

6

The rules of Scatterjack are very simple: five cards to a hand,
two cards to trade, and a knife up your sleeve if the game goes sour.
—THE INS AND OUTS OF TABLE BETTING

Before she died, Cayo's mother had often told him that he was born under the sign of Luck, the glittering constellation that greeted his arrival into this world. She used to trace it for him with her finger, following the stars that made the shape of a crown.

"He who is lucky is a king," she would tell him as she rested a hand on his shoulder. "And like a king, he must always watch for usurpers. Those who are not lucky will succumb to envy and seek his power for their own."

Cayo wondered now, as he sat across the desk from the Slum King, whether the man had also been born under the sign of Luck—or if he was one of the usurpers.

His office was within the Scarlet Arc, a gambling hall that the

Slum King owned. Although his name wasn't on the deed in case the city guard—lazy as they were—decided to use a paper trail to find him, everyone knew who truly ran it. Despite its respectable name, nothing respectable happened within the red-painted walls of the Arc. It was undeniably one of the most dangerous halls in the Vice Sector, rife with murderers and thieves.

Although Cayo had realized just this morning that he needed to return, he was fast coming to regret this decision.

The Slum King—also known as Jun Salvador—sat in his maroon wingback chair and steepled his fingers on the desk, eyeing Cayo with something that looked deceptively like patience. His dark brown hair was thin, combed into a stylish swoop above a large forehead. He was impeccably dressed as always, a trait that Cayo had once appreciated, yet now made him all the more conscious of his mussed hair and rumpled clothing. The man was lean and trim, but corded with muscle that he didn't bother to hide under his expensively tailored shirt and waistcoat. His face, however, was haggard and scarred, a long silvery line going from forehead to chin and a pinkish crater in his right cheek where someone had carved out a hunk of flesh.

"Well," said the Slum King. "This is the part where I'm supposed to say I'm surprised to see you, but that would make me a liar."

Even hearing his voice again sent a shiver down Cayo's spine. Low, steady, and rough from years of cigarillo smoke, it was the sort of voice that could convince you to trust it, that could lead you through a den of vipers simply because it asked nicely. It was the sort of voice that made you want to impress its owner.

Cayo had wanted to impress him, once. And he had.

And then he'd lost everything.

Now he was on that precipice again. But Soria's life was on

the line. This was the only way he knew how to save her.

Even if he had promised her he would never come back here.

For a brief moment, Cayo wished Sébastien were with him. Bas had always been good at making the Slum King laugh, at defusing the tension in any given situation. Cayo hadn't heard from him since giving him the last of his month's allowance, but then again, he hadn't expected to; he'd made it clear that Sébastien could expect no more help from him. Still, he hoped he had done enough.

Cayo took a deep breath and leaned forward in his chair. "I want to return to the tables."

Salvador laughed softly. "Has the itch finally come crawling back?"

Cayo ignored that. "I need back in."

Fast as a bullet, a pocketknife flicked into the Slum King's hand. Cayo flinched, but Salvador only reached into a drawer and pulled out a cigarillo, cutting off its tip with the knife and lighting it on the candle burning on his desk. He took a puff and leaned back with a deep exhalation. Smoke drifted through the study like fog, inching toward the brass chandelier above Cayo's head. The murmur and laughter of the Arc's usual crowd drifted through the closed door in the taut silence.

"Not a chance," he said at last.

"What? Why?" Cayo scooted to the edge of his chair, all too aware that the Slum King hadn't yet put his knife away. "I was one of your best winners at Scatterjack and Threefold. I know the dealers, I've networked within the casinos—"

"You *were* one of the best until you started getting reckless." Another drag of his cigarillo. His eyes never left Cayo's. "Until the thrill of it made you think south of your brain."

Cayo clenched and unclenched his hands. Chasing the high of winning had urged him to the casinos, to the gambling dens, to the racetracks—anyplace he could drop a sum in the hopes of doubling or even tripling it. It had made him drunk without a drop of liquor, convincing him that he was unbeatable, unstoppable.

"My time away from the dens has cleared my head," he said stiffly. "I'm ready to play again."

The Slum King continued to survey him through his cigarillo smoke. "Why?"

"I . . . I need the money."

"You'll end up losing more than you gain. Desperation makes for poor decisions. You didn't fold when you needed to, and you didn't cheat when you had to. You've lost my trust, Cayo."

Once, these words would have devastated him. Now they just filled him with a sense of panic. His only chance was slipping away.

"Please." He couldn't hide the urgency in his voice. Cayo was unwilling to draw Soria into this, but it was better to be truthful with the Slum King than get caught out in a lie. "I need medicine I can't afford. For ash fever. *Please*, I'll do anything."

The Slum King paused at this, cigarillo halfway to his lips. He toyed with his knife, spinning it in his fingers. Then, finally, he snapped it closed.

"Anything," Salvador repeated, the word slow and wicked on his tongue. It poured out like pomegranate syrup into a glass of Blood and Sand, a drink so sweet it disguised how strong the alcohol in it was until it came over you like a wave.

Salvador rapped his knuckles on the desk. The door to the office opened, and one of his staff members leaned in.

"Fetch my daughter." When the man withdrew, the Slum King

turned back to Cayo, a thin smile playing at his lips. There was no hiding the hint of cruelty in that smile, nor the hunger in his eyes.

"It seems people are always coming to me to tell me what *they* want, not what they can offer *me*. I'll give you the money you need, but it won't be won at the tables."

"What do you mean?" Cayo asked, his shoulders tense. Whatever game the Slum King was playing, he didn't know the rules.

Before the Slum King could answer, Romara herself strutted in. She was dressed all in black today, her bodice low-cut and form-fitting, with long tapered sleeves smudged with dust and glitter. Her skirt was plump with tulle and torn lace, her boot heels so sharp they could likely kill a man. In fact, Cayo was willing to bet they had.

"I see the puppy is back," she said, quickly readjusting her breasts and fanning out her skirt. She blinked lashes spidery and limp with mascara at him. He'd seen her do the same thing a million times before, but it sent a flicker of worry through him now. She was on full alert. "Is he going to play again?"

"Hardly." The Slum King sat back, crossing his arms with that same catlike smile on his marked face. "He's just become your fiancé."

Romara's smile froze in place.

Cayo tried to laugh, but only a dry cough came out. "You can't be serious."

The Slum King eyed him through a veil of smoke. "You'll marry my daughter and give her—and by extension, me—the status we deserve in this wretched city."

Cayo's whole body went cold. Marry the Slum King's daughter? Marry *Romara*?

The thought was so absurd it didn't seem plausible. It wasn't just the way she drank to the point of becoming feral; as smart as she was, a sharp cruelty ran through her very being. He knew how she enjoyed letting her father's men deal with those she didn't favor. He had once seen a young man dragged out of a gambling den for accidentally spilling his drink on Romara's favorite dress. His bloated body had been washed ashore two days later.

"No," Cayo said. "Absolutely not." Romara looked as shocked as he felt. Cayo had spent enough time with Romara to know what was an act and what was real, how she determined what pawns to sacrifice in the ongoing game of power she played with her father. And she wasn't acting now.

"You want to marry one of my sons instead? I'll warn you, they're both dense as rocks."

"I'm not marrying anybody!"

"Do you want the money, Cayo?" Salvador's voice had gone soft, his eyes half-lidded. Cayo shuddered, knowing the first stage of the Slum King's rage when he saw it.

Of course he wanted the money. He *needed* it. Soria needed it.

But Romara . . .

"Ash fever isn't cheap," the Slum King continued, tapping stray embers off the end of his cigarillo. "And from what I hear, without medication the disease advances rather quickly."

Cayo was having trouble breathing. But the Slum King was right. Soria was dying. Every minute he wasted here was a minute she was suffering back at home.

He needed the medicine.

He had no choice.

Cayo glanced at Romara again, and their eyes locked. Sometimes, when he wasn't quite expecting it, he glimpsed a girl who wanted more than what her father had made of her. But she hid that girl under heavy makeup and a vicious grin, always playing the game she knew best, the one that was her family's true inheritance: manipulation.

She gave him a barely perceivable nod. Understanding that he had to follow whatever act she had in store, he inclined his head slightly.

When he nodded in acceptance to the Slum King, Romara squealed and plopped down on his lap, nuzzling his head with hers. She smelled like sweat and dying roses.

"I'll be the best wife," she purred, tracing circles over his chest. "I can't cook or clean, but I'm good at other things." She was enjoying this far too much for his comfort.

"I . . . I'll need time," Cayo croaked. "To arrange it with my father. Romara needs to be properly introduced, a contract needs to be signed, a dowry secured. . . ."

Stall, was all he could think.

"The money for medicine should be dowry enough." Salvador adjusted the silk tie at the base of his neck. "But I'll give you time to settle things with your father. Just as long as you don't go back on your word." His thumb moved almost lovingly across the hilt of his knife. "It would be a shame for a different fate to befall your sister, wouldn't it, Cayo?"

Cayo momentarily stopped breathing, the back of his neck damp with sweat. Keeping his eyes locked on the Slum King, he knew without a doubt that there would be no getting out of this. Money or no money, he had entangled himself too deep.

Romara laughed softly near his ear, still sitting on Cayo's lap like she owned him.

"Yes, sir," he whispered.

"I'm glad you understand," Salvador crooned. "Because you know what happens to those who try to cross me."

The Slum King nudged aside the candle on his desk, revealing a jar that had been half-concealed behind it. It was filled with a pale liquid, and in that liquid floated two eyeballs of the most beautiful shade of bluish green.

Cayo stared in horror at the jar.

Sébastien's eyes stared back.

7

Court Ruling: The accused has been found guilty of the following—smuggling, robbery, arson, and minor treason. The court hereby rules that defendant shall be sentenced to Landless status immediately following prosecution.

—COURT RECORD FROM JUDICIARY LEDGERS WITHIN THE REPUBLIC OF REHAN

Silverfish slept in fits and starts, her dreams rarely drifting beyond the boundaries of her aching body. Every time her eyelids fluttered she caught brief flashes of light. The sound of waves rushed in the distance, and when she tried to move she could only twitch, sending pain along her limbs.

Eventually, she was able to open her eyes for longer than half a second. The sun was a vicious eye staring down at her, and she squinted at the brightness of the white sand around her. The world seemed washed out, the color leached like dye from a shirt laundered too many times.

She tried to roll over and gasped in pain. Her arms were heavy and sore, her legs deadweight. And her *head*. It was pounding with a sickly beat, like a funerary march. She barely lifted herself on her elbows before vomiting.

She had first thought she'd washed up onto an island, but when she lifted her head she realized it was a small atoll. It curved in an almost perfect semicircle around a shimmering blue lagoon, like a crescent moon fallen to earth. A handful of palms stood stubbornly along the south side, not too far from where she had been washed up on the atoll's soft white sand.

Silverfish rolled onto her back and groaned. Everything *hurt*.

But she was alive. Once again, she had survived.

She was hot and sticky, sea salt clinging to her skin and hair. Her tongue was swollen and dry in her mouth, the back of her throat burning with the need for water. A sickening shade of purple swam behind her eyelids—the blue of the sea mixed with the red of her blood.

After a minute to gather her strength, she crawled to the edge of the sand, toward the lagoon. The water was clear, and she could see where the sand descended into a black pit toward the middle. She cupped some water in her hand and tasted it, then spat it right back out. Salt water.

Damn it.

The shore of the atoll was stubbled with rocks and remnants of coral. Clinging to those rocks and coral were strange scallop-like creatures. Silverfish moved closer to inspect them. Their flesh was a delicate pink, and they were soft and spongy to the touch.

Brinies. Once considered a delicacy in Moray, they had been out-lawed years ago after guests at a duke's dinner party had been fed a bad batch. Most of the guests had died of the poison they had unknowingly ingested.

She couldn't risk eating them, then. But still, their discovery surprised her. She didn't know much about them other than their reputation and that they were notoriously difficult to find. The fact that they would be here, on this little forgotten atoll, seemed like a terrible omen.

"Ah, I see the monsters didn't eat you."

Silverfish turned quickly, her head pounding with a violent protest.

Boon. He was dripping wet, wearing a white shirt and a pair of cutoff trousers. "So you took my advice," he said with a little salute that made no sense to her. "I knew you looked smart."

"Where did you come from?" she rasped, her throat raw from salt water.

"I'm about to show you." He tossed something to her; it landed on the sand between them. Her shucker. "I owe you again, Silverfish."

Anger and confusion fought inside her, but eventually anger won out. "You were supposed to wait until I'd left the ship to escape. The captain knew I helped you."

Boon shrugged. "I did warn you to jump ship. Not my fault you lingered."

"He tried to *kill* me," she growled.

"Looks as though he failed, huh?" he said, unfazed by her anger. If anything, he sounded cheerful. "'Less I'm talking to a ghost."

He took a step forward, and she tensed. He stopped, waiting wordlessly for her permission to come closer. Eventually, she nodded, and he knelt beside her.

"The bullet grazed you, looks like." He indicated a tear in her sleeve she hadn't even noticed. Nor had she felt the thin red line on her skin underneath the tear, but now that she knew it was there it began to burn. "You never feel it in the heat of the moment, do you?"

She pulled away. "This is your fault. If I hadn't rescued you, I would have been able to walk off the *Brackish* and go home. I would have . . ."

She was about to say *I would have seen my mother,* but Captain Zharo's words came rushing back. Like the wound on her arm, the delayed pain suddenly came all at once, stealing the air from her lungs. She doubled over, whimpering.

"Whoa, what's gotten into you?" Boon demanded, but she ignored him.

My mother is dead. She died three years ago, and that bastard never told me.

She was too dehydrated to cry, but her eyes still stung, her throat tightening with the force of her grief. She pounded a fist into the sand.

"I'm going to kill him," she seethed.

"Hold on, now. Before we go killing anybody, there's something I gotta show you."

Silverfish looked around the blank shore of the atoll. "Show me?" she repeated. "What could you possibly have to show me?"

But he only gave her a funny little smile. "Think you can dive once more?"

She didn't want to dive. She needed to get off this atoll, to find Zharo and plunge a knife in his heart. Breathing heavily, she hauled herself to her feet, ready to swim to Moray if she had to.

At the sight of what awaited her, she froze. There were whirlpools surrounding the atoll, the waves churning in slow, spinning cyclones.

I see the monsters didn't eat you. Boon had been talking about Usaad and Broma, the twin sea serpents said to lurk to the southeast of Moray. They were fabled to cause devastating maelstroms that sank countless ships. The riptide was connected to the whirlpools, which must have spat her out on the atoll.

She was trapped.

Slowly, she turned and stared at Boon, who grinned at her knowingly. She suddenly saw the situation for what it was: She belonged to him now, much in the same way he'd belonged to her on the *Brackish*. He was the only one who knew how to escape. She had to follow him.

Silverfish grabbed her shucker and tucked it into her pocket. At least she had a weapon, however puny, in case this all went belly-up. As she finally approached the lagoon, Boon handed her a water skin. She greedily began to guzzle the freshwater, but he yanked it away before she could get more than three sips.

"It'll make you sick," he admonished. "You ought to know that. You can have more when we get there."

"Where is *there*?"

"You'll see."

She followed him toward the middle of the lagoon, sucking the residue of water off her lips. The sand eventually fell away, and she swam slowly behind Boon, her arms leaden as she tried to keep up.

"Ready?" he asked once they had made it to the middle of the lagoon. "Take a deep breath."

"I know how to dive," she muttered, but he had already plunged into the water. She gulped a breath and followed.

It almost felt like when she had jumped off the *Brackish* into the orange water, swimming down as far as she could go just because Boon had told her to. And now here she was, doing it again.

Down and down, through layers of aquamarine water. They swam past a ring of coral, a reef naturally formed from whatever island had once occupied this lonely spot on the sea.

Suddenly, a hole appeared in the reef, forming a natural corridor. Boon pressed on until he reached the end, where carved into the lava bed that had originally birthed this atoll was . . .

A door?

Boon pushed at a hatch-shaped hunk of rock, revealing a dark hole as it slid away. He beckoned her through first.

Silverfish's instincts told her to swim up instead of down. But Boon insistently gestured again, so she quickly swam through the hole and waited for him to do the same. He led her through the dark until he tugged on her arm and pulled her up.

They broke the surface of a pool. Silverfish, stunned, saw they'd surfaced inside a cave of blackish stone.

"What in Trickster's name is this place?" she demanded.

Boon hauled himself onto a lip of dark rock and helped her stand. "Back on the ship, you called me Landless. You weren't entirely wrong."

When a person committed crimes against their country or people, they were sometimes sentenced to become Landless, exiled from their homes and blacklisted in other empires. Some of them were also escapees of debtor ships. Their only resort was to either roam the seas or find a hidden community of other Landless.

"This is a Landless comm," she guessed.

"For simplicity's sake, yeah, it is." Boon wrung out his shirt. "Come on. The others will wanna meet you."

She once again followed him. She felt as if she were half-asleep, and there was a small part of her that didn't particularly care what happened to her now.

Her mother was dead. There was no one left in the world to love her.

There was only the promise of retribution.

The caverns they walked through were cramped and impossibly dark, the rock columns on either side damp and made of a black stonelike material. Boon kept clicking his tongue, and Silverfish was reminded of how a bat used sound to map out its surroundings. She wondered how much time he'd spent in darkness, alone.

The columns eventually opened up to a larger cavern with a lantern swinging from an unseen rope, water dripping down the walls like miniature waterfalls, glittering hunks of fluorite embedded in the rock. Stalactites branched downward in varying lengths, a few stalagmites reaching up toward them as if seeking to become one.

Beyond the forest of stalagmites, a series of wide natural arches in the rock walls led into caverns—*rooms*—filled with makeshift furniture and hammocks.

And people. There were about a half dozen she could see, most of them milling about in what looked to be a central common area, filled with benches they had no doubt carved themselves; the wood was old and rotting, likely taken from wrecked ships that had run afoul of the whirlpools or the reef. Lanterns hanging from dried ropes of kelp illuminated the black rock walls and the people who turned to look at her.

"What—what is this place?" she breathed. She was half-afraid, half-amazed. It was like a hidden castle underwater, and surprisingly beautiful.

Before Boon could reply, a man approached them. He also looked Kharian, tall yet slight of build, with thick black hair curling around his ears. He wore bracers on his arms and a bandolier across his chest that contained various knives and daggers. Silverfish pinned his age about a decade younger than Boon.

"This the infamous Silverfish?" he asked. His voice had an almost musical quality to it.

"The one and only. Let's get her some grub, and water, too. She's tired."

"*She* can speak for herself," Silverfish said. "And she wants to know why she's here."

"There's time for that later." Boon waved her questions away. "You need something in your system before you keel over."

They led her deeper into the Landless comm. Silverfish drew stares from the others, and she couldn't help but stare back. The system of caverns was like a honeycomb. They were mostly small and empty, but in one, she spotted something that nearly made her stop in her tracks. Inside lay piles and piles of crates, barrels, chests . . .

And the unmistakable glint of gold.

"The cave's been around for decades," Boon said suddenly, making her start. His friend stalked silently beside him, save for the clink and rattle of his bandolier. "I only made it back thanks to Avi here."

Avi sniffed. "You still owe me for picking up your sorry ass on that pathetic dinghy."

"It was a rowboat, thank you very much." Boon glanced over his shoulder at her. "When we first stumbled across this place a few years ago, it had been abandoned. We think some ancient Ledese tribe lived down here. We began to fix it up for ourselves." He spread out his arms, indicating the rocky homes around them. "It's grown nicely, I think."

Silverfish nodded absently, her mind still spinning at the sight of that gold. She caressed the shucker in her pocket.

Boon and Avi led her to a cavern they were using as a make-shift galley. A large pot stood over a smoldering fire, dirty wooden bowls piled up beside it. Silverfish suddenly felt very alone, missing the times she could sit in the *Brackish*'s galley and talk with Cicada or watch Roach nibbling his rations, trying to make them last for as long as possible.

She missed that simple trust between them. Down here, she couldn't trust anyone—Boon least of all.

Boon allowed her to take a few more sips from his water skin while Avi ladled whatever was in the pot into a bowl. Her mouth immediately watered as a yawning hunger nearly split her open.

"Briny stew," Avi said as he sat next to Boon. "It'll help get your strength back."

Silverfish paused with the bowl halfway to her mouth. "Brinies? But . . . they're poisonous."

Boon and Avi exchanged amused looks. "Not before they begin to molt," Boon said.

"You eat some, then."

Boon gestured lazily at Avi, who sighed and got him a bowl as well. Boon lifted it in a mock toast before guzzling its contents, spilling at least a third of it down his chin and onto his shirt. Silverfish wrinkled her nose in disgust.

"See?" he said as he tossed the empty bowl back toward the others. He wiped his chin with a sleeve. "Have at it. Or not—suit yourself."

Silverfish took a tentative sip. The brinies were soft and buttery, flooding her mouth with a taste so good it was almost painful. She must have made a sound, because Boon laughed.

"There's more where that came from." Boon leaned back and crossed his arms. "Whatever you want is yours, Silverfish. I'm a man who pays my debts."

She swallowed her second bite too fast and coughed. "What does that mean?"

"Answer her questions, Boon," Avi grumbled. "My binder's too tight and I'm getting a headache."

Boon rolled his eyes. "What I mean is that you saved my life. Twice." He spread his hands before him, the left still trembling. "So. Name your price."

Silverfish looked from Boon to Avi and back. She had no idea what game these two were playing, or how many of the other Landless were in on it. Boon had to be some shade of dense to think that she would willingly walk into whatever trap he was building for her. Boon was trying to get her to trust him, she could figure out that much, but the question was *why?*

She suddenly felt dizzy, her exhaustion dropping like an anchor on her shoulders. As she stared at the bowl of soup before her, aromatic and tasting vaguely of the sea, she knew that she had to get out of there. Quickly.

"I need to piss," she blurted.

"Third cavern on the left's what we got for a privy," Avi said with a barely suppressed smirk.

Silverfish got to her feet, still a bit off-kilter. She hurried down the pathway they had taken. Their "privy" was nothing but an arid cave hollowed out with troughs dug deep into the rock. She hurried quickly past it. She had only a few minutes to find what she was looking for.

Finally, she spotted the cavern she'd seen earlier and ducked inside, her heart racing and her head throbbing in time with her pulse. Silverfish carefully wended through the crates and barrels, many of them labeled with goods such as spices, dried meats, oil. Stolen from merchant ships, no doubt. But one barrel in particular caught her eye. Its lid was partially open, revealing a yellow mound of gold pieces within.

It was more wealth than she had ever seen in her life. More than her debt—more than enough to cover the costs of several Water Bugs' debts, if not all of them. Entranced, Silverfish raised a shaking hand and touched the cool surfaces of the coins, feeling how they slid and tumbled against each other, listening to the satisfying clinking sounds they made. Golden senas. It had been so long since she had seen real money, but she remembered what Rehanese currency looked like.

A memory broke across her like a wave. Her mother and father had taken her to the public gardens one hazy morning, the fog burning off to reveal a blue sky overhead. The sunlight had filtered down onto the plants around her, splattering the path like golden paint shaken from a brush.

But something along the path had actually glinted gold in that light—a sena coin. She had bounded toward it and picked it up, showing it to her parents with pride. They had looked at each other, debating whether to let her keep it, until her mother had said that it was hers—but only if she put it away in savings. It had been confiscated by the debt collectors years later.

Where Boon had been able to get this, she had no idea. But that didn't matter; all she had to worry about was stuffing her pockets and getting out of here. She grabbed handfuls of the coins and stored them wherever she could: her pockets, her boots, her underthings.

She was so preoccupied that she didn't hear the footfalls behind her until it was too late.

Boon grabbed her wrist and spun her around. She palmed her shucker and aimed to stab him in the chest, but her other wrist was caught in a similar viselike grip.

"Let go of me," she growled.

Boon looked unimpressed. "You really think I wouldn't notice some of my gold gone missing? You could have just asked for it, 'stead of sneaking around like a thief."

"And be indebted to you? No thanks." She twisted out of his hold, breathing heavily. She'd exerted what little energy she had left, and her hands shook. In the corner of her eye, she noticed Avi leaning against the cavern entrance as he looked on. "Where did you even get all this gold? Are you a pirate?"

He gave a sudden, loud laugh. "Hardly. I can help you, you know, so that you don't gotta resort to this. But you'll have to let me."

Her whole body was shaking now. She could feel the gold weighing down her pockets, but they all knew she didn't have the means to run.

"I meant it, you know," Boon continued. "Whatever you want is yours. But you have to know what you want."

What did she want most? She didn't have to think long about it.

"I want to kill Captain Zharo," she rasped. "I want justice for the life he took from me. I want him to feel fear. I want him to *suffer.*"

Boon clicked his tongue a few times. "I think you're setting your sights too low, Silverfish. The captain isn't the one you need to target."

"He ruined my life!"

"He may've made it miserable, but he's not the one who ruined it. If he's gone, someone else is just going to take his place. What you need is to aim higher. You want to kill a snake, cut off its head."

"You mean the merchant who owns the *Brackish*?" Silverfish shook her head. "Whoever he is, he's too powerful."

"That's why you need me. You're inelegant, impulsive. What you need is a back door." His head twitched a couple of times as he jerked his thumb at his chest. "And I'm the door."

She scoffed. "So what's this great idea of yours?"

"The merchant's name is Mercado. Kamon Mercado. We find his weak spots, exploit 'em, and tear down his whole empire. Take away the things he holds most dear." Boon grinned, all sharp edges and violent promises. "We make him weak, and then we take him for everything he's got."

"Kamon Mercado," she repeated slowly, testing the sound of it. "Are you sure?"

Boon gave that loud bark of a laugh again. "I wouldn't be here if it wasn't for that money-grubbing bastard. The gambling halls, they'd cleared me out, and I was strapped. But then I get an offer: Mercado says if I work for him on one of his ships, and if I rack up enough coin, my debt goes *poof*." He wiggled his fingers on either side of his head. "All gone. Bye-bye.

"But then the ship gets caught by the Port's Authority. And surprise, surprise, what did they find in our holds? Not the goods that were written in the ledgers, but the real backwater market stuff, all the fun things that're illegal in Moray. Mercado had me smuggling goods from the Rain Empire that he later sold up to the gentry, and Mercado, bastard that he is, played like he knew nothing about it."

Boon bared his teeth like a sick dog. "Me and the rest of the crew were exiled for life."

"That's when he came to me," Avi cut in. "I used to be Landless, until I found a loophole that restored my name and allowed me back on the continent. But it required going after the right people, so I know a thing or two about revenge." He grinned. "Now I make it my mission to help other Landless folks get their status back."

Nausea roiled inside her, as if Usaad and Broma were creating treacherous whirlpools in her gut. The idea of going after someone like Mercado was absurd; all she wanted was to bury a knife in Zharo's chest.

She studied Boon, the way he leaned most of his weight on the balls of his feet, the soup stains on his shirt, how his eyes gleamed in manic anticipation. He was too invested in this idea of vengeance, so much so that she knew she had found her opening.

"I'll help you," she said, "on one condition."

Boon's eyebrows went up, but he nodded for her to continue.

"You buy the *Brackish* and let me kill Captain Zharo. Then, and only then, will I help you take down Mercado."

Boon exchanged a look with Avi, who frowned in confusion. "Why're you so hung up on this man? He's nothing."

She looked down at her feet, dirty and callused and scarred after seven years on the *Brackish*. "I have nothing to live for," she whispered, realizing the truth of it as she spoke it aloud, the enormity of her loss.

Her father, gone. Her mother, gone. Seven years of her life, gone.

She fought to swallow. "I might as well ruin these men's lives, after all they've done to ruin mine."

When she looked back up, both Boon and Avi wore similar expressions of victory. Silverfish tried to school her own.

"I think this condition of yours should be easily met," Boon agreed. "I help you take out the captain, you help me take out Mercado. Everybody wins."

"Are we going to kill him? Mercado?"

"I like your enthusiasm, but picture something even worse than murder." He held his hands together and then pulled them apart, as if unraveling a banner. "Imagine seeking the perfect revenge."

"And how exactly do you plan to do that?"

"One, ruin the reputation he worked so hard to obtain. Second, target his family—make them fight among themselves, and turn his children on him. He has a son, an heir, who's ripe for conning. And third . . ."

"We take his money," Silverfish guessed.

Boon pointed at her. "Exactly. *Then*, when he's admitted to his crimes and he's lost everything, we go for the kill." He dropped his hand and took a few steps toward her, eyes glinting with feverish excitement. "What do you say?"

Revenge. It was a simple word when spoken out loud, but it was so much bigger, like the hidden city under the atoll. It was a word of fire and blood, of a knife's whisper and the priming of a pistol.

It was a word that consumed her, filled her entire being until she knew that she could no longer be Silverfish. Silverfish's will was to *survive*, to simply make it to the next day, and hopefully the day after that. But that was no longer her will.

Now it was *revenge.*

Captain Zharo. Kamon Mercado. Moray.

They would all pay.

Amaya looked up at Boon. "Where do we start?"

Never corner a man on a losing streak.

Desperation is deadlier than a bullet.

—*THE DEVIOUS ART OF DICE AND DEALING*

S urrounded by splendor and the empty comfort of rich, gilded things, Cayo could not stop thinking about Sébastien's eyes floating like dusty cue balls in a jar on the Slum King's desk.

Cayo had rushed to Bas's apartment as soon as he'd left the Scarlet Arc after speaking to Salvador, knocking for several long minutes on a door plastered with neglected debtor notices. Eventually, the superintendent of the building had come by and told him that Sébastien hadn't been home in days, giving the landlord no choice but to evict him.

But Cayo refused to believe that he was dead. He had gone by every place he could think of—the local clinics, the homeless shelter, even the opium dens. Bas was nowhere to be found, and there were no reports of an eyeless corpse being discovered by the city guard.

He wondered if his entire life's purpose was to fail everyone around him.

Although Cayo wanted to keep searching, here he was, again on his father's orders, peacocking around at another soiree thrown by Countess Yamaa. After the wild success of her first party, the gentry had been talking about it nonstop, practically clamoring for more.

Like new gamblers itching to come back to the tables because they had beginner's luck, Cayo thought. *But that luck never lasts.*

The partygoers gathered in the lush gardens of the countess's lavish estate, partially hidden by massive palmetto trees at the end of a winding road beyond the Business Sector. Thin columns supported the huge square-shaped estate, and a balcony ran the entire perimeter of the second story. It wasn't near the sea, but he could still smell salt as the wind ruffled his hair.

The gardens were the true spectacle, though. The first level branched away from the main house, sporting a large fountain and protective marble railing that spiraled down into two separate staircases leading to the lower level. Most of the partygoers mingled here, within a masterpiece of perfectly trimmed shrubberies and rows of blooming flowers, from the red and yellow bursts of hellebore and glory lilies to the flirtatious blush of hibiscus. Orchids, cypresses, and palm trees lined the paths the partygoers took, soft lantern lights hanging from their branches. It was the latest stage of dusk, the sky dark blue and pensive, lingering on the last of the day's light before succumbing to the dark.

It should have been peaceful, but Cayo's mind raced with panic.

His entire being had been stripped to just three senses: Sébastien's eyes staring at him from the jar, Romara's smell on his clothes, and his father's warning lingering in his ear. *Do not fail us.*

Standing before a wide pool in the center of the gardens, Cayo scanned the crowd for the strange young woman he'd met a week ago at the countess's last party, the one who didn't mind ruining her gown with snacks—and had unknowingly called him a drunken playboy. He found himself hoping she would be here tonight, longing to get in a fight just to still the restless agitation within him.

He glared down at the pool, its water lit with floating candle boats that made a few coins at the bottom glint. The candle boats were of Kharian origin, clay molded into lantern shapes painted with swirling designs. A bridge arched over the water, where couples were strolling to take in the romantic scenery.

It was convenient for them, Cayo thought, to completely dismiss the servant children lighting lanterns around the garden. He watched as one of them, a small girl with wispy brown hair and a sunburn, leaned over the edge of the pool to corral one of the floating lanterns her way. She, like the other children of varying ages, was dressed in the purple livery of Countess Yamaa's house.

Purple sails, purple livery . . . He was beginning to sense a theme.

Disgusted by the sight of the working children, he turned away. He hadn't wanted to come, but once again, his father had made him.

Since you're so desperate for options, here's one, Kamon had said. *Try to seduce the countess. Securing a marriage contract with her could be invaluable. Or, who knows, maybe you can make use of your unique talents and lift a crystal doorknob while you're there. She probably won't even notice if one goes missing.*

Cayo had suppressed a wince at the word *marriage.* He still hadn't told his father about Romara. He knew he had to do it soon, but every time the thought crept in, fear locked his muscles and dried his mouth.

Ever since he had foolishly agreed to marry her, Cayo had felt as if he were in a fugue, existing only because his lungs and heart stubbornly refused to stop. Since his father would never agree to an engagement with the Slum King's daughter, they were going to pretend that Romara was a member of the Rehanese gentry until the marriage contract was signed. And then the other shoe would drop, and the Slum King would get the status he so craved.

"Drink?"

He blindly grabbed whatever was on the serving tray offered to him. Soria would have frowned to see him drink again, but Soria wasn't here, and wasn't that the whole point? He took a big gulp and immediately recognized the taste of Calamity, the drink of choice for gamblers who were quickly spiraling into bankruptcy and needed something to fortify themselves. It was typically made with lupseh, a Ledese alcohol, and a mix of bitters and cherry syrup, with just a hint of coffee bean to deepen the flavor.

The taste brought him back to the dens, to the smoke-thick rooms and the hot press of bodies. His friends clapping him on the back, spurring him on.

One more round, Cayo?

He glanced at the server who had offered the tray. The Kharian man seemed to be in his thirties and had a wholly unprofessional look to him. His hair was a bit too long, his nails a bit too ragged.

"So where is the countess, anyway?" Cayo asked. "Shouldn't she be at her own party?"

The server righted his tray, which had been tilting to one side. "She's bound to make her entrance soon, m'lord." His words were flat and laced with annoyance. He quickly moved on to a flock of young women, muttering as he went.

Cayo took to his drink like a man dying of thirst. New plan:

He would get drunk, and then he would tell his father that he was gaining a criminal for a daughter-in-law. Cayo sputtered a laugh into his glass, his blood already fizzing after not having had alcohol for so long.

Then he blinked. As he stared into the crowd, he began to recognize one of the faces: Philip Dageur, the son of wealthy immigrants from the Rain Empire.

And Sébastien's ex-lover.

Would he know where Bas was, or what had happened to him? Cayo knew they were still friends—and perhaps a bit more than that—and that Bas would never want Philip to give him charity, but it was the one place Cayo hadn't tried.

As Cayo began to make his way over, a voice projected across the garden.

"Noble gentry of Moray, I present to you, Countess Yamaa!"

Cayo turned at the crescendo of applause. A woman with brown skin and black hair was descending one of the marble staircases. Although she wobbled on a stair here and there in her high-heeled shoes, there was still something commanding about her that spoke to him. He gravitated toward her, a wandering planet in need of a star to orbit.

But when she turned her face in his direction, his stomach gave a violent lurch.

It was the young woman who had spoken to him at the countess's last party—the one who had insulted him and claimed his father employed children.

She was Countess Yamaa?

His mind raced as he tried to recall exactly what he had said to her. He had disparaged her taste, her party, her attitude . . . everything.

Feeling sick, Cayo turned and frantically looked for a way out that wouldn't involve passing by her. Philip was gone—*damn it*—but he spotted Tomjen nearby, his lanky arm slung around a lowly lord's daughter. Cayo began to make his way to them when the countess's gin-strong voice easily broke through the din of the party.

"We meet again, my lord."

He froze in place. A few curious onlookers glanced his way, including Tomjen, who quickly read the scene and widened his eyes at Cayo in a way that said *don't mess this up.* Cayo quickly downed the rest of his Calamity, thinking the name too appropriate for the situation.

Countess Yamaa approached him, her smile reserved, subtle, like the outline of a weapon hidden under a coat.

He bowed in greeting. "Countess."

Her smile broadened. "Ah, so you do know me." She again wore her necklace of pearls, but the dress was wholly different. The bodice was an impossible patchwork of colorful embroidered flowers, woven through with green-threaded vines that snaked up her belly, ending in a few blooming buds over the curve of her chest. Her skirts were long and made of gauzy blue layers, each hem ending in another burst of flowers.

She was wearing her own garden.

It was exquisite.

"I should apologize for my forwardness when last we met," she said, fidgeting with the clunky rings she wore before clasping her hands together. Her hair was down tonight, curled elegantly over her bare shoulders and braided through with jasmine blossoms. Cayo could smell them even from where he stood, thick and fragrant. "Perhaps I'd had a bit too much to drink."

"No, it's . . . it's fine. I mean . . ." It wasn't fine. Nothing was fine. "All is forgiven, my lady."

"I'm glad." She nodded toward the tables at the back of the garden, sparkling with trays of silver and crystal. Her silver earrings swayed with the motion. "Have you eaten? I have the best cook in Moray under my roof."

From whose family did you steal him? Cayo wondered. "I'm afraid I have no appetite tonight." He looked around nervously, seeking an escape route. "It's a lovely party, though."

"You think so? Not gaudy, as my last one was?"

He winced. He had said that to her face, hadn't he? "Not at all, my lady." Cayo cleared his throat, heat crawling up his neck as he thought back to the way he'd insulted Countess Yamaa in front of a girl he'd mistook for a stranger. "I must apologize for my forwardness as well."

Amusement flashed in her eyes. "Everyone should hear a bit of critique now and then. Keeps one humble."

He couldn't forget all she had said. Still, there was something about the slope of her neck, the vulnerability of her bare shoulders, the sheerness of the gauze between the stitched flowers of her dress that tied his tongue into a useless knot.

"You seem distracted tonight, my lord."

"I'm simply wondering how many hours of labor it took to pay for this party of yours," he replied. He had the satisfaction of seeing her eyebrows go up. "After all, you own your own debtor ship, don't you? The *Brackish*?"

"Good memory," she murmured, almost as if to herself. "I can see you're trying to goad me, but it won't work."

Anger, sharp and sudden, hooked into him like a barb. What gave her the right to criticize his family? The Calamity swam through him, fortifying his backbone and sharpening his tongue. "Are the children in this garden paid for by their parents' debt? Do their earnings slide into your pocket when they're not looking?"

At last, a flash of true anger crossed her face. In that moment, he saw through the pretense and glimpsed something like truth in her eyes, something as dangerous as it was fathomless.

"Do not presume to know me, my lord," she said softly.

"And do not presume to know me, my lady. I'm much more than a . . . what was the phrase you used? Drunken playboy?"

The dawning realization on her face was even more satisfying than pulling a winning hand of Scatterjack. He could practically see the scene of that night flitting through her mind's eye, the wholly unabashed way she had stomped upon his family's name. Flushed, the countess held back a grimace of mortification.

"Lord Cayo Mercado," she murmured.

He bowed with a sarcastic flourish.

She was quiet for a minute, her teeth clenched. "I see. And you think you have the right to come here and judge me for the same rotting thing your father has exploited in order to build his fortune? As I said, you cannot presume to know me."

Cayo was startled by her use of the word *rotting*—he had only ever heard the servants use it—but he didn't let it distract him. "I know enough. You're Kharian, perhaps also Rehanese, with a fortune that likely came from dealings with the Rain Empire. Now here you are in Moray, flaunting all you have for those who think with greed instead of compassion. They don't see the children working around them. They don't see you as a *person*. They see you as a nothing but a lovely ingot of gold, and they're all itching to chisel off a piece of you for themselves."

The countess had begun to fiddle with the pearls on her necklace, watching him steadily during his tirade. A thin white scar lined the side of her palm. "Is that also what you would like to do, my lord?"

"No." The truth of his answer surprised him, and perhaps her as well. "I want . . ."

He wanted this city to run on something other than gold. He wanted someone to help him escape the Slum King and Romara.

He wanted Soria to get better. To not leave him like their mother had, like everything good did sooner or later.

But before he could finish, there was a short scream followed by a splash. The countess turned sharply, layered skirts fanning out around her. In the pool with the floating lanterns, the little girl Cayo had spotted earlier was flailing in the water. The partygoers yelped at the shock of it, but no one moved to do anything.

Cayo rushed forward, but the countess was faster.

In the time it took her to get to the edge of the pool, she had kicked off her heels and torn off the outermost layer of her skirts. Then, without hesitation, she arced gracefully into the water. It was more than graceful—she seemed to meld with the water, like molten metal. Like she had been born in it.

She swam to the girl and grabbed hold of her, using one arm to propel them back to the edge. A server helped them out onto the bank, the little girl coughing and sputtering.

The partygoers erupted into applause. Cayo stood there in shock, trying to parse out what he had just seen: a *countess*, ruining her gown for a servant. Where had she learned to swim like that?

The countess asked for the server's jacket, which she wrapped around the girl's trembling shoulders. The server led the girl back to the house to recover.

Cayo approached the countess, dripping wet and wringing out her long hair, as excited lords and ladies flocked around her to commend her for her bravery. He glared at them, thinking that they could have just as easily gone in after the girl if they'd thought to put down their drinks and canapés for one second.

"Thank you," he said when he caught her attention. He wasn't sure why he was thanking her, exactly, but it felt right.

She tossed her wet hair over her shoulder. Her dress was sodden, heavy and damp and clinging to her skin, and he once again had the impression that she was some kind of sea creature who'd mistakenly found herself on land.

Then she leaned over and spat. The lords and ladies murmured in surprise, then laughed in delight.

"It's a tricky thing, water," the countess said. The kohl smudged around her eyes gave her a wild, untamed quality that both frightened and fascinated him. "If you don't know how to navigate it, it can take everything from you."

She dismissed him as easily as turning her head and excusing herself politely to her crowd of admirers. She made her way back to the main house, and he followed her with his eyes.

Perhaps he had misjudged her. Perhaps there was something even rarer hiding under all that gold.

Trickster told the people that if they prayed to him, he would find them a suitable leader. The people prayed and left out bowls of sweet milk with herbs. They thought Trickster would find them a worthy emperor, as that was all they had ever known. But at dawn on the third day, they found a woman clad in red standing on the steps of the Ruby Palace. She was their empress, she said, and as the people bowed, Trickster fed on their confusion and lapped up their surprise, sweeter than the milk they had offered.

—KHARIAN MYTH

I t took all of the countess's willpower not to slam the door behind her.

Soaked and seething, she went to the window and peeked around the curtains at the party below. Cayo Mercado was still by the pool, gazing up at the main house with a complicated expression. He had all the fine features of one born to wealth: soft skin, glossy hair, an air of assuredness. And a smile that knew exactly what it did to those it was aimed at.

Of course—of *course*—he had to turn out to be the Mercado heir. Fate had never been kind to her; she saw no reason why that should change now.

She had actually enjoyed talking to him at the first party. She found his casual mannerisms and blunt speech refreshing after an hour of pointless niceties with the Moray nobility. She had dropped the Mercado name in the hopes that he might know them, that perhaps she could turn him into an ally. She had even been hoping to see him again.

In her room, she changed into a dress of peach and coral, the skirt filled with embroidery work of shells of different shapes. She had been planning on saving this one for the next party; she would have to get another commissioned so that the petty nobles didn't start whispering about how Countess Yamaa *recycled* her dresses.

Liesl, her "lady-in-waiting," bustled into the room after her. "What, may I ask, was that?"

"Don't start," she growled, flailing in her efforts to close the dress's clasp at the back of her neck. Liesl helped her.

"Eager to return to the party?" Liesl asked when she turned back around. She was a couple of years older than the countess and originally from the Rain Empire, pretty and plump with light brown skin and curly chestnut hair. Although Liesl called herself Landless, she was technically only exiled from the Rain Empire after having been caught spying in a nobleman's estate.

"No, but every second I stand here talking to you is a second I'm not getting closer to the Mercado heir."

Liesl's eyes widened, and she ushered her to the vanity table to fix her makeup and tie up her hair. But by the time the countess flew back downstairs, bursting out the front door and breathlessly scanning the glittering crowd for any sign of Cayo Mercado, he was nowhere to be seen.

Finally, she spotted him at the end of the winding path that led to the estate, hailing his carriage. Gritting her teeth, she clutched the skirt of her new dress and hurried to the stairs.

One of the nobles saw her and lifted his drink. "Behold, our fearless countess!" The others around him cheered and applauded.

She forced a smile and started down the stairs. These people only cared about two things: their money and their legacy. She could take money easily enough; any thief worth their salt could. But legacy . . . That was what would hit Mercado the hardest.

From her vantage point on the stairs, she watched as Cayo Mercado climbed into his carriage, its gilded edges worn and dulled—a sure sign of hard times.

He was in for much harder.

She wished it didn't have to be him. But wishes, like fate, had never done her any good.

After the party was over, she kicked off her wretched heels and changed out of her dress into a simple outfit of black, her trousers tucked into tall boots and her sleeves long and tapered. She braided her hair and washed off her makeup, stripping away the countess bit by bit. Outside the silks and jewels and rouge, she could finally take a full breath, the relief of coming back up after a long dive.

Downstairs, she found Beetle curled up on a stool in a corner of the kitchens, blowing steam off a big mug of tea Cicada had prepared for her. He was busy washing pots and pans now that the party was over, some of the other Bugs—former Bugs—helping him. The kitchens were warm and smelled of garlic and ginger.

"You told me you could swim," she scolded, arms crossed. The girl flinched. "Why did you lie?"

"I'm sorry, Silv—I mean, Amaya," Beetle murmured. No, not Beetle anymore—Fera.

"Shh!" She looked around until she remembered where she was. She still had to remind herself every day that they were no longer on board the *Brackish*, that they didn't have to conform to Captain Zharo's whims.

That Beetle was now Fera and she was now Amaya.

Except that she was also Yamaa: a mysterious and wealthy countess taking Moray by storm.

For a moment, she thought she might be overcome by incredulous laughter. How, *how* had she managed to trick so many people tonight? She still felt like the ragged girl who smelled of fish guts, but no one else had seen it; they had seen only a young woman with more wealth than she knew what to do with.

Roach, she thought sadly, her chest tightening, *what would you say if you could see me now?* It killed her that she might never know.

"How did you end up in the water?" Amaya demanded.

"There were coins at the bottom and I thought I could grab them."

"You were never trained as a diver. That was incredibly foolish of you."

And it had been incredibly foolish of Amaya to dive in after her, but the alternative would be Fera drowning, and she couldn't have that. But now the gentry would be talking about it nonstop; she had already gotten a taste of their hunger for rumormongering as she'd flitted from guest to guest.

Fera whimpered and wiped her nose on her sleeve. Amaya sighed and scratched at her head, hair still damp.

"Look," Amaya said, "I get it. I really do. But you have to be careful. No one can suspect who we are and where we came from. Remember?"

Fera looked up at her, her small face flushed and miserable-looking. But it softened as she nodded. She trusted Amaya; otherwise, she wouldn't have joined her.

On the Ledese island where Boon had first taken her, Amaya had forced him to make good on his part of the deal.

"Buy the *Brackish*," she'd said. "I want to be sole owner."

Boon had done just that, using Avi as an intermediary. But to her dismay, Captain Zharo had disappeared as soon as the gold had traded hands.

"It's just a slight delay," Boon had told her as she seethed. "You'll get his blood on your hands one way or another."

The Water Bugs had been given a choice: try to go home on their own, or follow Amaya to Moray and become part of Boon's plan until she got enough gold to send them back to their parents with riches of their own. Most of them had followed her, but a few of the older ones had taken off, barely pausing to thank her for their freedom. She couldn't blame them.

She had looked desperately for Roach, but he hadn't been on board. It had been too early for his seven years to be up, but the other Bugs claimed he'd just disappeared one day when they were docked outside a Ledese port.

Worry ate at her bones when she thought of Roach, but she wasn't in a position to go looking for him. Whenever she could, Amaya sent up a quick prayer for him to be safe, and that she would see him again. That they would meet in Moray, like they'd planned.

The Landless had then converted the *Brackish* into a proper vessel, renovating its rotting interior and redesigning its hideous exterior. She had asked for purple sails. Blue sea mixed with red blood.

"I don't want you anywhere near water again," Amaya said, pointing a stern finger at Fera. "Not until you learn to swim."

"I can teach her," said Spider from where he was helping Cicada with the dishes. Not Spider—his real name was Nian.

"Great. Do that, then." Amaya turned and rubbed her forehead. She had a headache after all the excitement.

Cicada flashed her a wide smile as she passed. "Did folks like the abalone cakes?"

"They were raving about them."

"And let me guess: You haven't had a bite." As soon as he said it, her stomach made a desperate noise. Cicada laughed.

"I'll fix you up a plate."

"You're beautiful."

In the hallway, she looked into a mirror and realized she still wore her earrings. She pulled them from her ears, letting them clatter on the top of the decorative table. Her lobes were sore, unused to the weight. She rubbed them and thought back to the day Boon had brought her to a jewelry stall in the busy market quarter of the nearest Ledese city.

"Becoming a countess will be no small feat," Boon had said. "Transforming you will be as complicated as alchemy. And alchemy is pretty damn complicated."

She had eyed the gems and chains nervously, wondering how many pieces would have been the equivalent of her debt. Wondering if he was going to tell her to pick out some necklaces or a bracelet.

Instead, Boon had exchanged words with the proprietor before ushering her to sit on the stool in the corner. She had shifted uneasily for a minute until the proprietor, a hulking man with a ridiculous pelt of arm hair, had come toward her with a needle.

"No, no, no!" she had screeched, prevented from running away by Boon's strong hands on her shoulders, keeping her on the stool.

"You're honestly telling me," Boon had said, "that you can withstand poisonous rockfish, a murderous ship captain shooting at you, and a lively jaunt with the riptide, but one little needle has you pissing yourself? Do you need me to hold your damn hand?"

Instead, she had sat as still as she could on the stool, refusing to even whimper as the needle went through, just to shut Boon up.

Later, her ears sore and bearing small silver hoops, she had moodily followed Boon through the rest of the market. He'd stopped by a stall selling sticky honey cakes and bought one for her.

"If you're that squeamish about a needle, I doubt you'd be able to handle yourself with a knife."

She'd licked up the honey running down her fingers. "I bet you're wrong."

Boon had lifted an eyebrow at her. "I'll take you up on that bet."

"If you lose, you have to pierce *your* ears."

His laugh had been loud enough to draw stares from the crowd.

But, true to his word, he had begun teaching her how to handle a knife the next day. A proper knife—not a shucker, not a gutter.

She had stared at her reflection in its blade, and in that moment she saw herself in halves: the girl who was still finding her land legs meeting eyes with the one who had sworn vengeance on the man who had ruined her family.

She had vowed to become only the latter.

Boon had been easy on her at first, showing her the proper way to grip the hilt, how to position her legs, ways to slash and block. But as soon as he'd realized she was a quick learner, he hadn't held back. He would come at her with that disarming grin and a barely perceivable restraint that prevented him from actually harming her. Instead he would make little nicks on her arms or legs, punishment for letting her defenses down or not moving the way he wanted her to.

The others had gradually come out to watch these sparring sessions, held in the patch of sparse grass behind the bungalow Liesl shared with her lover, Deadshot. After a month of losing to Boon, she had finally found an opening and swept the legs out from under him, pinning his arm and tipping his chin up with the point of her knife.

Everyone had held their breath as Boon looked up at her. His dark eyes had been difficult to read, but she had thought—or perhaps she only hoped—that she had seen an undercurrent of pride.

"Don't worry," she'd said. "You can hold my hand when you get your ears pierced."

Boon had laughed while the others cheered. As she helped him up, satisfaction had curled in her chest, warm and hungry for more. To wear her victories like the hoops of silver dangling from her ears.

She knew, then, that she wouldn't stop until they pulled this off. Taking down Mercado would be her greatest triumph.

Amaya returned to the main chamber. Walking through the estate still made her feel as if she were trespassing. She had no idea what to do with all this refinement, from the elaborately sculpted moldings on the ceiling to the black-and-amber polish of the marble floors. There were touches of gold *everywhere*, so much so that she had bitten a candleholder on her first day to make sure it was real. The estate had once belonged to an old duchess who died without any heirs, and it had been on the market for months until Amaya came along with Boon's money in her pocket.

"Spend as much of it as you can," he'd told her before she sailed to Moray, all the chests filled with coin stowed away in the hold. "It's going to a good cause."

He hadn't come with her—he couldn't, lest he violate his Landless sentence or was recognized by someone he'd once known—but he had sent three of his best crew members with her. She found them in the dining room, waiting to debrief now that the party was over. The room was just as absurdly elegant as the rest of the house, the walls a rich green and the table made of shining rosewood.

Liesl glanced up from her notes as she entered, a glass of red wine already before her. Avi, on her right, raised an amused eyebrow at Amaya. "Was the dunk refreshing?" he asked. She glared at him, but he just kept smirking.

"I bet it made quite an impression on the boy," said Deadshot on Liesl's left, her boots propped up on the tabletop. Another of the Landless Amaya had met on the atoll, she had gotten her name due to the pistols she always wore at either hip. She was of mixed race, Ledese and a nation from the Sun Empire, with dark copper skin and crimped hair that had been dyed red with henna. She wasn't recognized as Landless in Moray—only in the Sun Empire, where she had committed enough robberies and heists to earn her an unsavory reputation.

Amaya turned away so Avi wouldn't see her face redden at the reminder of her blunder with Cayo Mercado. Out of all the men in this cursed city, of course *Cayo* was the one who ended up being their mark. She thought back to all the things she had said about the Mercado family—about *him*—at the greenhouse party, how his father employed children and that his son was nothing but a rogue. It was no wonder he hated the countess, or at least, the idea of her.

Although Boon had told her the barest details about Cayo Mercado before she came to Moray, speaking to him in person was another matter entirely. She hadn't anticipated the way he parried her thrusts, or that he would have the balls to insult Countess Yamaa. There was something almost thrilling about it.

She could still see his expression after she had fished Fera from the pool. It had been a look of surprise and something else, something softer, as if his wariness had been whittled down to mere curiosity.

Maybe this had worked in her favor after all. Perhaps she had changed his impression of her, if only a little.

Remembering from Boon's notes that Cayo had a history of gambling, she said, "I think our next party should be game-themed."

Avi, still dressed as a server, gave her an approving look. "Smart."

"It would certainly help to lower his guard," Liesl agreed, consulting her notes as she pushed her glasses farther up on her nose. "Particularly if we do only card games. Apparently, that's his weakness."

"I'm more of a roulette girl myself," said Deadshot.

Cicada came in and put a plate of food before Amaya. She grinned up at him in thanks and began to scarf it down with her fingers, thankful she had put away the countess persona for the night and didn't have to bother with manners.

Boon had forced her to use forks and knives with every meal. She had grown out of the practice on the *Brackish*, and as a result her hands had cramped as she clumsily navigated the utensils. Boon had constantly barked at her not to stab her food, not to scrape the tines against the plate, to take petite bites—*What are you, an animal? Cut your damn meat!*

But it had only been the preface to a greater trial. Once the *Brackish* had been fully commissioned, they had left the Ledese Islands and sailed to the southern coast of the Rain Empire, to the cosmopolitan city of Viariche. Amaya had ogled it from the ship as they came into port, a city of beautiful white buildings and winding cobblestone streets lined with black iron streetlamps.

There, Liesl had been fully in her element, and her first order of business was to trade Amaya's trousers for fanciful dresses. In the spacious apartments where they had stayed, paid for by Boon, Amaya had been awakened their second morning by an assertive tailor eager to put his measuring tape in places Amaya didn't care to think about.

"That was one of the most reputable dressmakers in the city!" Liesl had yelled as the tailor, now sporting a black eye, stormed out of the apartment. "He's *supposed* to measure you all over!"

"Find one who's a woman, then!"

Liesl eventually did, though it barely made the procedure any easier; Amaya squirmed and fidgeted during the entire fitting, staying put only by the power of Liesl's glare. Deadshot, standing next to her, had merely crossed her arms and grinned at Amaya's discomfort.

It had taken a combined effort among the three of them to get Amaya into the first dress, a cobalt-blue ball gown with embroidered butterflies peeking through the ruffles of the skirt. Though Amaya had cursed and complained the entire time, when Liesl finally steered her toward the stand-up mirror, the grumbling had died on Amaya's lips.

She hadn't worn a dress since she was a little girl. Her mother had had a whole corner of her closet devoted to them, and would smile widely whenever she could wrestle Amaya into one. Her mother would brush her hair and pin it up, and even apply a bit of pink lipstick. Amaya had always fussed through the process, but once it was done, she would delight in how pretty she looked. She would spin around and make her skirts fly out until her mother reprimanded her for showing her legs.

Staring at a stand-up mirror hundreds of miles away from those memories, Amaya had run her hands over the expensive fabric of her first new dress in a decade and blinked back tears.

"Do you like it?" Liesl had asked. Amaya nodded. "Good. We'll debut it tonight."

For three months, Amaya had been expected to patronize ritzy establishments and attend extravagant parties. Walking through them was like walking through a fever dream. She hadn't laid eyes on such finery since living in Moray, and the sight of massive chandeliers, ballrooms of white-and-black marble, and dazzling arrays of colorful foods had constantly driven her speechless.

In some ways, it had been even more difficult than her work on the *Brackish*. Walking in high heels was not unlike walking across a slippery deck in the rain, and sometimes the bodices and corsets of her dresses were so tight she became short of breath and needed to lie down. When she complained about her bruised ribs to Liesl, the girl had merely shrugged and said, "Such is the price of fashion."

The worst of it, though, was the people. They asked her endless questions, their personalities were dull, and their compassion was nonexistent. Still, Amaya mirrored the nobles' motions and practiced their cadences when she spoke. She wrapped herself in a new persona the way sails are furled before a storm, hiding Amaya away and making room for the only person who would be able to deftly infiltrate the Moray gentry.

Countess Yamaa.

On the night before their journey to Moray, Boon had pulled her aside and given her a gift: a set of four knives, their handles inlaid with silver and pearl.

"I've been teaching you how to fight with real knives," he said, "so I figured you should have your own. Make sure you always have one hidden on your person."

Amaya had held each of them in her hand, felt their weight and tested the edges of their blades. She had easily read the message in Boon's gift: that she would never hold a shucker again.

"We will succeed," he had whispered, and she had believed him.

As Liesl, Avi, and Deadshot continued to scheme down the table, Amaya licked the last of her late dinner from her fingers, only half listening. She was tired. She wanted only to fall into a dreamless sleep. But she had more to do tonight, more than they even knew.

When she heard her name, she looked up to find all their eyes turned toward her.

"You should call on the Mercado boy soon," Liesl said. "Invite him to dine with you, or meet with him at a teahouse in the city somewhere. Get to know him better."

Amaya bit the inside of her cheek, still smarting over the way she had fumbled both interactions with him. But what choice did she have?

"I'll write an invitation tomorrow," she agreed, standing up. "Liesl, I need you for something."

The girl met her out in the entryway. "Do you need help getting ready for bed?"

"I think I can handle it," Amaya said dryly. "No, I wanted to ask . . ."

She had rehearsed the words, oddly nervous at the thought of speaking them out loud. But Liesl just looked at her calmly, patiently.

Amaya took a deep breath. "If you have a spare moment, I was wondering if you could look into a person for me. Find files on him, public records, that sort of thing."

"Of course," Liesl said. "That's why I'm here. Who do you need research on?"

Amaya's throat worked, but no words came out. She swallowed, tried again.

"Arun Chandra," she said, almost too soft to hear.

But Liesl heard, and her face shifted slightly to sympathy. She thought about it—after all, it was a request that wasn't a part of Boon's overall plan—until eventually she nodded.

"I'll see what I can find," Liesl said.

She breathed out in relief. "Thank you."

Amaya excused herself and retired to her bedroom. Her work as Countess Yamaa was done for the night, and she had plans elsewhere.

At a specific address, in fact, that she had written on a small piece of paper tucked in a jewelry box in her room.

She walked by the expansive canopy bed, the broad windows open to a view of Crescent Bay in the distance. Lifting the lid of the jewelry box on her dresser, she thumbed the note open and took a deep breath, reciting the address for the hundredth time before she tore up the paper and threw it in the bin.

The knives Boon had given her were laid out on the bed. She tucked them away one by one: the longest at her hip, two more in the hidden sheaths in her boots, and the smallest at the bracer under her left sleeve.

Briefly she brushed her thumb against the tattoo on her wrist, the knife pointing outward. It had once meant survival to her, a reminder that she had to fight for every single day. But now it meant something else.

It meant revenge.

Turning down the lanterns in her room, she climbed out the window onto the balcony. Moray was spread out before her, its lights a pale imitation of the stars overhead. Somewhere in that sprawl was her destination, the address that had been spinning in her mind for days.

The address where the retired Captain Zharo now lived.

She had been patient long enough. Now it was time to see if there was any difference between gutting a fish and gutting a man.

10

Light is the greatest tool in an artist's arsenal.
It sheds truth that would otherwise be buried by the dark.
—THE PAINTER'S PRACTICE

Cayo knew that, shaken as he was, he should have gone straight home to his waiting bed. But his mind was a viper's nest— every thought he grabbed at turned out to be venomous.

The countess was a contradiction. He was engaged to Romara and had not yet told his father. And Bas . . .

There had to be *something* he could do. Cayo was so tired of being useless, of being able to do nothing while Soria's life drained out of her a day at a time.

Then he remembered seeing Philip at the party, how he hadn't gotten the chance to speak to him.

Cayo pounded on the roof of the carriage. "Take me to the light-house," he told the driver. "Please."

They arrived ten minutes later, and when the driver opened the door for Cayo, he was greeted with a fresh, cool ocean breeze. The lighthouse was stationed on the edge of a tall cliff face overlooking the bay, the short, squat tower made of light brick and limestone. Night had blanketed Moray in navy and demure purple, but here, the lighthouse drove back a bit of the dark in flashes like dying stars.

It was one of Bas's favorite places. Cayo had often come here with him, as had Philip, and he hoped to find one of them—if not both—at the top. As Cayo walked the gentle incline of the road leading to the lighthouse, he remembered a night when he had stolen a cake from a duchess's party and how he and Sébastien had eaten the whole thing with their hands under the watchful light. Cayo absently licked at his lips, as if he could still taste the sugar.

When he reached the courtyard surrounding the lighthouse, he saw his gamble had paid off. A lone figure stood at the railing, gazing out at the ocean as he smoked a long, thin cigarillo. As Cayo approached, he made sure to clear his throat so as not to startle him.

Philip Dageur looked over his shoulder and, seeing Cayo, sighed in vexation. He turned around and rested his elbows on the railing behind him, leveling a glare in Cayo's direction.

"I saw you at Countess Yamaa's party," Philip said, his words inflected with a slight accent from his parents' homeland. It galled Cayo to admit it, but he was unquestionably handsome, his features soft yet refined, his sorrel-colored skin glowing with health. "I'd hoped you wouldn't see me. Or follow me. Then again, you were always a bit creepy."

Cayo held back from making an immediate retort. He and Philip had never gotten along, much to Bas's frustration. Cayo had always assumed that Philip was jealous of his friendship with Bas, and how they were always prone to some level of flirtation, even when Bas had gotten together with Philip.

But he didn't have the time or energy for that sort of drama right now.

"Tell me," Cayo demanded. "I need to know."

"Know what, exactly? I can't read minds—and even if I could, your skull would be too thick to penetrate."

"If he's *alive*."

Philip stared at him from under his eyelashes—scheming or seething, Cayo couldn't tell. And he didn't care. He was too focused on the labor of his heart, the desperate hope that shortened his breath.

Finally, Philip said, "He's alive. Barely."

Cayo nearly staggered back with the force of his relief. He shut his eyes for a moment of thanks, still seeing the flashes of the lighthouse behind his eyelids.

"Do you know where he is?" Cayo asked, once he'd collected himself.

Philip regarded him for a moment as the lighthouse flashed above them with the rhythm of a heartbeat. He took a long drag off his cigarillo, no doubt reveling in the way Cayo clenched and unclenched his hands, at the mercy of his information. And whether to divulge it.

After he sighed out a cloud of smoke, Philip said, "Bas is no concern of yours."

"Wha— Of course he is! He's my friend, he—" *He came to me when he was in trouble, and I didn't do enough to help him.* "Look, I know he's hurt. I know what the Slum King did to him." At the reminder of those beautiful eyes floating in that jar, he shuddered and pulled his jacket closer. "Just . . . tell me he's all right. Please."

"Why do you think I owe you that?" Philip snuffed the rest of his cigarillo against the railing before approaching him. He was shorter than Cayo, but his dark eyes blazed with contempt. The smell of smoke and alcohol had woven itself into the fabric of his jacket, his hair. "Why do you think you have the *right* to ask anything of me?"

"What is your problem?" Cayo growled. "I have the right because I'm his *friend* and I'm *worried*—"

"A friend?" Philip's eyebrows rose. "Is that all?"

Cayo groaned and raked his hands through his hair, the strands slightly hardened from the product he had run through it before the party. "Are we going to do this now? Seriously?"

"You were always leading him on, and you never acted on it. He came crying to me once, drunk and stupid, saying that you didn't want to be with him because he didn't come from wealth or carry any status."

"*What?* I never—"

"You didn't say it, maybe, but that's what he thought." Philip crossed his arms. "Eventually, he came to his senses and moved on. But even when he was with me, you were still too close for comfort. Of course, you were far too dense to see any of it."

"I thought . . ." Honestly, he hadn't thought much during those times. He'd always been in a haze, whether from drinking, taking part in Romara's stock of jaaga, or from the high of winning. The whole point of his existence had been to feel *good*. And whenever Sébastien had wrapped an arm around his waist, or planted a playful kiss on his cheek, Cayo had greedily accepted it without question.

It was no wonder Philip hated him. He hated himself, too.

"Whatever may or may not have happened between us," Cayo said, "we were still friends, and I deserve to know where he is. He

119

came to me for help, but it . . ." His voice broke, and he roughly cleared his throat. "It wasn't enough."

Philip let out a huff of laughter. "Nothing is ever enough where you're concerned." Still, he mulled it over, the sound of the ocean's waves like an encouraging whisper. Finally, he turned back to the railing and pulled out another cigarillo. "Bas is leaving Moray for good."

"Leaving? To go where?"

"He came to me, because he had nowhere else to go." Philip paused lighting the end of his cigarillo to throw another glare over his shoulder. "I told him he could go to my family's estate in the Rain Empire. At first he refused, but I made him come around. He'll be safe there. And he can heal."

"The Rain . . ." Cayo's gaze drifted east, where the cliffs of Moray gave way to the expanse of coastline outlining one of the vast empires that hemmed them in. "Where?"

"Soliere. Where my parents are from."

The country of Soliere—long since subsumed into the Rain Empire—was on the complete opposite side of the continent. Cayo swallowed against the tightness of his throat. He had experienced this before, suddenly having one of the constants of his life ripped away, but it never got any easier.

"Don't pretend to care so much for him now," Philip sneered, watching his reaction. "Or are you just like those other rich children, crying over a toy they can no longer play with?"

Cayo briefly considered pushing Philip over the railing. Taking a steadying breath, he squared his shoulders. "When does he leave?"

"At dawn." Philip hesitated, the smoke from his cigarillo drifting upward in a thin plume. "He's taking the *Sovereign*."

Cayo blinked at him, wondering if he was lying. At Cayo's shocked silence, Philip scoffed.

"I'm not telling you for your sake," he said, "but for his. For some reason I still can't comprehend, he cares for you." Philip took a long draw off his cigarillo. "He'll want to say good-bye."

For the first time, Cayo heard the misery in his voice. He lingered there a moment, wondering if he should apologize, if there was anything he could say that would help. But in the end, he figured the best thing to do was to leave Philip alone.

"Thank you," he murmured before heading back for the carriage. Philip gave him a rude hand gesture in farewell.

Bas was leaving at dawn. Cayo had only a few hours to figure out what he was going to say to him. He paused halfway down the road to stare at the ocean's restless surface, the lighthouse behind him flashing its warnings into the dark. Toward the places he would never see.

The *Sovereign* was a midsize galleon sporting the flag of Moray, as well as blue-and-silver pennants that represented the Rain Empire. Cayo only spared it a passing glance as he ran full tilt toward the dock. He had only just arrived and had had to scan the board outside the Port's Authority offices to figure out where to go.

The horizon was limned in dusky red, casting a pink glow over the harbor. It made Cayo feel as if everything around him were surreal, from the cry of the gulls to the creaking of the ships.

And the form of Sébastien just ahead, about to step onto the gangplank.

"Bas!"

His friend froze at the sound of his voice. There was another person with Sébastien, dressed in Dageur livery—no doubt sent by Philip to help Bas with the journey—who whispered something in his ear. As Cayo stumbled to a halt, gasping for breath, Bas murmured something back to the servant and nodded. Then he turned and made his careful way back to the dock, where Cayo waited.

A violent curse nearly tore from Cayo's mouth before he reined it in. He had tried to prepare himself, in the hours leading up to dawn, for the consequences of the Slum King's wrath. But the reality was so much worse.

Sébastien was sallow and wan, his hair lacking its normal luster, and his clothes—or perhaps they were Philip's clothes—hanging baggily on his frame. And then there was the linen bandage wrapped carefully around his head, hiding his eyes, or rather, where his eyes had once been. Although the bandage looked fresh, it was already stained with discharge, and the set of Bas's shoulders told Cayo of the pain he was trying to hide.

Cayo felt unable to move, like the shock of being plunged into icy water. It was one thing to imagine violence; it was another to see its result, to have to accept the messy aftermath. And to imagine it being done to Bas . . . Cayo choked on a gasp, a hot flash of horror replacing the ice in his veins.

"Bas," he finally whispered, reaching for his cheek without thinking. Bas flinched back at his touch, and Cayo dropped his hand. "Sorry, I didn't—"

"What are you doing here?" Sébastien's voice was low and rough, as if he were recovering from a sleepless night in the Vice Sector.

"Philip told me you were leaving. I've been trying to find you for days. I knew what happened, but . . ."

"Yeah?" Bas spat. "Did you hear about it from your new fiancée? Am I supposed to congratulate you for marrying the daughter of the man who did this to me?" He pointed at his face.

Now it was Cayo's turn to flinch. "It's not like that! And how do you know about Romara?"

"Back-channel gossip. They may have taken my eyes, but they didn't take my ears."

"I . . . I didn't know what he did to you until after I agreed to the engagement. Bas, I'm sorry. I know that isn't enough, that it doesn't really make a difference, but I am. I'm so sorry."

Bas turned his head away, seething. Cayo could see it in the way his jaw clenched, in the way his fists shook at his sides. Cayo couldn't stand that he was contributing to his pain, to his fury, to his spite for this city and the terrors that hid within it. He took a step forward, hand hovering in the air between them.

"I'm going to touch you again," Cayo murmured. "Is that all right?"

Bas nodded stiffly. Cayo wrapped his hand around Bas's wrist, feeling the strain there, the tendons pressed stark against his skin.

"What happened, Bas?" he whispered. "How did it get so bad? Was my help . . . Was it not enough?" It was all he'd had to spare at the time, but he should have done more.

"Stop making yourself out to be the cause of this," Bas snarled. "Your guilt doesn't allow you to become the victim here."

Cayo swallowed. "You're right."

Bas took a few deep breaths, and Cayo could feel him trembling. Suddenly, he deflated. "It wasn't anything you did, Cayo. You . . . You did what you could. But this was bigger than borrowed money."

Cayo stepped closer to him, gently squeezing his wrist. "What happened?"

Sébastien used his free hand to pull something from his pocket. It was small and round and oddly flat, like a piece of charcoal that had been compressed. He held it out, and Cayo warily took it.

"What is this?" Cayo asked, rubbing a thumb across its surface. It felt almost like graphite.

"What does its shape remind you of?"

Cayo studied the small object. Then he noticed the little ridges etched into its sides, almost like . . . "A coin?"

"A gold sena, to be exact." Bas had dropped his voice to a whisper. "Or rather, it was when I lifted it from the Slum King's tables."

Cayo frowned. "What does that mean?"

"I was scared when I took the money, so I spent the night with Philip." Bas swallowed. "We played a game. The one where you put a coin at the bottom of a wineglass and have to drink all of it to get the coin. Except we ended up falling asleep, and I never finished my last glass. When I fished out the coin the next morning . . ." He gestured to the black sphere.

A cold sweat had broken out on the back of Cayo's neck. "It's a counterfeit," he whispered in realization.

"And I'm sure it's not the only one." Bas's head twitched, as if he'd been about to look around before remembering he no longer could. "The Slum King must have thought I was the one planting the counterfeit money in his dens, or that I was at least part of the scheme. That's why he wanted to make an example of me."

Nausea gripped Cayo's stomach, and he tightened his hold on Bas's wrist. "You weren't part of it, were you?"

"Of course I wasn't!" He ripped out of Cayo's grasp. "You're a jackass. A complete . . . utter . . ." His breathing stuttered, and he bared his teeth in pain as he pressed a hand to his forehead. "Whoever *is* in charge of this scam, I hope they give the Slum King what he has coming. I hope they take their sweet time with him."

Cayo's eyes stung. He almost apologized again, wanted to apologize a hundred times, but he knew it would only make Bas angrier. Instead, he slowly leaned in and kissed the fever-hot skin of Bas's cheek.

"Thank you for telling me," he said softly. "Bas, if you . . . if you want to stay . . ."

Bas choked on a pained laugh. "I *can't*, Cayo."

Cayo nodded his understanding even as sorrow dug a trench inside him. "I'll miss you, Bas."

Sébastien sighed, leaning into him for just a moment. Then he pulled away, signaling for the servant to help him up the gangplank. Cayo watched them leave, then stood back and watched the ship prepare to set sail.

He even watched the *Sovereign* depart the harbor, carrying one of his oldest friends away. A friend he had failed in so many ways. A friend he might never see again. Dawn had grown stronger around them, gilding the water and lengthening the shadows, and Cayo couldn't help but see the painting it would make, a composition pieced together with regret and mistakes.

Finally, he turned and walked away from the docks. Realizing he was holding something in his hand, he unfurled his fist and saw the remains of the counterfeit coin.

Bas said he had lifted it from the Slum King's own tables. Bas's theory was that someone was trying to thwart Jun Salvador from the inside, but what if Salvador was fully aware of the counterfeit?

What if he was the *source* of it?

It wasn't that big of a leap, knowing the Slum King's penchant for controlled chaos. And if Cayo exposed him, or at least made enough of a case against him, it would break off his engagement to Romara. He could even get a reward from the Port's Authority for exposing Salvador's crimes.

Which meant finally breaking free of the Slum King's threats.

The carriage driver stifled a yawn and opened the door for him as he approached. "Home, my lord?"

"No." Cayo clenched his hand around the fake coin. "We're going to the Port's Authority."

11

SOLAS: What miseries, then, have you endured to become so heartless?

BRAEGAN: You must look to your own heart, for the answer lies within.

—*THE MERCHANT'S WORTH*, A PLAY FROM THE RAIN EMPIRE

The building was painted a shade of green that reminded Amaya of unripe guavas, and it left the same unappealing taste in her mouth. She crouched in the shadow of a balcony, dagger in hand, and stared intently at the street. Waiting.

She had been waiting now for two hours; the son of a bitch was likely in the Vice Sector, or whatever ale shop was lowly enough to accommodate the likes of him. But he had to return sometime, and when he did, she would be here to greet him.

Amaya hadn't been to the outskirts of Moray yet, where the smell of the sea was diminished and the wind carried instead the verdant scent of the jungle to the northeast. The breeze was warmer here, too, and sweat began to crawl down her ribs and between her breasts.

Finally, when the moon had fully crossed the sky, she spotted a dark figure lurching down the street just beginning to lighten with the silver threads of dawn. Gripping her knife hilt tighter, she watched the figure stumble up the shoddy iron stairs leading to the balcony. He fumbled for the key to the hideously green door and pushed it open with a squeal of its hinges.

Amaya melted out of the shadows and slipped through the door behind him. He didn't notice, rubbing a hand over his face while mumbling nonsense curses.

He *did* notice her boot kicking him to the floor.

Before he could cry out, she had the point of her knife pressed to his meaty neck.

"If you so much as move, I'll nick an artery," she warned.

"And I'll blast a hole through your guts," he growled back. Only then was she aware of the pistol trained on her stomach. She had underestimated his reflexes, even when he was sodden with drink.

Amaya cursed and backed away. He stood and dusted himself off, leering as he kept his pistol aimed at her.

Captain Zharo—except he wasn't a captain anymore, she realized—had been obviously enjoying his new life of retirement. Although his shirt was stained with sweat, drink, and food, it didn't have holes or tears like his shirts on board the *Brackish*. He had also added a couple more gaudy rings to his collection, fat bands of gold and gemstones twinkling against the weathered brown skin of his hands. A cursory look around the apartment showed a sparse yet decent setup, from the four-poster bed with mosquito netting to a kitchen area stocked with plenty of provisions. A door leading to another room had been left ajar, affording her a glimpse of a desk.

All paid for with Boon's gold.

"Didn't think I'd see you again, Silverfish," Zharo rumbled. "Thought the ocean had swallowed you right up."

"It did," she said, eyeing the barrel of his pistol. "It spat me back out."

"Not surprised, given how bitter you must taste." He grinned again, all rotting teeth and malice. "You here for revenge, then?"

It sounded so basic when he said it out loud, almost childish. Silverfish—*No, I'm Amaya, my name is Amaya*—gritted her teeth.

"Go 'head and drop that toothpick," Zharo said, indicating her knife with a wave of his pistol. "And let's get this over with."

When your opponent is cocky, you use that to your advantage, Boon had told her during his training. *Make 'em think the advantage is theirs, then swoop in and grab it for yourself.*

Amaya forced herself to toss the knife between her and Zharo, then lifted her hands as if in surrender. As Zharo approached, bending down to pick up her discarded knife, she kicked him in the head. He dropped to the floor with a grunt and she was on him within a second, pinning his arm down with her knee. She unsheathed the tiny knife hidden in her bracer and poised it above his left eye.

"I was going to do this quickly, but now I'm beginning to change my mind," she said. She rested the tip of the knife against the corner of his eye, and he flinched. A shiver of delight ran through her at that flinch. "Do you remember threatening to carve out Termite's eyes when she accidentally let a net of fish drop back into the sea? I do. I remember every single threat, every single punishment. I can re-create them all tonight."

She went into free fall, remembering the way his hand struck her face, his boots catching her in the ribs and stomach, his gravelly voice telling her that she was *nothing*. The way he laughed when she was forced to eat bugs in her starvation. The way he ordered her to *smile* while she worked.

This hadn't been her plan—she had wanted to get it over with, to feel some measure of relief at knowing this man's life had been erased from the world. But the more she opened herself to that familiar anger she had felt every day aboard the *Brackish*, the more she began to realize that Zharo was not worthy of the mercy of a quick death.

Zharo glared up at her, teeth half-bared. "You can try, Silverfish, but you've not the stomach for it."

"Let's find out together, shall we?"

"Or," he said, a hint of a smile in his voice, "I can tell you where your precious Roach is."

Amaya froze. *Roach.* The other Water Bugs didn't know what had happened to him, or what had caused his sudden disappearance. The worry had eaten at her ever since they'd acquired the *Brackish* a few months ago.

"Tell me," she said, surprised at how calm she sounded, "or I pop this eye out of your skull."

"I know some folks what'll have the right connections to find out where he is. But it'll take a day or two to get."

Amaya narrowed her eyes. She couldn't be sure if he was telling the truth, and her instinct told her to simply aim for his heart and be done with it.

But if there was any possibility of finding Roach . . .

She increased the pressure of her knee on his arm until the pistol fell from his loosened grip. She grabbed it and stood, aiming it at his chest. Although she had never shot a pistol before, Zharo didn't have to know that.

"Up," she ordered. "Come with me."

She forced him to walk into his office, where she found a chair covered in red velvet. *This is what he spends his money on?* she thought as she made him sit in the chair. Taking the rope she had coiled at her belt, she lashed his thick wrists together behind the chair's back. She tried not to shudder in revulsion whenever her fingertips grazed his skin.

"I'd almost say I'm proud of you, Silverfish," the man drawled. "Never thought a girl who whined at a coupla lashings could dole it out herself."

Amaya gritted her teeth as she felt the echo of his belt on her back, raising welts on her skin. She tightened the rope around his wrists and was satisfied with his grunt of discomfort. Then, pistol still in hand, she began to rummage around his office.

"These people you know who can find out where Roach is. Who are they?" she asked as she checked the cabinet. "Where can I find them?"

Zharo gave a single bark of laughter. "You think I'm dumb enough to let you walk outta here with that information? Why don'tcha untie me first and we'll make a deal."

"I'm not making a deal with *you*." Amaya looked through the cabinet's contents and found multiple ledgers that Zharo had kept on board the *Brackish*, documenting debts. She briefly flipped through them, glowering as the numbers went higher instead of lower.

"Only a few months on land and look at how rebellious it's made you," Zharo mumbled. "You were better off scrubbin' decks and shying away from my hand."

Amaya didn't respond. She told herself it was because she had risen above his threats, that she could handle his taunts. In reality, her mind went pure white with rage, so strong and bright that the only way to control it was to sit perfectly still until it faded. Breathing deeply, she shut the cabinet door and turned to his desk next, opening drawers and pulling out files. Zharo frowned at her, nonplussed by her silence, no doubt expecting her to have risen to his bait.

Silverfish would have. Amaya had bigger worries. She looked through invoices and receipts of the things he had bought within the last six months, including a document detailing the sale of the *Brackish* to a nameless buyer. *Boon.* Still, she saw nothing that would be of help to her.

"I still remember the day you were dropped off at the docks," Zharo went on. "Miserable, skinny thing that you were. All elbows and teeth and those big, hauntin' eyes."

Amaya ignored him, feeling around the drawers for secret compartments. She found one and popped it open, revealing another ledger underneath the false bottom.

"Wasn't even expecting a shipment that day, but there was a special seller who said it was a rush case. Guess your folks must've gotten on the wrong side of the wrong man. But then when I saw you, I knew you weren't nothin' special—another family lookin' to throw a hungry mouth away. Happens more often than you'd think, parents getting sick of their brats and doin' anything to get rid of 'em."

Amaya's hands tightened around the ledger, but she kept her face blank. Zharo's words poked and prodded at the soreness around her heart, the unanswered questions that dogged her day and night: Who had sold her, and why? What were the debts attributed to her father that her sale would have paid off?

But there had never been any indication that her father had raked in debts, or gambled. He'd always had enough money to feed her and her mother, and even to buy her a small present every month if she had behaved well.

The people around her—Boon, Zharo—didn't know the full truth either, and that was the whole point of why she was doing this. She would clear her father's name and restore her family's dignity.

But first, she had to restore her own dignity.

She flipped through the pages of the ledger until she came across some familiar names. Looking closer, she tried to decipher the numbers underneath them, as well as the names she didn't know.

Fredrique G. (Scarab)—4,500 senas, A. Zhang

Yaomin X. (Mantis) —3,000 senas, J. Vedasto

Fera B. (Beetle)—2,000 senas, C. Melchor

Amaya's stomach churned. Scarab had been the Water Bug who had given her the tattoo on her wrist. Mantis had fallen and died aboard the *Brackish*. And Beetle . . .

Zharo kept talking, but she paid him no attention. The price next to their names was undoubtedly the price paid for taking on these Bugs, and the names next to them had to belong to debt collectors. She scanned the rest of the ledger for her own name, but it wasn't listed. Just dozens upon dozens of children with prices affixed to their names. As if they were mere objects instead of living, breathing people.

Her heart pounding under the swell of her anger, she ripped out the page with Fera's name and stuffed it into her pocket. She wasn't sure yet what she would do with the information, but she knew it couldn't hurt.

Amaya stood and walked around the desk. She met Zharo's gaze and held it.

"I'm going to give you one last chance," she said, leveling the pistol at his head, "to tell me how to find Roach."

But Zharo only grinned, and she didn't know why until he launched himself from the chair and slammed into her.

She fell with his weight on top of her, crushing the air from her lungs. The stink of sweat and alcohol filled her nose as he reached for the pistol—he must have been loosening the rope while he spoke to her, to cover up the sounds of his rustling—and Amaya gagged as she twisted futilely under him.

She had had endless nightmares of being helpless and in his grasp. Her lungs tightened and her breathing stuttered, the same terror that took hold of her when she dreamed of being unable to run, unable to fight back.

But now she knew how to fight back.

Lesson number one, Boon had told her on the island, *is to always aim for the cock and balls first.*

Pivoting her hips, Amaya jerked her knee up and between Zharo's legs. The man wheezed and fell to his side, allowing her to wriggle free and whip out a knife from her boot.

This was it. In one thrust of her arm, she was going to put an end to this wretched chapter of her life. Zharo would no longer be the author of her misery. He would never hurt her or the other Bugs ever again.

Zharo heaved himself up and cocked the hammer of his pistol back, just like that fateful day on the *Brackish*. "I'll see you in the hells, Silverfish."

But before he could fire or she could stab him, he convulsed with a strangled yell. He twitched once, twice, then fell back onto his side, the light leaving his wide, murky eyes.

Amaya panted as she stared at him, uncomprehending. A voice wormed its way into her head, until it was practically yelling in her ear.

"Amaya!"

She started and swung her knife up, but it was blocked by another. Liesl stood before her, dressed in black as Amaya was. The knife she held was dripping blood onto the floor.

"You really should have told me you were planning this before going out on your own," Liesl said, gesturing to the still body of Zharo. A pool of blood was spreading from his corpse, inching toward Amaya still sprawled on the floor.

"Wh-what—" Her mind struggled to catch up to what had happened. "You killed him?"

Liesl shrugged and offered a hand to help her up. "Boon said not to leave any witnesses."

Now that the shock was beginning to wear off, Amaya bared her teeth and smacked Liesl's hand away. "He was supposed to die by *my hand*!"

"What difference does it make? Look, he's gone." She nudged his body. "You don't need to worry about him any longer."

Amaya got to her feet, shaking. Nausea gripped her stomach, and looking at Zharo's body didn't help. "It was supposed to be *me*! He was— He was always—"

She couldn't tell her that it wasn't so easy to simply *not worry* about him any longer. He would always be there, laughing at her, taunting her, ready to remind her she was nothing. Maybe, if it had been her hand on the knife, she could have severed that connection with him—but now she would never know.

"Amaya." Liesl looked her in the eye. Although Liesl was a girl who loved frills and flowers, Amaya could see the steel in her, hinting at a difficult life. "Trust me, you don't know what it means to kill a man—to have someone's blood on your hands. You aren't ready to face that yet. For now, you just need to be Countess Yamaa and focus on charming the city. Leave the dirty work to us. That's why Boon sent us with you."

Amaya was breathing hard, the room flooded with the metallic scent of Zharo's blood. It coated her throat and choked her. She swayed on her feet, and Liesl took her by the arm.

"Let's get you home and cleaned up," the girl soothed. "We can discuss this later."

As Liesl led her from the room, Amaya looked over her shoulder at the remains of the man who had helped ruin her life, the pitiful mass of useless flesh he left behind.

Then Liesl gently closed the door, putting an end to Silverfish for good.

12

If opportunity does not find you, you must create your own.

—*THE DEVIOUS ART OF DICE AND DEALING*

The office of the Port's Authority was situated in the Business Sector, its facade of marbled columns and elaborate window fittings blending in perfectly with the rest of the buildings along the main, cobbled thoroughfare. Golden letters gleamed in the dawn light above the entryway, spelling out the name of Moray's infamous system of authority.

As Cayo climbed out of the carriage, he was hit with the same disorientation he experienced every time he visited the Business Sector. Most sectors in Moray harkened back to a time when the city state was a part of Rehan, but after its colonization by the Rain Empire long ago, there were areas—like this one—where the architecture was so extravagant and pretentious that Cayo had to wonder if he was even in the same city.

He told the exhausted carriage driver to find some tea and take a break, and the driver touched his forelock in thanks. Cayo then turned to the office's wide double doors, the counterfeit coin held snug in his fist.

The main floor was quiet, the benches on either side mostly empty save for a woman with a black eye and a couple of men with crossed arms speaking in low tones. Cayo approached the young man at the desk near another set of doors.

"I'm looking for Petty Officer Nawarak?"

The young man waved him toward the doors beside the desk, not bothering to look up from his book.

Unlike the main floor, the back area was bustling with workers shuffling papers and running files into offices, all overlaid with the din of officers talking and cursing and laughing. It smelled strongly of parchment and burnt coffee. Cayo asked around until he found Nawarak's desk near the far wall.

She was sitting with her head propped on her hand as she glowered at a file spread before her. Although she was only in her early twenties, a wrinkle was already beginning to form between her eyebrows due to all her frowning. Her bluish-black hair was tied into a tight braid, showing off a round, pleasant face that clashed with her no-nonsense eyes.

She flicked that no-nonsense gaze up to him when he sat in the chair before her desk.

"You smell like alcohol," she said before he could greet her. "Good night, or rough night?"

Cayo thought back to the troubling events of the countess's party, his encounter with Philip, saying good-bye to Sébastien. "Rough."

"You'll get no sympathy from me." She leaned back and closed the file she'd been studying. "Although I hear you've reformed your ways since I last saw you. I'm sure your father is thrilled." She grinned, but like her eyes, it held no warmth. "Then again, knowing him, he's just found another thing to be disappointed in."

Cayo couldn't decide if he wanted to laugh or sigh. Nawarak had always been like this, ever since they were children. She was the daughter of his mother's best friend, and his mother had always called Nawarak his cousin despite the lack of blood connection. And, much like a cousin, Nawarak took pleasure in finding any opportunity to poke fun at him.

"I'm not here to listen to you trample on my character," Cayo said.

"Then why are you here? And at the ass crack of dawn, no less?"

Looking around to make sure no one was watching, Cayo leaned forward and placed the black lump of the counterfeit coin before Nawarak. She lifted an eyebrow at it.

"Wonderful. I just cleaned my desk, but please, feel free to sully it again."

"Do you know what it is?" he asked in a hushed voice.

She picked it up and inspected it. After a moment, she used her thumb to flip it up into the air and caught it.

"Counterfeit sena," she said.

"Yes!" He gripped the armrests of his seat, leaning even closer. "And I can tell you where it came from: the Slum King."

He held his breath, the weight of potential crushing his lungs. The potential to put an end to the Slum King's reign and make sure that nobody else ended up like Bas. The potential to sever his engagement with Romara.

Then Nawarak shattered that potential with a laugh.

"Cayo, we already know." She flipped the fake coin at him, and he fumbled to catch it. "We were on a lead with the case, but it's been put on hold."

"Put on hold? Why?"

"Ash fever." Nawarak leaned back in her seat, looking tired. "Some of the officers have it, and two have already died. One of them was actually on the counterfeit case. About a third of us are looking into the origins of the fever, in the event this is some sort of pathogen-like weapon being wielded by the Rain or Sun Empire."

A wave of cold swept through Cayo's body. "Why would they attack us?"

"You know they hate each other." She shrugged. "And they've been fighting over Moray for dozens of years. The city is a pawn to them."

"But isn't there a . . . whatever it's called, a statement of neutrality?"

The Prince of Moray was often called a figurehead, although his family were the last remaining vestiges of Rehanese royalty. When Rehan became a republic, the family had been able to buy the colony of Moray from the Rain Empire on two conditions: that they demilitarize, and that they remain neutral between the empires. Naturally, the Sun Empire didn't take kindly to this, and skirmishes had cropped up over the years.

But thanks to the prince, the casinos in Moray had flourished, bringing in enough money to rebuild the colony into a proper city-state. Over the last few years, though, Cayo had noticed wealthy citizens without business ties leaving Moray's shores. Something had changed—the first cracks in the gilded facade of the city, a rot hidden under the cobblestone.

"Good to know you paid *some* attention during your home-schooling," Nawarak drawled. "But neutrality means nothing when a multination world power wants control over the best trade routes."

"So you think they're preparing for another war?"

"I don't know. All I can say is that we have more serious issues to face than some fake gold cycling through the gambling dens."

Cayo looked down at the black disc in his hand. This small, worthless thing had cost Sébastien his eyes. Had driven him to pain and fear and suffering, and now self-imposed exile.

"What if I help with the case?" he asked. "I have plenty of contacts in the Vice Sector, including the Slum King himself."

Nawarak tried to hide her surprise. "You fancy yourself a for-hire detective?"

"Maybe not that, but someone who's invested and wants to bring Salvador down. Also . . . if I bring you information, I want to be compensated for it. Like a reward." *Enough to buy Soria's medicine.*

She stared at him in confusion, but eventually she shook her head. "Well, who am I to dissuade you from community service? Just don't, you know, kill anyone in the name of the law or something equally ludicrous."

"I'll try my best." Already his mind was racing with ways he could find dirt on the Slum King. "Do you have any leads for where I can start? Something the officers may have found before putting the case on hold?"

"I don't have access to that information, but my best guess would be to find any sailor who's spent a long time at sea and made port within the last few months."

"That certainly narrows it down, thank you."

She gave him her sharp grin again. "Hey, it's all part of the job when you're a for-hire detective."

"Don't call me that."

"Actually, I do have a lead for you. We picked up someone not too long ago who had counterfeit coins on him."

"Who is it?" he urged.

She hesitated, a conflicted look on her face. "It's probably not connected, but he *was* employed by your family until recently," she admitted. "He claimed he was retired when we picked him up, though, so I doubt there's anything there."

"Employed? How?"

"He was the captain of a ship called the *Brackish*."

Cayo frowned at the familiar name. The *Brackish* was like a ghost ship following him around, haunting him. "How many counterfeit coins did he have?"

"Just a dozen or so. Claimed he won them in the Vice Sector. There was no reason to think otherwise, and no hard evidence, so we had to let him go."

Cayo nodded. "Thank you for the tip." He stood up, preparing to leave.

"Cayo." She hesitated, looking uncomfortable. "I'm sorry. About Soria. If there's anything I can do . . ."

"Just promise there'll be a fat reward for me when I bring the information you need."

She huffed out a relieved laugh. "Deal."

The best place to start, Cayo figured, was his father's records. Kamon kept meticulous notes on all of his employees, and information about the *Brackish*'s captain would surely be in there.

Mercado Manor was eerily quiet as he padded down the hall to his father's office. Cayo was used to seeing maids scurry about and hearing the sounds of the kitchen staff preparing the day's meals, as well as Miss Lawan's voice as she instructed Soria on subjects like poetry, arithmetic, and etiquette. All they had now was a cook who only came to make dinners; the carriage driver; and the footman, Narin.

Narin had been on his father's list of those to let go, but the man had been in the Mercados' employ ever since Cayo could remember. Instead, Narin had offered to take a reduced pay, which Cayo found distinctly unfair given the fact that he also had to help take care of Soria now that Miss Lawan was gone.

When Cayo peeked into his sister's room, he was shocked—and elated—to find her sitting by the window instead of in bed, a pamphlet open on her lap. Narin was preparing tea for her and nodded in greeting to Cayo when he walked in. Soria turned her head and smiled weakly.

"You're up early. Oh," she said, noticing his party clothes, "or should I say, you're up late."

"It's been a long night." But strangely, he didn't feel tired—his deal with Nawarak had given him new energy. He bent down and kissed the top of her head, briefly feeling the heat that radiated off her. "What are you reading?"

"The new designs coming in for next season. Look at this." She practically shoved the pamphlet under his nose. "This is an unconscionable amount of lace."

Cayo swept his eyes over the dress in question, wrinkling his nose. She was right—much too much lace when a simple satin sash would work better. Then he noted the designer. "Well, what else do you expect from Girald? He wouldn't know fashion if it rose out of the sea and bit his backside."

Soria giggled as Narin set her tea before her. It wasn't her usual Kharian black, but some swampy-green brew that smelled like grass.

"A message came for you, my lord," Narin said, handing him a small envelope. The seal of red wax was stamped with a curly Y. Cayo broke it with his thumb and pulled out the paper inside.

"Who is it from?" Soria asked.

"Countess Yamaa." He narrowed his eyes at the elegant script, a blush heating his face at the reminder of their encounter last night. "She wants to meet at Laelia Teahouse later today."

Soria gasped. "I've wanted to go there for months!"

"Well, don't be too jealous. The countess is . . . ah . . ." Really, what word could best describe her? "Eccentric."

"I want to meet her," she whined. "And drink tea that doesn't taste like bathwater. Not that you don't make excellent tea, Narin." The footman gave an amused half bow. "But why does the countess want to see you? Do you think she's taken a liking to you?"

He choked. "Absolutely not." *Not after all the things I said about her—to her face.* "I might not even go. Now come on, drink your bathwater."

Cayo encouraged Soria to keep taking sips of the medicinal tea as they went through the pamphlet together, dog-earing their favorite pieces even though they both knew they could no longer afford them. For the first time, Cayo noticed a ring on her finger, a band of green rock.

"Where did you get that?" he asked, worried that she'd recently bought it.

"This?" She glanced at the ring. "It's been in my jewelry box for forever. I think Father gave it to me as a present a few years ago."

He deflated in relief. "Oh. Good." Before, the purchase of a ring would have been of little consequence. Now it sent panic coursing through his veins.

Eventually, Soria's energy flagged and she went into a coughing fit. Cayo and Narin helped her back to bed, where she fell into a light doze. Cayo kissed her forehead and stole into his father's office, determined to find a lead that would help her.

He spent the next hour going over his father's records, often glancing at the door in case Kamon walked in. He had to weed through the most recent documents first, some of them detailing his father's attempts to purchase unclaimed Widow Vaults, possibly as a means to inflate their coffers a bit. It wasn't an uncommon practice to bid on a Vault that couldn't be opened by a blood heir once its statute of limitations was up.

Finally, he found the workman records. But after several minutes of scanning the sheets, he came up frustratingly empty-handed.

Then he realized it wouldn't be in the current employee records, but in records of sale.

Cayo searched for the transaction document and found it near the top of a stack of papers to be filed. It detailed the passing of ownership of the *Brackish* from Kamon Mercado to a nameless buyer from the Ledese Islands.

The *Brackish*—that was the name of the ship that Countess Yamaa owned. Then why would it have been bought anonymously? Unless the countess wanted to be discreet for some unknown reason.

Although he found it odd, all his attention turned to the ship captain's name: Zharo. There was an address scribbled underneath in his father's handwriting, an address here in Moray. Now all he had to do was pay the captain a visit, ask him how he acquired his counterfeit coins, and follow whatever new lead that gave him.

A grin split his face as hope surged within him. This was going to be easier than he thought.

Half an hour later, Cayo stood outside the address he had copied onto a scrap of paper, blinking at the swarm of officers and curious onlookers who flocked around it.

The midmorning sun was bright and hot, making it painful to look at the lime-green apartment building on the outskirts of Moray. Cayo had to squint to make out the officers on the balcony above the street coming and going via an open apartment door.

The same apartment where the former captain of the *Brackish* was supposed to live.

Cayo approached the nearest officer who was keeping curious citizens away. "Excuse me, what's going on?"

"Investigation," the officer said. "There's been a murder."

"M-murder?"

"If you have a queasy stomach, best leave now," the officer said, looking toward the balcony. "They're removing the body."

Cayo followed his gaze. Two officers were carrying a large body on a stretcher. It was shrouded, but as they went down the stairs, an arm slid off the stretcher, revealing a heavily ringed hand.

Cayo stepped back as they passed and caught the unmistakable scent of blood. His gorge rising, Cayo turned away from the murmuring crowd and walked back to the carriage.

His best chance at a lead, and now the man was dead. He couldn't even enter the apartment, swarming with officers as it was. The captain's death seemed too close to his arrest to be a coincidence. But who would want to kill him?

And then he realized: the Slum King. Salvador had to be behind this—nothing else made sense, not with the coincidence of the counterfeit coin and Zharo being briefly held by the Port's Authority. It would be little effort for the Slum King to cover his tracks and do away with one of his unwilling peddlers.

He sat in the back of the carriage for a moment, thinking about what to do next. When the driver popped his head in, he startled.

"Sorry, my lord, but you haven't said as where you'd like to go."

"Oh. Um . . ." He could go back home to get some much-needed sleep, wait for his father to leave the house again before he dove back into his records. Frustrated, Cayo reached into his pocket to double-check that he had the right address, but the paper he pulled out wasn't the captain's address—it was the countess's invitation.

"My lord?"

Cayo hesitated. His father's words came back to him, the idea to try to flirt the countess out of some pocket change. After all, if his plan to dethrone the Slum King worked and his engagement to Romara was severed, he would need to get the money for Soria's medicine some other way.

"Laelia Teahouse," Cayo told the driver. "But take the long way. I'm going to take a nap."

13

A lady must always keep her guests engaged. Begin by inquiring after their day, or offering them tea. Please note that the offered tea should not be steeped too long, lest your guest become as bitter as the drink.

—*A LADY'S GUIDE TO ENTERTAINING*

Laelia's was the finest teahouse in Moray, frequented by the gentry and those who saved up for special occasions. Amaya had a vague recollection of passing by with her mother and being stunned by the beauty of it, but when she'd asked if they could go, her mother had laughed and claimed she could make better tea at home for a sixth of the price.

Now Amaya sat in one of the most coveted spots within the teahouse, a round glass table on a mezzanine overlooking the main floor. The railing was low and crafted of gold-veined marble, affording a grand view of the rest of the teahouse. She had to admit, it was absolutely stunning—from the domed glass ceiling to the moldings of leaves and flowers along the walls, it was easy to see why so many longed for a few hours within this place.

She had almost not come. She had almost dressed in disguise to visit Zharo's apartment, to confirm what she already knew: that he was dead, and he was never coming back.

But she had to do her part in learning more about the Mercados. She had to follow Boon's plan in getting closer to the son, Cayo, in order to create a door to Kamon Mercado.

And besides that, since returning to the estate last night Amaya had been in a mild state of shock, even when Liesl helped her wash off the blood and gave her a mugful of warm milk with a pinch of turmeric. Sleep had evaded her, making her toss and turn. She kept seeing Zharo's murky, lifeless eyes. Kept smelling his rancid odor on her clothes, in her hair.

Amaya scratched the back of her hand, still a little raw from all the times she'd washed it last night.

Trust me, you don't know what it means to kill a man—to have someone's blood on your hands. You aren't ready to face that yet.

Amaya bared her teeth. Liesl was wrong; it should have been *her* work. She had not only been robbed of the opportunity to find out where Roach was, but her revenge had gone unfulfilled.

She closed her eyes and sent up a quick prayer for Roach, willing him strength for whatever had befallen him. Apologizing for the delay in finding him.

A scrape and a call made her open her eyes again. On the ground floor of the teahouse, men were setting up a dais against the left wall. Once it was in place, they brought up a podium, as well as easel stands hidden by sheets.

"Excuse me," she called to a passing server, "what's going on?"

"Ah, today's an auction day," the server said. "They're usually held in the Business Sector, but once every few months we get to host them at the teahouse."

"And what is an auction day?" She tried her best to keep her voice level and snippy, an heiress demanding answers rather than a curious orphan peeking into another world.

"You're aware of the Widow Vaults here in Moray?" She nodded; they were purchased and handed down from family to family. "Every so often a Vault is left abandoned when an heir doesn't claim it. About a month after it passes that mark, the Vault is up for auction to the highest bidder. That is, unless no one gets wind that it's for sale and swoops in to buy it for themselves."

Amaya tried not to frown. "Why is it auctioned?"

The server's eyes widened slightly, as if unable to fathom her ignorance. "There's all sorts of treasure in them, of course. I've never seen the contents of one myself, but I've heard rumors—rich silks, forbidden spices, blood jewels, even parts of ships! And *gold*. Piles and piles of gold." He was nearly salivating at the idea.

"I see. Thank you for the explanation."

He nodded and hurried away to the next table. Amaya shifted in her seat, suddenly overcome by a heavy curtain of sorrow. She had lost everything of her parents—their belongings, their clothes, their furniture. They had never been wealthy enough to afford a Widow Vault, and she wondered now what she could have reclaimed of her past life if they had.

Sighing, she leaned forward to take in the sea of lovers and friends at the tables below. The riot of flowers and potted ferns around the teahouse made for a fragrant atmosphere when combined with the aromatic steam and the underlying scent of fresh baked goods. The chatter of the patrons was a soft background roar interspersed with the twinkling chime of teacups and saucers, occasionally interrupted by a man who kept coughing into his napkin.

"You look besotted," Avi mumbled from his place near the railing, acting as her bodyguard and footman. "Don't tell me *you* of all people enjoy places like this?"

Amaya leaned back from the railing with a scowl, heat crawling to her face. "No. It's just . . . a different experience."

Besides, so what if she liked it? She was fulfilling a wish from her childhood. But with her lingering rage from last night paired with the unexpected grief of this morning's reminder of all she'd lost, she was finding it difficult to properly enjoy herself.

"Well, save some of that for the boyo," Avi said, jerking his chin toward the spiral staircase. "I'm sure it'll do wonders for his ego."

Amaya turned. Cayo Mercado was being escorted to the table by one of the servers, who was dressed in the pink-and-white uniform of Laelia's. Cayo, in contrast, wore a jacket of deep navy and dark breeches. They were colors that must have matched his mood, for his eyes were glazed and his brow furrowed until he looked up and spotted Amaya.

The server held out a seat for Cayo, who took it with the ease of one who was used to having others pull their chairs in and out for them. Amaya's fingers twitched in irritation under the table.

"My lord, my lady, welcome to Laelia's," the server said. "We have an excellent array of blends today, a fresh shipment straight from the heart of Khari. I personally recommend the white starlight blend, which carries notes of lemongrass and mallow blossoms."

Amaya put on a bland smile as the server spoke, unable to resist studying Cayo as he politely gave the server his attention. Up close she could discern the bags under his dark eyes, and the way his hair had started to droop out of its styled look. A black strand of it had fallen across his forehead, curled and stiff with pomade.

Although the lines of his jaw and nose were sharp, there was something almost soft about him, the more she stared. Perhaps it had something to do with the tender slope of his neck, or how his lips weren't as thin as most boys'. Or maybe it was just that he was sleepy, blinking slow and often as the server went on.

The show of weakness only stoked her rage. To him, she wasn't a threat.

Not yet.

"Do any of those strike your fancy, my lady? My lord?"

Amaya shook herself. "The last one, please," she said with a smile, although she had no idea what she was ordering.

"And I'll have your strongest blend," Cayo said.

"Excellent choices. I'll return shortly."

Once he was finally gone, Amaya turned her smile to the young Lord Mercado. Cayo glanced at Avi before offering her one of his own smiles, somewhat forced and guarded.

"I'll admit, Countess, that I'm surprised you asked to see me."

His voice was like the rolling of a gentle wave, mild enough to disguise the strength that hid beneath it. She would have to tread more carefully than she thought.

"Well, you made such an impression at my party," she said. "I couldn't help but be curious to find out more about you."

"I'm really not that interesting." One of his eyebrows lifted. "Not as interesting as a countess who dives into a pool to save her servant."

"Would you have preferred the girl to drown?"

"Of course not. Although it might have been avoided altogether if you didn't hire children in the first place."

Shaky as she was, she grinned. He was ready to spar today. And that was just what she needed: to let loose some of the tension coiling within her.

"I took her away from a violent lifestyle," she said. "And this is how she wanted to repay me."

Cayo frowned at that. "What do you mean, a violent lifestyle?"

The sound of wood knocking on wood echoed through the teahouse then, saving her from answering. They looked down as a man in a nice suit stood at the podium, his spectacles gleaming with the light coming through the glass dome.

"Good morning, fine patrons of Laelia's. As you must know, today is considered an auspicious day in the Rehanese calendar, one that promises fortune and favorable odds. It only comes once per month—which is why we conduct our auctions on this specific date. This month, we're delighted to partake in this day with you in the hopes of bringing you the wealth you desire."

There was a polite round of applause, peppered with coughing. Amaya suspected today's patrons were frequent attendees of these auctions. Contempt simmered low in her gut as she considered them, dressed up and glittering like a magpie's den, having nothing better to do than to flaunt their expendable wealth.

Briefly, the image of Zharo's ringed hands flashed through her mind. She winced even as she fisted her own hands under the table.

"We have two Widow Vaults to auction off today," the auctioneer went on, signaling to his workers to unveil the easel stands. They held canvases with paintings that depicted vases, golden statuettes, jewelry. "Vault one contains an exquisite collection of artifacts from the second and third Yomir eras, which I think will impress quite a number of you. I'm looking at you specifically, Lord

Nadim." A gentle wave of laughter rose from the crowd.

As the auctioneer began to list the items, Amaya again took a moment to study Cayo as he watched the goings-on below. His question still rang in her head.

She wondered how he would react to the truth.

"The girl was sold by her parents to a debtor ship," she said.

He blinked and swung his gaze back to her. "What?"

"The girl in my employ. She spent quite a few months on a debtor ship before I came upon her. It was on the *Brackish*, actually."

The name sparked something in him, and she felt her chest go cold. Something like muted horror crossed his face, and she realized then that she had made a mistake.

"The *Brackish*," he repeated slowly, sitting back. "Your ship, you mean."

"Yes. When I bought it, I knew I wanted to provide a better life for the children who were being subjected to cruelty on a daily basis. So I gave them a choice: work for me, or continue to gut fish until their indenture was up." She shrugged. "It wasn't a difficult choice."

He took a moment to reply, the auctioneer's steady, fast-paced voice filling up the silence. "Why do you care about the children but not the rest of the debtors?"

Amaya took a breath to steady herself, knowing a boy like this would never truly understand the next words out of her mouth.

"Because children are the victims of their parents' crimes."

He thought on that as his attention seemingly drifted back down to the auction. Amaya continued her unabashed study of him, wondering if he had any idea what his father had done. Her fingers tingled in her lap; her chest tightened with inaction. She needed to get up and walk away, she needed to yell at the auctioneer below to shut up, she needed to pick up the small knife beside her plate and—

"Did you hear the news this morning?" he asked suddenly. "The former captain of the *Brackish* was found dead in his apartment."

The cold in her chest spread. Waves beat against her ears, the deafening madness of the sea at night. She breathed hard through her nose as she fought against it, tried to clear her vision and compose herself before he knew, before he guessed.

Amaya forced her hand up to her throat, widening her eyes in what was only a partial imitation of shock. "You . . . You can't be serious."

"I am. I . . ." He cleared his throat. "I saw the crime scene this morning. They brought his body out on a stretcher. You knew nothing about it?"

"No, I'm afraid not." *Why in Trickster's name were you there?* she wanted to growl. *He was no business of yours!* "I've never even had contact with the man. I heard he was vile, though. He beat the children on board and worked them to the bone."

"Do you think he deserved to die, then?"

The tone wasn't accusing. It was curious, almost dispassionate, as if the act of discussing murder over tea wasn't a new experience for him. It was a question she had asked herself before—if the punishment truly fit the crime, if Zharo's conduct could have only been balanced with death.

"Perhaps the gods were only meting out justice," she said at last.

He frowned but was prevented from asking about it further when the server arrived with their teas. They were each given a teapot and cups painted a delicate shade of green. It reminded Amaya of the color of Zharo's apartment building, and a sudden wave of nausea overtook her. She began picking at her fingernails, certain they still smelled like blood.

The server poured their teas with an expert hand and gave them a three-tier tray of pastries and fruit, then bowed and took his leave. Cayo waited until the server was on the stairs to address her again.

"Are you well, my lady?"

Amaya stilled her hands in her lap. "Perfectly fine, my lord. Although you seem the worse for wear. Did you have too much fun at my party?"

"One could say that," he muttered. He lifted his cup and took a sip even though steam was still billowing out of it. "You seem to have had a sleepless night yourself."

"It's difficult work, playing hostess." She lifted her own teacup, willing her hand not to shake. The tea smelled of jasmine, and when she took a small sip, the heat nipped her tongue.

I have to kill him, before he suspects.

The thought came unexpectedly, like a rock smashing through a window. She wasn't even sure if the thought was actually hers—it almost sounded like Boon's voice, whispering in her ear. There had been moments when he'd done that during her training, when he had placed a callused hand on her shoulder and murmured directions.

Try to take that lad's coin purse, he would instruct while they were out walking at night, teaching her the ways of deception. *Compliment that woman until she gives you her address. Rip your dress and run up to those guards, pretend you've just been mugged, and then knock 'em out.*

Amaya set her teacup down a little too hard, making Cayo and a couple of nearby patrons turn their heads. Her whole body flushed, but not with embarrassment—with an almost feverish conviction.

Liesl had prevented her from acting last night in the way her body craved, yanking her revenge out from under her. Her limbs jumped and twitched with it, and without her realizing it her hand drifted to the small knife on the table, caressing the blade with a thumb.

She could do it in a multitude of ways. She could lure him outside, or follow him back to his manor. Or she could simply lunge across this table and cut a line across his throat, watch it yawn open as he choked and stained the tablecloth.

"—bolt from the northern province of Rehan, highly valued for its durability and shine."

Cayo was in the middle of placing a berry tartlet on his plate when his attention quickly returned to the auctioneer. Amaya forced herself to do the same and saw a painted depiction of fabric on one of the easels.

"This blend of silk is one of the finest you'll find on the continent," the auctioneer said. "Valued at a thousand senas per bolt."

"He could have at least brought one to show," Cayo muttered to himself. "Some of the tailors in Moray could benefit from using a higher grade of silk."

A surprised laugh bubbled up in her throat. She couldn't believe it; Cayo Mercado enjoyed *fashion*?

"Is this . . . an interest of yours?" she asked, trying to keep her voice light, trying not to reveal the darker thoughts lurking beneath the surface. "How did you get involved in such a thing?"

You're supposed to be asking him about his father, she reprimanded herself. *Not about his hobbies.*

Cayo shrugged. "I've always admired clothes, I suppose. When my sister was growing up, I'd help her pick out dresses." He glanced at what Amaya was wearing today, a lavender dress of typical Kharian design, with a length of fabric draped over her shoulder and embroidered with golden suns. "I was fascinated by tailors and how they worked to create such beautiful pieces with just a needle and thread."

Amaya's throat tightened unexpectedly. She thought of her

mother sitting bent over coats and skirts, her needle glinting like a miniature sword as she sewed.

She struggled to regain her voice. "I . . . take it you go shopping often, then?"

"We used to." Cringing as if he'd said the wrong thing, he took another sip of his tea and turned his gaze to the patrons below.

Amaya felt a flutter of opportunity seize her. She recalled the battered state of his carriage, and the fact that he had once been a frequent gambler. Were the Mercados not as wealthy as they led others to believe? Her heart quickened at the thought.

"Tell me more about your family," she said. Feeling Avi's watchful eyes on the back of her head, she slowly let her hand drift away from the knife and instead take up the silver tongs. She carefully selected a chocolate-drizzled pastry and put it on her plate. It was filled with a decadent cream spotted with black vanilla bean. "You mentioned you have a sister?"

"Yes." He used a tiny fork to spear a glazed strawberry on his tartlet. "She's a couple of years younger than I am."

"How come I haven't seen her at my parties?"

His fork stopped halfway to his mouth. He hesitated, then followed through and took a bite of the glistening fruit.

"She's been ill," he said after swallowing. "But should hopefully recover soon." He gave her another forced smile, showing off a dimple.

"Oh." Amaya leaned back against the chair, disappointed to feel a spike of regret cut through her lingering rage. Wracking her brain for one of those ridiculous phrases Liesl was always making her recite from a book on etiquette, she added, "Please give her my regards."

"I'm sure she would be thrilled, my lady." At the sound of a patron coughing down below, his shoulders tightened. It was then that Amaya saw through the polite veneer of Cayo Mercado and glimpsed a boy who, despite his smooth words, was afraid.

Just how ill was his sister?

And then another part of her—the Silverfish part of her, perhaps not so dead after all—wondered how she could use that to her advantage.

"I can't imagine the worry you and your father must feel," she went on, digging into the sore spot as far as she dared. "To have someone you love so much be in the clutches of such a serious illness. It is serious, isn't it?"

"One could say that," he murmured down to his tartlet. Whatever intentions Cayo had brought with him today, they seemed to be unraveling. Which told her that she was right—it was much more serious than he let on.

She knew about the deadly sickness running through Moray; she and the Landless had been checked by a doctor when they docked at port. It wasn't that big of a leap to conclude the girl likely had ash fever.

But should she play that hand now, or wait until she could use it as leverage? It was no surprise the family didn't want the news public. To have someone like Countess Yamaa know, with the possibility of spreading the gossip among her many acquaintances like a dandelion spreading its seeds, would have been a living nightmare.

She was tempted to blurt out that she knew, to figure out if her guess was correct, but the look on Cayo's face stopped her. There was a muted terror there, in the wariness of his eyes. In the tight way he held his mouth.

It chipped back her rising bloodlust, still roiling and unsated. Her anger turned from him to herself—for showing her own weakness, the way her misery made it easier to detect it in others.

Children are the victims of their parents' crimes.

No, she decided, she would not kill Cayo Mercado. She would reserve her vengance for his father alone.

Cayo picked up a small silver spoon and began to nervously dance it between his knuckles. Amaya blinked. The young Lord Mercado may not have been good at concealing his emotions, but he was certainly skilled with his hands. She wondered if it was a result of his interest in tailoring.

"I would appreciate it," he finally said, his voice low, "if you kept my sister's illness to yourself. My father . . . We can't . . ."

"I understand." She was only too eager to have information on the Mercados no one else had.

Another brick in the foundation of their ruin.

When you go after the boy, be sure to lay it on thick, Boon had told her. *Trust me, most young bucks have mud for brains, and a lotta them hunger for the touch of a pretty girl.*

Amaya steeled herself before reaching over the table and touching his hand. She wasn't used to touching people she did not know; it had taken her almost a year to be comfortable enough to hug Roach. But when Cayo looked up, surprised, she knew she had made the right move.

"I admire how you care for your sister during this difficult time," she said.

He stared at her hand, somewhat darker than his. Cayo took a deep breath, shedding even more of that veneer of detachment. *Good.*

"I'll do whatever it takes to help her," he said to the tabletop.

Keep going, Boon's voice whispered in the back of her mind. Her fingers slid across his skin until she was clasping his hand. Cayo hesitated, then returned the soft pressure. His touch was warm and dry.

"I hope things improve for her," she said, and was distantly surprised to realize she meant it. "And for your family as a whole." That, she did not mean.

"Thank you, my lady. I'm beginning to learn the only way to move forward is by confronting the mistakes of one's past." He shrugged a shoulder. "Otherwise history will just repeat itself, and everything falls apart again."

This boy was full of curiosities. But before she could prod more into what he meant, the auctioneer banged his gavel against the podium.

"Vault one is *sold* to Mr. Hirana at twenty-one thousand senas! Please come up, sir, and sign your name on the contract of transfer."

The crowd erupted into gentle applause as a man stood from a table and made his way up to the dais. It was the same man who had been coughing since she arrived at the teahouse. He was coughing even now, the noise muffled by the napkin pressed to his mouth.

When he pulled it away, it was speckled with blood.

The man wobbled and fell against a table, knocking over cups and plates that smashed on the floor. People yelped as he toppled over and lay unmoving, sprawled against the marble.

Amaya tore her hand away from Cayo's and leaned over the balcony. The man's companion rushed forward to put his head on her lap, and that's when Amaya saw it.

A splotch of gray on the man's neck.

"Ash fever!" a patron screamed, knocking their chair back.

The teahouse erupted into chaos.

14

The greatest key to pulling off a con is misdirection.

—*A HUNDRED AND ONE VICES FOR THE EVERYMAN*

Cayo walked the counterfeit coin across his fingers, watching it roll as fluidly as any normal sena would.

It was amazing, he thought, how easily a simple disguise could fool so many people.

Sighing, he pocketed the false coin and gazed at the mouth of the alleyway. The familiar din of the street beyond made his blood sing, his fingers buzzing with excitement, with the promise of chance and fortune.

But Cayo had not returned to the Vice Sector to play. He had come here to find clues with which to take down the Slum King.

Straightening his jacket, he stepped out of the alleyway and onto Diamond Street, the central artery of the Vice Sector. The bright multicolored lanterns dazzled him and made him blink, and the riot of the crowd stirred the nervous energy inside him. The people were a curious mix of seasoned locals, grubby alley dwellers, glitzy nobles, and naive tourists. It was the only part of the city where one could find this unexpected assortment of Moray's citizens, the only part where luck mattered more than status.

Cayo had once considered it more home to him than Mercado Manor, a place where he could be unapologetically himself. Where excitement nipped his ankles and fed the flame of his recklessness. He remembered first feeling that recklessness after his mother died, an urge to fling himself into danger and fun—to distract his broken heart with broken morals.

He didn't quite feel the same now, walking down Diamond Street with his hands in his pockets, keeping an eye out for thieves. It was as if that recklessness had evaporated off him, leaving him tired and unsatisfied.

"Cayo!" someone cried down the street. A petite woman with short, curly hair waved at him and grinned. He recognized her as Mariposa, a gambler roughly his age who had often sat at the same tables with him. Her girlfriend, a tall Rehanese girl, glowered at him, no doubt remembering his penchant for flirting. "We haven't seen you in so long! Welcome back!"

His neck heated under his collar. "Well, I actually . . ." He shook his head; they didn't need to know this was hopefully a onetime visit. "Have you seen Romara?"

Mariposa made a long-drawn-out sound of delight. "Of course you're here to see your *fiancée*. She's in the Hart and Bell."

Cayo cringed before thanking Mariposa and continuing on, passing street musicians who flooded the air with brash drums and shrieking fiddles. One of them even had an old-fashioned

Rehanese lute that warbled over the babbling crowd.

So the gossip had spread about him and Romara. That meant he only had so much time to tell his father about the arrangement. If Kamon heard it from someone else first . . .

But if Cayo succeeded in finding a link between Salvador and the counterfeit, then he wouldn't have to. The engagement would be called off, Nawarak would give him a reward, and he could take care of Soria.

Thinking back to yesterday, to the man who had collapsed in the teahouse, he shuddered. It had reminded him too much of how Soria had fallen at their dinner with the Hizons. He and Countess Yamaa hadn't said a word to each other as the fallen patron had been carried out on a stretcher. At least, not until the countess had laid out the money for their tea.

My invitation, my treat, she'd said in response to Cayo's protest, paired with that small, secretive smile she was so good at.

Well, he *had* wanted to see if he could weasel some money out of her, hadn't he?

Still, even the idea had sat wrong with him. Cayo rubbed a thumb against his palm, remembering the countess's touch. How she had shown sympathy instead of scorn.

He stopped in front of the Hart and Bell, recognizing the bronze sign above the door of a stag wearing a bell on its collar. His mind still spinning, he drew a deep breath to prepare himself and walked in expecting the worst.

The den was lively with the sounds of rolling dice and shuffling cards under the roar of the losers and the cackles of the winners. The layout of the Hart and Bell was open and spacious, affording him a view of crowded tables and a long bar in the back.

He spotted her almost immediately. She was near the bar, in the nook of couches and chaises that were usually reserved for the den's most frequent—or richest—players. She was sprawled on a cream-colored chaise, swirling a red drink in her hand. As he watched, she threw her head back and laughed over something a young man sitting on the arm of the chaise had said. There were three others with her, all with the same hungry look that Cayo was used to seeing on the Slum King's followers.

Cayo clenched and unclenched his hands, stretching out his neck in an attempt to look more relaxed. Plastering on his dimpled smile, he approached Romara's makeshift court.

She was taking a sip of her drink when she spotted him over the lipstick-stained rim of her glass. Her eyes narrowed.

"Romara," he greeted her, not bothering to spare a glance at the others. "I—"

"Stop." She pointed a gloved finger at him. "Not another word out of you. I know exactly why you're here."

His heart gave a violent lurch. How could she already know what he was up to? "You—you do?"

Romara waved impatiently at the young man sitting on the arm of her chaise, who stood and rounded up the others to slink back into the hubbub of the den. Cayo didn't miss the nasty looks they gave him as they passed.

Once they were alone, Romara draped an arm above her head and sipped at her drink, gazing at him like a hawk sizing up a mouse. Her black-and-purple dress spilled across the chaise in a waterfall of silk and tulle, and she was barefoot, her black heels discarded haphazardly on the rug below. Her eyes were rimmed in kohl that winged out into sharp points.

"I know you're here because you don't want to get married," she finally said. "But just so you know, I have every intention of having this wedding."

Cayo was momentarily struck speechless. Out of everything he had expected her to say, that had been at the very bottom of the list. "Excuse me?"

"Oh, you're playing the prim-and-proper boy now, are you?" She revealed her teeth in a grin. "Have you been spending too much time with your dear daddy?"

"Looks like you've been doing the same," he muttered, glancing at the vacated seats. He was stalling for time, trying to wrap his head around this new direction.

"I don't need that fool to tell me how to make a name for myself," she said. "I can do that just fine on my own. In fact, it's why I need this wedding to happen."

Cayo crossed his arms. "I thought neither of us wanted that. That we were going to play along until we found a way out of it. Or did I misunderstand?"

"You didn't misunderstand anything." She sat up slowly, making sure her drink didn't spill. "I merely changed my mind."

"But *why*?"

"Because Daddy Dearest is playing a game with me, too. I didn't see it at first, but now I know the stakes. If I marry you"—she stuffed a hand into her décolletage and pulled out an iron key—"then I get the key to the business. Literally."

That explained her growing number of followers. But more importantly, Cayo had finally found an opportunity: He had to get that key from her. It no doubt led to the Slum King's office, where he could find all sorts of incriminating evidence.

166

He watched as Romara shoved the key into a pocket, immensely thankful she hadn't put it back in its original holding place. Putting on his dimpled smile again, he sat next to her.

"If that's the case, then I agree with you," he said. "We should go through with it."

She gave him a skeptical look, sipping again at her drink. "What's with the eagerness all of a sudden?"

"Profit," he said, shrugging. "If you become the next Slum King, then as your husband I'd get a cut of your earnings. You already know that my family's purse strings are drawn tighter than they used to be."

She hummed in thought. "And in exchange, I get more status among the gentry."

"Exactly. It's a win-win situation." Cayo tapped back into the flirtatious manner that used to come so naturally to him and leaned into her, wrapping an arm around her waist. He rested a hand on her hip. "We could be the most powerful couple in Moray," he whispered into her ear, his lips skimming the outer shell. "We could *run* this entire city."

Romara shivered at the prospect. Cayo sat back, still maintaining his smile. She was flushed, but not from his embrace—from the promise of power at her fingertips.

"I'm glad we're in agreement, Cayo," she said, breathless. "And to think, here I was worried you would be shaking in your shoes."

"I'm craftier than I look."

"So I'm learning." She lifted her glass to his lips. He obediently took a sip of the fiery drink before she took one of her own. "Here's to tearing apart our fathers' legacies."

"May it be swift," he added, feeling the impression of the key within his fist.

15

The sun and the moon play an eternal game,
A celestial chase, one after another,
Never knowing the tricks they play,
Never knowing each fools the other.
—FROM "THE LIGHTS OF THE NORTH," A REHANESE POEM

The garden was still littered with party debris. The hanging lanterns waved gently in the sea breeze, some having fallen into bushes or onto the ground. Glasses had been left on tables, several only half-drunk, and an errant garland had drifted into the pool to float forlorn and forgotten.

If the estate had been properly staffed, Amaya supposed that all this would have been taken care of already. As it was, she only had a small detail of spies and a crew of children at her disposal. She herself had been too preoccupied to do any cleaning, especially since meeting with Cayo Mercado a couple of days ago at Laelia's.

He had mentioned something about confronting the past to prevent history from repeating itself. Since then, she had become obsessed with the list of debt collectors taken from Zharo's apartment, now her only link to figure out what had truly happened.

She looked to the list she had brought out here with her, weighted down with a rock so it wouldn't fly away. The inked words glared up at her, almost taunting her.

Amaya had had Liesl reach out to all the listed debt collectors under the guise that the countess had an important, undisclosed job that needed doing, and she was searching for the right candidate. In reality, Amaya would use the countess's influence in order to get at the heart of what she wanted: information about why she had been sold all those years ago.

She had to move forward with Boon's plan. But first, she had personal business to settle.

Footsteps sounded behind her. Her hand drifted to her knife by instinct, her shoulders stiff.

But it was only Cicada. She relaxed as he gave her one of his infectious grins, a flash of white against the striking darkness of his skin. It crinkled the corners of his eyes and stretched the white tattoos on his upper cheeks. Amaya tried to return it, but it sat weak on her face.

"You only picked at your breakfast, so I figured you might be wanting for something else," he said, placing a silver tray on the glass table beside her. It contained a small teapot, a cup, a plate of fried plantains, and a bowl of colorful fruit.

Unexpectedly, Amaya's eyes began to sting. It may have been a small kindness, but it felt so much bigger. It reminded her of all the times he snuck her a bit of what Zharo ate—always better than what the Bugs got—and how that, to them, was only one method of survival.

This, though—it wasn't survival. Not really. It was merely kindness and friendship, and Amaya had no idea what to do with either.

The *Brackish* had taught her that such things were practically nonexistent; that the world was cruel, and it forged cruel people to inhabit it. It had been a miracle that she had had Roach, considering how many of the older Bugs grew to turn on each other. Once, a Bug had told her that if she snuck one of the fish she gutted down her shirt, she could dry it in the Bugs' cabin for jerky. But Zharo had seen through that in an instant and given her a black eye. The Bug had merely shrugged and said, "I wanted to see if it would work."

People were not designed to be trusted.

"Thank you," she whispered. "How . . . How are the others?"

He shrugged and took a speckled piece of pitaya from the fruit bowl. "Managing. Waiting. The smaller ones seem fine, but the older ones are itching to get home. I try to keep them busy with housework and meal prep and the like."

Amaya didn't blame them for being impatient. Again she thought of Roach, missing him desperately and wishing he were here to tell her what she should do. He had always been much better with the younger Bugs than she was, telling them fantastical stories and pulling laughs out of them when he could.

"I appreciate you looking after them," she said. "Just let me know what else I can do."

"You're already doing plenty." He gave her a mock salute before heading back inside.

Amaya sat back with a sigh, nibbling on a plantain. She didn't feel like she was doing plenty. She felt like she was swimming in circles, knowing that as soon as she grew too tired she would drown.

Sunlight filtered through the overhead branches, spangling the ground and her table with coins of gold. A thin breeze ruffled the wide leaves of the palms surrounding her, creating a susurrus that kept her calm as she cycled through her troubled thoughts.

She didn't hear Liesl until the girl was standing beside her. Jumping halfway out of her seat, Amaya dropped the plantain and pressed a hand to her chest.

"What in the *hells*, Liesl!"

"I apologize. I should have stepped on a twig to let you know I was coming."

Amaya caught her breath and glared up at Liesl. One of these days she was going to ask the girl how exactly she had come to learn all these unique . . . skills.

"Is the first candidate already here?" Amaya asked, looking for the sun's position. It was far too early for them to be starting.

"No, it's not that." Liesl hesitated, keeping her hands clasped before her. Amaya noticed then that she held a folded piece of parchment. "You asked me to look up your father. Arun Chandra. I went through some public records, pulled some things from his business that might be of note."

Amaya's heart beat faster. She had worried about asking this favor of Liesl, not wanting Boon to know that she was poking into places he didn't want her poking. But she had to know what had happened to her father, and why the Port's Authority would go after him the way they had.

That, and she wanted to prove Boon wrong.

"What did you find?" she demanded.

Liesl looked down, the sun glaring off her glasses. She handed the parchment to Amaya, who took it with shaking fingers. As she opened it, Liesl explained at her elbow.

"Chandra's Pearls was making good income for a few years, and then something happened to create a significant dip in earnings. I don't know if it was because of loss of business or some other factor—debts, perhaps"—Amaya flinched at the memory of Boon telling her that her father had gambled—"but he was in need of a loan to keep the business afloat."

Liesl paused, then sighed. "He took out a loan with Mercado."

Amaya's fingers went cold. She scanned the words and numbers on the page before her, though she could barely understand them.

"That isn't everything," Liesl said, gesturing to the parchment. "Just the initial loan."

"What . . . what does this mean?"

The girl moved to the seat on the other side of the table, fanning out her blue skirts before she sat. "Arun Chandra took out a loan with Mercado, and there was a plan to pay it off over the course of five years, plus interest. Merchants, you know—they're greedy. Your father was able to pay off the first year, but after that . . ."

Every man carries his sins a different way.

"I couldn't find every record, but from what I could gather, your father fell further into debt with Mercado. A debt he couldn't repay."

The parchment crumpled between Amaya's hands. She stared blankly at the garden before her, revelation opening a pit underneath her.

She didn't want it to be true. She didn't want to have something in common with Boon, hatred toward a man who had torn their lives apart.

"I'm sorry," Liesl said when Amaya stayed quiet. "The fact that Mercado was tied to this is . . . Well, it doesn't surprise me, but it can't be easy. At least we're going to be striking back. That's the whole point of coming here, isn't it? Boon gets his Landless status revoked, we get paid, and you get revenge for your father."

So simple when she said it. It wasn't simple where it sat in Amaya's chest, a tangled ball of rage and grief that threatened to grow a briar around her heart.

Had Mercado been behind all of it? Her father's debt, his punishment, her being sold?

"We don't have to go through with this today if you don't want to," Liesl said, tapping the paper that Amaya had taken outside with her. "We can reschedule."

Amaya took a deep breath, her chest shaking under the weight of this new information.

"No," she said, standing. "This is perfect timing. Now I know specifically what to ask of them."

Liesl nodded her approval. "I'll go prepare, then."

Amaya still had no definite answers to her questions, but that was going to change. Today.

A few hours later, Amaya ran her thumb over the crinkled edge of Zharo's list, glowering at the far wall of the sitting room as she slouched in her cushioned, gilded chair. She was fairly certain the furniture under her backside cost more than the *Brackish* had, and it only worsened her mood.

At the doors to the sitting room, Liesl was busy ushering away a stocky man. "We thank you for your time, Mr. Vedasto," she said in her best lady-in-waiting voice, all musical and charming. "We will contact you if you seem to be the right fit."

Amaya watched the man leave. He passed by Deadshot standing guard at the door, the mercenary trailing his movements with hungry eyes, as if itching for any excuse for a fight.

Liesl waited until the man was gone before pecking Deadshot on the cheek and walking back into the room with a sigh.

"Boon has trained you well," the girl said, pouring herself some tea and splashing in a bit of brandy from the drink cart. "If it were me, I'd have stabbed one of these bastards by now."

"Yes, you're very good at stabbing, aren't you?" Amaya muttered.

"Shush." Liesl took a moment to sit and rest, sipping daintily at her tea. "I did you a favor with Zharo."

Amaya ground her teeth together and looked over the list in her hand, already crinkled from her handling throughout the day.

"We'll find something," Liesl said. "One of these men ought to have a lead."

But they had been at it all afternoon—a steady stream of investigation under the pretense of Countess Yamaa conducting interviews. So far, there had been no luck. Every man who was shown into the sitting room left roughly ten minutes later, confused. The most recent debt collector, Jin Vedasto, had blinked vapidly at her under thick, wiry brows as she asked him questions.

"Who was your employer? How long did you work for them? What would you say was the most fulfilling aspect of your former employment?"

Vedasto had given slow, drawn-out answers, as if he suspected this to be the trap that it was. Then Amaya had gone for the final blow.

"I'll be honest, Mr. Vedasto. I was given your name by Lord Mercado," she said as Countess Yamaa, her hands folded in her lap to disguise how her fingers tightened. She hoped the name would inspire them to discuss the merchant in more detail. "He knows I'm searching for someone with your specific . . . talents. I've done some research on your past jobs, though I couldn't help but wonder if you knew anything about a certain job that wasn't documented. Specifically, the sale of a child from a family named Chandra."

Vedasto had swung his head from side to side. "Beggin' your pardon, lady, but I don't know nothin' about that."

So Amaya had signaled Liesl to see him out, the sixth debt collector she had dismissed that day. She didn't know how much more she could take.

"It makes me sick to sit across from them," Amaya said. "Knowing *exactly* what they did but having to look into their eyes and pretend that I admire their actions."

"And many are retired now," Liesl observed, pushing her glasses up her nose. "Must have been good money, selling children."

Amaya exhaled through her teeth.

"We have three more to go. The next one is waiting in the foyer. Should we tell them to come back tomorrow?"

Amaya took a moment to look up at the ceiling, at the intricate golden designs and dark wood paneling. Although the sitting room was spacious, it felt cramped with all the elegant furniture and molding and the thick bluish-green rug of Rehanese design under her slippers.

"No," she decided, bringing her gaze back to Liesl. "Send the next one in."

When Liesl left, Amaya nervously plucked at the cream fabric of her Rehanese wrap dress. It had a high collar that felt constricting against her throat whenever she swallowed.

If Boon were here, she had no doubt he could have gotten an answer by now. After all, what it did cost men like these to lie to a frilled-up countess? If she had been conducting these interviews as Silverfish, she could have just cut straight to the matter using the tactics she'd learned from observing Zharo for seven years.

Amaya shook her head. Zharo was dead. So was Silverfish.

Instead, she would use what she had learned from Boon in the months before coming to Moray.

"Manipulation is about more than just lies and tricks," Boon had once said as they strolled down a narrow cobblestone street in Viariche one evening. He had often kept to the ship, but sometimes meandered the outermost quarters of the city during dusk and dawn and the dark cover of night. "It's about really gettin' into the act, to the point where you almost *believe* the things you're saying."

Boon had pointed out a woman down the street. The woman had been standing before the window display of a haberdashery, despite the hat of rich felt and ribbon atop her curls.

"Go get me that hat," Boon had ordered.

"Huh? Why?"

Boon had clicked his tongue a few times. "'Cause then I'll have something nice to wear while I dine with the queen," he'd growled. "Just go talk that lady outta her hat."

"But I don't know how to do that!"

He'd sighed and straightened his new jacket, thankfully not yet torn or stained, the buttons gleaming silver in the gloaming. "Fine, then. Watch me."

So she had tucked herself into a stone niche and observed as Boon made his casual way over to the woman. He stood a distance from her at first, hands in his pockets, shoulders relaxed, as his gaze roamed the wares on display.

"That one would look great on you," he said eventually, indicating the hat the woman pined over. The woman had a hand curled wistfully at her throat, but at Boon's voice—less harsh than it normally was; Amaya supposed that was *acting*—she started and dropped it to her side.

"Oh," the woman had said in a throaty accent, "do you—you think?"

"Absolutely. I got an eye for this stuff." Boon had flashed her a wide smile that nearly bowled Amaya over with the level of charm behind it. Where had *this* man come from? Where was the disgusting, eccentric Landless rogue she had come to know?

The woman flushed and ducked her head. She touched her hat uncertainly.

"I bet you deserve to do somethin' nice for yourself," Boon had said, practically a croon as he edged a little closer to the woman. Amaya had tensed, as if watching a shark approach a seal. "Buy yourself a little present."

"I don't know . . ." the woman had murmured.

"C'mon, there's no harm in it. In fact, I'll help—why don'tcha give me the hat you have on now? Then you'll have an excuse to get that one." He'd winked. Boon had actually *winked*.

The woman had blushed harder with a giggle. Amaya had rolled her eyes; how did people give in to their baser urges so quickly? Still, it was effective, since the woman slowly removed her felt hat with its shiny ribbon and shyly presented it to Boon.

"There, y'see?" he said with another damn wink. "Now go treat yourself."

He had come back to where Amaya had been watching and plopped the hat on his head once the woman was in the shop. "Easy," he'd said, offering her his arm. "Now let's find you a young chump to dupe. It'll be good practice for the Mercado lad."

But Cayo Mercado was not the person she was dealing with today. Liesl brought in the next debt collector, who eyed Deadshot as he passed her. Deadshot's hand strayed toward one of her pistols, but a warning quirk of Amaya's eyebrow made her drop it.

He was taller than Vedasto, and thinner, though he had formed a small gut that came from frequent drinking. His brown eyes were bloodshot, but he was mostly clean shaven, his brown hair swept away from his face in a queue.

Amaya forced herself to put on the bland smile of the countess as Liesl directed him to sit on the chaise opposite from Amaya's chair. Like Boon, she had a part to play. She had to believe it if she wanted the man before her to believe it as well.

"Good day, Mr. Melchor," Countess Yamaa said.

"Suppose it is," he said with a barely concealed leer at Liesl, who had gone to stand attentively at the drink cart. Unlike her lover, Liesl was good at schooling her emotions so her disgust didn't show. "Especially if I get money out of it."

"Then we both want the same thing. For if you meet my requirements for this job, it's yours. You just need to answer a few questions first."

"Sure." He leaned back with his arms and legs spread wide, as if determined to take up as much room as humanly possible. "Got the time."

Amaya swallowed her grimace. "I'm so glad."

The interview went on as it had for the others. Christano Melchor had worked as a debt collector for twenty years; he had been recommended by a friend who had worked for Mercado; he had semiretired a mere six months ago and was now only looking to take on commissions.

Remembering the name that had been written next to his on

Zharo's list, Amaya fought not to follow Deadshot's example and reach for the knife hidden behind her. *Fera.* She must have been Melchor's last job before his retirement from the debt collectors. She tried to imagine his wide, scarred hands on Fera's small shoulders and felt a shiver of revulsion and fury go through her.

"These all seem like serviceable answers, Mr. Melchor," she said. "But I do have one last question for you. Lord Mercado gave me your name personally, as he knows I'm searching for someone with just the right set of talents to get the job done. Someone who will do whatever it takes to track people down. I've conducted some research on your past jobs but noticed that one wasn't documented. It was a job relating to a family named Chandra. Do you recall it?"

Melchor tipped his head back, dangling from his fingers the now empty glass of lupseh that Liesl had given to him during the interview. "Chandra . . . it does ring a bell."

Amaya straightened in her seat. "Does it?"

"Yeah. Chandra. The job was to bring a Kharian brat to one of the debtor ships, but I can't remember which one." He brought his head back up and shrugged. "S'all I recall of it."

Her heart beat a fierce tattoo in her chest. She felt Liesl's gaze on her, urging her on.

"Do you remember who hired you for that specific job, and why?" she asked, hoping her voice didn't betray the weight of her question. "Did . . . Did Mercado have anything to do with it?"

After all, if her father couldn't pay back his loan, it made sense that Mercado would force his only child onto a debtor ship.

"Mercado?" Melchor gave a half grin, revealing stained teeth. "Nah, he didn't hire me for that. This wasn't a traditional job."

"Wh—" Amaya reined in her surprise before it could show,

before her act could unravel around her. Instead, she focused everything on tilting her head to one side in curiosity. "But I thought you were a debt collector?"

"Sure, but I took commissions on the side. We all did."

"Then who hired you?"

"The same sorta folk who always end up making these commissions. It was the girl's own mother."

A coldness sank to the center of Amaya's chest and spread outward in numbing veins, erasing all feeling in her body as her mind went blank.

Staring at Melchor's face, she began to think about that hazy day, about the man who had pushed her toward the dock with a grating laugh and his breath smelling like alcohol.

She couldn't tell how long she sat there—a second, a decade. She could barely process Liesl approaching the debt collector and saying that the interview was over, that he would be contacted should the countess decide to hire him for the job.

Amaya was staring at the rug when Liesl's freshly shined shoes appeared before her. The young woman knelt down to peer into her eyes.

"Are you all right?" Liesl asked carefully. Deadshot stood behind her, looking on in worry.

Amaya merely stared at them, lips parted. That numbness had pervaded her so thoroughly that she was sure she would never move again.

"He . . ." It was a monumental effort to speak. "He was lying."

Liesl exchanged a look with Deadshot. "I'm very skilled at detecting liars, and he seemed to be telling the truth. Or at least, the truth as he knows it."

"It . . . can't be true. It can't. It doesn't make sense."

Her voice was rising, climbing into hysteria. Amaya took a deep breath, then another. Deadshot poured her a glass of lupseh, but Amaya merely cradled it between cold hands.

"Let's go over the facts," Liesl said, standing and brushing out the skirt of her dress. "We know that it was a commission and didn't go through the proper channels. Easy enough to double-check, if the statute of limitations on the debt collectors' data is up. We know that Melchor was the one who . . . took you," she said delicately. "Maybe we can use his name to—"

"He's wrong!" Amaya pushed herself out of the chair, the coldness giving way to fiery heat. "He's lying, and I don't know why! Maybe he was told to keep the job secret for some reason."

"Ama—"

"My mother would never sell me!"

"I didn't say she did, but—"

Amaya screamed in helpless rage and threw the glass of lupseh at the wall, reveling in the destruction, the crash, the shards that flew toward them. One nicked her on the ankle, a glorious pinpoint of pain.

Breathing hard, she looked over her shoulder, through the fallen strands of her hair. "Get out."

Liesl hesitated, but Deadshot touched her arm and the two of them walked out of the sitting room, closing the doors gently behind them.

Amaya collapsed to the floor in a pool of silk, shaking and nauseated. She stared at the shattered glass, the lupseh soaking into the rug like spilled blood.

It was the girl's own mother.

He was wrong. Mercado was behind all of this—the sale, the lies, the deceit—and once she knew exactly how, she would break his world apart.

16

"Lady," said the magician from the clouds,
"I saw you descend from the stars, and it was my wish to follow."
—"NERALIA OF THE CLOUDS," AN ORAL STORY ORIGINATING FROM
THE LEDE ISLANDS

Cayo slipped on gravelly dirt and cursed. At this rate, he was going to scuff his shoes beyond repair. Grabbing hold of the steadiest rock, he swung down past a patch of shale, inching closer to the grass and scrub that lined the steep incline.

It didn't help that the sun kept a beady eye on him as it sank toward the horizon, making him sweat under his collar. It cast the rocks and succulents around him in a gentle shade of pink that reminded him of the morning Sébastien had left Moray.

Was Bas doing all right? When would he reach Soliere? Would he send word back to Philip, at least, that he had arrived safely?

The counterfeit coin and the key to the Slum King's office

jostled together in Cayo's pocket as he climbed closer to level ground. Mercado Manor loomed above him, gleaming in the late afternoon light. The manor sat on a hill overlooking the bay and had the luxury of no neighbors due to the low cliffs hugging the shoreline. He had come this way not for exercise, but because he didn't want his father to know where he was going—which meant sneaking past the carriage driver and not using the main path leading to the manor.

He was going to break into Salvador's office and find the evidence he needed to prove the Slum King was behind the counterfeit. He was going to make him pay for what he'd done to Bas.

And he was going to get money for Soria's medicine.

The biggest hurdle would be Romara. That is, not getting stabbed by her once she realized who must have taken her copy of the office key last night.

Cayo paused to swallow the nervous laughter creeping up his throat. The protagonists in the adventure novels he read made it look so easy—confronting the villain, saving the day, evading death. They always had *some* idea of what they were doing. Cayo, staring down the imposing barrel of a harebrained scheme, envied them and their predetermined fates.

Panting lightly, he finally reached the bottom of the incline and wiped the sweat from his forehead. He needed to start taking the carriage less often, build up some endurance. He set off toward the city, knowing that by the time he reached the Vice Sector it would be dark enough to sneak around undetected.

He admired the view of the Southerly Sea beyond the bay as he walked. His mother would often sit at one of the manor's balconies and watch the water for hours at a time, sometimes with a smile, sometimes with an expression that had been too complicated for

Cayo to understand back then. Sometimes he would sit in her lap and watch the sea with her, or carry a book outside for her to read to him over the gentle roar of the waves.

Fresh ocean air is the best remedy for any ailment, his mother would say. He wished that were actually true. That it had been enough to heal her lungs, strengthen her body, force her heart to keep pumping.

Cayo was so wrapped up in his nostalgia that he almost didn't notice the figure standing on the edge of the nearest cliff. When he did, he slowed to a stop, caught off guard by their presence. They stood beside a pile of discarded clothes, their gaze fixed on the wide curve of the ocean.

Before Cayo could call out and ask if they were all right, the figure lifted their arms and jumped.

"No!" Cayo hurried to the cliff, yanking off his jacket and hopping on one foot and then the other as he pulled off his shoes. "Hold on, please don't die!"

He only had a fraction of a second to realize the discarded clothes were a finely tailored dress and a shift before he leaped in after. The fall was short, and as soon as he hit the water he arced back up to the surface and looked around frantically, shaking wet hair out of his face.

"Hello?" he called. "Are you all right?"

"What in Trickster's name are you *doing*?"

Cayo spun around in the water and came face-to-face with Countess Yamaa.

Her hair was unbound and hung in damp strands. Her dark eyes were wide and wild, staring at him as if he were a ghoul who had crawled out of the hells.

Cayo only noticed then that they hadn't dived straight into the sea. The cliff face overlooked an inlet that extended like a small arm into a deep, secluded pool of seawater. He blinked in consternation at the rocky walls around them, kicking his legs to keep himself afloat.

"Uh," he said, forgetting every single word in any comprehensible language. "Ah . . ."

"Did you follow me here?" the countess demanded, her tone sharp. "If you touch me, I *will* drown you."

"Wha— I— No! I'm not— I wasn't— I thought you were jumping! I was going to save you!"

Yamaa's eyes were still spooked, but at this her eyebrows climbed toward her hairline. "You were going to *what*?"

Cayo's heart was finally settling down, his mind racing to catch up with the situation at hand. "You . . . You weren't jumping to . . . ?" He looked around at the secluded inlet again. "Did you come here to swim?"

The countess flushed. Cayo's own face was a miniature inferno, and he briefly toyed with the idea of letting her drown him after all.

"Answer me, Lord Mercado," the countess said, a warning woven around the word *lord*. "Did you follow me here?"

"No! I was on my way into the city when I saw you jump."

"What were you doing by the cliffs?"

"I . . ." He thought of the coin and the key he had abandoned up above in his jacket pocket. "I was taking the long way around. Our manor is just up that way." He lifted a hand from the water to point, bobbing a bit as he lost his balance.

Yamaa stared at him a moment longer, as if assessing whether he was telling the truth. Finally, she sighed and said, "Yes, I come here to swim. Usually alone."

And his so-called heroism had ruined that. Swimming into the bay and getting washed out to sea was beginning to sound like an excellent way to escape this situation.

"How did you even know about this place?" he asked, a little breathless from the constant effort to stay afloat. "I mean . . . you're a countess. You have a pool in your gardens. Why come all the way out here?"

"So that no one can disturb me." The iron still hadn't left her voice. "I'm sure you would understand the desire, considering you were taking the 'long way around.'"

He grimaced. "I may know something about it, yes."

Spotting a group of rocks nearby, Cayo swam up to them. The water was somewhat cold in the shade, but it felt good against his skin, and the rock he heaved himself onto was sunbaked and warm.

"I'm sorry I disturbed you," he said, wringing out his shirt.

Yamaa sighed again and followed him. Although the simple act of treading water had left him out of breath, she seemed completely unaffected. He watched the graceful way she moved, remembering when she dived to save her servant at the garden party. Did she use to swim wherever she came from? Had her family's manor also sat by the ocean?

She lifted herself onto the rock near his, dripping water everywhere. She was only in her underthings, and Cayo's face heated again as he briefly glanced at the curves of her thighs and hips. But she didn't seem to care about modesty or covering herself around him. She merely squeezed excess water from her long black hair as she studied him with narrowed eyes.

"Do you often go about trying to save young women?" she jabbed.

Cayo let out an embarrassed laugh. "Not usually. I'll admit that I'm surprised to see you here, though. Alone." After all, she had brought a servant with her at their meeting at the teahouse.

"You're not the only one who likes to sneak around."

"I wasn't—" He cleared his throat. "I'm not sneaking. Just taking a walk. Sometimes I prefer it over taking the carriage."

She hummed in a way that said she obviously didn't believe him. Then her eyes cut back to him. "If you're going to keep staring at me, you might as well undress, too."

"Wh—" God and her stars, why couldn't he *talk*? "Undress?"

The countess pointed at his shirt. "It looks expensive."

That was true enough; it was tailored by Ferdicand, one of Cayo's favorite shops in the city for everyday wear. His fingers hesitated at his collar as she leaned back on her hands, observing him unabashedly.

"Go on," she urged.

"Why do I feel like I'm putting on a show?"

"You could, if you wanted to. I'm a tough critic, though."

That made him laugh and start unbuttoning his shirt. He'd been shirtless plenty of times around others, had enjoyed the attention he got as a result. But something about the way her eyes grazed his bare shoulders and slid down his chest was different. It didn't feel sensual, exactly—but it wasn't analytical, either. Something in between, as if she were trying to figure out what to make of him.

That calm appraisal made him shiver. There had been something about her at the teahouse as well—an intensity that rooted him to the spot, focused acutely on how her gaze trailed over his neck. Like she wanted to follow the path her eyes left with her fingers, or her lips. Or her teeth.

He was so used to blatant flirtation that the lack of it was startling, and somehow even more tantalizing. For the first time, he wondered if he actually *wanted* her to want him.

Cayo balled up the wet shirt and dropped it onto the rock next to him. "Better?"

"It'll do."

They fell into an uneasy silence. At least, for Cayo it was uneasy. He still couldn't help but feel like a trespasser, the skin along his arms prickling with guilt and the lingering effects of her gaze. He tried to speak a few times, maybe to apologize again, maybe to say that he should get going and leave her be, but for some reason he stayed glued to his rock.

"I also wanted to come here," she said at last, eyes on the water that lapped at the rocks, "so that I could clear my head. Get away from everything and just . . . think."

"Oh." Cayo rested his elbows on his knees, his feet still submerged in the water. The air smelled of salt and sunshine, much cleaner than what he had to breathe at the docks. "I know what that's like."

"Do you?" She turned to look at him again. It struck him then that for the first time, he was seeing her without flourishes or makeup, without the elaborate dresses and perfectly styled hair. Every time he had encountered her she had been so . . . put together. Picturesque. Almost as if she were donning a costume instead of an outfit.

But now she had been stripped—literally—and all he saw was a girl without a mask to hide behind, flawed and fierce and beautiful. Someone Cayo could actually relate to.

"Yes," he admitted. "It's funny, isn't it, how you can only ever see the surface of a person? I feel like most of the time, beneath my surface, I'm drowning. And no one can see it."

Her eyebrows gently furrowed together, thoughtful. "That's it," she agreed. "That's it exactly."

That initial admission had unlocked some door within him, and now it was beginning to creak open. "A lot's been weighing on me lately," he went on. "It helps to be alone with your thoughts. My mother . . . she used to sit on the balcony and stare at the ocean." He gestured to the mouth of the inlet that led toward the bay. "That was her way of handling things, I suppose."

Yamaa's expression was cloudy, but her eyes were bright. Some of the tension left her shoulders, or perhaps he was only imagining it.

"My mother used to sew," she said quietly.

Cayo thought back to their discussion at the teahouse about his interest in fashion. "What did she sew?"

"A bit of everything. Dresses, sheets, dolls." Yamaa turned her face to the sun and closed her eyes, some of her wet hair slipping over her brown shoulder. "But that was a long time ago."

Cayo wanted to ask more, but he was struck by the sudden vulnerability in her, the way the sunlight caught drops of water on her eyelashes. They spangled across her body like diamonds, as if she were worth more than any amount of gold.

He thought back to his halfhearted plan to charm money out of her. His father's plan, really. Seeing Yamaa like this, more a girl he could have met in the Vice Sector than a noble in a gilded house, he realized that he could do it—he could get her to warm to him, sympathize with him, play a slow yet steady game of seduction.

But after only a moment of planning, he shook his head and looked away. It would be wrong to use her. Wrong to ignore this new and sudden fascination that drew his gaze back to her like the sun toward the horizon.

Eventually, he found his voice. "You mentioned needing to clear your mind. Has something been troubling you?"

"I . . ." She hesitated, startled by the question.

"I shared something about myself," he said with a half-teasing grin. "Only fair you should, too."

She scoffed, but it was more amused than annoyed. She smoothly slipped back into the water and crossed her arms on top of the rock. "I lost someone recently. Someone I thought I knew well, but now I'm realizing that maybe I didn't know them at all."

Cayo watched her legs slowly treading under the semiclear water. "I'm sorry to hear that. I know what loss is like, and it never gets any easier." He thought of his mother on the balcony, humming her favorite songs. Thought of Soria coughing weakly into her pillow. "Especially when you have to watch someone you love waste away before your eyes."

Yamaa looked at him as if for the first time, her guardedness dropping. "Yes," she said. "Or you realize someone you love wasn't who you thought they were. When someone who was supposed to protect you ends up betraying you instead."

Cayo blinked at the cryptic words but decided not to press it. Yamaa rested her cheek on her arms, staring at the water, and the two of them were silent as they listened to the distant cries of gulls and the sound of the wind blowing past the cliffs. Cayo finally relaxed, his mission in the Vice Sector momentarily forgotten.

How long had it been since he had sat beside the ocean to merely exist and think? Probably not since his mother was alive. It was a sad thing, to realize that there was no one in his life he could completely be at ease with. Not his father, not his friends. There was Soria, to an extent, but even then he was always on watch.

But here, he could share this with Yamaa: this careful removal of their masks, the outward shell of polite young members of the gentry. Here in this inlet, they could be the messy, flawed, tired truths of themselves. And that was something to be thankful for.

As the light of afternoon began to wane, Cayo slipped back into the water with her. As if by some unspoken agreement, they swam lazily around the inlet, sometimes passing one another and sometimes swimming together.

She still had that thoughtful, mournful expression on her face. Suddenly, he was overcome with the desire to wipe it away.

"Hey." He pointed to the far cliff wall. "I'll race you. Last one there has to tell an embarrassing secret."

She gave him an incredulous look, but before she could reply he was already speeding away. She yelled at his back and kicked off, slicing through the water like a blade. Within a few seconds she had outpaced him, water frothing at her heels. In another few seconds, she was slapping the cliff face victoriously.

Cayo slapped it a moment later, panting for breath. "You're fast."

"And you have to tell me an embarrassing secret."

He groaned and floated on his back, lacing his fingers on his stomach. "Fine. Let's see . . . Once, when I was eight, I got my fist stuck in a vase at a duchess's manor during a dinner party. I was trying to tug it off when everyone came into the foyer and saw it go flying." He re-created the spectacular arc it had made with his hand over the shimmering water. "And crashed at the duchess's feet."

"It's not a secret if people saw you do it."

"No, the part that's secret is that my father spanked me when we got home. I couldn't sit down without crying for days."

Although Cayo had lost the race, he was rewarded all the same by the sound of her short, clear laugh ringing over the water.

Unwilling as he was to leave the calm they'd created, the water was getting choppy. They climbed back onto the rocks, which created a makeshift shore. Cayo shielded his eyes and looked at the path of rocks they would have to climb to get back up to the cliff side.

When he turned to ask her if she needed any help, his breath caught in his throat. The fabric of her undergarments had clung to her with water, revealing the outline of a body threaded with corded muscle. The way she stood revealed the strength of her arms and thighs and stomach, a strength that was constantly hidden under silks and corsets. Water droplets rolled down her smooth skin, pooling in the crooks of her elbows and the hollow of her collarbone.

She met his heated gaze, and the two of them stood there, frozen, as if waiting for the other to move first.

Cayo swallowed. What would happen if he reached out to tuck back her hair? If his fingers skimmed the side of her exposed neck? There was a speck of water at the corner of her mouth. He could brush it away with his lips.

But before he could decide whether to take a step toward her, she shook herself and headed for the cliff face.

"It would be best if we forgot this happened, Lord Mercado," she said as she began to climb, her limbs flexing as she moved.

It took him a moment to come to his senses, his blood warm and buzzing through his veins. "You can just call me Cayo," he called up to her.

She paused, looking down at him. She seemed something born of the earth itself, power and beauty mixed with something almost feral.

"Thanks for your company," she said at last. "Cayo."

She climbed the rest of the way up, leaving him to shiver in the breeze as evening began to streak through the sky.

And wonder how in the hells he was going to climb up after her.

17

And so Punisher drove his sword point to Trickster's chest,
where welled a bright berry of blood. The drop fell to the earth and
an orchard grew around them, the trees silent witnesses to the price
Trickster paid for deceiving the gods and thwarting their whims.

—KHARIAN MYTH

Following Cayo Mercado's example, Amaya took the long way home. The night was dark yet carried a balmy warmth, and her wet hair dried frizzy and soft about her shoulders. She still smelled of the sea, her skin coated by a patina of salt.

She went largely ignored as she wandered through the streets of Moray, her slippers dangling from her fingers. Her feet had long since dried, but she didn't like the constricting fabric of her shoes, so used to going barefoot on the *Brackish* and on the islands where they had made their diving stops. She almost missed the feeling of a deck under her soles and the kiss of too-warm sand.

That was why she had gone to the inlet: to rekindle her connection with the water, to be alone for a blessed hour in order to parse out her thoughts. To mull over what the debt collector had said about her mother.

And then Cayo Mercado had barged in, refusing her a moment of privacy. Yet . . . Amaya wasn't as mad as she would have expected at his unexpected company. It had helped, in an odd way, to see that she wasn't the only one in some state of misery.

Amaya came across a street musician with a lap harp and stopped to listen a moment. He had collected a small audience, but no one looked twice at her; with her untamed hair and plain day dress, she wasn't the remarkable Countess Yamaa, but just Amaya, a long-forgotten child of this city.

There was a pressure in her chest, a dreadful weight that pulled her shoulders down in such a way that would cause Liesl to order her to keep her posture straight. But Amaya's mind was filled with conflicting thoughts. Her throat was tight with the fear of facing the consequences that rose before her.

Cayo Mercado. Everything Boon had said about him made him out to be a fop, a careless merchant's son with no head for business. Perhaps those things were true, but the Cayo Mercado she had seen today was . . . different. Just as she hadn't had the visage of the countess to hide behind, Cayo hadn't had the visage of Lord Mercado. They had merely been a boy and a girl swimming in the sea.

When they had spoken of loss, she hadn't missed the aura of hurt that surrounded him like a fine mist, the depth of loneliness—of helplessness—in his dark eyes. She had felt that mist coat her like a second skin, had taken it into her lungs. His pain tasted like hers.

They had both lost their mothers. Cayo was in the process of losing his sister.

And thanks to Boon's plan, he was going to end up losing a lot more.

Yet she couldn't help but feel a twinge of envy toward him. If Amaya was water, always moving, then Cayo was a tree, planted firmly into a patch of soil called home. Digging roots into the earth—grounded, connected.

Amaya staggered away from the lilting music and wandered deeper into the city, barely conscious of where she was going. She felt feverish, hot and numb all over.

Did Cayo really deserve to suffer for the sins of his father? Just as the children sold to the *Brackish* had been forced to pay for their parents' debts, Cayo was merely the unwilling victim of his father's crimes. They had all been ravaged by the generation that had come before them, told to feast on scraps and to be thankful for it.

Amaya stopped to lean her shoulder against the nearest building and passed a hand over her eyes with a shaking sigh. She couldn't go through with this. Cayo Mercado did not deserve her revenge, no matter how spoiled and strange he was.

Dropping her hand, she looked around to get her bearings. She was in one of the traditional Rehanese districts, full of wide, short homes with green roofs like mountaintops and pointed eaves. Some homes bore statuettes of star saints, animal-like beings who carried out the work of the sky god. Lanterns had been lit along the street, dancing across the cobblestone in whirls of amber and orange.

It seemed vaguely familiar to her, like recalling a dream from a long time ago. Looking closer, she found the plaque bearing the street name. Guen Street.

She knew this place. It was the district where she had once lived with her mother.

Her lips dry and her heart beating faster, Amaya pushed off the side of the building and hurried down the street. She passed ghosts along the way—memories of holding hands with her mother as they went to the fish market, climbing onto roofs to keep a lookout for her father coming home for the day, the local neighborhood festivals held every season. Her mother had always loved those, for any excuse to dress herself and Amaya in Rehanese wrap dresses with their hair done up in the traditional styles. She had always splurged for freshly roasted nuts and balls of sticky rice coated with sesame seeds.

Amaya's eyes were full of tears by the time she stopped before the door that had once led to her home.

If another family lived there now, she didn't know, as the lanterns inside weren't lit. But it still looked the same, from its red-painted door and the owl statuette on the corner of the roof. It was missing its beak from the time Amaya had thrown rocks at it. Her father had laughed, but her mother had been so furious, claiming that the star saint wouldn't be able to protect their home if Amaya shattered it.

Grief surged up and seized her by the throat. She collapsed at the base of the outer wall and buried her face in her skirt, choking down the sobs that threatened to escape. Ghosts crowded her and touched her back, reminding her of when her father hauled her up onto his shoulders, or when her mother swept the dust out of the house while humming off-key.

The things she could no longer have. The comfort and love she had been denied by an unjust world.

Without her parents to be proud of her—without them to love her—who even was she? Did she mean anything to anyone? Would she ever have that unconditional support again, or was she destined to be alone, relying on no one but herself?

When the worst of her grief had passed, she was hollowed out and exhausted. She stared at the door and willed it to open. To walk the same floors her parents had walked. To somehow force time to run backward, to warn them of what was to come.

As she sat there, ensnared by memories, one in particular began to tug at her. She had been in the garden at the back of the house, an overgrown patch of herbs and morning glories. She had been playing with a doll her mother had made, but at the sound of a rustle, she had looked up and gasped.

A fat spider had been sitting in the bush beside her. A Rehanese Blueback, named for the triangular patch of bright blue on the back of its bulbous body. It had been crafting a web before her eyes, made up of shining strands of silk and gossamer.

But Amaya hadn't been afraid. Her mother had always told her not to harm spiders. *Look at how diligently they work,* she would say, pointing them out in the garden or on their walks through the city. *Most think of them as pests, but they create such lovely silk. That's their gift to us.*

So she had watched it work in awe, marveling at the level of skill it must have taken to make such a fine web. But her peaceful moment hadn't lasted long. The front door to the house had slammed, making her start, and Amaya had abandoned her doll to see what was wrong.

Her mother had been pacing the front room, her eyes shining as she pressed a hand against her mouth. Amaya stared at that hand, realizing that something was different—her mother's jade ring was gone, the one her father had given her when they'd been married. In its place was only a thin band of paler skin.

When she had spotted Amaya, her mother had dropped to her knees and grabbed her by the shoulders.

"Amaya," she had whispered, her lips trembling and her eyes overflowing with tears. "It can't . . . It can't go on this way. I have to." She had broken down then, hugging Amaya tight to her as she wept. "I have to!"

The next day, the debt collector had come for her.

Amaya opened her eyes. Her mother's behavior had confused her, scared her, made her wonder what was wrong.

Now she knew. That had been the day her mother had sold her to the *Brackish*.

Slowly, Amaya got to her feet. She felt mechanical. Distant from her body.

But she was no longer hollow. Cayo Mercado perhaps did not warrant her revenge, but she knew someone else who did.

In Viariche, she had once found Boon in a decrepit tavern by the docks. He had been playing a game that involved throwing knives at a crudely drawn target on the wall, eliciting taunts and shouts of encouragement from the other patrons whenever he landed a hit.

Amaya had watched at a distance, observing how he acted much drunker than he actually was. Manipulation; he always seemed to be in the midst of it.

He'd finally noticed her as he paused to take a swig of his drink and rolled his eyes.

"You wanna compete?" he asked, gesturing to the target embedded with knives and daggers.

"No thanks."

Boon had squinted at her. "Couldn't sleep?"

She'd shifted uneasily on her feet. He read people entirely too well.

"Boon," she'd said under the cheers of the tavern dwellers and the thud of steel against wood, "how can you tell who to hurt and who to spare?"

The man had recoiled a bit, as if the question were a fist aimed at his head. But he hadn't dismissed it. Instead, he had taken long pulls of his drink as he blearily watched the next round of knife-tossing.

"I think you know who to hurt when the hurt they've given you makes nothin' else they do matter," he said slowly, slurring his words. "When you can't see them as a *person*, but just a vessel for your hatred, your pain. Then you know."

That's how Amaya came to find the vessel of her pain pissing against the wall of an alleyway. Christano Melchor swayed as he did his business, his aim wide and sloppy. He chuckled to himself, as if pleased with his mess.

When Liesl had done the work of finding all the debt collectors on Zharo's list, she had used Avi to find their most frequented spots in the city to ensure that they all got the invitation from the countess. Unlike the others, who visited a wide array of dens, Melchor only went to an alehouse called the Rooster.

Which was how Amaya came to be crouched on its roof in the middle of the night, gazing down at Melchor in disgust. The knife she had brought with her to the inlet was in hand, which she had used to split the tighter seams of her dress in order to climb up the building. She was still barefoot; her slippers wouldn't have given her the right traction for the climb.

And she couldn't afford to lose her balance tonight.

Keeping quiet in the shadows, Amaya swung off the ledge of the Rooster and plopped down into the alleyway. It stank of urine and old vomit, and she had to resist the urge to gag as the odor momentarily overwhelmed her.

When Melchor turned to head back inside for another round, he started at the sight of her. She knew she had to look ragged and scraped, a haunting half-bathed in shadow. He didn't seem too well off himself, his jaw carelessly stubbled and his eyes bruised from lack of sleep.

"What's this?" he slurred, his breath carrying the scent of cheap ale. "Little pigeon wants to steal my money?"

"I don't want your money," she said, her voice low. He had only met her as Countess Yamaa, with her lighter, more enunciated way of speaking; she doubted he would recognize her with her hair curled from seawater and her dress frayed and dirty. "I want you to repent."

Melchor squinted at her, still swaying on his feet. "What'd you say? Repent? For what?"

"For the lives you ruined," she growled. "All those children you gleefully shipped off just to get some coin in your pocket. How does it feel, knowing that you likely sent them to their deaths? To torture and labor and trauma?"

He stared at her, as if thinking it over. Then he let out a loud belch.

"How's it feel? Feels like nothin'," he slurred. "Each of those soft little heads paid for a month's worth of drinks. Best job I ever had."

Amaya breathed hard through her nose, trying not to shake. She again thought of her mother weeping as she held her, the day before this man came to shepherd her to seven years of torment.

How could you sell me? she demanded of her mother's ghost. *How could you hand me over to this man?*

She bared her teeth and tightened her hand around her knife's hilt. It glinted in the starlight, and Melchor's eyes widened.

"Whoa, now," he said, hands raised before him. "Put that sticker away 'fore you take an eye out."

"It's not your eyes I'm after."

She launched herself at him. She knocked him into the wall of the alley hard enough to wind him, but he was a grown man nearly twice her size and had no trouble shoving her off so that he could scramble for his own weapon. Melchor brandished a small boot knife at her, his hair beginning to fall out of its queue.

"Just turn around and go home," Melchor warned her. "I don't want none of this tonight."

Amaya ignored him and rushed in again.

Use surprise to your advantage, Boon had taught her. *Speed, ducking and weaving, feinting—they're all the friends you need in a fight.*

She ducked under Melchor's wild swipe and slashed him on the thigh. He yelped and backed away, limping. Amaya faced him again, knife lifted before her to show off his blood along its edge.

"The children you helped sell faced years of degradation," she said. "Of hopelessness. They cried for their parents. They cried for someone to help them. Some died performing their work, and some—" Her voice broke. "Some chose to jump into the sea instead of facing one more day of it. You did that. *You* caused their suffering. *My* suffering."

He squinted at her again. "Your—"

She didn't give him time to finish—her nerves were screaming for action. She yelled and rushed in, blocking his arm and stabbing him between the ribs, angling up toward his heart, just as Boon had shown her.

She wasn't prepared for the jarringness of it, the way the blade glanced off bone and sank through muscle.

He exhaled with a grunt, taking a few steps back. Amaya held on to his arm and walked with him, keeping her knife buried in his body, her grip turning slippery on the hilt.

Her fingers wet and warm with his blood.

She could feel his stuttering breaths on her face, his eyes wide and full of pain. Amaya flinched back, releasing her knife and scrambling away from him. Melchor uselessly pawed at the protruding hilt, the shirt around it dark and damp. The scent of his blood flooded the alley, metallic and rusty.

"I hope you regret it," she whispered. "The day you sold me to the *Brackish*."

He fell to his knees. His gaze was still on her, his mouth opening and closing uselessly.

"Ah," he sighed after a moment, sinking toward the ground. "Yeah, it's you. I get it now. Should've just . . . done what I was told . . ."

And then he fell over. Unmoving.

Dead.

Amaya stood there for what felt like hours, bathed in starlight and blood. She couldn't move. She couldn't look away from Melchor's body. His eyes were still open, still looking at her, the flash of recognition now faded.

His last words perched on her shoulders, echoing in her ears. *Should've just done what I was told.*

What had he been told to do?

A raucous sound from within the Rooster made her come back to herself. Amaya hurried forward and grabbed at the knife, trying to pull it out of his chest. It was slippery, and the body refused to give up the blade. She gritted her teeth and put her foot against his chest, yanking until it pulled free with a sickening squelch.

She turned and threw up.

She heaved until her stomach was sore and tears poured down her cheeks. She wiped her mouth against her wrist, shivering despite the warmth of the night around her. Inside she was cold, frozen.

Trust me, you don't know what it means to kill a man—to have someone's blood on your hands.

Now she knew.

She didn't know how she got back to the estate. She just remembered staggering through the door and hearing someone gasp, and then the Water Bugs were there, asking if she was all right.

"Did someone hurt you? Why were you in the city? What happened to your shoes?"

Amaya saw Beetle—Fera—in the back, her eyes wide and fearful. She wanted to go over and hold the girl in her arms the way her mother had held her after she had sold Amaya to the debt collectors. She wanted to tell her that the man partly responsible for their suffering was gone.

Then Liesl came and ushered her away, up to her room, where the knife was pried out of her tight fingers and her bloodied dress was shucked off of her. She was scrubbed clean and given a nightgown.

She sat before the vanity as Liesl brushed out her hair, taking care of the tangles. Amaya couldn't look at herself in the mirror. Her hands were buzzing, and it was silent in her mind, although she couldn't stop smelling blood underneath the lavender of her soap.

It reminded her of being on the *Brackish*, the way the odor of a fish's innards could cling to her for days and weeks at a time. The infuriating knowledge that she couldn't escape it—that she just had to live with it, tolerate it, until it became a part of her.

Finally, Liesl asked, "Who?"

Amaya closed her eyes. "Melchor."

Liesl set the brush down, sighing. "Amaya."

"Don't lecture me."

"If anything, this is my fault. Perhaps I should have let you kill Zharo after all. Then you would have seen what a horrible mess it makes. Not just on yourself, but here." She tapped Amaya's temple.

She swallowed. "I wanted . . . He had . . ."

"I know." Liesl came around and rubbed some lotion onto Amaya's hands. It was scented with lemon. "But you need to keep an eye on the bigger picture. Zharo was found dead, and now a former debt collector who sold to Zharo's ship. It's going to look suspicious, and we can't afford any more obstacles."

Amaya nodded that she understood. Liesl moved away, then came back with a sealed envelope.

"This came today," Liesl said, handing it to her. "It's from Boon."

Amaya hesitated, her heart beating sorely against her chest. She took the envelope from Liesl and broke it open, reading the short message inside.

Heard about Zharo. Don't get too cocky. Remember what you're there for, and how you got there in the first place. If the countess is found out to be a fraud, it won't only be your head on the line, as mine'll be sitting on the pike next to yours.

Our goal is Mercado. Focus on the son and getting him wrapped around your little finger.

I can expose you at any time, Amaya Chandra. It's up to you whether or not to make me.

—B

"What does he say?" Liesl asked.

Amaya set the letter down, steadying her voice so as not to give away her rising panic. "As if you didn't tamper with the seal."

Liesl smiled. "Guilty. He's right, though. Mercado needs to be our only target from now on, and the young heir is the best way to get to him."

Amaya thought back to that afternoon, swimming with Cayo and feeling that strange, unexplainable connection. The way his eyes had lit up when she had won their race, the smile on his face at the sound of her laugh.

She didn't want him to become a casualty of her and Boon's revenge. But what other way was there to strike Mercado where it hurt most?

There was still a bit of Melchor's blood under her thumbnail. Scraping at it, she turned to Liesl.

"Get some paper," she said. "We're inviting Cayo Mercado to dinner."

Women with knives are sharper than any mind.

—KHARIAN PROVERB

The scrapes on his hands and feet throbbed, but Cayo barely noticed. He was still swept up in the dusk spell between him and the countess, the diamond shine of the water and the warm kiss of the air that dried him off as he climbed out of the rocky inlet. It made him feel the way that looking at her felt: as if possibilities were fruit he could pluck off trees, sweet and ripe and easily within his grasp.

He carried that feeling with him as he walked deeper into the city, the key he'd lifted from Romara heavy in his pocket. The lantern light and the deep blue of the night sky kept his spirits lifted until he got closer to the Vice Sector. Then dread began to seep back into him like water into a porous rock, reminding him that most things in this world weren't possible after all.

Such as sneaking into the Slum King's office without being noticed.

Cayo leaned against a building on the outer fringes of the Vice Sector, chewing nervously on his lip. He could already hear the din of debauchery nearby, nipping at his blood and making his fingertips buzz.

That's not why you're here, he told himself. But his body so thoroughly remembered this place it was like muscle memory, phantom pangs and reflexes that had no place in the outside world.

Sometimes he wondered if the real Cayo existed only in the Vice Sector. The Cayo who didn't care what anyone thought, who wasn't afraid to get his clothes dirty and his hair mussed, who always had someone eager on his arm. Perhaps more than the high of winning, he missed the sheer freedom of it, stripping off the gilded varnish of the merchant's son and revealing the rusted foundation beneath.

He couldn't be that Cayo again. He couldn't afford to be. Soria needed him, and his father needed him. They both preferred this Cayo: shining and bland and obedient.

Countess Yamaa didn't seem to prefer that Cayo. She'd seemed to prefer who he was in the inlet: messy and flawed and honest.

Gritting his teeth, he pushed off the building and followed the familiar path to Diamond Street. The crush of people strangely calmed him, and he let them push him down the street like a school of fish, passing jugglers and musicians and even a Kharian fire swallower.

The Scarlet Arc was on a side street the locals called the Gauntlet—tourists only knew it by its original name, Malachite Street—as the dens there were infamous for their abysmally low chance at payout. Everyone knew it was because the owners and their dealers cheated, but that was part of the fun: Could a cheater cheat another cheater?

In a sense, Cayo thought, that was exactly what he was trying to do with the Slum King. At the sight of the red sign hanging above the Arc, fear swooped low in his belly at the idea of even catching a glimpse of him.

But he had to do this. For Bas. For Soria. For himself.

He waited until a group of drunken toughs walked out the door to slip in past them. He was immediately assaulted by the crimson walls and dripping red chandeliers, pressing in against him like the walls of a bleeding heart.

His own heart pounded in his chest as he kept to the shadows, staying out of eyesight. It was probably pointless, given how loud and distracted everyone was as they tried their best at the card and roulette tables. Still, he hugged the far wall and followed it to the back, the smell of strong, cheap alcohol burning in his nose.

Cayo hurried into the hallway leading to Salvador's office. He pressed his ear against the door; nothing. The Slum King was usually out this early in the night and likely wouldn't return until midnight or later. He only had a short window in which to do this.

Fumbling with the key, he breathed out in relief as the lock clicked under his hand and he could push inside. As he closed the door soundlessly behind him, he regarded the office as a soldier would survey a battlefield, calculating his best chance at survival.

The only thing that would help him now was haste. So he began to pore over the bookshelf, pulling out tomes and flipping through their pages. He found secret compartments containing drugs, and even a volume on alchemy, which he eagerly skimmed through—but there was nothing in its contents about the manufacture of counterfeit coins.

He turned to the desk and froze. The jar with Sébastien's eyes was still there.

The Slum King was using it as a paperweight.

The breath shuddered in Cayo's chest. He thought back to Bas on the dock, the bandage around his eyes and the fury in the set of his mouth. The softness of his cheek under Cayo's lips.

His hand hovered above the jar. He wanted to smash it, or take it with him—he wasn't sure which. After a moment of painful deliberation, he turned instead to the desk drawers and began to pull them open. His chest was tight and hot, his eyes stinging, but he had to put that aside and focus. Once he got the evidence he needed, the Slum King would get what he deserved. But all he found were invoices for the Arc, shipment supplies, signed transactions with other dens—

"Is the puppy sniffing for a treat?"

Cayo jumped and slammed the desk drawer shut, banging his finger in the process. He cursed and shook it out as Romara looked on from the doorway, unimpressed.

"I knew you had to be the one who took my key," she said as she closed the door behind her, the words menacing on her black-painted lips. "I think I underestimated you, my dear fiancé."

Cayo held his throbbing finger, watching her cautiously as she approached the desk. He had entertained the notion of the Slum King catching him, but Romara was a whole other species of threat.

Salvador was somewhat predictable. His daughter was not.

Romara stopped on the other side of her father's desk and crossed her arms. She wore a sleeveless red dress with a scalloped hem and a low neckline. An opal pendant sat in the hollow of her throat, and he wondered if she had received it from a recent admirer.

"I'm feeling generous today," she drawled, "so I'll give you three chances to explain yourself." Then she sniffed and furrowed her brow. "Did you just crawl out of the ocean?"

"I . . ." Cayo's mind was still trying to make sense of the situation he had stumbled into. His thoughts were jumbled like a rat's nest: *Countess Yamaa counterfeit Soria the taste of seawater medicine Romara Bas's eyes Countess Yamaa—*

Romara sighed and gave an impatient wave of her lace-gloved hand. "My father comes back in about an hour, so I suggest you start talking."

"I was just . . . coming for this." Cayo grabbed the jar and pulled it toward him. The eyeballs sloshed sickeningly within the liquid.

"Two more chances," she warned.

He sighed and tilted his head back, closing his eyes. How much could he get away with telling her? He hadn't come to the Vice Sector to gamble, but now Romara was forcing his hand.

His only advantage was that he knew her loyalty to her father was stretched thin. The fact that she was beginning to cultivate her own followers was proof enough that there was a low chance of her repeating what he said to Salvador.

So he met her hawklike gaze and said, "Your father is making and distributing counterfeit money."

He had the unique pleasure of catching her by surprise. Her thin eyebrows shot upward, stretching the wings of kohl at the corners of her eyes.

"Counterfeit," she repeated blandly.

Cayo dug into his pocket and took out the black disc that had masqueraded as a sena. He extended it to her, and she picked it up with her long, filed fingernails as if it were a used napkin.

"Sébastien figured it out," he whispered. "He saw this coin dissolve in alcohol and realized what it was. Then the Slum King punished him to keep him quiet." He glanced again at the jar and

210

suppressed a shudder. "Think about it. Your father has a lot to gain by manufacturing his own coin. He has the resources and the connections for it."

Romara studied the black disc for a silent minute. Cayo realized then that she looked the most composed he had seen her in a while. There were no tears in her dress, and she didn't smell like alcohol. Was she doing it for her new followers? Was she finally beginning to put away the messy, violent girl she wanted everyone to believe she was?

Then she dropped the disc onto the desk between them. "It's cute how you're playing detective and all," she said, "but my father isn't involved in this."

Disappointment shot through him like a harpoon; maybe she was more loyal than he'd bet on. "How can you know for certain? You don't know everything about your father or the business he does. Out of everyone in Moray, he's the best equipped to get away with this."

She placed her hands flat on the desk and leaned in, a wry smile twisting her dark lips. "You think I don't know everything about his business because I'm . . . what, younger? Because I'm a woman? Because I'm his precious only daughter?"

"I never said that. I mean, hells, I don't know everything about *my* father's business!"

"You might want to correct that," she said with an earnestness he found not a little disturbing. "Unlike you, I've done everything in my power to make sure I know my father's every move. His every. Single. Move." She leaned in closer. "I know things that would make your delicate little self toss and turn at night. I know things that would make you hurl up your guts in the back alley. But there is nothing—*nothing*—about manufacturing counterfeit coins."

Cayo couldn't find the words to reply. Just a couple of hours ago he had been full of light, but now that familiar darkness was stealing over him, disappointment and terror clasping hands.

If he couldn't bring any evidence in to Nawarak, how else was he going to fix things?

"Normally intruders would be severely dealt with, but seeing as you're my fiancé, I'll let you go this once," Romara said, straightening. She gestured to the door. "You better go before my father decides you'd look prettier without a finger or two."

Cayo clenched his hands into fists, but he was powerless again. Romara had the winning hand this time.

On his way to the door, she lunged at him. He grunted as his back hit the wall, and it took him a moment to realize she had pinned his jacket to the wood with a knife; where she had hidden it until then, he had no idea.

With her free hand, she rummaged in his pockets until she found her key. She held it before his eyes, smiling sweetly as his face heated. She kissed the warm metal and pressed it to his lips.

"Don't ever steal from me again," she whispered. She yanked her knife out of the wall and stepped back. "By the way, do you like black lilies?"

Cayo forced himself not to scramble for the doorknob as he turned to her in confusion. She was twirling her knife absently, watching him with a keenness that almost made him feel naked.

"I've ordered about ten thousand for the wedding," she explained. "They're my favorite. I heard they were your mother's too."

Heat stole through his chest and stomach as he yanked the door open. "Fuck you."

"Wait." She caught his wrist. Stabbing the knife into the wall again, she used her free hand to draw something out of her own pocket: a vial of cloudy liquid. She pressed it into his hand.

"For your sister," she said.

Cayo stared at her. The amount of medicine in his hand likely cost a thousand senas, at least.

She shifted uncomfortably at the look in his eyes, turning her head away. "It's my dowry, remember?" she muttered. "Now go."

He hesitated, wondering how to thank her. Wondering if she even deserved thanks. In the end, he only shook his head and hurried down the hall, eager to remove himself from this crimson nightmare.

Narin tried to stop him as he crossed the threshold of the house.

"My lord, you received correspondence from Countess Yamaa," the footman said as he trotted after him. "She's invited you to dinner at her estate tomorr—"

"I'll get to it later," Cayo threw over his shoulder, bounding up the stairs two at a time. Although the countess's name sent a thrill of excitement through him, he couldn't think about her now, not when his sister needed him.

Soria was laid up in bed, the lantern at her bedside making her a playground for restless shadows. She looked sallow today, her breaths struggling in her lungs, the skin beneath her closed eyes bruised.

Cayo poured the necessary amount of medicine into a small tumbler, careful not to spill a drop. Then he came to sit beside her.

"Soria," he called, gently brushing hair away from her face. Her skin was feverish under his touch. The spot of gray behind her ear had grown larger, spreading down to her neck like a splotchy rash.

Her eyes fluttered open. She tried to smile when she saw him, but even that seemed to cost her energy she didn't have. Cayo didn't have the experience of a doctor or Miss Lawan, but he tried his best to sit her up and make her take the medicine, even watering down the last of it to make sure she drank it all.

When she was done, she leaned back on the pillows with a somewhat deeper breath. He held her hand, wanting to simply be with her, grateful for this fleeting moment of relief. A moment made possible by Romara, of all people.

Cayo took out the counterfeit coin and restlessly walked it over his knuckles. How could the Slum King not be part of this? Romara may have known plenty about her father's business, but surely there were some things even she didn't know.

"Where did you get that?"

Soria's eyes were half-open, watching him fiddle with the black disc.

"A . . . friend gave it to me," he said.

"It looks like something I've seen before," she whispered, her voice cracking from disuse.

"You've seen something like this?" His heart gave a violent thud. "Where? How?"

"It was . . ." She stopped to suppress a cough. "Downstairs, in the cellar, where Father keeps his wine. It was where he put my chest containing my dowry for the Hizons. I would go down there and run my hands through the coins sometimes. It felt nice. Then a couple of the wine barrels broke, so I went down to check on it. Father must have moved the dowry, because it wasn't there anymore. Instead there was a trunk full of those." Soria weakly pointed at the counterfeit coin. "Just a bunch of worthless black discs."

The last word broke apart as the suppressed coughs ripped through her, tearing up her throat. She convulsed with each rattling cough, curling onto her side as tears streamed down her face. Cayo hurried to fetch her water, but she couldn't even come up for air, let alone drink anything.

Finally, what felt like a thousand years later, she stopped. She lay there, exhausted and bathed in sweat, as Cayo stared numbly at the blood that speckled the pillow under her.

He collapsed to his knees, grasping her thin wrist as he leaned his head against the side of her bed. The world had gone spinning around him, forcing him to look at the truth, to bear the burden of its terrible weight.

The truth that the Slum King was not behind the counterfeit after all.

Kamon Mercado, his father, was.

19

There are some who are lured to the Vice Sector not by greed,
but by love. Yes, there are those who lust for these streets,
for the desire to slip into the murk, into the same shadows
that line their hearts.

—A COMPLETE GUIDE TO MORAY'S SECTORS

As a fresh wave of pain swept over her, Amaya ground her teeth and glared at the ceiling of her canopy bed. She grabbed a fistful of the expensive maroon silk sheets and waited for the worst of it to pass before relaxing back into the pillows, panting.

Of course, *of course* her cycle had to come now. She had only bled on board *Brackish* a few times, her body usually too malnourished for it, and it seemed now her body was trying to make up for lost time.

"I don't see why I can't just cut it out of me," she mumbled.

Liesl snorted and set a fresh cup of tea beside her. "Is violence your solution to everything?"

"The best way to retaliate against pain is pain."

Amaya couldn't quite remember where she'd heard those words before. That is, until Liesl raised her brows and readjusted her glasses.

"You really are Boon's pupil," the girl said.

The statement made her clench her fists into the sheets again. As if Amaya could not belong simply to herself—she had to be Arun Chandra's daughter, Captain Zharo's prisoner, Boon's pupil. Silverfish. Countess Yamaa.

The best way to retaliate against pain is pain, Boon had muttered into the mouth of a wine bottle one night, his eyes bloodshot and faraway. *Pay them back everything they gave to you.*

She had thought then that it was only the ramblings of a drunken fool, someone so embittered toward the world that compassion was a distant memory. Amaya had felt sorry for him.

But then she had come here, home to Moray, to the seat of her rage and loss. She had unpacked the truth like a fragile artifact from a crate, and now all she wanted to do was smash it to pieces. Pain—it made up the whole of her, driving her to inflict it on others, to almost revel in it.

Captain Zharo's last breath rattled through her. Melchor's lifeless face burned like a brand in her mind. She could still smell their blood on her, layering her dreams with copper and steel.

Everything smelled like blood—theirs, hers. She even lifted shaking fingers to her wet temple only to find that it was just sweat. Her body was a crossroads, her hands remembering the blood of death, her womb remembering the blood of life.

What would Roach say, if he knew what she had done?

Panic flared within her, a stray ember from a growing fire. She again tried to convince herself that she had done the right thing, that the lives of two terrible men meant nothing when weighed against the consequences of their actions. But perhaps that was only a rationalization given to her by a bitter man who had nothing else to live for.

When she looked at the wreck that was Boon, was she seeing her future?

She didn't want that future. But what else was possible for someone like her, after the choices she had made?

Her lower abdomen clenched with a pain that was both sharp and dull, spreading its fingers possessively over her hips. Amaya groaned into the pillow as she writhed.

"Drink the tea," Liesl advised. "It'll help."

She managed to wrangle Amaya into a sitting position. While Amaya alternated taking sips and making faces at the bitter drink, the door opened and Fera peeked in.

"Has there been word?" Amaya demanded, lurching forward so suddenly that some of her tea spilled.

Fera shuffled in carrying a plate that Cicada had sent up for Amaya. Fera placed it on the bedside table and stepped back, twisting her fingers together. "N-no, not yet. I'm sorry, Si—Amaya."

Amaya fell back so hard she nearly rapped her skull on the headboard. Disappointment threaded through her, disguised as hot anger.

"Don't you dare throw that cup," Liesl warned her, folding laundry at the foot of the bed.

"Wasn't he raised to be the perfect merchant's son? Isn't he supposed to be a *gentleman* and respond to a lady's invitation for dinner?"

"Perhaps something came up. We can try again."

But Amaya remained piqued, her cheeks flushed and her breathing too fast. She thought back to swimming in the inlet with Cayo Mercado, to wondering what would happen if she truly let her guard down. There had been something about the way his eyes caught hers that made her feel stripped, torn open, her ribs bared and ready to be snapped.

The fact that he would so easily dismiss an invitation from her after that . . .

Amaya knocked back the rest of the awful tea and slammed the cup down on the bedside table. She told herself that her disappointment was due to prolonging the next stage of her revenge.

Fera took the cup and held it carefully between her hands, as if it were a newborn bird. Amaya forced herself to relax her face, to give the girl a tight smile of thanks.

"Has Spi—I mean, Nian been giving you swimming lessons?" she asked, idly picking at the food that Cicada had sent up: dried bananas, coconut cookies, and taro cakes.

The girl's face lit up. "He's been taking me down to the beach. I didn't really like it at first, and it hurts when I get the water in my eyes, but I like kicking while he pulls me around."

Amaya's mouth softened into a true smile. "I'm glad."

"I can't wait to go home and show Mama and Papa," Fera continued, bouncing on the balls of her feet. "They'll be so surprised!"

Amaya's smile fell, and guilt tightened her chest. Her belly tightened as well, and she weathered another stabbing cramp, screwing her eyes up tight.

All of the Water Bugs were waiting for the money she promised them—that Boon promised them. But she hadn't gotten to Mercado yet. She was still keeping them from their families, these children who were too young to travel on their own, who had no idea how to reunite with the parents who had sold them in the first place.

If only Cayo had come to dinner, or even responded to her invitation . . .

Amaya took a deep breath. It was her own fault. She had been too engrossed in her personal vendettas, and the truth about her mother was a weight pressing on her chest, deterring her from moving on.

Maybe when Cayo looked at her, he could see the truth of what she was and all she had done. Maybe that was why he avoided her.

"I'm sure they'll be thrilled," she made herself say. Fera beamed and scurried out to return the teacup to the kitchens.

Liesl came to sit beside her. "I think I know what you can do. If the Mercado boy isn't responding to your missives, try to run into him in the city. Make him see you. Corner him, if you have to."

"And how do I do that?"

Liesl nibbled on one of the coconut cookies. "According to my notes, there are a few places he likes to frequent. Or rather, he used to. Apparently, he visited the Vice Sector several times a week, then stopped going."

Amaya thought back to the dexterity of Cayo's hands. She had thought them the hands of a would-be tailor, but they were the hands of a gambler, too. "I'll visit tonight and see if I can get any more information on him."

"Would you like me to come with you? Or I can send Deadshot or Avi."

"No," Amaya said, harder than she intended to. "I want to do it alone. I'll attract less attention that way."

"Suit yourself." Liesl stood and grabbed another cookie. "I'll make you more tea."

Right on cue, Amaya's next cramp tore through her. She held her stomach with a small sob. "Are you *sure* I can't cut this horrible thing out of me?"

Liesl gestured to the door where Fera had gone. "Don't you want a sweet child like that someday?"

Horror descended on her. "Absolutely not!"

"Well, then, I guess I can't stop you." Liesl made a resigned motion with her hand as she left. "Just try not to get too much blood on the sheets."

While the sun was setting, Amaya dragged herself out of bed to get dressed, the tea reducing the sharp spikes of pain into a duller ache. She chose soft trousers and a dark green bodice, and opted not to tie her hair back, as she wanted the ability to hide her face if she needed to.

When she went downstairs to return the plate of mostly uneaten food, she found some of the older Water Bugs at the scoured wooden table in the kitchens. They were all listening to Cicada, one of the few of them who could read and write, as he read out loud from a broadsheet.

"'It is with greatest sorrow that we report the advisor to the Prince of Moray, Sir Carden Behlor, has passed due to the affliction known as ash fever. According to local sources, Sir Carden was diagnosed a mere two months ago, but the fever progressed too quickly for any remedy to take effect. The funerary rites for Sir Carden are as yet undisclosed.'"

The Bugs murmured among themselves, and Amaya frowned, remembering the man who had passed out at Laelia's. Ash fever again. If even the richest citizens of Moray were dying despite being able to afford the medicine, the lower classes wouldn't stand a chance.

"Seems like a good thing if the nobs are getting axed," Weevil said, rubbing the island of a birthmark on his jaw. "Who needs 'em?"

A fifteen-year-old girl named Cricket scoffed. "Don't you know anything? They're the only thing that holds the empires back."

"I thought the Prince of Moray didn't even do much?" Cicada asked. "That it was just a title?"

"A title that they bought from the Rain Empire in exchange for neutrality," Cricket snapped. "The prince has no heirs—he's the last of his family's line. So what'll happen if the prince's court falls to sickness and death? Moray will be weakened. The Sun Empire might decide to try their hand at us again."

The older Bugs argued while the younger ones looked on, vaguely worried. Amaya imagined their small bodies riddled with gray marks.

Shivering, she set her plate down and headed for the front doors. She had to hurry and fulfill Boon's plan. The Bugs were already unsafe—she couldn't risk anyone coming down with ash fever on top of that, or a potential attack by the Sun Empire.

There was so little she could control. Finding one boy and getting him to speak to her was the least she could do.

Amaya had never set foot inside the Vice Sector before, but she had heard stories. As she walked the darkening streets of Moray, her lower belly clenching and unclenching, she imagined what she would find: knife fights, copulation in the streets, brazen thieves who didn't care if they had witnesses.

None of it prepared her for the real thing. It was almost as if she had stumbled upon a festival rather than a district infamous for debauchery, fooled by the warm multicolored lights and the singing and the raucous laughter that wove through the crowd like strands of sugar. Amaya stopped and stared at the sight of it.

"Long as your mouth's hangin' open, pop somma these in," called a boy nearby. He stood at a small cart used for roasting nuts.

Their smell wafted over her, caramel and sea salt, and it reminded her of her mother.

Amaya was about to dismiss him before she remembered that she actually had money. A thrill shot through her as she pressed a coin into his hand and received a paper cone of roasted nuts, feeling silly at the flutter of her heart.

She had never done something as simple as this before.

The sign above her read DIAMOND STREET, the main thoroughfare of the sector. Amaya roamed through the crowd and merely took in what she saw, popping treats into her mouth and occasionally stopping to observe a musician or juggler or dancer.

Just the other night she had plunged a knife into a man's body, and now she was treating herself. The juxtaposition almost made her stumble, but she forced the terror crouched in the back of her mind to be shielded for now, to focus only on what was in front of her.

There was a lively house farther down the street, with folks drinking and dancing outside. Amaya watched a young woman pull another dressed as a boy over the threshold, meeting in a passionate kiss. A third young woman, her hair henna-dyed, leaned against the doorway and looked Amaya up and down.

"Only a drina for an hour," she called, arching her back to better show off her assets.

"Oh," Amaya said. "Um. Maybe some other time?"

The woman blinked at her, then laughed drunkenly before shooing her away. Amaya hurried on with a reddening face.

Still, she couldn't help but smile. She felt so much freer in these clothes, in a sector of the city that didn't care about pretension.

She forgot about her pain. The residue of her nightmares faded. The truth of her mother fled.

She existed only for sound and sight, lost in the simple and unique pleasure of being alive.

Amaya momentarily abandoned her plan and instead lost herself in that feeling, that brief window of sunshine on a cloudy day. She allowed herself to laugh at a puppet show. She joined a shell game, even though she knew the busker would cheat. It didn't matter—she was immersing herself in her city, in the nooks and crannies hidden by daylight.

In some ways, this place felt more like home than her actual home had.

She wished desperately that Roach was with her. Whenever she'd spoken of Moray, he had always been most fascinated by the Vice Sector.

"How many casinos do you suppose they have?" he'd asked.

"I don't know. I wasn't old enough to gamble, let alone visit the Vice Sector."

"Well, when we go, I want to gamble."

"With *what?*"

He'd shrugged in that easy way of his, unconcerned. "I'd figure something out."

She continued through the mazelike streets of the sector, finding the area with the highest concentration of gambling dens. A large casino loomed above her, winking with lantern light and spilling over with laughter and chatter. The sign displayed across the facade had a bare-breasted mermaid luring a sailor toward her.

This had to be the Grand Mariner. According to Liesl, it was one of the casinos where Cayo Mercado had liked to not only play, but to do his own fair share of dealing.

How does a merchant's son end up dealing at card tables? she wondered with a frown.

She rolled her shoulders back and entered through the wide double doors. The guards gave her a once-over, not even bothering to pat her down for weapons. If they had, they would have felt her knives.

As charmed as she was by the Vice Sector, she was still aware of its dangers.

The Grand Mariner was composed of three floors. The ground floor was laid out with card and dice tables, its ceiling crimped with ornate molding and a long cherrywood bar hugging the right wall. Amaya stood there, overwhelmed and unsure where to go first.

She began attracting the attention of the guards standing watch on either side of the doors, so she hurried to find a card table. Liesl had briefly gone over some of the easier games, making sure that Amaya at least understood the rules.

"Scatterjack seems to be one of the Mercado boy's favorites," Liesl had told her. "He was a dealer for several months, until he stopped going to the Vice Sector altogether."

Amaya wove through the crowd of well-dressed patrons until she found a Scatterjack table. She watched a round from the sidelines, then slid into a chair once it was vacated by an irritated player.

The dealer was a young person with curly brown hair and sparkling blue eyes, and wore a diamond-shaped pin at their collar that signaled to others that they didn't wish to be called *him* or *her*, but rather *they*. They had a flirtatious smile and weren't shy about using it. When they dealt the cards, Amaya studied hers and felt a flush start from under her collar.

She had no clue what she was doing.

Still, she faked it as best she could. When she inevitably lost, she shrugged like she had predicted it and stayed for another round, and then a third.

"Your luck is a little off tonight, miss," the dealer said with a hint of an accent that pointed to the Rain Empire.

"That seems to be the case," she agreed. "Do you know any remedies?"

"My only solution is to continue drinking," they said with a wink.

She continued to exchange small talk with them as she played the next round, then another. She ordered a Blood and Sand and sipped at it carefully, wanting to make sure her mind didn't get too fuzzy.

"You seem to be enjoying the game despite the fact that you keep losing," the dealer said with their charming smile.

"Perhaps I'm enjoying the view more than the game."

It was the sort of ridiculous thing Boon would come up with, and she nearly cringed as she said it, but it worked—the dealer laughed at the compliment.

"Don't think you can win your money back with just a little flirting," they said with a playful wag of their finger.

She smiled and took another sip of her drink. Gods, how could a drink this cloyingly sweet be this strong? "I'll admit, I came here looking for another dealer, but I think I like you even better."

"Is that so? Who is this dealer that I must now be jealous of?"

"I never got his name, but he was about my age. Black hair, mostly Rehanese features. Small nose, perfect eyebrows."

"Aha," the dealer said, "you must mean Cayo. He hasn't dealt here in a while, unfortunately."

She pretended to be disappointed, her lower lip extending in a pout. "That's a shame. Any reason why?"

"I'm actually not sure." They greeted the other players and dealt out the cards. "But I know he was beginning to slip, toward the end.

He was one of the best at Scatterjack, and then all of a sudden he couldn't concentrate. Ended up losing quite a bit of money."

Perhaps that was why Cayo hadn't returned to the Vice Sector. "Pity. I would have liked to see him again."

"I know he used to hang about near the Scarlet Arc, down on Malachite Street."

Hope surged within her. After losing her eighth round, she thanked the dealer and left her unfinished drink there, her mouth coated with pomegranate and her head a little too light.

She got lost trying to find Malachite Street, tangling herself deeper within the bowels of the Vice Sector. She quickly realized that Diamond Street was merely the outer visage, the "safe" part where tourists liked to go. Beyond that visage were streets littered with trash and stinking of vomit, men relieving themselves against the sides of buildings, and grubby children fingering knives that were too large for them. Amaya stared them down, daring them to try. Although they sneered, they left her alone.

It reminded her of the sea: As beautiful as it first appeared, there was peril layered under that beauty.

Malachite Street was cleaner than the alleys surrounding it, if not less intimidating. Finding the Scarlet Arc, she headed inside and was immediately assaulted by *red*. It was everywhere, from the painted ceiling to the vivid wallpaper to the crimson rug spread across the floor. The Arc was much smaller than the Grand Mariner, and Amaya's trepidation rose, especially when patrons turned to stare at her. Patrons who were scarred and didn't bother to hide the weapons they carried.

Swallowing, she hardened her expression and walked toward the bar. *Pretend like you belong*, Boon would have told her. *So long as you can fake it, they'll believe it.*

She overheard someone ordering a drink called Toxin and ordered one as well when the bartender turned to her. It came in a square tumbler, its color a light green due to some sort of syrup and the muddled leaves at the bottom. Amaya took a tentative sip and nearly gagged at how strong it was.

"That's one of my favorites. How do you like it?"

She turned in surprise. The smooth voice belonged to a tall, trim man dressed in a finely tailored suit, his hair combed back and his bearing regal. She would have thought him a member of the nobility had it not been for his viciously scarred face—the sign of a man who had grown up in these streets, where violence ran like currency.

"It . . ." Her voice tried to leave her, but she dragged the words out. "It's quite good."

He smiled, and it sent a shiver down her spine.

"I haven't seen you at the Arc before," he went on. "What brings you by this evening?"

Amaya hesitated, her scalp prickling with warning. She shouldn't have come here. She should have just stuck to the Grand Mariner, waited until that dealer with the curly hair was off shift, and . . . what, tried to seduce them in the alleyway?

Maybe she had wanted to come here to avoid that. Maybe there was a part of her that felt more comfortable in filth and danger than flirtatious smiles and witty words.

Is violence your solution to everything? Liesl had asked her. Perhaps it was. Apparently stabbing a man in the chest was easier to her than kissing someone.

"I got tired of the big casinos," Amaya said. "I wanted to explore more of what the sector had to offer."

This time his smile showed his teeth. "Is that so? Well, then, I'm glad you came to partake at my establishment." He held out a hand, equally scarred as his face. "Jun Salvador."

Amaya took his hand as if to shake, but he lifted the backs of her fingers to his lips. Her scalp prickled again.

"Forgive me, but you look familiar," Salvador said, releasing her hand. "Perhaps this isn't your first time here?"

The heat of dread filled her chest. Had this man seen her as Countess Yamaa? Had he attended any of her parties or seen her on the streets?

Before she could flounder with an answer, a girl appeared at his side. She was dressed in a sparkling black gown with a low neckline and a slit in the skirt that exposed a brown, curvy leg when she cocked her hip and planted a fist there.

"Father, you're needed," she said in a flat voice.

He looked at her with some annoyance. "It can wait."

"Tell that to your investors," the girl said with a grin similar to his: sharp and hungry.

He sighed and gave Amaya a small bow. "If you'll excuse me."

As he walked through the tables, the girl huffed and sat heavily on the stool beside Amaya's.

"Sorry about that," she said as she rapped her knuckles on the counter. The bartender hurried to fill her a glass with amber liquid. "He's like a vulture, isn't he?"

Amaya had no idea what to say, so she only watched as the girl—she couldn't have been much older than Amaya—downed half her drink in one go. She had traditional Rehanese features with a bit of Sun Empire mixed in, her long black hair pulled into a sloppy bun. As she set her glass down with a happy sigh, Amaya noted her glittery eye shadow and dark painted lips.

"So," the girl said, turning to rest her elbows back against the counter, "what's a countess like you doing in a place like this?"

Amaya stiffened. The girl watched her, as much a vulture as she claimed her father was. Amaya couldn't help but feel like a helpless rabbit under her knowing stare.

"I've seen you," the girl said, taking smaller sips of her drink. "All dolled up in those fancy costumes. This look fits you much better."

"I . . . don't recall seeing you at any of my parties."

"Wasn't there. Not exactly my type of scene. But I like to keep track of what happens in this city. Countess Yamaa," she murmured, her brown eyes drifting toward the ceiling. "A mysterious visitor to Moray's shores, wealthier than god herself, and as secretive as an eel refusing to come out of its den."

Seeing the distrustful look in Amaya's eyes, the girl laughed. "Don't worry. As long as I'm with you, you're safe. That's why I sent my father away. He likes to exploit. Me, on the other hand? I like to invest."

"I see," Amaya murmured.

The girl held out her hand. "Romara."

Amaya shook it. "So . . . your father owns this place?"

"You really are a stranger to Moray, aren't you? He's the Slum King. He owns the entire Vice Sector."

The center of Amaya's aching belly went cold. Of course she had heard of the infamous Slum King, but to know that she had been speaking to him, *touching* him . . . A shudder went through her.

"Yeah, he gets that reaction a lot," Romara said, polishing off her drink. "But you still haven't answered my question. What brings you to this piss-stained corner of the city?"

"I . . . I'm looking for someone."

"Then you're talking to the right person. I know everyone. I can help you find them in no time." She leaned in with a smile, stroking Amaya's jaw with a slim finger before using it to lift her chin. "For a price," she crooned.

Amaya flushed, her heart beating harder. With a shaking hand, she reached into her inner pocket and drew out a gold sena coin, pressing it into Romara's palm.

"Cayo Mercado," she whispered in the space between their mouths.

Romara pulled back as if she'd been bitten. She stared at Amaya, her eyes narrowing.

"What would a countess like you need with Cayo Mercado?" she drawled.

"We're friends. Um, sort of."

The girl's eyebrows rose. "What kind of friends?"

"What does it matter to you?" Amaya bit the inside of her cheek, cursing at herself. This was the daughter of the Slum King—she couldn't afford to get on her bad side.

Romara leaned in again, danger written in the curve of her painted mouth.

"It matters to me," she said softly, "because he is my fiancé."

Amaya's lips parted, but words wouldn't come. She looked at this girl, glittering and perilous, and tried to make sense of what she'd said. Tried to understand how someone like her could ever possibly be matched with someone like Cayo.

I'll do whatever it takes to help her, Cayo had told her at Laelia's, when they had discussed his sister's illness.

You complete and utter ass, Amaya thought, forcing herself not to bare her teeth.

How had this come to happen? Why hadn't Liesl or the others caught wind of this?

"Why does no one know, then?" Amaya asked. *Why didn't I know?*

Romara flipped her hand dismissively. "Oh, people know—those who like to keep their ears open. Word will spread once Cayo finally tells his daddy. And he will, if he knows what's best." She stood and pocketed the coin Amaya had given her. "You won't find him here, though, I can tell you that much. Oh, and you better not show up here again either, unless you want my father to recognize you as well."

Romara blew her a kiss and walked away, leaving Amaya reeling at the counter. Amaya gripped the edge of it, worried she would fall off her stool otherwise.

Cayo was engaged to the daughter of the Slum King.

Was this why he wouldn't respond to her? Why he hadn't come for dinner?

But she remembered the look in his eyes when they had swum together in the inlet, the way he regarded her as not a countess, but a person. Not Boon's pupil or Silverfish or any of that.

He had seen her as Amaya that day, and she had been grateful for it.

Her limbs tight and her body burning, she knocked back the rest of the Toxin and gasped for air as her insides clawed themselves to ribbons.

She had her secrets, but so did Cayo. And she was going to do whatever it took to drag them out into the open.

20

BRAEGAN: You claim harm and misery at my hand,
and yet yours holds the key to all my undoing.
SOLAS: Shall we pretend, then, that we are equals?
BRAEGAN: There is nothing equal about
vengeance—only the victor and the defeated.
—*THE MERCHANT'S WORTH*, A PLAY FROM THE RAIN EMPIRE

Cayo stared up at the sign of the Port's Authority, clenching and unclenching his hands. The street was busy at his back, yet all he heard was a distant roaring in his ears, like a wave about to crash down on a dinghy.

Just a few words from his mouth would become that wave, capsizing his father's business, their family, and everything they had ever worked for.

The weight of it slammed into him, made him stagger back. His throat was tight, his breathing thin. The space behind his eyes flared and pulsed through his temples with a steady, pounding pain.

He hadn't slept at all last night—not since Soria had given him that unbearable revelation. Not only had he been tormented by its implications, but his sister had had a bad night as well, tossing and turning with fever interspersed with terrible bouts of coughing. Cayo had stayed beside her, sweating and shaking as if he were also feverish, dabbing the blood from her pale lips and patting her forehead with a cool cloth.

When she finally fell into a doze, Cayo had crept downstairs to the wine cellar. Walking from the humid warmth of Soria's room to the cool cellar beneath the manor had been a shock to his system, pebbling the skin of his arms and raising the hairs on the back of his neck. The cellar had smelled of cold stone and aged wood, with a slight vinegary tang left from the recent barrel spill.

Cayo had spotted the stain on the floor and followed it to where the chest must have been. But it was no longer there, leaving only a vague rectangular impression of where it once sat. Suddenly furious, Cayo had heaved the remaining cluster of barrels onto their sides and rolled them to the far wall until he spotted the corner of a small stained box.

It had reeked of the wine that had ruined it. Pushing open the lid, Cayo had staggered back from its contents, his breath catching in his throat.

Hundreds of black discs, all identical to the one in his pocket.

Cayo wasn't sure how he managed to pass the rest of the night without pounding down his father's door. He'd put the chest in his bedroom closet before going back to Soria's room, where the heat had lulled him into a trance-like state that wasn't quite sleep, but neither had he been fully awake. When Narin had shaken his shoulder hours later, he said that Kamon was out on business for the day.

Cayo had been relieved to avoid a confrontation with his father. After all, he had the evidence that Nawarak needed. It would be enough to claim his reward money.

But it would cost him so much more than whatever he would be paid.

Which was why he could only stand and stare at the office of the Port's Authority, his head and his heart at war with each other. Nausea sat coiled in his gut, spiking painfully whenever he moved to take a step forward.

What if he was wrong? What if his father was being set up? What if Cayo single-handedly destroyed whatever was left of the Mercado name, ruining the business his father had worked so hard to cultivate?

Cayo pressed the heels of his hands to his eyes, cursing. What could he do? What *should* he do? Condemn his family, or condemn the city?

It felt as if he stood there for an hour, a boy turned to stone, betrayal and fear compressing his bones into faceted mineral. One more blow and he would shatter.

His feet refused to move forward. His mouth had forgotten how to form words. In the end, he turned away from the Port's Authority and wandered down the main thoroughfare of the Business Sector, his chest sore from the weight of indecision and his heart in his mouth. Disappointment threaded through him at his cowardice.

But Soria didn't deserve to have this unleashed on their family. His duty was to protect her, not use her as an exhibit in court. His father, though . . .

I have another child to think about, a blood heir who can inherit our family's Vault when I'm gone.

Kamon's meager excuse to let his daughter wither away to nothing. Just like their mother.

What if he wanted her to die to protect his secret?

Cayo shuddered and leaned against the nearest building, his arms crossed tight across his chest. He willed himself to turn back around to the Port's Authority, but he was too heavy, too uncertain.

He had gambled all his gold away, but he couldn't gamble his father's reputation or their livelihoods.

As if inspired by his thoughts, his feet had led him to the Widow Vaults, a massive structure across the street supported with columns and curved eaves. The marble shone in the daylight, the stairs leading to the entrance inscribed with words from an old language of the Rain Empire:

Blood to blood, name to name, bone to bone.

An admittedly macabre way of stating that only those descended from the owners of these Vaults could open them, after the owner's demise. Cayo had often wondered what was in the Mercado Vault—jewels, gold, bolts of silk? Surely his father would have swept it clean by now, bankrupt as they were.

Kamon wanted at least one child alive to inherit a Vault full of dust and cobwebs.

Or perhaps it was full of counterfeit coins, ready to be spread throughout Moray.

Cayo laughed dully, mirthlessly, and leaned his head back against the wall. Everything was unraveling like a poorly stitched hem. He was tripping and stumbling in the dark.

A shout and a short scream made him pop his head back up. A young boy had fallen into the road, an old, lanky man looming over him. The man was well-dressed in a Rehanese-style suit and gold-trimmed glasses, a walking stick in his hand. Judging by the way he held it, he'd just used it on the downed boy.

"Were your filthy fingers in my pockets?" the man roared. The boy remained curled up, protecting his head. "Answer me, dog!"

The man kicked him in the stomach. The boy coughed and wheezed, his face contorted in pain. The man lifted his walking stick again, intent on smashing in the boy's skull with the heavy crystal handle.

Cayo lunged forward, getting between the walking stick and the boy. The handle caught him on the shoulder, making him stumble as a bright flare of pain shot across his collarbone.

"What is this?" the man demanded.

"Sir, please don't harm this child. Whatever wrong he's done—"

"He was trying to pilfer from me!" the man shouted. They were drawing stares now, people stopping in the street to watch the spectacle. Cayo's face heated, but he remained where he was, arms spread to prevent the man from getting to the boy again. "I'm a hardworking businessman! He has no right to my money!"

"I'm sure he's just hungry and frightened," Cayo said in a softer voice so that it wouldn't carry. "People in his situation tend to do desperate things for some coin."

"If he's so desperate for coin, all he has to do is go to the Vice Sector and learn some tricks."

Cayo grimaced at the implication. "Kindly walk away before I make this situation worse for you."

"You can't speak that way to me! How dare—"

A woman ran down the steps of the Widow Vaults wearing a horrified expression. "Father, please, don't make a scene! Let's go."

The man kept yelling and swinging his walking stick about, but the woman determinedly pulled him down the street, her face hardened with embarrassment.

Cayo rubbed his shoulder with a wince, knowing it would bruise. He turned around, fully expecting the boy to have dashed off, but received a surprise when he saw the boy sitting in the street, staring up at him in awe. He was small and mousy, a birthmark as irregular as an island on his jaw.

"Are you all right?" Cayo asked, extending a hand to help him up. "How badly did he hurt you?"

But the boy remained silent. After a moment, he finally jumped to his feet and took off running, nearly tripping over himself in his haste to get away.

Cayo sighed. The counterfeit money—his father's counterfeit money—had the potential to break the city, but perhaps it was already too broken to fix.

In the end, he just couldn't do it.

He'd turned his back on the Business Sector and returned home, his relief spoiled by regret.

Coward, his mind spat at him.

But he kept telling himself he had to know for certain, despite the insistent clawing in his skull that whispered he already knew.

Cayo waited in his father's office until he returned home, but Kamon went straight to his bedroom, claiming he was too exhausted to even sit for dinner.

"Father, I have to speak with you," Cayo said, his voice tight and on the verge of breaking.

"Not now, Cayo. I have an early meeting tomorrow, and I need to get rid of this headache."

"It's important. I found—"

"Cayo." Kamon turned to him, a hand on the knob of his bedroom door. He wore the frown that Cayo remembered most from his childhood, the lines between his brows warning Cayo that he was trying his father's patience. But there was also genuine weariness, as if Kamon was finally beginning to bend to the pressures he had exposed them to. "Have you fallen back on your vices?"

"What?" Cayo shook his head. "No, it's not that."

"Then whatever it is can wait," his father said before disappearing into his room.

So Cayo stayed in bed for hours, feverish and sore. His whole body ached, as if to physically repel the truth. As if that was all it took to reverse the fact that his father was a criminal.

Somehow, he managed to sleep throughout the night. When he was fully aware of being conscious again, a watery gray light softened the edges of his widow curtains. His stomach was hollow, his shoulder and neck were stiff, and his mouth tasted like rot.

Still, he hauled himself out of bed, not bothering to glance at himself in the mirror like he usually did before he shuffled down the hall to check on Soria.

But his sister wasn't in her rooms. Instead, he found Narin changing her bedsheets.

"The lady decided she wanted to go downstairs to eat," the footman said with a tone of pride.

Relief loosened Cayo's limbs. The medicine Romara had given him was already taking effect. "My father?"

"Meetings all morning."

Cayo sighed and scrubbed a hand through his hair, wincing when the motion pulled on his bruised shoulder. How was he supposed to talk to his father about the counterfeit when he refused to sit still long enough?

What would happen if I just turned him in? he thought as he went downstairs, taking in the manor that his father had worked so hard to obtain. *What if I can end this now?*

The prospect was an arrow aimed between his eyes, sharp and unavoidable.

As he neared the dining room, he heard two voices in conversation. Cayo frowned. Who else was around other than Narin?

Pushing open the door, he took two steps into the dining room and froze.

Soria looked up with a grin, dressed only in her nightgown and robe. The young woman beside her turned and met his incredulous gaze, the thinnest razor-sharp smile on her face.

Countess Yamaa.

"Good morning, Lord Mercado," she said. She swept her eyes over him, from his mussed hair to his wrinkled sleeping shirt to his baggy trousers and bare feet. Cayo flushed hot all over, desiring nothing more than to run back to his room and put on his best suit with a healthy spray of Ladyswoon.

But he made himself stand still, carefully clearing his throat. "Countess. What . . . Ah, to what do we owe the pleasure of such an early visit?"

"Early?" She quirked an eyebrow at the nearest window. "It's past noon."

Cayo swallowed a curse. The overcast sky had deceived him.

"The countess was telling me her ideas for her next party," Soria jumped in, barely able to contain herself. "Sit down and eat, Cayo."

He looked between them, shoulders tense. Although the countess knew his sister was ill, he hadn't told her about the ash fever. Yet there was no disguising the gray mark on Soria's neck. The countess said nothing about it—in fact, she didn't seem troubled by it at all—so he could only hope she would keep it to herself.

He moved awkwardly to a chair opposite theirs, his body jerky and uncoordinated under Yamaa's intense stare. Unable to resist the urge, he tried to flatten down his hair, wondering just how wild it looked to her.

"How are you feeling?" he asked Soria.

"Good," she said. There was some color in her cheeks to contrast with the gray spread along the side of her neck, her eyes brighter and her breathing more even. Cayo couldn't shake the memory of blood touching her lips, her ragged gasps for air. "I wanted to take a walk in the garden, but Narin said it's too cold."

"And I agree with him. Maybe tomorrow, if it's warmer."

If we still have a garden then.

She huffed but didn't argue further as she nibbled at her egg bun. Cayo smiled despite the tightness of his chest, happy just to have his sister up and talking.

The countess watched the exchange with fascination. He suddenly wondered if she had any siblings. He burned to ask her questions, to put away his worry and his indecision and merely focus on a girl he wanted to know more about.

A foot kicked him softly under the table. Soria pointedly looked at the teapot between them, then at the countess's nearly empty cup. Since they no longer had servers for this sort of thing, Cayo stood to pour the countess fresh tea, accidentally spilling some when he pulled the spout away. Cursing, he wiped it up as Soria sighed and shook her head. The countess tamped down a smile.

"So, ah." Cayo wasn't particularly hungry, but he took a rice noodle pancake and began tearing it into pieces on his plate. "What's this about another party?"

"It sounds amazing," Soria said with a dreamy sigh. "It'll be on a ship and catered by Kastille's. They make the *best* cakes. And the theme of it is—"

"Gambling," the countess finished with another thin smile.

Cayo stopped tearing at his pancake. There was a stiffness in the countess that he hadn't seen before, a wholly different persona than the girl he had raced in the inlet. She looked at him with weight behind her dark eyes, as if she also bore a knowledge too heavy to hold on her own.

"Soria," he said softly, "you should go back to bed."

"But I feel fine."

"If you want a walk in the garden later, I want you to be rested for it."

Soria rolled her eyes and got up from the table, giving the countess a small curtsy before heading toward the stairs.

Once they were alone and out of earshot, Cayo faced the countess again.

"I know your secret," she said without preamble.

Cayo's heart tripped. The theme of her next party was no coincidence; she must have figured out, somehow, that he was embroiled with the Slum King, that he had drained his family's coffers, that—

"Who would have guessed that the young Lord Mercado was engaged to the Slum King's daughter?"

242

The words were a punch to the solar plexus, leaving Cayo winded. He stared at Yamaa with an open mouth. When she did nothing but stare back, he desperately reached for his voice.

"How . . . How do you know that?" he croaked.

"All information can be bought, for the right price." She winced, as if hating the words even as she spoke them. As if she were quoting someone she disliked. "I happened to be curious about you, and one thing led to another."

Although the engagement with Romara was far and away the least of his troubles, the fact that Yamaa now knew—even before his father knew!—filled him with a strange sense of shame. He realized then, in that moment, that he cared far more about what she thought of him than he had initially guessed.

"So." She laced her fingers together on the tabletop. "How exactly did *that* relationship start?"

"It's not a relationship," he growled. "It isn't like that."

"Don't tell me it's a marriage of convenience? Because somehow I don't find the idea of marrying a criminal very convenient."

He sighed and rubbed his face. There were too many voices crowding inside him, whispering his fears and doubts in continuous loops, all pressed and cramped together so that he felt as short of breath as Soria.

Eventually he dropped his hands, also dropping all his masks, so that when he looked at the countess, he was merely Cayo and nothing more.

"Let's take a walk," he said.

He didn't dress in his best suit, but he did put some care into his outfit of soft breeches and a light blue shirt, over which he pulled on his long coat. Yamaa was a bit understated today as well, wrapped in a simple dress of dove gray with embroidered leaves around the hem. She wrapped a shawl about her shoulders and nodded for him to lead the way.

Cayo didn't have a destination in mind; they didn't need one. He just needed to get away from the manor, from the possibility of his father coming home early and interacting with the countess. For some reason, he wanted to keep them as far from each other as possible.

"You've probably heard the rumors about me," Cayo said as they walked down the long, winding road leading to the manor. "You must have, considering you called me a drunken playboy."

Was that a hint of a blush he saw, or were her cheeks merely warming from the exercise? "I may have heard a rumor or two, yes. Including that you liked to frequent the tables. I didn't know for certain if that was true until recently."

"Well, it used to be true. That used to be my life: gambling dens and countless drinks and getting good-luck kisses from strangers. I suppose that was my way of creating freedom—overindulgence, addiction, not bothering to think about the consequences of what I was doing." He looked up at the pearlescent sky, hands in his pockets. A sea breeze was coming in off the bay, cool and sweet. Beside him, Yamaa hugged her shawl tighter around her. "It made everything seem simpler. And all I wanted was for things to be simple."

He had spent so long thinking about these words that speaking them out loud now was akin to peeling off the dead skin of a sunburn, revealing the tender, healing skin beneath.

"I'm the reason my family is in this mess," he said quietly. "It wasn't just enough to overindulge. I wanted more. So I got in with the Slum King, and I played for him. I dealt. I cheated. I lined his pockets with money."

He rubbed a hand over his mouth, feeling the bristles starting to come in at his jawline. "But I got in over my head, and I lost . . . everything. I drained all my coffers, and some of my father's. I was so far gone that I hadn't even been keeping track, and my father didn't notice until it was too late. And then Soria got sick, and . . ."

"You couldn't pay for the medicine for ash fever," the countess finished softly.

He nodded, teeth clenched. "My sister is the reason I got out of that life. She literally dragged me from the gutter and slapped me awake. Without her, I . . . I don't know where I would even be now. I'd do whatever it takes to care for her, even if it means condemning myself to something I don't want."

The countess stopped under the shivering leaves of a ceiba tree. "Such as marrying yourself off to the Slum King's daughter."

Cayo sighed. "I made a bad deal with the Slum King, and Romara was the price. But at least my family stays safe, and we get the medicine Soria needs."

Yamaa's eyes were pinched. "You could have come to me for the medicine. We could have struck a fairer deal."

"This happened before we properly met. And besides, we haven't known each other that long," he said with a small smile, though a part of him warmed at the idea that she cared enough to suggest it.

"Still," she muttered. "Is there a way you can break off the engagement?"

"Not without making the Slum King very, very angry."

They continued walking, entering the main city and wandering aimlessly down its streets. Although he had taken the lead at first, he noticed that the countess now seemed to be picking out their path, as if her feet were guiding her somewhere. There were few citizens out today, everyone no doubt preferring to keep inside and wait out whatever storm was on its way to Moray. He could smell it in the air, sharp and earthy.

They walked in a direction that Cayo typically never went, but the countess was deep in thought and he didn't want to disturb her, so he was content to follow. Her hair was half tied back with a butterfly pin, a couple of locks strategically curled and framing her face. He wanted to reach out and brush one behind her ear. To skim his fingertips against her smooth cheek.

God and her stars, what was wrong with him? He was engaged to another woman, his sister was potentially dying, his father was a criminal . . . And yet all of that fell away when he was with her, this girl made out of salt water and steel.

The countess looked up and blinked at their surroundings. Cayo recognized it as one of the poorer districts, a traditionally Rehanese neighborhood where the houses were guarded by statuettes of star saints. She shrank back suddenly, looking uncomfortable.

"Are you all right?" he asked. He recalled all the times his father would tell him not to go near neighborhoods like these for fear of theft and getting roughed up. "Are you afraid?"

She scowled. "Why should I be afraid?"

"Well, you know, places like this . . ."

"Just because the people who live here have less money doesn't mean they're dangerous," she said. "They live their lives as best they can, just like you and me."

Cayo studied her, the flame of her eyes and the white-knuckled grip on her shawl. It was true that he was brimming with secrets, but he was certain she was, too.

"You're right," he conceded. "I'm sorry to imply it. Sometimes the things you're told as a child follow you through the years, whether they're correct or not."

That seemed to calm her down, and she gave him a little nod. Wordlessly they agreed to pass by the neighborhood. The countess's shoulders didn't ease until they were several blocks away.

Why was it that whenever he spoke to her, he felt as if different parts of himself broke open? He wondered if she felt the same, oddly pleased with the idea that he might have the ability to make her as off-kilter as she made him. But more than that, he was drawn to tell her things, to unleash those frantic whispers inside of him so that he didn't have to carry them alone.

Cayo drew in a deep breath. "Do you remember when you said something about knowing a person well, only to realize you never truly knew them at all?"

She looked at him with those heavy, dark eyes and said nothing. As if she were plagued by her own restless whispers.

"How do you cope with it?" he asked softly.

The countess bit her lower lip and stared at the cobblestone road as they entered a district near one of the city's public parks. The sky churned overhead, the air thick and damp.

"It depends," she answered at last. "What did this person do?"

He thought of the chest hidden in his closet. The specks of blood on Soria's pillow. The jar containing Sébastien's eyes. "Something bad. Something that can hurt people—that *has* hurt people. People I care about."

She stopped and faced him. He turned to her.

"Then you have to stop them," she said, the certainty in her voice robbing him of breath. "Even if you love them."

His throat worked as he tried to swallow. "Even . . . Even if it means they'll be taken away?"

"Even if it means they'd die."

The breeze sent a chill down the collar of his coat, and he shivered. She took a step toward him, so earnest and confident that it was the only thing preventing him from simply crumpling to the ground.

She was right—he knew she was right. His father had done so much harm already, and if Cayo allowed him to continue dispersing the counterfeit coins, even more people would be harmed.

He had to turn his father in.

He began to feel feverish again in the wake of that impossible decision, but there was also relief hiding beneath it, the chance to do the right thing. To try to make up for the harm that Cayo himself had caused.

The countess lifted a hand as if to touch his sleeve, then dropped it again. She parted her lips to speak, but the sky chose that moment to rumble and burst open, unleashing a sheet of rain over the city.

Yamaa yelped in surprise, and it startled Cayo out of his reverie. He held his hand out to her.

"Come on," he yelled over the deluge. "I know a place we can wait this out!"

She hesitated, her fingers hovering over his. When she finally took his hand, it was like the sun and moon colliding, a brilliant and thrilling crash.

Cayo pulled her forward, and together they raced through the rain like stars shooting across the sky.

21

The magician smiled, and Neralia felt as if she were back among the stars. Together they danced through the ocean's depths, leaving trails of radiant light in their wake so as to make the sky jealous.
—"NERALIA OF THE CLOUDS," AN ORAL STORY ORIGINATING FROM
THE LEDE ISLANDS

The touch of water to Amaya's skin woke her from the dread at seeing her old neighborhood again.

When Cayo had asked if she was afraid, she had almost wanted to say yes, but not for the reason that he thought. She had been afraid of the ghosts that still lurked there, the shadow of her old home against the street, a garden overgrown with weeds. She had been afraid that if they stayed there a moment longer, she would erode like rock washed with seawater, turning into a ghost herself.

But as Cayo gripped her hand and led her toward the park, the two of them racing through the rain, her fear dissolved. She spent so much time living in the past that she had forgotten what living in the present was like—until now. Now, with soft, thick raindrops soaking her hair and her dress, her legs keeping stride with Cayo's, a surprised laugh spilled over her lips as if she could hardly contain it.

Cayo pulled her toward a stone bridge. Amaya vaguely remembered it from when she and her mother would walk the paths on sunny days, when the humidity wasn't strong enough to choke. The bridge had been built over a man-made creek that ran a serpentine track through the park, but the creek was running low after the summer months, only a thin trickle that would swell with the rainfall.

They ducked under the arch of the wide bridge, panting and soaking wet. They looked at each other and burst out laughing.

"You look like a drowned dog," Amaya said as she pulled her hair over her shoulder and squeezed out the excess water.

"Oh yeah?" Cayo shook his head like the dog she'd compared him to, water flying from his hair and hitting her in the face. "You look like a shipwreck survivor."

"What?"

"You know, like in the books." Cayo gestured to her sodden dress, the mud from the creek bed staining the hem. "There's a harrowing shipwreck, and it's always the woman who escapes and gets washed up on some deserted island. And of course, there she meets a man who helps her survive on the island, they eventually fall in love, et cetera. . . ."

Amaya grimaced at the memory of waking up on the atoll above the Landless comm. But she wasn't some romantic heroine—she had more important things to do.

Like trying to pry more secrets out of the boy beside her. She had gotten too wrapped up in their conversation to think properly, to ask the right questions when he was so obviously baring his soul to her.

Someone he knew and cared about had done something wrong. Was it his father? Had Cayo discovered something that could help her own plans in bringing Kamon Mercado down?

But the pain in Cayo's eyes had been so stark that it had stripped away her motives. She understood that pain; she felt an echo of it in her bones. It was the pain of asking yourself, *How could someone I love do something so horrible?*

"Sorry, I didn't mean it as an insult," Cayo said, noting her dark expression. "It's actually a good look on you. Just that, you know, you can pull it off. Like you and water belong together."

He was beginning to ramble, so she gave him a wry smile. "Thanks?"

He raked fingers through his hair, pulling it back. Looking around, he hummed in surprise. "Looks like others have been here recently."

Amaya followed his gaze to the underside of the bridge. It was covered in drawings and words and symbols she didn't recognize, some done with paint, some done with the reddish clay runoff from the creek. A few of them looked old, but the ones done with clay were more recent, almost as bright as blood against the dark stone.

"People like to come here and leave their mark," Cayo explained, putting his hand against a drawing of a sea serpent that was actually quite good. "It's like a rite of passage. I remember daring one of my friends to do it, but he got caught. They usually have a patrol that comes around to check that no one is vandalizing anything new."

"I know," Amaya said without thinking. "I remember."

She had once seen two teenagers chased out of the park by an irate member of the city guard, one of them carrying a bucket of white paint. When she had asked her mother what they were doing, her mother had explained that some people were graced with the gift of art, and sometimes that made them want to share it with the whole

251

world. *If you have a special talent,* she would say, *it would be selfish of you to keep it for yourself.*

"You remember?" Cayo echoed, frowning.

Amaya realized her mistake and stiffened. "They . . . do something similar, where I'm from. That's all I meant."

"Oh." He still looked a bit confused. "Where exactly *are* you from? I think no one really knows the answer to that, yet."

"Does it matter?" she asked, already rebuilding her protective walls.

"I think it does, yes." He dropped his hand and studied her as intently as he had studied the graffiti surrounding them. "Where you're from . . . I think it helps inform who you are as a person, in some ways. A home is something you can't easily forget. It stays with you no matter where you go or who you become."

Amaya stared at him, again sensing the ghosts that called her back to the street where her mother and father had carved out a simple yet happy life. For a time, anyway.

She had carried that seed of remembrance during her years on the *Brackish.* She carried it still, that pocket of memory that reminded her of all she'd lost, of everything she would never have again.

She looked away from Cayo, drifting to the far end of the bridge. Placing her fingers against a word she couldn't read, she traced the lines and curves as if to discern its meaning through touch alone.

"I come from a place where happiness was more important than money," she said, her voice nearly overtaken by the hiss of rain outside their shelter. "Where spiders are revered and myths were eaten up like candy."

She heard him come closer, stopping just far enough to give her space. "What sort of myths?"

Amaya took a deep breath and delved into memories of her father, his low, amused voice and the way he used his broad hands to add inflections to his stories. Turning, she bent and scooped up a handful of clay from the edge of the trickling creek.

"Trickster was born from a seed of the oldest acorn tree and the blood of the cleverest snake, and the heart of a star was his womb." She took some of the cold, wet clay with her fingers and drew a star on a bare patch of stone, with Trickster's symbol in the center: a diamond with a forked line in the middle. "When he emerged bright and hungry from the star, he descended to the earth and disguised himself as human. He wanted to learn about people by becoming one, to better understand what they wanted and how they deceived one another."

Cayo listened raptly to the Kharian myth her father had often told her—her favorite one, the one she would always request before bed. She drew as she spoke, outlining Trickster's life and his most notable deeds.

"He grew trees when there was famine, stealing them from the forests of Khari's enemies. He instated the first empress of Khari, and was even said to stay with her in the Ruby Palace for many years as her lover." She drew the spiraling dome-shaped towers of the palace. "But when the other gods began to look upon him with disdain, he knew he was in trouble."

"But he was doing good deeds," Cayo interrupted, the first time he had done so. "Why would they object?"

"Because the gods like order and balance, and Trickster was a being of chaos," Amaya explained. "He opposed all their orders and never listened when Protector warned him not to overstep his bounds. Then, one day, Trickster offended Protector greatly when he pretended to be him, ordering the other gods to perform his whims.

When Protector found out about the impersonation, he challenged Trickster to combat."

Amaya drew a knife, its shape a familiar comfort. She checked to make sure the tattoo at her wrist was covered by her sleeve, but some part of her didn't mind if Cayo saw. In fact, she *wanted* him to see it, to share a bit of who she truly was.

Taking an uneven breath, she drew a tree. "Protector spilled Trickster's blood, and an orchard grew where he fell, bearing enough fruit and nuts to feed five villages."

"So he died?" Cayo asked.

"Gods can't really die, but he disappeared for a while to lick his wounds. The orchard is still there, though. There are people who visit to pray to him, and some claim they can hear him laughing through the trees and raining acorns down on the heads of unsuspecting visitors."

She turned to find Cayo smiling at her drawings. The softness of that smile was like a kick to the chest, and when his eyes met hers, she stood rooted to the spot. They were no longer full of pain; they were gleaming with discovery, with contentment.

For a moment, she felt as if she, like Trickster, were encased within a star. Bright and hungry and eager to right the wrongs of the world.

As she watched, Cayo also scooped up a handful of clay and began drawing on the stone. He told her about his favorite book, a story about a boy who joins a pirate ship and sails on adventures all around the world. He drew sea monsters and swords and chests of treasure.

"What's that supposed to be?" she asked, pointing at an oblong shape he had made.

"It's a mermaid," he mumbled.

"Oh." She tilted her head, as if seeing it at another angle would throw it into sharper clarity. "I think I see it now."

"Don't you dare make fun."

"No, no, I think it's quite good. Is the mermaid supposed to be part manatee?"

Cayo threw the rest of his clay at her. She jumped back, but the clay hit her dress, a splatter of red and brown.

Cayo's eyes widened. "I'm so sorry, I didn't mean—"

She immediately retaliated, throwing a handful of clay at his coat. It hit his shoulder and splattered on the side of his face.

"All right," he growled, gathering more clay. "Now it's war."

They threw and dodged and yelled, hurling insults at each other as they launched clay from their hands and ran from the other's counterattacks. When Amaya proved to be too good at dodging, Cayo changed his strategy and came straight at her, his hands full.

She shrieked in a way she hadn't done since she was a child, being chased by her father in the backyard as he pretended to be a monster. She ran from one side of the bridge to the next, but Cayo eventually cornered her and grabbed her arms, the clay squishing between them.

"Nooo," she groaned around a laugh as he smeared it all up and down her sleeves. Liesl was going to have a conniption, but in that moment, Amaya didn't care. She scraped some clay off her sleeve and rubbed it against Cayo's cheek.

"Agh!" He reached for her face to retaliate, then hesitated. The sudden stillness between them made her highly aware of their heavy breathing, the way her chest moved so close to his.

Swallowing, Cayo reached up and touched her cheek. Slowly he began to draw, and even without a mirror she could tell what it was: Trickster's symbol, the diamond with the forked line. She stared at him the whole time, invested in the concentration on his face, the solemn line of his mouth. Although her body was cold from the rain and mud, the skin under his fingers flared with heat, purling through her limbs and diving down into her chest as if she had taken a sip of warmed wine.

When he was done, they shared another moment of stillness. Then she reached for the hollow of his throat, the triangle of skin revealed above his shirt where he hadn't done up the last button.

She had touched him before, at Laelia's. She had forced herself to do so, uncomfortable with her skin meeting his, this stranger full of secrets and tied to the man she detested most.

But Cayo no longer felt like a stranger. Their words had built a bridge between them, one that Amaya thought she could finally cross, a small step at a time.

She placed her fingertips on the space between his collarbones. He shivered beneath her touch, and it intensified the heat in her chest, made her as drunk as the wine would have. She didn't dare look at his face; everything would shatter if she did. Instead, she focused on crafting the symbol at the base of his throat, the traditional Kharian design that meant protection.

What she was protecting him from, she wasn't entirely sure. His father, perhaps. The Slum King.

Herself.

When had he gotten so close? She dropped her fingers and finally looked up at him, the rawness in his expression beckoning her to cross the bridge between them faster, to meet him in the middle.

Before she could, a shout emerged from the rain.

"Move it, vandals! I'll drag you home to your parents if I have to!"

Cayo's eyes widened. "Shit," he hissed before he took her hand, and they ran back out into the rain.

"The city guard patrols even during a storm?" she called as they ran deeper into the park.

"I didn't think they got paid enough for that," he called back with a sheepish laugh.

They didn't stop until they were hidden in a copse of aloe trees, rain sliding down the long, thin leaves. Amaya held her palms out and let the water wash away most of the clay.

"I guess they really do hate vandalism," she said.

Cayo laughed again, but it was quiet. He nervously shifted on his feet, lifting a hand to run it through his hair, but winced at the motion.

"Are you hurt?" she asked.

"It's nothing." He rubbed his shoulder. "Some old man clobbered me with his walking stick yesterday. Must have been in a bad mood."

Amaya's lips parted. Yesterday, Weevil had come back to the estate with a bruise on the side of his head, a hand curled protectively around his stomach. When she had demanded to know what happened, he'd admitted to scouting the Business Sector for easy targets.

"I was just going to pick a couple of pockets," he'd murmured into the tea that Cicada had made for him. "I didn't know that old man was strong enough to wallop me."

Amaya had pinched the bridge of her nose. "You don't have to resort to thieving like you did on the *Brackish*, Matthieu. I told you, once this job is over, all the Bugs will have enough money to get home."

"How'd you even get away without getting arrested?" Cricket had asked Weevil.

He'd sniffed, his nose running from the steam of the tea. "A man stood in front of me. Got walloped for his trouble, too. If he hadn't done that, I'd likely be scraps on the street."

Amaya stared at Cayo, her lips still parted. His eyebrows lowered in confusion.

"It was you," she said softly. "You helped Wee—I mean, Matthieu."

"What? Who's Matthieu?"

"The boy who was pickpocketing in the Business Sector. He works for me at my estate. He said a man got between him and his attacker. That was you, wasn't it?"

He blinked, trying to absorb the information. "Oh. I guess it was. I didn't know he belonged to you. I mean, not belong as in you *own* him, or at least I hope not, just that if he works for you—"

He was rambling again. She put a hand against his chest, leaving reddish fingerprints on his shirt.

"Thank you," she said.

He nodded, as if he didn't know what to say. What design had the gods woven to keep bringing this boy back into her life in unlikely ways? Amaya didn't understand it, this push and pull, this interlocking of fates. It was too big for her to comprehend.

Maybe she wasn't supposed to. Maybe she was supposed to allow herself to be shipwrecked, to find someone who could help her through the jungle. To help her step out of the past and remain in the present, to turn her eyes to a future she'd thought she didn't deserve.

"I'm glad," he said suddenly, "that you came to Moray."

Her breath shuddered out of her. He took a step closer, the rain washing off the clay from his cheek but not touching the symbol of protection at the base of his throat. She was hyperaware of his body so close to hers, how he breathed and moved, the heat trapped under his coat.

"Can . . ." His eyes dropped to her lips, longing. "Can I kiss you?"

From anyone else, the question would have sounded innocent, imploring. But in Cayo's voice, it was a question that burned through her. In just four words he had opened a door to his desire, allowing her to see it. To do with it what she would.

Wordlessly, she nodded.

She thought it might be a sudden thing, but Cayo was slow, careful, as if he had spent a long time thinking of this moment. One of his hands settled at her hip, and heat spiraled from the touch, coiling in her stomach. His other hand cupped her jaw, his thumb brushing the skin beside her ear. She shivered at the sensation, almost angry with herself for the involuntary admission that he was doing something to her that no one ever had before, that she had never wanted before. Until him.

When he touched his lips to hers, she was shocked by the softness of it, the tentative heat and exploration. As if he had guessed that this was all new to her, that she had no idea how to navigate these waters. The second brush of their lips was more insistent, and Amaya found herself clutching her shawl, trapped between Cayo's hands and having no idea what to do with her own.

He pulled away a little, and she opened her eyes to find his half-lidded. Waiting. Patient. She nodded again, and he brought her in closer, fusing their mouths together with such intensity that she gasped against him.

The surrender was terrifying, but she let herself melt into it, into how Cayo's hand swept up her back and cupped the other side of her face, his fingers scrunching into her hair. She let go of her shawl and clung to him instead, feeling the expanse of his chest as he breathed, the frantic beating of his heart.

His tongue brushed her lips, and she staggered against him. Her head was hot and light, and she barely understood what she was doing when she opened to him, some animal instinct taking over.

You can't, a part of her cried. *Remember who he is. What you have to do to him.*

What was she doing?

Amaya pulled away, pressing a hand against her mouth. It was warm and buzzing, her lips carrying the impression of Cayo's.

He stared at her, out of breath, as rain rolled down his stunned face. The water ran over his throat, breaking the symbol of protection she had made.

He took a concerned step toward her. "Ya—"

"No." She held a hand up to stop him, to prevent him from calling her a name that was not her own. When he had held her, she had forgotten about Countess Yamaa, about Silverfish, about what she had come here to do.

She had been Amaya, a seventeen-year-old girl with hopes and desires, and she had been free.

But she wasn't free. Not yet.

"I'm sorry," she whispered.

She turned and ran from him. Breaking through the copse of aloe trees, she headed out of the park, wiping the rain from her face and forcing herself not to look back. If he followed, she couldn't hear him, and she would lose him within the alleys anyway.

She couldn't do this much longer. She had to use Cayo to get to Mercado, to turn his desire into a weapon for vengeance.

But as she tried to look to the future that had seemed possible only moments ago, she saw nothing but a barren orchard, the memory of Cayo's lips on hers grown cold.

22

Do not be afraid to fold. Do not be ashamed to walk away. We all must know our limits, and to recognize when we have been beaten.

—THE INS AND OUTS OF TABLE BETTING

Cayo didn't chase after her. He had seen the spark of something in her eyes—not regret, exactly, but something close to fear, or surprise.

When he had kissed her—*I kissed her*, he thought in wonder—he had sensed that she had never done this before. With a boy, or with anyone. He still remembered his first kiss, an awkward exchange between him and some merchant's daughter, and he had been just as stiff, just as unsure.

But then Yamaa had eased against him, her lips pliant and allowing it to happen. He could still feel that phantom touch, bright and sparking against the rain.

Cayo closed his eyes and leaned his head back. The rain washed over him, and he longed for it to strip away his doubts and shame, to leave him with a new skin that only knew the touch of Yamaa's.

Her words blazed within him like a brand.

You have to stop them. Even if you love them. Even if it means they'd die.

Cayo had been sitting in his indecision for too long. Love and loyalty had restrained him, kept him from doing what had to be done. But no longer. He had to be someone as strong as Yamaa thought he could be—someone just as resolute as she was, made of salt water and steel.

He had the means to put a stop to this, to drag the truth into the light and do something good, for once. Something that could actually benefit others.

He had to turn his father in.

Opening his eyes, Cayo barely felt the tear on his cheek before that, too, was washed away.

He walked all the way home. As he crossed the threshold, sodden and shivering, Narin exclaimed his dismay.

"My lord, you'll catch sick! Let me draw you a warm bath and bring you some tea."

"I'm afraid I don't have time for that," Cayo said. "Can you tell the driver to bring the carriage around?"

The footman hesitated, his eyes pinched. "I'm sorry to say that your father dismissed the driver yesterday, my lord."

"What?" Cayo rubbed his hands against his face, his shoulders tightening with stress. "Then can you please find a carriage to take me to the Business Sector?"

"In this weather, my lord? Surely it can wait—"

"It can't," he snapped before he could rein it in. He took a deep breath, forcing himself to find the calm that Yamaa had instilled in him. "I'm sorry, Narin, but I must go immediately."

The footman gave a small bow, his eyebrows furrowed in worry. "I'll see it done."

Cayo bounded up the stairs, his heart climbing into his throat. The walls of the manor seemed to press against him, as if it wanted to trap him here, prevent him from doing what had to be done. As he peeled off his soaked clothes and put on a fresh, dry outfit, his stomach churned the way it did when he knew he was on the losing side of a game. That dreadful anticipation sank fangs into his gut, clawing at his ribs and hips.

He held on to the side of his dresser and bowed his head, his hair still dripping water onto the floor. He focused on breathing, on calming the anxious monster curled up within him.

Kamon believed his son was the sole cause for the gradual decline of their family, that his time in the Vice Sector had put them all at risk. Perhaps Cayo had had a hand in this, but he hadn't been the one to put flame to the pyre, to see everything Kamon had worked for go up in smoke and ash.

Cayo could still save himself and Soria from that pyre.

He went to his sister's room and found her reading in bed. She looked sleepy, likely from the weather and her spirited conversation with the countess that morning. When she saw him, she smiled and put the book down.

"Did you and the countess go for a walk?" she demanded. "What happened? Tell me everything."

Cayo's heart gave a hard, mournful *thump*, and he wished he could simply sit and gossip with Soria like they used to. Swallowing, he sat in the chair beside her bed and clasped his hands between his knees.

"We talked about stories," he said quietly, over the gentle patter of rain on the window. "A bit of the past, and a bit of the future."

"Are you going to marry her?"

Cayo shook himself in surprise. "What?"

"It seems the sort of thing Father would want. Especially after . . ." Soria averted her eyes in shame, likely remembering Gen Hizon and how her illness had ruined their engagement. "And besides, she seems fairly well off."

"That would be an understatement," he murmured. "I . . . I don't know."

Even as he said it, he knew it couldn't be. Not only would their lives be changed once he revealed the truth about their father, but the Slum King would kill him in an instant if he married Yamaa instead of Romara.

"I think she enjoys your company," Soria said with a teasing grin.

Normally, he would have been pleased to hear it, but instead he just nodded, feeling the ghost of Yamaa's lips on his.

Soria frowned at his solemn demeanor. "Is something the matter?"

He shook his head. "No. Or at least, not for much longer."

"You're acting strange." Soria noticed his outfit. "You're dressed to go out again? It's getting late. And Father said he'll be home tonight so the three of us can have dinner together."

Cayo closed his eyes tight, clenching his jaw.

You have to stop them. Even if you love them.

"Cayo?"

He looked at his sister, wanting to tear apart the world and

264

remake it for her, a world where she was healthy and happy and nothing bad could ever touch her.

Reaching for the handkerchief on her bedside table, he dabbed at the sweat lining her brow, then kissed her forehead.

"It can't go on this way," he whispered. "But no matter what happens, I'll protect you."

She called his name when he turned to leave, then dissolved into a coughing fit. Cayo gritted his teeth and hurried out of her room, down the hall, to his bedroom. Throwing open the closet, he stared at the chest, panting for breath and delirious with purpose. When he grabbed it, the discs inside rattled like bones.

"There's a carriage waiting for you at the front, my lord," Narin said as Cayo came downstairs. "It's a bit battered, but it was the closest one I could find at such short notice."

"That's fine. Thank you, Narin." Then he stopped, looking at the footman who had been a part of this household ever since Cayo could remember. What would happen to him? Guilt tightening his throat, Cayo put a hand on the man's shoulder, squeezing. "Thank you."

Narin still wore his confused frown. "You're quite welcome, my lord."

Cayo gave the driver his instructions and then ducked into the carriage. It bumped and rattled its way into the heart of the city. Cayo hugged the chest the entire time, staring numbly down at its stained lid, enveloped in the smell of wood grain and vinegar.

When the carriage rolled to a stop, Cayo barely paused to pay the driver with the little spending money he had left before storming his way into the offices of the Port's Authority.

"I need to speak with Petty Officer Nawarak," Cayo demanded of the person at the front desk. *"Now."*

The doors opened, and Cayo strode straight to Nawarak's desk toward the back. She was standing with a hip leaning against the side of the desk, her arms crossed as she spoke with another officer, laughing at some joke.

When she noticed him, her eyes widened in surprise. Before she could say anything, he slammed the chest down onto her desk.

The sound it made was like a door slamming shut. Final. Decisive.

He met Nawarak's gaze, his own burning.

"I have the evidence you need," he said.

23

As I lay upon my father's grave, the map of my bones above his,
I felt what it was to love and hate at once.

—FROM *PATHWAY OF STARS*, THE MEMOIR OF CHAIRAK BOUGHN,
CELEBRATED REHANESE ADVENTURER

In Viariche, Amaya had been miserable. Her feet were constantly sore from high-heeled shoes, her ribs crisscrossed with the impressions of corsets, and her scalp always stung from having to pull her hair up all the time.

At first she had borne it in silence, conditioned from the *Brackish* to keep her head down and say nothing lest Captain Zharo find an excuse to throw her overboard. But as the weeks went by, her frustration grew, her useless rage sitting like boiling water under a lid.

One night, she had come home from an art gallery showing in near tears. Her feet had been throbbing, her toes almost entirely numb. As soon as she'd entered the apartment, she had thrown her shoes at the wall with a loud *bang*.

"Gods above, it's like the siege of Gravaen in here," a familiar voice had rumbled from the depths of the apartment.

Amaya had frozen. Boon rarely came to the apartment, choosing instead to prowl the waterfront. She'd limped into the main sitting area and found him lounging by a small fire he'd built in the hearth, nursing a bottle of wine. He looked ragged and torn, like he'd just escaped a street brawl.

"What are you doing here?" she had demanded.

"Relax," he'd muttered, taking a swig from his bottle. "No one's seen me. 'Sides, not like I've got broadsheets up with my face on 'em in a place like this." He'd appraised her then, dark eyes scrutinizing even when glazed with drink. "You're home early."

Amaya had sunk into one of the chairs and pulled her right foot toward her lap, hissing as she began to massage it. "I had to. I was going to fall over otherwise."

Boon lifted an eyebrow at her stockinged feet. "Thought you'd be used to the shoes by now."

"Well, I'm not." Suddenly, inexplicably, tears had begun to prick her eyes. Amaya drew in a sharp breath and scowled, disappointed in herself for acting this way over something so trivial. "They *hurt*. Everything hurts, and I have no idea if I can even pull this off, and . . ." She'd stopped, knowing if she kept going, then the dam would break.

Boon was silent a moment, drinking and staring into the fire. She'd thought he would reprimand her like he usually did, but when he spoke, his voice was quiet.

"The siege of Gravaen," he had said. "Have you heard of it?" She had shaken her head. "A years-long campaign against a city fortified with an impenetrable wall. They held all the world's knowledge—a library so big it could likely block the sun. Even the gods were jealous of it. The demon Arjar, though, he wanted all that knowledge for himself. So he set his hordes of minions upon the city to break down the wall."

Amaya had stopped kneading her foot as she listened, caught within the simple cadence his voice had taken. She had heard of Arjar before, once or twice, in the Kharian myths her father used to tell her: a demon king in constant opposition to the gods.

"Arjar called on all he had at his disposal," Boon went on, still staring at the fire as if hypnotized. "Shadow beasts, ifrits, the ghosts of murderers. They launched themselves at that wall, but it still stood firm. At night, wraiths would sneak into the city and take children from their beds, and Arjar held them hostage in exchange for the library. But the city refused, and every day they refused, Arjar ate another child."

Amaya had shivered. The stories her father had told were fanciful, mysterious, and full of magic. This story was darker, stranger, but nonetheless held her in its thrall.

"This went on for so long that nearly all the children in the city had been eaten, and the wailing of their mothers could be heard all over the world. Finally, the gods saw fit to intervene. They met with Arjar and his demonic hordes on the field outside the city and battled. The demon king was defeated, and withdrew.

"The city thanked the gods and promised to build them bigger shrines, but that wasn't enough for 'em." Boon had taken a slow pull from his bottle. "The gods wanted access to the library."

Amaya roused herself. "What did the gods do with the knowledge?"

"Hells if I know. They were probably so disgusted with us by then that they decided we were on our own." He'd finished his wine, wiped his mouth on his sleeve, and set the bottle down carefully beside him. He clicked his tongue a few times. "Don't blame 'em, really."

There was something sorrowful about him in that moment, and suddenly Amaya realized that he'd never told her who he had been mourning the day she rescued him at sea, covered in marigold petals.

"So what's the point?" she'd asked. "All stories come with some sort of lesson. What's the lesson of this one?"

Boon had sat so still and silent that she almost thought he hadn't heard her. Then he took a deep breath, looked at her, and grinned wide enough to show wine-stained teeth.

"That knowledge comes with a price."

Water lapped gently against the side of the porcelain bathtub, spirals of steam lifting the scent of rose from the surface. Amaya leaned back and watched those ghostly tendrils and their lazy movement, not quite seeing, not quite feeling.

Her mind was a labyrinth of nightmares. Zharo's death-glazed eyes. Melchor's bloody chest. The last hug Roach had ever given her. Boon's story of child-eating demons. The feeling of Cayo Mercado's heart under her hand.

If only she had reached in and squeezed it to pulp. Then she wouldn't have to worry about him; she wouldn't keep touching her lips and remembering the shape of his.

Liesl entered the bathing room with a soft knock. As soon as Amaya stumbled into the estate, Liesl had practically screamed at her condition: wet, bedraggled, mud-stained, shivering with cold and shock. The Water Bugs had gathered curiously, looking on in amusement and confusion as Liesl had shepherded Amaya upstairs, grumbling at her recklessness.

"I don't know how many times it needs to be said," Liesl had growled as she none too gently helped Amaya out of her soaked and torn clothing, "but you need to remember that you are a *countess*. And countesses don't run around in the mud and muck!"

Amaya had stayed silent, not even daring to tell her about Cayo. It still felt too close to her, a secret that could tear the world apart if she so much as whispered it aloud.

Liesl now came to sit on the stool by the tub, removing her fogged-up glasses to wipe them on her skirt. When she replaced them, Amaya noticed the look on her face wasn't disapproval but rather trepidation.

"There's been some news," the girl said. "The Prince of Moray has succumbed to ash fever. He's dead."

Amaya frowned. Her first thought was, *Who cares? That means nothing to me.* But then she remembered the Bugs talking in the kitchen, about how the tension between the empires was escalating again, with Moray sitting helpless between them. A pawn ripe for the taking.

If the ruling figurehead of Moray was gone, with no successors or replacement chosen, what did that mean for them? Was the treaty of neutrality dissolved?

"One of the empires might try to install a regent, or a governor," Liesl answered Amaya's unspoken question. "They both want access to Moray's waterways. They want a claim on the best trade routes. The city will be batted around like a mouse between a cat's paws."

Amaya took a deep breath of humid, rose-scented air. "We'll have to leave before that happens."

"I agree. Now get out of that water before you get wrinkles."

Liesl helped her into a robe. As soon as it was tied, the door pushed open to reveal Deadshot, a letter clenched in her fist.

"News," the girl gasped, shoving the letter at Liesl.

"Is it about the prince? I've already told Amaya—"

"No." Deadshot shook her head, pushing the letter into Liesl's hands. "Read it."

Liesl did so; her eyebrows lowered. Then they lifted in shock.

"Is this true?" she demanded. Deadshot nodded fervently.

"What is it?" Amaya clutched the front of her robe. "Are the empires already making a move?"

"No, it's . . ." Liesl's gaze strayed from the letter to Amaya, disbelieving. "It's Kamon Mercado. He's been arrested."

Amaya's knees weakened, and she sat heavily on the stool. Her head was full of fog. "On—on what charges?"

"The manufacture of counterfeit money."

Amaya withdrew into herself as Liesl and Deadshot speculated how this had come to pass, remembering Cayo's words about someone he cared for doing a bad thing. Asking her what he should do about it.

Cayo had turned in his own father.

It was exactly what Boon had wanted: turning the Mercados against one another, using the son to take down the father. Mercado's name was now ruined, his prospects destroyed. Whatever wealth he still possessed would be taken away, and Amaya and the others would divert it into their own pockets. She would have enough to send the Bugs home.

So then why didn't she feel victorious?

There was nothing but a hollow gnawing in her gut, in her heart. She realized it was because nothing had changed—all her questions had gone unanswered. She still didn't know why her mother had sold her. She didn't know why her father had had to die.

In all this time, she had not yet faced Mercado, but now she found she had no other choice.

In order to get the answers she craved, she would have to confront him. Not as Countess Yamaa, or even Silverfish, but as herself. Amaya, the girl who had helped plot his downfall and urged his son to betray him. If she didn't, she would never know the truth. She would forever be wrapped in falsehoods and lies.

She was the greatest counterfeit of all: a ragged girl masquerading in gowns she should never have been able to afford, the pieces of her sewn together like a patchwork doll.

Slowly she stood, gaining the attention of Liesl and Deadshot.

"I'm going to the Port's Authority tomorrow," she said. "And I'm going to end this."

Although the rain had stopped by early afternoon the following day, the sky was still bruised with clouds, the air heavy and thick. Almost as if it expected that change was coming.

The city seemed affected by it, the people talking in hushed voices and throwing uneasy glances over their shoulders. Mourning flags had been raised outside of homes and shops, white pennants and banners bearing the crest of Moray: a cutlass crossed with a rolled-up scroll.

Amaya wondered why they were mourning a man revealed to be a fraud when she remembered that the prince was dead. Now Moray felt like a held breath, a deep inhale before a plunge.

She noticed all this as she walked to the Business Sector, her boots splashing through puddles and her hair frizzing out of her braid from the humidity the storm had left in its wake. Liesl had tried her hardest to get Amaya to take a carriage, but she had refused.

"I can't go as Countess Yamaa," she had insisted. "I'll attract too much attention." And besides, she wanted to speak to Mercado without pretense, so he could see what had become of her.

"Fine," Liesl had sighed. "But Deadshot will be following behind, and I'll have Avi on standby just in case."

"I'm sure that won't be necessary."

"Don't let your guard down just because Mercado is behind bars," Liesl had warned her, eyes flashing. "This news on the heels of the prince's passing is going to throw an unexpected wrench in the gearwork of this city. Stay sharp."

Amaya was breathing harder by the time she reached the Port's Authority, but not from the walk; the more she imagined facing Mercado, the more her stomach shrank in on itself in a writhing, confusing mess. She had imagined this moment in many different ways—stealing through his window and putting a knife to his throat, confronting him at the docks, walking into Mercado Manor beside Cayo. Never like this, in broad daylight, with bars separating them.

But when she asked the receptionist at the front about visitation, she only received an odd look and was told to sit on a bench and wait.

She sat there for nearly half an hour, her legs jogging with nerves, until the doors opened and an officer stepped out.

"Mercado?" he repeated when she told him her reason for being there. "He was released this morning."

The floor tilted beneath her. "*What?* Why?"

"Not enough evidence yet to prove anything. The case is still open, though. If he really is guilty, we'll bring him back in."

"But he could escape the city! He could cover all his tracks and—"

"Miss, this really isn't the time or place," the officer said, glancing at the folks still waiting on the benches, listening in. "The city is in mourning. Once things calm down a little, we'll be picking up where we left off."

Amaya couldn't believe what she was hearing. She turned on her heel and stormed out, fingernails driving into her palms. All her work, for nothing. Mercado had still slipped free, and she still had no answers.

Damn it. Damn him.

She wasn't going to let this go. She was going to play out one of her fantasies after all: barge into Mercado's house and use that as her battleground, the stage for the revenge her blood cried for.

Before she could even reach the end of the street, a familiar figure barreled around the corner and nearly ran into her. Avi, out of breath and shimmering with sweat, grabbed her arms.

"Mercado," he gasped out. "He's been released."

"I know," she growled, ripping out of his hold. "I'm about to break down the door of his house."

"He's not there. Liesl—she found out—he's at the Vaults," he panted. He must have run straight here from the estate. Deadshot trotted up to them from where she had been stationed on the street. "The Widow Vaults."

She frowned. "Why would he go there?"

He wiped the sweat from his brow with a shaking hand. "There's a Vault he's been trying to buy for years. The statute of limitations for its heir to claim it ended today."

"So?"

Avi exchanged a look with Deadshot, whose hand rested on one of her pistols.

"The Vault belonged to Arun Chandra," he said.

Her ears roared. She was running before she could fully process what he'd said, the other two calling after her.

Arun Chandra.

How had she not known that her father owned a Vault? Why did he even *have* a Vault? He had died penniless, in debt to Mercado!

She found the familiar building and raced up the stairs, still slick with rain. Stumbling through the open front doors, she looked around for some sign of Mercado, unsure what she would do once she saw him but knowing that she had to face him.

"Can I help you, miss?" asked a startled guard by the doors.

"The Vaults," she gasped. "Where are they?"

He pointed to a marble staircase leading down to an underground floor. She sprinted for it, ignoring his call asking if she was all right.

Amaya nearly fell down the last few steps, gripping the banister before she could break her neck. She barely even noticed that it was colder down here, the walls made of limestone and the floors shining marble. Her boots squeaked as she hurried down the corridor, passing wide, gleaming metal doors that had been painted gold.

The sound of crashing echoed down a nearby corridor, and she turned the corner to find one of the Vault doors thrown open, a collection of papers and junk piled in the hall. Men were hauling it out from the Vault and placing it into stacks. They didn't notice her creep closer, eyeing the things they were handling so roughly.

Her father's things. Hers to inherit, by birthright.

It didn't amount to much. Just some old furniture, most of which she recognized from her home, and papers. So many papers and files and ledgers, stacks and stacks of them.

Amaya knelt and grabbed the nearest file, flipping through it quickly while the men went to grab their next armfuls. It contained reports and transaction receipts and handwritten notes, some in her father's hand, some not.

She stopped when she saw the name Jun Salvador. The Slum King.

Cold washed over her. Individually, the papers didn't make sense, but together they painted a terrible picture: Kamon Mercado had been, or perhaps still was, in business with the Slum King. The file contained various accounts of their dealings within the Vice Sector, from Mercado liquidating gambling dens that were taking profit away from the Scarlet Arc to the Slum King supplying thieves to hit Mercado's biggest competitors.

The most recent transaction was dated the year of her father's death. He had scrawled a note over it that read:

Thousands from Mercado to Salvador for use in the Arc. Fake coins. Distribution?

Amaya's teeth chattered as she stared at the note, then at the mountains of paper before her.

Blackmail. All of it. Her father had been gathering it for years, all to take Mercado down and expose him for who he truly was.

And Mercado had killed him for it. Not because Arun couldn't repay a loan, but because of the havoc that would be unleashed with this information.

The men's voices snapped her out of her thoughts. She stood, only slightly comforted by the weight of the knife at her wrist.

Then she walked into the Vault.

She recognized him not because he looked like Cayo, but because of the way he stood, the arrogance of his expression and the indifferent crossing of his arms. Cayo had the same dark, teardrop-shaped eyes as Kamon, but that was where the similarities ended; Kamon's hair was deep brown, not black, and his features were broader.

He was directing his men with words only, not bothering to lift a finger to help. When he saw her, though, his arms dropped and his carefully blank face folded into a frown.

"What are you doing here?" he demanded.

He said it as if he knew her, as if she were a pest he couldn't get rid of. Amaya stood her ground and forced herself not to flinch, to look her father's murderer in the eye. Her blood ran hot, itching under her skin.

"Because you weren't where you were supposed to be," she growled. "In a cell."

One careful eyebrow rose. "They released me because there's no substantial evidence."

"That they know of," she countered, lifting the file she'd taken. "Now I have all the proof I need to show the city who you really are."

"We seem to have fallen into quite the predicament," he said, signaling his confused men to wait outside, "as I could say the same of you, *Countess*."

Amaya swallowed her gasp and fisted her free hand, the other holding tighter to the file.

"I don't know what you mean," she lied.

He laughed. It was an unnervingly attractive laugh, all low and controlled, meant for dinner parties and soirees.

"Countess Yamaa," he murmured to himself. "I doubt Yamaa is even your real name. When my son began to take an interest in you, I made sure to do my research, and guess what I found? Nothing. Absolutely nothing. Countess Yamaa only came into being a little over a month ago, when she docked in Moray. Before then, she may as well have not existed."

Amaya tried to swallow. She and the other Landless had worried about being found out, recognizing that they only had a certain amount of time before it became an inevitability. Still, to have it happen now, falling from the mouth of her enemy, sent thorns of panic tangling around her spine.

"A fake name, a fake reputation, and I'd even wager fake wealth," Mercado went on. "My dear, the only counterfeit you should be worried about is yourself."

She bared her teeth at him. "What do you mean, fake wealth?" She didn't bother to try to lie—it would have been pointless.

He shook his head, almost as if in pity. "It was a good job, I must admit, to have lasted this long. The coins are barely distinguishable from the real thing." His eyes gleamed with sudden intent. "Tell me, who are you working with?"

"I don't . . ."

"Whoever they are, I can offer you protection from them. But only if you give me a name."

She stared at him blankly. What was he even talking about? She had hoped to enter this arena on even playing ground, but everything Mercado said was tripping her and making her stumble.

"You're . . . just trying to evade blame," she said. "To pin your crimes on others, like you've always done."

"Am I?" he said softly. "Or are you choosing to ignore the truth? Whoever this person is, you must have been working with them for some time. You must have had *some* indication of what they were doing."

Even as she opened her mouth to insist she had no idea what he meant, she thought back to the barrels of gold in the Landless comm, the unexplainable wealth at Boon's fingertips. She had never been able to figure out how such riches were possible for a Landless man with nothing else to his name, and though she'd asked, she had never been given a straight answer.

Horror bloomed in her gut. Seeing it spread across her face, Mercado smiled coldly.

It couldn't be true . . . and yet, she realized, it must be. The last several months blurred together in her mind: Boon teaching her a move to take down an enemy, laughing at the extraordinary amount of frill on one of her dresses, betting her a handful of gold she couldn't steal a woman's parasol.

Boon luring her to work for him, how easily he had manipulated her the same way he did all his victims.

She had constantly told herself not to trust him, not to let her guard down so easily around him. And yet, she had. She had somehow convinced herself that this man, who had sat before a fire and told her the story of the siege of Gravaen, was more than just a drunken thief. He was a fellow countryman who had been scorned and spat on, who craved vengeance as much as she did.

He was someone that an orphan like herself could latch on to for protection.

But this . . . this was not protection. This was throwing her into a pit of vipers armed with nothing but lies.

Knowledge comes with a price.

She dropped the file, its papers spreading out in a fan. Mercado fashioned his expression into one of false sympathy.

"I understand the difficult position you've been put in," he said in that calm, measured voice. "As I said, if you just give me a name, I can help you. Not only for justice, but because I know my son cares for you."

Amaya felt her heartbeat in her jaw. She remained silent, although she couldn't understand why. If Boon had tricked her, as she had always known he was capable of doing, then why did she continue to protect him?

And why did she feel so *hurt*?

She couldn't answer him, didn't know how. Instead she looked down at the scattered papers, moving her dry tongue until she could speak again. "These files . . . How did you know they were in this Vault? Is that why you hate the man who owned it?"

He seemed surprised by the subject change. "One could say that. The man who owned this Vault was a villain. A criminal, and a thief, and a liar of the highest order who did his absolute best to slander my name and take down my family. He was the sort of man who wouldn't hesitate to take his life and abandon his own family rather than face punishment for his crimes."

Boon's words from the *Brackish* came creeping back: *Every man carries his sins a different way.*

"He wasn't a criminal!" she shouted before she could stop herself, her voice ringing off the metal of the Vault. "And he didn't take his own life, you *killed him!*"

The silence that fell was dense with shock. Amaya was unable to look away from Mercado, and likewise, he seemed morbidly fascinated by her, slowly putting together the puzzle pieces in his mind.

"I see," he said at last, soft and sneering. "Good luck proving that, 'Countess.' I may have had to do that eventually, just to shut him up. But in the end, I didn't need to." He approached her, his polished shoes stepping over the years' worth of blackmail her father had curated. "You believe your father was murdered? You might want to double-check with whoever told you that was true, because they're lying. In fact, they probably know how your father truly died." He leaned in closer, his cologne smelling of ambergris, a weak imitation of the sea. "They're probably the one who killed him."

Amaya couldn't move. She was shaking, unable to withdraw the knife at her wrist. He was so close, all she had to do was thrust up. . . . But then Melchor's face swam across her vision, the sickly sound of her blade in his flesh.

She thought of what Cayo would say if he saw his father's blood on her hands.

Mercado was behind all of this—he *had* to be—but a quiet voice in her mind reminded her how much information Boon possessed, and how much he had not disclosed to her. He had orchestrated all of this. He had known her father, and Mercado, too.

Everything she had done up till now had been at his direction, his insistence.

Because he had been using her to play a long con.

All the fury, all the resentment, all the hatred she felt for the man before her shifted like a sail in the wind toward Boon.

Mercado bent down to pick up the fallen papers. Tucking the file under his arm, he gave her another thin, unfeeling smile, knowing he had won.

Amaya took a step back, then another. She was being pulled apart, twisted in opposite directions.

What was she supposed to do?

She did the only thing she *could* do: She turned and ran.

"My offer still stands," he called after her. "A name for your clemency!"

Liar, he was a *liar*; he had killed her father and sold her to Captain Zharo and destroyed her family.

But she didn't know him, and she didn't know Boon, either. She didn't know anything.

She was at the bottom of the dark ocean, under the crushing weight of water, with no way to tell if she was swimming up or down.

24

You could ask any man on the street what the sweetest things in life are,

and he will surely respond in threes: wine, women, and winning.

Little do they suspect these things come with bitter edges.

—*A HUNDRED AND ONE VICES FOR THE EVERYMAN*

Cayo never went home.

A feverlike fear gripped him as soon as he left the Port's Authority, leaving him shaking and sweating. The carriage driver had taken off, as Cayo had only enough money for the single trip, but the rain had lightened considerably during his couple of hours spent with Nawarak and the rest of the officers assigned to the case.

They had asked him questions in a tone that made him feel as if he were the criminal mastermind. They had asked where he'd found the chest, when the gold coating had dissolved and by what means, if he knew of any other caches in the city.

He had provided them what little information he could. He had done what was right. What Yamaa had given him courage to do.

But now all that courage had drained out of him at the thought of returning to the manor, of facing his sister and his father, waiting for the Port's Authority to come bang on their door and drag Kamon Mercado away.

No. He couldn't go home. Not yet.

So he walked. The Business Sector faded away in muted blues and grays, the rare sparkle of gold winking in his eyes and refracted in raindrops. The district had never been his favorite; it was too foreign, too precise, a contributor to the misconception that Moray was all gilt and glamour.

Before he was fully aware of it, his feet had led him to the outskirts of the Vice Sector. The gray clouds grew dark as night approached, like tea steeping in water, and glass lanterns were lit as excited patrons rushed to Diamond Street with their hoods pulled up or carrying umbrellas of colored silk.

Cayo's heart leaped, his fingertips buzzing. Although he was damp from the rain, his mouth was paper-dry, and the thought of sipping on something that would warm his chest and burn away his fear created a monstrous longing in him.

It was a longing similar to the ache he'd felt before kissing Yamaa, like nothing else in the world mattered other than slaking that bone-crushing desire.

He stumbled into the bowels of the Vice Sector, letting it clamp its vicious arms around him, welcoming him home.

He had only meant to lie low, to grab a drink and nurse it slowly while he watched others play. He chose to go to the Lusty Kraken off Diamond Street, a den known for its lively band and lighthearted atmosphere. They played some of his least favorite games here: Midshipman, Tempest, Seven Fronds.

Less temptation, he hoped.

Ordering a drink of gin stained blue with a splash of butterfly pea tea, Cayo joined the onlookers at a table where the dealer was soundly beating the other players. He sipped and closed his eyes, letting the sounds of the den wash over him like a balm, the sting and velvet of the drink loosening his limbs.

That is, until he heard his name called from across the room.

He spun around and found Tomjen and the Akara twins coming at him, beaming. Tomjen wrapped him up in a hug of long, messy arms and pointy elbows, and Cayo grunted while trying not to spill his drink.

"Stop making us think you've died!" his friend cried, gaining the attention of the nearest onlookers.

Cayo's face heated as he pulled the three of them toward a corner. So much for lying low. "And stop jumping to the assumption that everyone you haven't heard from is dead."

"Well, can you blame us?" one of the twins, Chailai, said. "What with this awful sickness going around."

Cayo's stomach clenched at the reminder that Soria was at home, waiting for him or his father to return. But Narin would be with her; he would make sure she took her dose of medicine before bed.

He forced himself to take a deep breath. "I'm not planning on staying long. I just wanted to"—he gestured at the den, the band setting up their instruments for a long night of music and dancing— "get away for a bit."

"To piss with that!" Tomjen said. "What you need is a good, healthy dose of fun."

"We're hopping around tonight," said the other twin, Bero. "We have the whole night planned out."

"Join us," Chailai pleaded, pulling on his arm.

Cayo stared at them, stared at the smiles of the patrons around them. His heart was sore from longing, the buzzing at his fingertips traveling up his arms and gripping his shoulders possessively.

Since he couldn't go home anyway . . .

He downed the rest of his drink in one go, and his friends raised a victorious cheer.

"Where to next?" he asked.

They visited the Ferrier, where Tomjen bought them three rounds of shots. Cayo barely thought as he flung his back, the routine having settled into muscle memory. The alcohol momentarily numbed his tongue and burned down his throat, and he laughed at the sensation of it, the giddiness of knowing that his belly would warm and his head would lighten. That his fear would dissolve like gold paint in a glass of wine.

Everything was wrong. But here, in this moment, there was something that felt *right*.

The twins urged him to get in on a game of Threefold, but Cayo hung back, still hesitant. The buzzing was everywhere now, rattling his bones and making his teeth ache.

"Just one game," they wheedled. "One!"

Finally, he relented to more cheers and Tomjen squeezing his shoulders with an encouraging shake. Cayo slid onto a stool and grinned at the dealer, a young woman with black skin and a brilliant, flashing smile.

"You look hungry," she said in a rich alto voice.

Cayo scooped up his cards with a practiced hand. "Starving."

Even while tipsy he knew which cards were throwaways and which would bring him fortune. They were imprinted onto his mind, scratched onto his skin like ink. Cayo dropped a hand that resulted in an effortless win, and Tomjen and the others screamed at his back, jumping up and down.

"Next round on Cayo!"

He gradually lost his sense of direction. He allowed them to pull him onward, into a wine bar where Tomjen nearly got into a fight with a man twice his size, through a street packed with half-dressed callers who whistled as he went by, and eventually into a casino that Cayo recognized as the Grand Mariner.

"You're back," said the dealer with the curly hair, the one he'd always been sweet on. They sounded happy, and that made Cayo happy, because finally there was someone who was glad to see him, someone he hadn't disappointed yet.

"I've been away on business," Cayo slurred, nearly falling in his attempt to sit at the Scatterjack table. "Top secret." He put a finger to his lips, but it landed more on his nose.

The dealer laughed and dealt the cards, only one other person joining them for the game. "Sounds exciting. Want to tell me about it?"

Cayo made up a mess of a story about sailing the Southerly Sea, how he'd wrestled a squid and rode a whale to an underwater kingdom. The other player kept glancing at him in irritation. Then Cayo won, and the other player huffed before stalking off. Cayo ordered another drink.

"Might want to take it easy," the dealer warned him.

"I've been taking it easy for forever," Cayo mumbled as other bettors filled the seats beside him. "But nothing is easy. Nothing, nothing."

He won that round, and the next. Where were Tomjen and the twins? He took a drag of someone's cigarillo, but he wasn't sure whose. His mouth tasted of pomegranates and smoke.

And then he lost, most of his winnings pushed to the far side of the table where a man had played his victorious hand.

"Wait," Cayo said, unsure what had happened. "That's my money."

"That's what you put on the table," the dealer said, watching him with concern. "Maybe you should choose a different game? Or call it a night?"

"No." He pushed a handful of coins forward, wondering what would happen if he upended his drink over the tiny mound of gold. Would they turn black? "I'll win it back."

The dealer sighed and kept going. Cayo lost the next round. And the next. His coins dwindled, and his glass was empty.

"What did you *do* to these cards?" Cayo demanded, the bite of anger in his voice.

"I can assure you, they're not tampered with."

"I'm not supposed to lose!" He lumbered to his feet, swaying. "Don't you know the constellation I was born under? *Luck!* I'm the king of luck! I'm unstoppable!"

"Sir—"

"There you are!" The twins took him by the arms, they and Tomjen steering him out of the casino. "C'mon, let's go somewhere less crowded."

Cayo lifted his face to the drizzle of rain outside, laughing in delight at the simple pleasure of it, his anger forgotten. Who cared about money? He was feeling good, and he wanted to keep feeling good, because once he stopped then the bad things would come and devour him again.

"Don't let them eat me," he murmured to his friends, but they didn't hear him over their own chatter.

He didn't know where they went next. It was dark, cast only in a dim red light that reflected in the liquor bottles along the back wall and shone weakly through the haze of jaaga smoke. The people dancing in the center were a shadowy mass of limbs, and the air carried the tang of sweat and fermented things.

One of the twins danced with him, then he was getting another drink. The room was spinning funnily, his feet on backward. The entire world had shrunk to this one spot where he stood, laughing at nothing and everything.

Then he was leaning against the wall, a young man before him. He was handsome, with light brown hair and jet-colored eyes. When he smiled, it plucked a chord in Cayo's stomach.

The young man said something, and Cayo responded, but he could barely hear or understand the words. The young man's arm rested beside him against the wall, trapping him.

Lips found his. The young man kissed him, swiping his tongue through his mouth. Cayo hummed in surprise, his lips mostly numb but still feeling how they reacted, how he kissed him back because that was what he was supposed to do, wasn't it?

And then something was in his mouth. The young man pressed a tablet to his cheek using his tongue, and Cayo felt the scythe of his smile against him.

Cayo mumbled a question, panic only a thin trickle in his bloodstream. The young man laughed and patted his cheek.

The tablet dissolved quickly, even as he doubled over and tried to spit it out, only making a mess as saliva dribbled down his chin. It left a medicinal taste in his mouth, his tongue tingling as it already began to take effect.

Tomjen. He had to find Tomjen. Colors surrounded him, noises he couldn't discern. Someone swept him up into a dance. There was a mouth at his neck, biting. Hands rummaging through his pockets. Laughter in his ear and rumbling in his chest.

He couldn't feel his body. He couldn't maintain a single thought.

It was oblivion. It was peace.

He was woken with a swift kick to the sternum.

Choking, Cayo turned over and vomited, all the excess of the night rushing out of him at once.

"Attractive," drawled a familiar voice above him.

His stomach sore from contracting, Cayo pushed himself away from his sick and coughed, face screwed up in disgust. There was a terrible ringing in his head that sent an ache down his neck and shoulders, and he was fairly certain the taste crouched on the back of his tongue was that of death.

"No, by all means, take your time. I've got all day to watch you writhe around like a worm."

"Shut up," he mumbled around coughs. He could barely open his eyes without sending a stabbing pain through his skull. Moaning, he felt around for something to grab hold of and encountered a wall. He shifted backward until he could lean against it, wanting nothing so much as to curl up and die.

When he could finally keep his eyes open longer than a second, he blinked as they watered and tried to make sense of his surroundings. He was in a kennel, in the back of an empty dog pen. The sounds of scratching and whining and barking surrounded him, and the strong odor of wet fur and dried urine almost made him vomit again.

Before him stood Romara, hands on her hips and a glare leveled down at him.

"What in the hells," he groaned, rubbing his face.

"I should be asking you that. What happened to you last night, puppy?"

"I . . . Shit. I don't know." It was all fragmented, like light off a crystal. He could only remember certain images, certain words. "I was drinking."

"That's apparent," Romara said with an indelicate snort. "Probably more than just drinking, too."

"No, I—" It emerged through the fog then. He'd been drugged. "Someone slipped me something." No wonder he felt so terrible, like his limbs would pop off if he moved wrong.

Romara cursed and crossed her arms over her chest. She wasn't wearing a dress today, but rather tight red hose and a black, high-collared Rehanese tunic.

"You know better than to get yourself in a situation like that," she said. "What were you thinking?"

"That's the thing," he murmured, squinting at the nearest window to gauge the time of day. The light was gray yet bright, either late morning or early afternoon. "I didn't want to think."

Rolling her eyes, Romara stepped forward and helped him up.

Their movement prompted the curiosity of the nearest dogs, who barked playfully. The sound sent peals of pain through Cayo's head, and Romara snapped at them with a command to be quiet.

He shuffled after her out of the kennel, across a damp alleyway, and into the back of the Scarlet Arc. The dogs must have belonged to Salvador, then. But any fear of running into the man was absent, likely because the thought of a swift death at the man's hands was oddly comforting.

Romara led him up a flight of stairs near the kitchen, to the place where she and her father lived. It was surprisingly modest, with touches of Rehanese art on the walls. Cayo felt like an intruder, like his presence here was a strangely intimate experience.

"Go wash," Romara ordered, pointing to the bathing room. "There's some clothes in there for you."

"Wait. What happened to my friends?"

She shrugged, looking irritable. "Does it matter? You must have gotten separated from them somehow. I found you last night stumbling around near the Gauntlet, babbling to yourself. You didn't even recognize me."

Cayo winced with embarrassment. "I'm sorry."

"Yeah, I'm sorry, too, now that you smell like dog." She pointed again. *"Wash."*

The tub was half-filled with lukewarm water. Romara had prepared it for him, had likely been ready to drag him here if she needed to. Cayo felt an unexpected surge of gratitude toward her, even if she was one of the many people determined to ruin his life.

He scrubbed away the dirt and grime from the night, hoping to wash his shame along with it. Dried and dressed in clean clothes that were slightly too big for him—hells, did they belong to the

Slum King?—he sheepishly shuffled into the main sitting room.

Romara was drinking a cup of black coffee and staring out the window at the street below. She saw him, gestured to the pot of coffee in a silent invitation to help himself, and continued her observation. Cayo was thankful to taste something strong and bitter to wash away the horrible staleness in his mouth.

As soon as he sat on the chair across from her chaise, she turned to him. "Well," she said flatly, "congratulations. You've ruined everything."

Cayo blinked. "What?"

"Don't play ignorant. We heard about the warrant for your father's arrest. I did some digging this morning and found out that you had a hand to play in it." She leaned forward, slamming her empty cup on the low table between them. "Now my father wants nothing to do with you or your messed-up family. In fact, in all his raving and ranting he may have mentioned something about sending his goons after you, to teach you a lesson like he taught Sébastien."

The center of Cayo's chest went cold. He imagined his eyes floating in a jar next to Bas's.

"He . . ." Cayo looked around, as if the Slum King were about to materialize from the walls. "He knows I'm here?"

"No, he's out all day visiting contacts to erase the trail. If I'd known this last night, I wouldn't have even bothered dragging you into the kennels. It would have been better for everyone if you'd just died of exposure."

Cayo leaned back with a sigh and closed his eyes. "I had to do it, Romara. He's the one behind the counterfeit."

"So's my father, but you don't see me marching to the Port's Authority!"

His eyes snapped open. "What?"

"You were right, to a degree." She crossed her legs and stared him down. "About him being involved in the counterfeit. I dragged it out of him this morning. Your father provides the coins, and mine is responsible for distributing them throughout the casinos in the Vice Sector, like the Arc. They've been in business together for years, apparently."

He felt as if the air had been knocked out of him. Kamon Mercado and the Slum King—business partners.

All this time, and he'd had no idea.

"I suppose this'll make it easier to break the news of the engagement to your dear old daddy," she said with a twist to her mouth.

"Engage— I thought your father wants me dead?"

"That was just him being cranky. I convinced him to let me keep you." As if he really were a puppy, or some trivial possession. "In fact, he's agreed to speed up the wedding date to next month instead of next year."

"Hold on . . ." Cayo held his aching head in his hands. His thoughts were sluggish, struggling to keep up. "How were you even able to do that? I thought that with my father in custody, he didn't want to have anything to do with my family?"

"Ah, but your father's not in custody anymore. He was released early this morning, thanks to a generous donation by Jun Salvador."

Broken. This whole city was broken.

And if his father was free, that meant there would be repercussions waiting when he returned home.

Home. Soria was no doubt worried about him. He had to go and see her, and try to avoid his father, if he could.

"This will be a good thing, Cayo," Romara said. "Together, you and I could be powerful enough to run this city. Especially now, with the prince out of the picture."

"What are you talking about?"

"He died last night, from ash fever." She leaned forward, eyes glittering. "Moray is poised on a knife's edge, Cayo. It's ready for change. *We* could be that change."

His head swimming with the news, Cayo decided that Romara was a lot scarier when she was sober. He dragged a hand through his wet hair and shook his head.

"Romara . . . I can't marry you. My life is in shambles. My father will very likely disown me. If it weren't for my sister, I would have probably left Moray by now." *Like Bas.*

Her head snapped back slightly, as if dodging a slap. "Are you serious, Cayo? You're *this* close to achieving power, and you just don't care?"

"I don't care," he agreed. "I just want to be left alone. And I want my sister to live."

Romara looked at him as one looks at a bug, unimpressed and having no clue how he'd gotten into the house. Sighing, she rubbed the space between her eyes with a knuckle.

"You really try my patience, Cayo," she said. "You know what? Fine. I can let you out of this engagement, but considering you need to repay the price of my dowry, it'll cost you something."

"Of course it will cost me." He sighed. "What do you want?"

"The recipe for the counterfeit. Is it a type of paint? Is it alchemy? If you can get it from your father, I'll tell mine to leave you alone, to cut you free."

Then he would just be making the situation worse. There was no way to tell how much of the counterfeit had already spread across the city; with Romara at the helm of the operation, how much more would be dispersed? The economy would go under. They would be ripe for the picking for either of the empires.

"Come on," Romara purred with a suggestive smile. "Isn't there something you're still willing to live for? Something you'd be willing to stay in Moray for?"

His thoughts flitted to the countess, to the feeling of her lips on his. Her demeanor like salt water and steel, the conviction and mystery that surrounded her like layers of a dress. He wanted to slowly peel them away, to find the heart of the girl buried underneath.

Cayo's shoulders slumped as he said, "I'll see what I can do."

"There's a good puppy. Now get out before you start tossing up your stomach again."

He stood, resigned, and was halfway to the door when she called him back. She walked to him with something held fast in her hand. When she pressed it against his palm, he could only stare down at it in confusion.

It was a black disc, just like the one Bas had given him. Like the ones he'd used as evidence against his father.

"Where did you find this?" he asked.

Romara's smile showed her teeth. "Your countess."

Startled, Cayo couldn't even muster the words to reply. He only slipped it into the pocket of his borrowed trousers and grabbed his coat on his way to the door, heart racing.

Had Yamaa managed to get caught in the counterfeit scheme, too? Was she one of the many victims of his father's ploy? He could barely think as he weaved through the city streets, head down, eyes on the ground. Everything *hurt*. He had to stop to throw up again, battling the urge to just lie down until his body felt substantial.

Climbing the hill to Mercado Manor was torture. He finished it on hands and knees, doused in sweat and shaking with exhaustion. Pushing himself to his feet, he stumbled toward the doors, his need for water and a bed just barely eclipsing his fear of his father.

But when he walked into the manor, the back of his neck prickled. He stood there a moment, wondering at this odd feeling, until he realized that Narin wasn't there to greet him like he normally was.

The footman was likely taking care of Soria. Cayo slowly climbed the stairs, the air around him unnervingly still, his skin gone taut from apprehension. Any moment, Kamon would round the corner and spot him. He just had to make it to his room first. He had to send a message to Yamaa that he had to see her, to warn her about the counterfeit before it was too late.

He smelled him before he saw him—the scent of seawater and an unwashed body. Pushing open the door to his bedroom, Cayo walked in and froze, unable to make sense of the man waiting there for him.

The man was Kharian, his skin brown and weathered from a life on the sea. He was stocky and middle-aged, his black hair shaggy and unkempt, his clothes torn and ragged for all they looked like they had cost a bit of coin. Upon seeing him, the man nodded in solemn greeting.

"Cayo Mercado," he said, his voice gruff. He made a series of clicking noises with his tongue.

"Who are you? What are you doing here?"

"I'm here to settle a debt."

A scream echoed down the hall from Soria's room. As Cayo turned to run to her, figures hiding in the shadows jumped forward and knocked him to the ground. He yelled and tried to fight back, but his body was weak and his head was spinning. The masked figures yanked his arms behind his back and lashed his wrists together, then stuffed a gag in his mouth when he kept calling Soria's name.

He was yanked up onto his knees, swaying woozily. The Kharian man stood before him, hands behind his back. The man's head twitched once, twice.

"Don't worry, we won't hurt her," he said, but in that rough, gravelly voice, it was difficult to believe. "Or you, for that matter. We're only using the two of you as leverage, see? Mercado'll want his precious heirs back."

Cayo tried to scowl at him around the gag. Little did this man know that his father was already willing to let one of them die.

But the Kharian man interpreted his look a different way. "It's simple," he said, spreading his callused hands. One of them held a tremor. "As soon as he reinstates my good name, you'll be free to go. I'll no longer be Landless, and he gets his darlin' children back."

Cayo breathed heavily around the gag. There had to be a way to warn someone—Yamaa, Romara, *someone*—but the man only grinned at him with stained teeth, as if he knew as well as Cayo did that there was no escaping this.

"Let's go check on your sister, huh?" The man walked by and patted his head like a dog. "This'll all be over soon."

25

SOLAS: A crow's caw. Either the gods laugh at us,

or they warn of ruin.

—*THE MERCHANT'S WORTH*, A PLAY FROM THE RAIN EMPIRE

*Y*ou *might want to double-check with whoever told you that was true,* Mercado had said, *because they're lying. In fact, they probably know how your father truly died. They're probably the one who killed him.*

Amaya had to stop and rest against the rough bark of a palm, barely able to take a full breath. Avi and Deadshot lingered behind her. They had been stopped from going down to the Vaults by Mercado's men, but when Amaya had burst out of the building, they had followed and tried to get her to tell them what had happened.

But she couldn't. The implication, the consequences . . .

Was Mercado right? Was Boon's money all counterfeit?

Did he know how her father truly died?

Wiping a sleeve against her eyes, she turned to the Landless. They regarded her warily, unsure if she would bite.

"We need to talk to Liesl," she said.

The estate loomed against the dark backdrop of the sky, the evening made of somber clouds. Although it had stopped storming, the air was still charged, raising the hairs along her arms and legs. She was a lightning rod prepared for the strike.

Or at least, she thought she was. She stopped before the double doors, staring at the lock that had been broken, the scratches and splinters surrounding it. The way the right door was open a crack, revealing a line of inky dark beyond.

The tension from Avi and Deadshot at her back made her shoulders tighten. She turned to look at them, to gauge if they had had anything to do with this. But Avi was ashen, and Deadshot already had two of her pistols out.

Amaya unsheathed her knife and pushed inside. The entryway was dark with shadow, the window on the left wall smashed open, gauzy curtains fanning out in the breeze. It was the only movement in a room full of destruction.

She inhaled a sharp breath. Pottery lay smashed on the marble floor, houseplants overturned and spilling dirt, the walls peppered with bullet holes.

And lying near the stairs . . .

"No," she whispered, rushing forward. She sank to her knees in the blood that had spread from Spider's body. He was on his back, his arms spread at awkward angles, staring lifelessly at the ceiling. A bullet wound marred his thin chest.

Spider. Only eleven years old, and yet he had never complained.

He had helped Cicada in the kitchens and had been teaching Fera how to swim.

Not Spider—his name was Nian. He was a boy named Nian who had been taken from his family, and now he was dead.

Avi joined her. He stared down at Nian, horror tightening his mouth. Deadshot raced past them, up the stairs. "Liesl!" she called, desperation cracking her voice. "Liesl, where are you?"

"What the fuck happened?" Avi asked hoarsely. "We were . . . We were *just* here. Who . . . ?"

But Amaya knew. The coldness within her thawed to simmering rage, and she gritted her teeth even as she kept staring at Nian, at all the possibilities of his future that had ended with his final breath.

"Silverfish!"

She whirled around. Weevil stood in the entrance to the kitchens, pale and shaking and eyes wide as coins. He sobbed and ran to her, grabbing her with scratched-up hands. She barely caught him, so stunned at the sudden burst of life when all around her screamed death.

"Matthieu," she whispered. "Matthieu, tell me what happened. Who did this? Where are the others?"

He hiccuped and wiped his face with trembling hands. "That man," he choked out. "The one from the ship."

The confirmation stoked her rage into a furnace. *Boon.* She would find him and rip him apart, feed his bones to the gulls.

"The others hid," Matthieu said, tugging her toward the kitchens.

She and Avi followed him inside. The pantry door was wide open, and inside lay Cricket's body, slumped against the shelves. Her blood flecked the jars and vegetables around her. Avi swore and Amaya felt herself grow distant, unable to properly digest what she was seeing.

She could not give in to grief now; it had to wait until this fire within her was extinguished.

Matthieu pulled open a segment of the floor, which Amaya guessed was used for storing root vegetables. It blended in so well that she hadn't even noticed it until the boards came apart, revealing the rest of the Bugs underneath.

"Thank the gods." Avi knelt to pull them out. Cicada helped him from below, lifting up the smaller Bugs, his face tight and blank with shock.

As soon as Fera was out, she scrambled to her feet and raced for the entryway. "Nian!" she called.

Amaya ran after her, but it was too late. The girl froze at the sight of his body, her own held stiff. Slowly, so as not to scare her further, Amaya crouched and wrapped her arms around the girl, rubbing her hands against the cold skin of Fera's arms.

"I'm sorry," Amaya whispered. "I wasn't here to protect you. I'm so sorry."

Deadshot reappeared at the top of the stairs. "Liesl!"

Amaya turned her head and saw the girl standing in the entryway, gaping at the scene before her. Her glasses were askew, the hem of her dress stained. Before she could say anything, Deadshot bounded to her and wrapped her up in her arms with a relieved cry.

Amaya stood but kept her hand on Fera's shoulder. Fera was still staring at Nian's body, her eyes glassy, uncomprehending.

"What happened here?" Amaya demanded. "Did you know this would happen?"

Liesl untangled herself from Deadshot and took a few staggering steps toward her, out of breath. She saw Nian and put a hand to her mouth.

"Answer me," Amaya growled.

Liesl lowered her hand and shook her head, tears shining in her eyes. "I didn't know. None of us did. I left the estate because I had word that Boon was in port, but he wasn't supposed to arrive yet, so I went out to get information." The tears fell from her eyes, and she heaved a shuddering breath. "This wasn't supposed to happen, Amaya. None of this was in his plan. He lied to us."

"Why is he here, then?" Avi asked as he left the kitchens. "His name hasn't been cleared yet."

Amaya thought back to her conversation with Mercado. "Because he has other business," she said. "He's behind a counterfeit scheme. All the money he told us to use? To distribute throughout the city? It's fake."

Liesl swore. "Of course it is. I should have known better."

"We need to leave Moray," Deadshot said. "If Boon is planning on ruining the city, then we have no further business with it."

"What about our cut of the money?" Avi demanded.

Amaya looked down at Fera, who had started to cry silently. Amaya wiped a tear away with her thumb, her insides twisting with guilt. She had wanted to protect them from Zharo, but was this much better?

"Cade," she called.

Cicada came to her, tall and silent, the oldest of the remaining Bugs.

"Come with me," she said. "Please."

The two of them went down to the cellar beneath the estate, where they had hauled in the chests full of Boon's gold. Amaya lit an oil lantern and examined the chests, unadorned and unassuming.

Cicada watched silently as Amaya went to the shelves of wine and selected a bottle at random. Opening a chest, she examined the contents for a moment, the coins gleaming in the lantern light.

Then she smashed the bottle against the side of the chest.

"What're you doing?" Cicada finally demanded.

"A test," she said.

He came closer, eyes fixed on the pile of coins now covered with wine. Amaya's breath turned shallow as she watched the coins, waiting to have the truth unveiled.

And then, after a couple of minutes, some of the coins began to turn black at their edges.

Amaya shut the lid of the chest and closed her eyes. A wound ripped open inside her, so sudden and painful that she had to clamp her teeth down around a scream.

"What . . . What does it mean?" Cicada asked.

She took a few deep breaths, trying not to remember the contempt in Mercado's voice. "This money is fake, but it should fool whoever you hand it to." She had been saving it for her takedown of Mercado, to potentially bribe the officers at the Port's Authority, but Boon's arrival had negated all her plans. "I want you to use whatever remains to get all the Water Bugs home. Will you do that for me?"

He looked toward the stairs. Above their heads, Amaya knew the other children had crowded together, crying at the sight of Nian. Cicada's dark locks swayed as he nodded.

"I'll do it for them," he said.

"Thank you. I want you all out of the city as soon as possible." She stood and squeezed his arm. "Keep them safe." *Because I couldn't.*

They returned upstairs and Cicada approached the children, speaking to them in his low, calm way. Amaya knelt and hugged Fera again, her heart splintering under the force of her mistakes. The girl barely reacted.

She had been so reckless to trust Boon. To let things get this far.

Amaya glanced at the Landless, who were quietly arguing about what to do next. She approached Matthieu, who was no longer crying but looked at her with bloodshot eyes. There was no reason for a child to look so haunted, she thought.

"The man who attacked you," she said softly. "Did you see where he went?"

The boy swallowed and shook his head, then paused. "I . . . I did hear him say something to the others who were with him, when we were hiding. Something about getting to a ship."

The spots where her knives lay against her body flared with promise.

Sometimes you can only see the way forward when all other options have failed you, her father had once told her.

She ran past the Landless, who called her name in confusion, and into the swelling night.

Revenge. It was a simple word hiding a bigger meaning, a layer of glitter over grit, a silk dress over a scarred and battered body. It was a word that pumped through her blood and set the stars on fire, and she wanted to rake her hands across the sky to grab them, to let them burn down everything in her path.

Even if she had to sacrifice the city, she would not allow Boon to get away.

It was late by the time she arrived at the docks, sneaking around its perimeter so that she wouldn't be spotted in the filmy moonlight that occasionally peeked out from the rolling clouds. There were no dockworkers at this time of night, which made the presence of a few shadowy figures all the more suspicious.

Amaya kept a knife in her hand as she slunk closer, trying to grab snippets of their conversation. They wore masks, and she would have bet her entire wardrobe that they were the rest of Boon's Landless crew, recruited to replace Avi, Deadshot, and Liesl. They were hauling crates up onto a small frigate bearing signs of battle damage, its hull scratched and a piece of its rail missing. It bore nondescript sails, in order to look as inconspicuous as possible. Boon had very likely stolen it.

As if the thought had summoned him, Boon appeared at the railing, calling something down to the Landless that was too soft for her to make out. The sight of him sent off a spark in her gut, and her hand tightened around her knife's hilt as her breathing grew uneven.

The best way to retaliate against pain is pain.

She would make him feel pain. She would return to him all he had done to her, payment for his lies and deceit.

But before she could rush toward the ship, a hand caught her arm. She whirled to find Avi there, a finger pressed to his lips. Liesl and Deadshot were behind him.

"We'll take care of the masked bastards," Avi whispered, nodding toward the dock. "You go get Boon."

Her brow furrowed. "Why are you helping me? Isn't he one of you?"

"He went back on his plan and abandoned us. He killed *children*. He's unstable, and he needs to be stopped."

She looked past him to the others, who nodded their resolution. Amaya's chest briefly tightened, suddenly thankful that she wasn't alone. Taking a deep breath, she nodded once and signaled them to go.

The three Landless slipped out before her. They were so silent that the others weren't aware of their presence until one turned and gave a warning cry, cut short with a gurgle as Avi slit his throat.

The dock seethed with fighting. Amaya used the distraction to run to the ship, avoiding flailing arms and waving weapons as she scurried up the gangplank, unsheathing a second knife in preparation.

It ended up saving her life. She felt and heard the whoosh of air by her head and only barely managed to block the downward swing of a short sword, its blade crossing between her two.

On the other end of the sword, Boon grinned down at her.

Amaya summoned her strength and pushed him and his weapon away, hopping backward to put more space between them. Boon idly swung the sword as he stared at her, his grin turning into a displeased frown as the sound of fighting rose to the deck of the frigate.

"I was hoping to avoid this, y'know," he said. "If you'd followed the plan, we could've all made a profit. Now everything's in pieces."

"What are you talking about?"

He pointed the sword's tip at her. "You betrayed me, girl. You let Mercado get into your father's Vault. You let him burn all the evidence that would've put him away for good!"

She shook her head slowly, heart racing. "You knew what was in my father's Vault? Why didn't you tell me?"

"Because you'd've gone and tried to open it for yourself!" He rushed at her, and she blocked again, grunting under the impact. "Don't lie and say you wouldn't have."

He was right, damn him.

"That doesn't mean I betrayed you," she growled, trembling

under their locked blades. "He had information I didn't!" She kicked the spot under his knee, but he seemed to have been anticipating it, for even as he stumbled he didn't buckle completely. It was enough for her to worm away again, backing up toward the railing as moonlight striped the deck with silver fingers.

"And you're one to talk," she panted. "All those chests filled with counterfeit coins. You were using me to spread them."

He barked a laugh, his head twitching a few times. "Surprised it took you this long to figure out."

"Why do it?" she demanded. "Any of this? Why couldn't you just leave Moray alone?"

"I told you," he growled. "Mercado—this city—took everything from me. My life means nothing until I can pay them back in kind."

"At what cost? At what point do we stop trading pain for more pain?"

"Don't get philosophical on me, girl," he said, twirling the sword again. "You won't like where it leads."

A sudden clatter made her turn her head. Her breath caught at the sight of the two people tied up on the far end of the deck, the rope around their middles pressing their backs together.

"Cayo!" she called. He was gagged and bound like his sister, but he had managed to knock over a barrel to grab Amaya's attention. His eyes were wide and pleading, his eyebrows drawn low in confusion at the scene unfolding before him.

She made to rush over to free them, but Boon got in her way and pushed her back. She deflected with her knives, aiming high then low, spinning to try to nick his shins. Ducking, weaving, feinting— those were the techniques he had built her training on. But he guessed all her moves and blocked them easily, always meeting her advances with an air of almost boredom.

Of course. He had trained her—he knew these moves because they were his own.

"That all you got in you?" he taunted.

"What are you doing with them? They're innocent, they're not involved in Mercado's schemes."

"It's called a ransom, girl. Mercado'll get his children back once he clears my name and pays me back what he owes me. I won't harm a hair on their pretty heads."

"Unlike the Water Bugs, right?" she countered, her voice wavering under the grief that suddenly gripped her. Her knees were still damp with Nian's blood. "You showed no hesitation killing them!"

His face shuttered into a darker expression. "The fellows I hired were a bit too eager, I'll admit." He cocked his head toward the continuous sounds of fighting, clicking his tongue. "Sounds like they're getting their due."

"That doesn't absolve you of anything. Their deaths are still your fault. And my father . . ."

They probably know how your father truly died. They're probably the one who killed him.

"Did you kill him?" she whispered. "Did you kill my father?"

Boon looked at her with a sobriety that she had never seen him show before. Even the tremor in his left hand seemed to grow still. His eyes were dark and unreadable, but there was something in the lines of his face that made her ache.

"In a sense," he said quietly, "I suppose I did."

Amaya's chest shook under the swelling of her lungs, her jaw clenched hard enough to ache. She launched herself at him, barely planning her attacks before she made them, hoping to throw him off course. He cursed when she got his forearm, a line of red welling from under his torn coat. But he countered expertly, driving her back and showing off moves he hadn't had time to teach her. He knocked one of her knives away and she reeled backward, falling over a crate and rolling into a crouch on the deck.

Boon approached her slowly, sword in hand. "Face it, girl," he said. "You're still too weak. You have too much of Silverfish in you."

Amaya grimaced, hatred hardening her heart. "The day we rescued you from drowning. Why were you there? Why did you have marigolds?"

Marigolds were the symbol of death and funerals in Khari. Who had Boon been mourning? Her father?

Boon almost wavered, genuinely surprised by the question. She waited for him to draw closer, crouched and ready to spring.

She had practiced what she would do if Captain Zharo ever went too far. With only a shucker or her hands as weapons, she had gone through the movements until she memorized them, hoping never to resort to using them.

It was the one move Boon hadn't yet seen.

"You wouldn't like the answer," Boon said at last.

"I already don't like anything you have to say." A few steps nearer. Amaya's fingers twitched. "What's one more transgression?"

"Trust me, you're not ready to hear it yet."

Once Boon was close enough, she jumped. She grabbed his blade in her bare hand and jammed her elbow into the crook of his arm, loosening his grip on the hilt. She tore away with the sword in her grasp and flipped it around to point it at him.

"You're wrong about me," she said, blood dripping from her

hand onto the deck. "Silverfish is dead, and you'll shortly follow."

Boon stared at her, a disbelieving smile crossing his craggy face. He barked that laugh of his and raised his hands as if in surrender.

"Point against me, I s'pose," he said.

The sound of a loud, muffled cough broke through the humid night air. Amaya looked to Soria at the same time Boon ran for the railing.

"No!" she screamed, chasing after.

But it was too late—he jumped over the railing and dived into the water with a splash, leaving her with no other choice than to prepare to jump in after him.

Then Soria coughed again, a great heaving sound that struck Amaya with the fear that she was dying. Amaya hesitated for only a second before swearing and dropping the short sword, rushing toward Cayo and his sister.

She used her knife to hack through their bindings and tore the gag out of Soria's mouth. The girl doubled over, shaking and coughing so hard that her entire body convulsed. Blood splattered over her lips and onto the floorboards.

Cayo wrenched his gag away, his mouth red and raw underneath. "Soria!" He knelt beside her, curving his body over hers as if that was all it took to protect her. "Soria, hold on, we'll get you out of here."

"She needs a doctor," said Liesl. The three Landless had climbed onto the deck, a bit bloodied but otherwise all right.

"Boon escaped," Amaya told them.

Avi nodded and ran off, and Amaya hoped he could track him down. But in the dark, she knew it would be all too easy for the man to slip away.

She had missed her chance.

Turning, she met Cayo's gaze. He was looking at her as if he didn't know her, as if he had no idea what to make of her.

And really, she thought, he *didn't* know her. Not yet.

Cayo roused himself and turned to Liesl. "My sister has ash fever. No doctor in Moray can help with this."

"What about a doctor somewhere else?"

Deadshot turned at the new voice, pistol ready, but Amaya flung out a hand to stop her.

That voice . . .

It can't be.

Amaya scrambled to her feet and took a few faltering steps toward the bow of the ship, where a young, lanky man melted out of the shadows.

He grinned at her. "Hey, Sil."

Amaya cried out and ran to him, wrapping her arms around Roach and holding him as tight as she could.

26

If all the world were made of gold, lies would still be richer.

—PROVERB FROM THE SUN EMPIRE

Cayo was in a nightmare.

That was the only way to explain the series of events that led him to carrying Soria down into the hold of a foreign ship, feeling the eyes of the countess on his back as he descended the stairs in the companionway.

No—not the countess. Cayo had no idea who she was.

His sister coughed weakly against him as he fumbled for the door handle the young man had told him to find, opening it to reveal a small cabin with a thin mattress on a wooden bed frame. He gently lowered Soria onto the bed, pulling down the sheets to throw them over her shivering body. Her face was dirty, her nightgown torn, and he shook with helpless fury at the man responsible for doing this to them.

Soria opened her eyes. "Cayo? Where are we?"

"We're on a different ship. It belongs to the Rain Empire's navy." He took a deep breath. "We're leaving Moray for a bit."

Cayo had watched as Yamaa—or whoever she was—embraced the stranger, a lanky boy wearing a naval uniform. She called him Roach, of all things.

"What are you doing here?" she had demanded, wiping tears from her face.

"Fetching you, silly. And I'm here on behalf of the Rain Empire to investigate the source of ash fever. Some cases are already popping up in Viariche."

"Wait . . ." She had stepped back, looking him up and down. "Roach, what *happened* to you? The Bugs said you just disappeared one day!"

The young man, Roach, had sighed and scratched the back of his head. "It's kind of embarrassing, but I was trying to sneak into a Ledese port when the *Brackish* was anchored off the coastline. I was worried about you and wanted to find you. But then I was caught by some naval officers and didn't have any paperwork on me, so I was conscripted. At first I fought against it, but they gave me three meals a day and didn't beat me, so I considered it a significant improvement."

"Then . . . how did you know I was here, in Moray?"

"Because we promised to meet here, and you always talked about coming back. That, and as soon as I heard about Countess Yamaa I knew it was the sort of reckless thing you'd be part of." He'd rolled his eyes. "Why you're parading about as a countess, though, I have no idea."

Soria had started coughing again, and Yamaa, or the girl who had once been Yamaa, looked over with pinched eyes.

"I'll explain later," she'd said. "Can you help them?"

"I can." Roach had approached Cayo then, dropping to one knee. Cayo had stayed back, untrusting, despite the warmth in the young man's eyes. "I can help your sister get better, but it would require leaving Moray. If you're all right with that, then we'll need to head to my ship before the Port's Authority starts snooping around."

Cayo had no idea what he was doing, or why he had agreed. As he now stared down at Soria, standing on a stranger's ship, the immensity of what had happened flooded over him. He sat hard on the edge of the bed, barely feeling the pain of the wooden frame as it dug into his thighs.

"Cayo?" Soria wormed an arm out from under the sheets and grabbed his hand. "Why are we leaving Moray? What about Father?"

He closed his eyes and clenched his jaw. He had to tell her the truth—all of it.

It came out of him like a frayed thread. Cayo told her about the counterfeit, about Kamon's dealings with the Slum King, about how their father had been willing to let her waste away. It hurt, as if he tore that thread from his own skin, ripping apart his seams and undoing all that made him Cayo.

When he opened his eyes, Soria was crying quietly, her face half-turned into the pillow. He squeezed her hand.

"We need to get away from him," he said. "And this man, Roach, says that there's a way to help you. That's why we have to leave." He pressed her fingers to his lips. "I'm sorry, Soria. I wish I could fix this."

But she shook her head and sniffed. "There's no fixing some things, Cayo. I just . . ." She sobbed brokenly, her breath rasping. "I thought he loved me."

He leaned over her. "*I* love you. And I'm going to do whatever it takes to save you."

Soria scrubbed a wrist against her eyes and looked at the jade ring on her finger. "I wasn't honest with you before. When I told you where I got this."

Cayo frowned, not sure what it had to do with anything, but nodded for her to continue.

Soria brushed a thumb against the ring, her lips trembling. "It was a long time ago, but I remember it clearly. It's because Father was so angry, and it scared me. I was supposed to be in a lesson with Miss Lawan, but instead I was going to the gardens because I'd left a toy out there. That's when I heard Father yelling at someone. I peeked around the corner and saw he was with another man, who was dirty and clearly drunk."

His sister closed her eyes, as if to better focus on the memory. "Father was saying that the other man had screwed up, that he had ruined his plan. That he was supposed to deliver a girl to the manor, not sell her to a debtor ship."

"Deliver a girl?" Cayo's frown deepened. "Was this a debt collector?"

"He must have been. He was nervous, but he laughed to hide it. He said something about needing to repay a debt to a captain. Father was . . ." Soria shuddered. "I'd never seen him so furious before. He hit the man and he went down."

It didn't surprise Cayo to hear about his father being violent, but the image still made his stomach ache.

"The debt collector told him to wait, that he had payment for his troubles, and showed him a ring. 'The girl's mother gave it to me as payment,' he said. 'For smuggling her out of the city. It'll make up for the cost of you hiring me.' But Father wouldn't accept it and flung the ring into the garden. He said that it was worthless compared to the

317

price of the girl. That if the man didn't want to die that day, he would leave and never come near him again."

Soria opened her eyes and fixed them on the jade ring. "I chased after the ring and picked it up, kept it in my jewelry box until I was old enough to wear it. I don't know why—maybe because it was pretty, or because I wanted to remember that day. As hard as I tried to convince myself that Father was a good person, that he was someone I didn't have to fear . . ."

More tears slid down her face. She angrily tore at the green band, scraping her knuckle as she popped it off her finger and threw it weakly across the room. It bounced against the wall and landed in a clatter.

"I'm glad we're leaving," she whispered.

He stayed with her until she stopped crying, until she let her exhaustion make way for uneasy sleep. Cayo stood and swayed, not quite used to the movement of a ship despite his childhood longing to live on one. But more than that, he was still dizzy and sore from last night, from his reckless descent into debauchery.

If he had simply gone home, would he have been able to avoid this? Had his vices finally ruined his family for good?

Cayo pocketed the ring before he climbed the stairs to the deck with a pounding head. The others were there: Roach, a man and two women he vaguely recognized from the countess's estate, and the countess herself.

The girl who had pretended to be a countess.

She felt his gaze and turned to meet it. She opened her mouth as if to say something to him, then looked away.

Cayo bristled. Fine, then.

He walked up to Roach. "You said you came here to investigate the source of ash fever. What do you know about it?"

Roach sighed and dug something from his pocket. The buttons of his blue uniform jacket winked in the meager starlight as he pulled out a folded handkerchief.

"I've been here for a couple of weeks, trying to connect the pieces," he said.

"Wait, you've been here for *weeks* and didn't try to find me?" the girl said.

"I did try to find you! In fact, I heard there was a sale for a Vault belonging to the name Chandra and I stopped by to see if there was a connection to you." He shrugged. "But when I got there, it was being raided by some men. I grabbed some random papers they'd hauled out, just in case, but I haven't had time to look them over yet."

She swallowed. "You . . . You must have just missed me."

"I've been looking for you all day. Didn't realize you'd show up here." He held out his hand, and the girl briefly took it with a weak smile. "Anyway," he went on, addressing Cayo, "the final piece fell into place once the prince died. I did some digging, tracked various transactions, and found that the deaths all had something specific in common."

Roach peeled back the layers of the folded handkerchief, revealing a flat black disc.

"Counterfeit currency," Roach said. "They're not just painted gold—they've been alchemically altered. And the substance coating them has properties that cause ash fever."

Cayo reeled, and not-Yamaa gasped. Roach solemnly wrapped up the disc and returned it to his pocket.

That meant his father wasn't just the cause of the counterfeit, but responsible for an illness that had already taken lives. Would very likely take his sister's life. Kamon Mercado wasn't merely a criminal—he was a murderer who had brought death upon his own daughter.

But that still didn't explain one thing. Cayo felt for the disc in his pocket and held it out to the girl he had kissed in the rain, the girl who had convinced him to turn in his father.

"Were you in on it?" he asked, his voice low.

She frowned as she stared at the disc. "What—"

"Romara. You gave her a coin, didn't you?"

She looked like she would be sick. Silently, she nodded.

"What were you doing with counterfeit money, other than pretending to be nobility? Are you working with my father?"

"No, it's nothing like that."

"Then tell me the truth!"

He hadn't meant to shout it, his voice ringing across the deck and over the water. Roach looked at the docks worriedly while one of the women swore.

The girl took a deep breath and met his gaze. "The man who kidnapped you and your sister. His name is Boon. He enlisted me—and these three," she said, gesturing to the others, "to help him carry out his plot for revenge against your father, who made him Landless."

The Kharian man crossed his arms with a stormy expression. "Wish I'd caught the bastard. He'd be much worse off than Landless."

"Boon sent me here with his money, but I didn't know it was counterfeit. I didn't know that it . . ." Her eyes drifted to the companionway, where Cayo had taken Soria.

Then she frowned and turned back to Roach. "You said there are cases of ash fever showing up in the Rain Empire. How is that possible, if the counterfeit is localized to Moray?"

"It's not as localized as you think. Part of my research led me to this man, Mercado, and I found that he's been sending money there for the past few years. Apparently, he has debts he needs to pay off, although I couldn't find the exact source of those debts."

Cayo shook his head. "What do you mean, he was sending money? It's illegal for any merchant in Moray to have dealings with the empires. We're supposed to stay neutral."

Roach laughed, and it grated against Cayo's ears. "I hate to be the one to tell you this, but nearly all of Mercado's estate belongs to the Rain Empire, and about a quarter of Moray as well. Coin has been flooding out of the city, and hardly anything is coming in. The city is broke."

"But that means . . ."

The young man nodded. "If Mercado is taken down and the counterfeit revealed, Moray will become economically dependent on the Rain Empire. It'll force an end to neutrality, and likely bring the Sun Empire to your shores. It'll mean *war*."

Cayo drifted back, as if to avoid the words. The consequences of his father's actions. His heart was a dull weight in his chest, dragging him down, down, until he thought he would merely fall through the floorboards.

He moved to the railing, gripping it in his hands. The others went on talking behind him, but the girl came up to his side, cautious.

"I'm sorry," she said. "For all of this."

He didn't bother to look at her. "Who are you, really? Why were you working with that man?"

She sighed and leaned her elbows on the railing. "I suppose I should start by saying that my name isn't Yamaa. It's Amaya Chandra."

Cayo repeated the name silently, his lips shaping the unfamiliar sound.

She told him her story: how she had grown up in Moray until her father was killed and her mother sold her to a debtor's ship. Her years diving for pearls and doing whatever it took to survive. She stared at her wrist as she spoke, and for the first time he noticed a small tattoo of a knife.

Fitting, he thought, though he wasn't quite sure why.

She explained how she met Boon, and how they had prepared to ruin his father's name. How she had been instructed to use Cayo, but that she had realized he wasn't part of his father's plans, how she had tried not to drag him into it. If she hoped it would soften him, she was wrong; it only cinched his bitterness tighter.

All this time, he had been an unwitting pawn. He had decided not to use her for her money, when all along she had been using him for her plans.

"Did you kill that man?" he asked when she was done. "The former captain of the *Brackish*?"

She paused long enough that he had his answer. Still, she replied, "Not directly, but I might as well have. He was a bad man, Cayo. He tortured children."

He understood that—he did—but the reminder of that lifeless arm swinging off of the stretcher turned him cold. She was stained with blood.

"We're going to find Boon and pay him back for what he's done," Yamaa—no, Amaya—said. "And we'll do whatever it takes to help your sister. It's the least I can do, after . . . everything."

Cayo didn't speak for some time. During her story, he had taken the jade ring from his pocket and fiddled with it, its weight insubstantial yet unbearable. When she looked over at what he was playing with, she stiffened.

"Where did you get that?"

He turned at the sudden change in her voice. Her dark eyes were wide, as if she had encountered a specter.

"It's not mine, it's Soria's." Cayo held out the ring in the palm of his hand. "Although I doubt she'll want it any longer."

Amaya reached out, then shrank back. Shaking her head, she took the ring from his palm, the graze of her fingertips white-hot against his skin. She cradled the ring in both her hands, one of them wrapped in a bandage, staring down at it as if it were a bird with a broken wing. She drew in breath to speak but released it as a shuddering sigh as tears fell from her eyes.

"It was my mother's," she whispered, brushing a thumb reverently against the band. "The day she sold me, she came home in tears, and her ring was missing. The ring my father gave her when they married."

Revelation opened a pit in his stomach as he thought back to the story Soria had just told him. "I . . . I think there's something you have to hear."

He related Soria's story to her, watching as her face hardened, then went slack with shock. She clamped her hands over the ring and held it to her chest, staring at the deck with overly bright eyes.

"This man, this debt collector, was told to bring you to my father for some reason," Cayo said. "But the debt collector sold you off to that captain instead, Zharo, because he had a debt with him. The debt collector tried to give my father that ring, saying that the mother . . . your mother . . . had given it to him in exchange for smuggling you out of the city."

"My mother didn't sell me," she whispered. She closed her eyes and let her tears fall. "I knew it. I knew he was lying."

"Do you know why my father wanted you? Why he would pay a debt collector to bring you to him?"

Amaya heaved a breath and wiped her face. "My father. He'd collected blackmail on Kamon Mercado and was planning on using it. But then he died, and I was the only one who had access to his Vault, being a blood heir. Mercado must have wanted to use me to gain access to all that blackmail, to destroy it." She shook her head and peered down at the ring again. "He got exactly what he wanted."

Cayo swallowed, hardly knowing what to say. Every secret that was revealed only seemed to turn his father more and more into a monster, into a man he couldn't even recognize.

"Well, you can keep it," he said, pushing away from the railing to return to Soria. "My father might be a thief, but I'm not."

"Cayo."

He turned to her. The way she stood there, her fist held to her chest, her hair loose and waving in the sea breeze, made his throat tighten. He had first seen this girl in the inlet, sad and stubborn and strong. To see her again now, when he knew the truth, made him mourn for all the time they could have had together, if only they had both been honest.

His mother's songs had been right: Nothing could stay, and everything was temporary. You could never trust what you had, only what you were capable of.

"Can you forgive me?" she asked softly. "It doesn't have to be now, but someday?"

He thought about it. But nothing made sense anymore, including whatever feelings he had, or thought he had, toward her.

"I don't know," he answered truthfully.

Then he descended the stairs, disappearing into the dark.

27

She searched, but her magician had vanished. Neralia wept,
for again she was alone, trapped in the cradle of
the ocean's dark and all the stars gone cold.
—"NERALIA OF THE CLOUDS," AN ORAL STORY ORIGINATING
FROM THE LEDE ISLANDS

Amaya stood at the railing of the quarterdeck, watching the lights of Moray grow distant. She had already lost sight of the *Brackish*, still docked with its pennants waving in the wind and its purple sails furled.

The last time she had watched Moray disappear on the horizon, she had been ten years old, and her name had been Silverfish. She had wept then, but she didn't weep now.

Because this time she was leaving nothing behind.

Cicada would take care of the Water Bugs, make sure they got home to their families. And by the time the Port's Authority caught wind of the strange events of this night, they would already be far out at sea.

Amaya looked down at the ring in her hand. Proof that she hadn't been betrayed, that her mother had done all she could to try to save her from Mercado. She remembered how well it fit her mother's slim finger, how the jade perfectly complemented the light brown of her skin. She tried to slip it over her fourth finger, but it was too small; she had inherited her father's broad hands.

Sighing, she drifted toward the front of the ship, turning her back on Moray and facing the expanse of ocean that stretched before them. Liesl, Deadshot, and Avi were below in the galley, but she didn't feel like joining them yet. Instead, she leaned on the railing and inhaled the briny air, letting it play with her hair as she remembered what it was like to be on the water, its rolling movements and fathomless depths.

Her need for revenge had brought them all to this place of uncertainty and fear. She had ignored all the warnings and tended only to her desires, unknowingly spreading the counterfeit and ash fever with it.

She was no better than Mercado. No better than Boon.

"You've changed."

Roach had joined her at the railing. He looked more like himself out of his uniform—more like the boy who had survived those seven years alongside her, making her laugh and sneaking her food. He gave her his familiar two-finger salute, and she gave one back. *I'm all right. I think.*

She rested her head against his shoulder. "The countess was only an illusion," she murmured. "As soon as I put on a pretty dress, all anyone could see was a rich girl."

He hummed in disagreement. "It's more than just clothing. It's in the way you hold yourself, the way you speak. Like you're more . . . you."

She lifted her head with a frown. "How can I be more *me* when I was pretending to be someone else?"

"I've no clue, but somehow it happened. And I'm glad it did."

"That makes one of us." But at least now she could drop all her masks, perhaps finally figure out who she truly was.

And maybe, hopefully, that girl would be someone worthy of Cayo's forgiveness.

Still, they had a long way to go until they reached that moment. Once they arrived in the Rain Empire, they would have to try to find a cure for Soria before the disease progressed more than it already had. She would try to find a lead on Boon's whereabouts and expose his lies. And then . . .

Well, she didn't know. She supposed the only definitive plan was the one she had stuck to for the last seven years: survive.

"It feels good," she said softly, almost to herself, "to be back on the water."

Roach huffed a fond laugh and tightened his arm around her shoulders. "It feels good to be on the water with you by my side. I've missed you, Sil."

She winced and looked away, focusing again on the sea before them. "Don't call me that. I'm not Silverfish anymore."

"Then what should I call you?"

Breathing in deep, she allowed herself a moment to admire the patches of sky where the stars shone through, listening to the way the water curled in whispers against the ship's hull. Her mother's ring pressed insistently against her palm.

"Amaya," she said at last. "My name is Amaya."

ACKNOWLEDGMENTS

I remember watching the Disney version of *The Count of Monte Cristo* movie years and years ago, falling in love with the epic tale of vengeance and sword fights and romance. So that makes the fact that *Scavenge the Stars* found a home at Disney all the more appropriate. (Also, Amaya is an official Disney princess now—sorry, I don't make the rules.)

I've been thrilled and honored to have so many people have a hand in this book's publication from start to finish:

First, a huge thanks to Patrice Caldwell for seeing the potential of this story and giving it the chance to find readers, and for being such an amazing advocate and cheerleader. I'm very glad you stormed my launch of *Firestarter* to shout about what I was working on next. Thanks also to Hannah Allaman and Laura Schreiber for their assistance and making sure everything was running on time. Thank you to the Disney team at large, especially Marci Senders for that magnificent cover (I'm going to storm the offices for that knife), as well as Melissa Lee, Seale Ballenger, and Dina Sherman.

Thank you to the folks at Glasstown for all their help and dedication, particularly Lexa Hillyer, Emily Berge-Thielmann, Deeba Zargarpur, Rebecca Kuss, and Diana Sousa. Lots of love and gratitude to Kamilla Benko and Kat Cho for their support and kindness through this process.

I would likely lose my head if it weren't for my fabulous agent, Victoria Marini, and her assistants, Maggie Kane and Lee O'Brien, who make sure I'm taken care of even in the midst of birthing a *whole human baby.*

Eternal gratitude to my friends for sticking with me even though I complain about practically everything on the planet. To Traci Chee, Emily Skrutskie, and Jessica Cluess: You three are the OG hoes of my heart. To T. J. Ryan: thank you for being my petty buddy and for taking me to Disney World. To Ellen Gavazza: thanks for adventures in sushi and movies. To the writing cult for encouraging me to post gross snippets in the Slack: Akshaya Raman, Katy Rose Pool, Alex Castellanos, Kat Cho (yes, you get to be named twice), Axie Oh, Claribel Ortega, Meg Kohlmann, Mara Fitzgerald, Janella Angeles, Maddy Colis, Ashley Burdin, Amanda Haas, Melody Simpson, Amanda Foody, and Christine Herman.

A hundred million thanks, always, to my readers, as well as the booksellers, librarians, and reviewers who helped spread the word about *Scavenge.* Also to my $5+ supporters on Patreon: Alyssa Tarr, Amanda Wheeler, Amelie Fournier, Arianne, Ash Hardister, Caitlin O'Connel, Carlee Maurier, Carolyn, Cody, Common Spence, Dani, Lisa, Mae Nouwen, Sen Scherb, and Sylph.

I couldn't do what I do without my family's support and love. The biggest thanks to my mother for making me pancakes, taking me out to dinner, picking me up from the airport, and feeding the cats when I'm out adventuring. Thanks as always to my father for encouraging me to do what I love.

And thanks to you, dear reader, for picking up this book. I hope you make your fortune and punish those who've wronged you.

(But like . . . legally.)

(Please don't stab anyone.)